TRAVIS BALDREE

First published 2025 by Tom Doherty Associates / Tor Publishing Group

First published in the UK 2025 by Tor
an imprint of Pan Macmillan
The Smithson, 6 Briset Street, London EC1M 5NR
EU representative: Macmillan Publishers Ireland Ltd, 1st Floor,
The Liffey Trust Centre, 117–126 Sheriff Street Upper,
Dublin 1 D01 YC43
Associated companies throughout the world

ISBN 978-1-0350-3594-6 HB
ISBN 978-1-0350-3595-3 TPB

Copyright © Travis Baldree 2025

The right of Travis Baldree to be identified as the
author of this work has been asserted in accordance
with the Copyright, Designs and Patents Act 1988.

All rights reserved. No part of this publication may be reproduced,
stored in a retrieval system, or transmitted, in any form, or by any means
(including, without limitation, electronic, mechanical, photocopying, recording
or otherwise) without the prior written permission of the publisher.

Pan Macmillan does not have any control over, or any responsibility for,
any author or third-party websites (including, without limitation, URLs,
emails and QR codes) referred to in or on this book.

1 3 5 7 9 8 6 4 2

A CIP catalogue record for this book is available from the British Library.

Frontispiece artwork by Carson Lowmiller
Map by S.E. Davidson

Printed and bound in the UK using 100% Renewable Electricity by CPI Group (UK) Ltd

This book is sold subject to the condition that it shall not, by way of
trade or otherwise, be lent, hired out, or otherwise circulated without
the publisher's prior consent in any form of binding or cover other than
that in which it is published and without a similar condition including this
condition being imposed on the subsequent purchaser. The publisher does not
authorize the use or reproduction of any part of this book in any manner
for the purpose of training artificial intelligence technologies or systems.
The publisher expressly reserves this book from the Text and Data Mining
exception in accordance with Article 4(3) of the European Union
Digital Single Market Directive 2019/790.

Visit **www.panmacmillan.com** to read more about
all our books and to buy them.

Sometimes the storm clears away the wreckage.

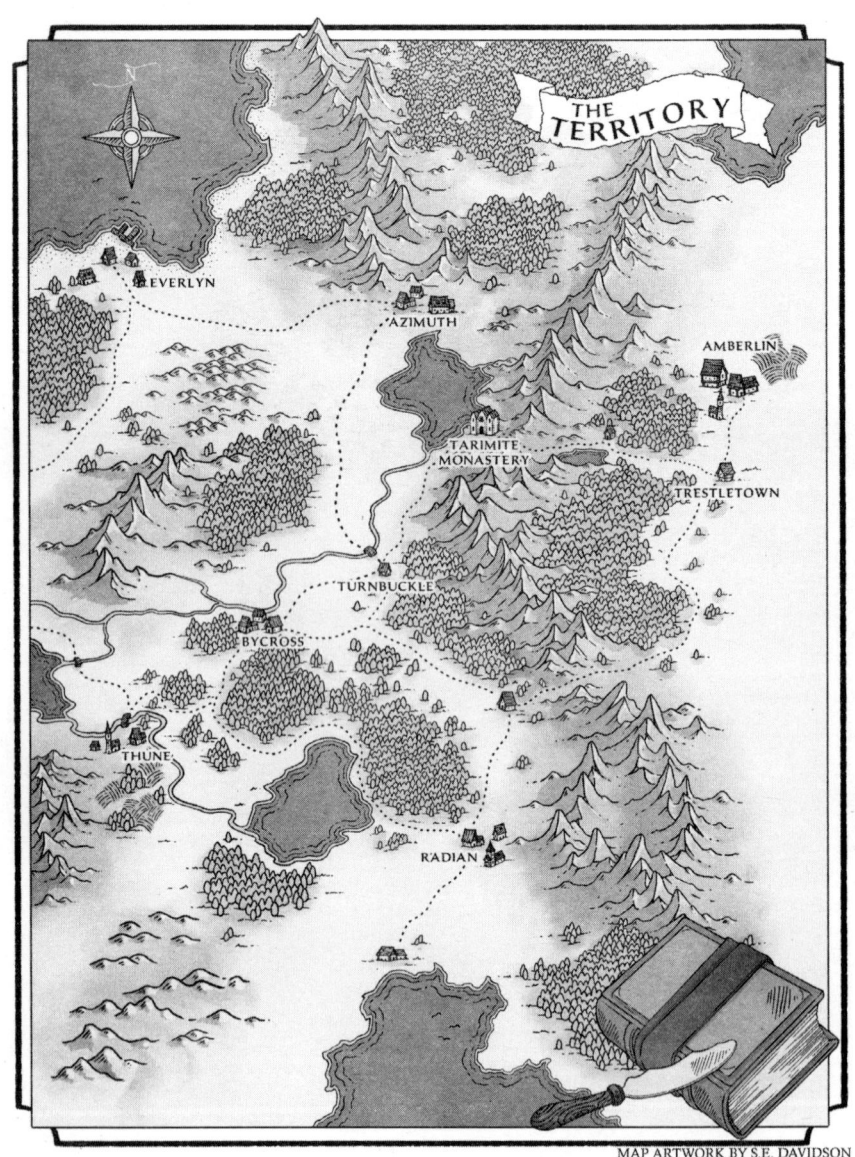

PROLOGUE

"Fuck!" cried Fern, ducking back inside the carriage a whisker before a clawed and scaled hand sailed past. A noxious ribbon of blood trailed in its wake, the owner no longer properly attached.

Fishy gurgles and bubbling roars arose on all sides, and the carriage rocked from another impact as the rattkin tipped back onto the bench, leather satchel clutched to her chest. No sooner had she bruised her own tail than she lunged forward again, flinging the bag aside to wrap furry arms around the gryphet scrabbling at the inside of the door.

Her pet's bedraggled feathers fluffed around his head, his graying hair bristling along his back. He hooted and huffed hoarsely at the commotion outside, and Fern hugged him against her belly. "Hush, Potroast," she soothed in a fierce whisper. "Somebody out there is on our side. I know you're brave, but you're *far* too old for this."

His wing tufts fanned her face indignantly.

When a fishy face and a needle-packed mouth appeared at the window—croaking and hissing and oozing all over the sill—concerns over Potroast's advancing age were blown clear out of her head.

The door rattled in its frame as the pescadine clawed furiously at the wood, jamming its head into the opening and spraying spittle in all directions. White, staring eyes gleamed like peeled eggs above an overcrowded maw.

The top hinge snapped and bounced off the opposite wall with a cheerful metallic *ping*.

Fern's deep well of profanity temporarily ran dry.

In the next moment, the nightmare at the door vanished with a sound like a melon in a mangle.

Through the slimed and splintered window frame, Fern caught moonlit flashes of silver as shrieks rose and were hacked off one by one, each more distant than the last, until eerie silence prevailed. Even Potroast's wheezing pants subsided.

A strangled moment passed. Then two. Then five.

The chirr of swamp frogs stirred into a relieved chorus.

She caught the wide eyes of the carriage driver taking refuge across from her, his long hands clapped over his mouth as though he couldn't trust himself not to utter a sound. His knees were drawn up to his chin as he cowered on the opposite bench.

Both their gazes snapped to the door again at the sound of muddy hoof clops approaching.

A sonorous voice echoed from the gloom outside.

A fussy voice. A pompous voice.

The sort of voice that could stultify the unlucky at a thousand paces.

"Ah, the common pescadine. Maltheus famously wrote of them in *The Eighty Verses*, where he likened them to his in-laws at winter solstice festival. Droll, indeed. My lady, did you know that they have *four* stomachs? Ha! Yes, and only two are reserved for food and digestion. It's quite fascinating, really, as unlike their upcountry brethren, the third and fourth are filled with small stones, which they—"

A deep sigh then, and the hiss of a blade finding its sheath.

"Hello?" ventured Fern.

The terrified coachman moaned behind one hand and used the other to frantically beg for her silence.

The sloppy hoofbeats drew nearer.

Gloved fingers wrapped over the windowsill and tugged, wrenching the door half out of its frame on a final, protesting hinge.

"You want to unlatch that?"

A different voice. Un-fussy. *Not* pompous.

Fern reached across Potroast's body to flip up the latch, whereupon the coachman squeaked, and the door fell out of its jamb entirely.

Framed there, amidst bearded moss and fireflies, a figure out of legend.

Silver hair cropped short and wild as though with a dull knife.

Eyes the blue of northern ghostlights, deep as glacial pools.

A body rangy and hard, forged by centuries of deeds of the blade.

The white, star-shaped pommel of that blade glinting above one shoulder . . . beside the slender, pointed ear of an eldest elf.

Only *one*, the other cut cruelly close and centuries scarred over.

"By the shitting *Eight*," breathed Fern.

Astryx One-Ear, Blademistress and Oathmaiden, glanced around the interior of the coach, nodded, and held out a gloved fistful of reins.

"Found your horses. They seem fine. Looks like you are, too."

When none of the carriage's occupants moved to accept them, she shrugged and wrapped them over a coat hook set inside the door.

Then she vanished, muddy footfalls marking her departure.

Fern scrambled to lean out the doorway, bringing one paw up to her mouth to holler after the retreating figure, "Um, *thank you!*"

And then in a smaller voice meant only for herself, "Fucking hells."

"You swear a lot," whispered the coachman, joining her to peer after their departing savior.

Fern narrowed her eyes at him, gesturing with a slow sweep at the wreckage of pescadine anatomy radiating outward from the carriage and into the bog beside the road.

The coachman appeared to finally comprehend Astryx's handiwork.

"Oh. Fucking *hells*."

The second, considerably less eventful half of Fern's journey seemed to take three times as long as the first. She wasn't sure who was more prone to the spooks, the coachman or the horses. Careful pauses were frequent, the pace positively leaden.

Still, no further perils beset them.

Days after their dramatic rescue at the hands of Astryx—Blademistress, Oathmaiden, etcetera—Potroast hooted in his sleep beside Fern as she read and reread her most recent correspondence with an old friend.

Decades ago, she'd met a brash young orc in the beachside town of Murk. Since then, in a move Fern would once have considered unimaginable, her friend had sheathed her blade for good and opened a "coffee shop" that was apparently extraordinarily successful. Fern didn't even know what coffee *was*.

Still, on the strength of fond memory and a series of lengthy letters, Fern had sold Thistleburr, the crusty little bookshop to which she'd dedicated twenty-five years of her adult life. She'd gathered the proceeds of the sale, a preposterously paltry valise of belongings, a satchel belonging to an absent companion, and an increasingly spherical and elderly gryphet, then booked a carriage to the city of Thune.

A new life awaited her there. A new start. A new bookshop. The embers of an old friendship to fan. Perhaps even something she might one day call family.

Also, she was clearly fucking insane.

There was one other letter packed into the satchel, a parting message from another old friend. She fished it out and her eyes fell upon the final lines, although by now she knew them by heart.

Always remember, although the unimaginative see life as a thread stretched from one point to another, birth to death, a life truly lived is a glorious tangle.

One is never lost.

And if one is lucky, one is never found, either.

Yours in the wilderness,
Zelia Greatstrider

1

Fern stared up at a wooden sign in the shape of a kite shield. A hammered hunk of metal representing a sword ran diagonally across the front. Two words bracketed the blade, chiseled above and below—

LEGENDS
— & —
LATTES

She'd never been more terrified in her life.

Well, that wasn't *entirely* true. A harrowing night a lifetime ago at the mercy of a certain necromancer still held pride of place as far as raw fear went.

But eight hells, this was a close second.

The two-story building's plaster was freshly whitewashed, with heavy corner posts and the half timbering stained dark. Light and color shifted behind leaded-glass windows. A pleasant murmur issued from within, like the whisper of a distant river, while rich scents of cinnamon and butter laced the air. The shop's front door was closed against the chill breath of a late spring evening.

And beyond that door?

"Just a friend you last saw when your fur was still brown, and neither of us knew our ass from an abacus," she muttered. "Hardly the stuff of nightmares."

A friend I knew for a single summer, and me with nothing to scamper back to if the friendship doesn't hold, she thought, but did not say.

The journey on foot through Thune's streets was already a misty memory. Navigating with the directions Viv had provided, Fern hadn't noted much more than the smell of the river, the twisty lanes, and the hodgepodge of buildings. If the city hadn't contrasted so starkly with Murk's salty air, sand, and regimented streets, even those details might not have registered.

Potroast wheezed at the level of her knees as he settled onto the cobbles beside her valise, letting his great golden eyes drift half closed.

She frowned at him. "Can't have you napping in the street, can we?"

In the end, that was what got her moving again. As folk had done since time immemorial, she got on with things, because otherwise . . . who would feed the dog?

"Come on then, old man." Fern gently nudged the gryphet with her toes.

As her red cloak fluttered in another gust, she hoisted the valise, hitched up the ancient satchel, and reached for the iron pull.

The door swung wide before her paw could touch it, and at the appearance of a familiar orcish face on the other side, Fern's own traveled through wild geographies of expression.

It arrived somewhere hopeful, but with cheeks wetter than when the journey began.

⁓

"So, what do you think?" asked Viv, nodding to the mug in Fern's paws and crossing her forearms on the table between them. Still impressive forearms. Still the same face, too, but fuller, less hungry somehow. And definitely expectant. A face Fern really knew . . . ? She thought so. *Hoped* so. She'd bet everything on that assumption.

Behind Viv, steam hissed from the gleaming machine on the

counter, flanked by an enormous slab of slate on the wall. A menu was printed across it with colored chalk in a tidy hand, ornate flourishes decorating the corners. Neat rows of polished mugs hung on pegs, and baked goods sparkled with glaze under fine glass domes. Customers bustled to and fro with drinks and nibbles.

Fern carefully set down her mug. She contemplated the unfamiliar bitterness on the sides of her tongue, the earthy heat in her belly.

She became aware that her answer was increasingly tardy.

"It's . . . *nice*," she ventured.

Except it wasn't.

Her claws tapped the side of the mug nervously.

Viv's still-the-same-but-less-hungry face fell, and it was so much like her disappointment when Fern first offered her a book those many years gone, that the rattkin almost laughed aloud in delighted recognition.

The laugh got lost somewhere under the guilt though.

Fucking hells, I've rejected her happily-ever-after.

"Well, it's maybe an acquired taste," said Viv. "You don't *have* to like it, of course!" She leaned back on the bench so her crossed forearms rested against her chest.

"Oh, yes, I mean, I'm sure with time I'll . . ." Fern trailed off as the rest of her thoughts decamped for other territory.

All the fear she'd left on the doorstep came back in a tidal swell, and she thought she might heave her guts—including a single mouthful of coffee—all over the table at the following wave of nausea.

Then, somewhere inside she found a pawhold and dragged herself out of the sea.

She pushed the mug away decisively. "Gods, it's just a *drink*. You got *married*?"

Viv slapped the table and leveled a finger at her. "There's Fern. It's so damn good to see you again."

And then it was okay.

"You should have led with the cinnamon rolls," Fern mumbled around a mouthful of one. She closed her eyes, and an involuntary shiver found its way from her shoulders to the ends of her whiskers. "Gods, it seems like you're really burying the lede with the name of this place."

She glanced at Tandri, who stood with one hand braced on the end of the table, eyeing Fern with a small but amused smile. A pair of horns the dusty magenta of the succubus's skin parted the hair at her brow, and her whiplike tail swayed languorously. Potroast lay curled around one of Tandri's feet, and she'd made no move to disturb him, even though she probably had something better to do. Fern thought from the start that she liked Viv's wife, but this clinched it.

She licked a sticky claw. "Put another one in front of me, and I might marry you, too."

The succubus laughed, tucking a lock of hair behind one ear.

"Paws off," called Viv, opening the front door just long enough to hang a CLOSED sign on its nail. She grabbed a cloth off the counter as she returned to the long table that Fern occupied very little of.

Fern affected a speculative look. "Tandri, did Viv ever tell you about the summer fling she had when she was still swinging metal around? *That* girl was a baker, too. Probably a whole *ovenload* of jilted bakers in your wife's wake, I bet. So, when the inevitable happens, just know I'm here for you." She fluttered her fingers magnanimously.

"Oh, I'm no baker. That's Thimble's handiwork." Tandri's smile became secretive. "You'll meet him soon enough, I'm sure." She switched her attention to Viv. "How did you never mention him in your letters?"

Viv settled across from Fern and scrubbed at an imaginary scuff on the table with the cloth. "Spent most of them conning an old friend into moving her bookshop next door, that's how. There must not have been room on the page."

"Have you seen the shop yet?" The succubus used the toe of her other shoe to scratch between Potroast's shoulder blades, to his audible, but dozy, approval.

"Honestly? I must have passed it on the way in, but I was so, um . . . flustered at the thought of *this*," Fern waved a guilty paw at the both of them, "that I couldn't pay much attention."

"Dread'll do that," said Tandri.

"Dread?" Viv's brows went up.

"Yes, I wonder what it's like to leave your entire life behind and move to a new city where you don't know anybody, and then start a new business?" observed Tandri wryly.

Fern shot her a surprised and grateful look.

"*I'm* here. She knows *me*," protested the orc.

Tandri gently extricated herself from Potroast and moved to wrap her arms around Viv's broad shoulders, delivering a peck to her temple. "I think she's just getting to know this version," she replied, in a whisper meant to carry.

Fern *definitely* liked her. Double-clinched.

A sharp rap at the entry elicited a hooting bark from the sleeping gryphet, and they all glanced that way as the door swung wide.

A hob entered first, clad in coveralls and a cotton shirt that had both seen a lot of hard wear. Tugging the brim of his flat cap in greeting, he held the door for a sleek gray rattkin laden with bags, boxes, and tins.

"Kid wouldn't let me carry a thing," complained the hob.

The rattkin squeaked something indecipherable, paused to stare at Fern with wide eyes, and then disappeared around the counter.

Fern thought Tandri's expression turned positively smug.

Viv cleared her throat. "So, that was Thimble. I'm sure he'll be back. And Fern, this is Cal, who I *know* I've mentioned." She leaned close and held a hand beside her mouth. "He's the *real* reason you don't have anything to worry about."

"Hm," said Cal, whose long ears heard just fine.

Fern thought he looked both put-out and pleased at the same time. "Glad as hells to know you," said Fern, rising and approaching to extend her paw. They were both about the same height.

The hob took it in a firm, dry grip and pumped it once, offering the grizzled ghost of a smile. "Plain speaker. Ain't that a relief."

"Some of the words Fern uses are a *long* way from plain," called Viv. "But if you ever need to strip some paint, I bet she can make it a lot easier."

"Oh, fuck off," replied Fern mildly over her shoulder.

Cal barked a startled laugh, and that clinched her opinion of him, too.

⁓

"Windows'll come, o'course," said Cal, tipping his cap back as they stared together at the vacant frames.

To Fern, the building bore an expression of horrified surprise, not unlike that of a rattkin who'd sold her bookstore and most of her worldly possessions to travel halfway across the Territory and set up shop in a moldering derelict.

Fern had been honest about paying no attention on her way to the Redstone district and the coffee shop. Now, she wondered if she would have made it in the door if she had noticed the place.

She swallowed hard.

"Don't worry!" Viv clapped a hand on Fern's shoulder. "My shop used to be a crumbling livery with a hole in the ceiling. *Then* it burned down. You're already leagues ahead. It's going to be *perfect*. You'll see."

Cal studied Fern from under his cap. He nodded once. "Hm. S'going to be fine."

Somehow that was a lot more reassuring.

It was only one story tall. Separated from Legends & Lattes by a narrow alley, the bright whitewash and neat stonework of its neighbor only made the peeling paint and sagging eaves look more desolate. Still, it wasn't as though her old shop in Murk wasn't in need of a lick of paint. Maybe if Fern's nerves hadn't already been thoroughly frayed, her first impression might've been gilded with a bit more optimism.

"The bones are good," she muttered to herself, but when she said it a second time even quieter, it felt more like a prayer.

"I've got something to show you," said Tandri gently. She gestured for Fern to follow, then opened the door to lead her inside.

Cal and Viv came after.

The interior wasn't much more encouraging. Evening light slanted through the gaping window frames, revealing raw beams and heaps of sawdust marking Cal's efforts thus far. Pale stains on the floor described the ghostly shapes of furniture long since removed.

"It does seem bigger once you're inside." Fern tried to sound optimistic. "Should hold plenty of books, at least."

"The bones're good," said Cal, gruffly repeating her earlier words. "She'll clean up smart."

Fern became even more aware that the worry sloshing around inside her was over-spilling enough for all of them to notice. Hells, the tension in her tail alone probably gave it away.

"This isn't what I wanted to show you though," said Tandri, opening a door at the back of the echoing storefront and passing through. At the rasp of a striking match, soft lantern-glow buttered the walls inside.

Fern stepped into a cozy bedroom, Viv and Cal crowding into the doorway behind her. They'd tucked a narrow bed in the far corner, complete with a quilt and a big, squashy pillow. A side table holding the lit lantern squatted beside it. A writing desk crouched against the near wall, and a wardrobe sat to the right of the door. Just above the desk hung a watercolor painting of a long swell of shoreline tufted with beach grass, and low clouds pinking at evening.

At the foot of the bed waited a large wicker basket with a blanket tucked around a cushion nested inside.

"Oh," managed Fern, remembering Potroast asleep back in the coffee shop.

Then she burst into tears.

~

"You're sure you're all right?" Viv had one enormous hand curled around Fern's outstretched paw on the tabletop back in the coffee shop.

Fern sniffed, then used her other hand to bring a mug of tea to her lips. "Oh, hells, I'm *fine*. The shop, the room, it's all lovely. *Thank* you." She nodded meaningfully at Tandri. "I just feel all . . . rattled around. Like I crossed a bridge that collapsed the second I reached the other side. You're relieved you made it, but weak in the knees at the same time."

Viv looked thoughtful. "I know exactly what you mean."

"Huh. You would, wouldn't you? I bet you had a lot of near misses in your time." She grimaced. "*In your time.* Bleagh. That makes you sound like an octogenarian."

Then she remembered her own near-death experience on the road not a week past. "Eight hells," she breathed. "That's *it*. No wonder I'm not myself!"

"What?"

And then she told them about Astryx and the pescadines and the coach door torn off its hinges.

"Astryx One-Ear," sighed Viv in obvious admiration. "Gods, I'd love to meet her."

"Who?" asked Tandri.

Viv looked affronted. "The Blademistress? The Oathmaiden? The most famous elven adventurer for the last thousand years?"

"I've read *three* different histories about her," added Fern. "Which is pretty impressive, considering she's still alive. *Scarred by Purpose*? *Steel Maiden*? *Flight of the Silver Hawk*? Amazing they got written, since she never seems to stick around after any heroics, which I personally can attest to."

"Not ringing any bells." Tandri shrugged. "A thousand years seems like an awfully long time to do the same thing, though."

While they argued good-naturedly, Thimble appeared out of nowhere and slipped a plate piled with some sort of long, brittle cookies in front of Fern.

"*Hello,*" he whispered.

Then he wrung his paws in front of his apron and vanished as quickly as he had come in a dusting of flour.

Fern didn't have the energy to puzzle him out.

She was simply relieved to have found a plausible reason for the sick feeling in her stomach that required no further investigation. A near-death experience would make anyone feel that way, obviously.

Also, the cookies were mighty fine.

2

"That's the last load," said Viv, grunting as she lowered a stack of lumber to the floor. She shrugged her arm a few times and rubbed life back into her shoulder. "I've got to head over to the shop. You going to be all right for now?"

Fern glanced up from a set of shelves, a paintbrush heavy with wood stain in one paw. She fanned her cheek with the other. With the window glass in place, the interior of the shop was choked with midday heat. She blew out a breath and waved the brush. "Sure. With Cal here, there's no possible way I can damage anything load-bearing."

Viv searched her face.

She was smiling, but Fern thought she was also trying to figure out whether there was any lingering panic in the joke. The prognosis must have been good, because her smile deepened. "See you after I close up, then. But come on over if you need anything."

In their letters, Viv had been clear that she would handle all the organizational work in advance of Fern's arrival. She'd been true to her word, and if there was any consideration she *hadn't* covered, Cal clearly knew what he was about. After a few days to give her bruised tail a chance to recover from the long carriage ride, Fern threw herself into transforming the shell of a building into a shop worth the upending of her entire life.

Watching her purse flatten also turned out to be a powerful motivator. Fern knew Viv would've been happy to assist there, too, but her old friend had already sunk plenty of sovereigns into the place. She couldn't countenance letting her add any more.

"Front counter?" prompted Cal. The hob stared down at a few planks he'd arranged to mark the perimeter of the structure in question. Potroast snored between the boards in a makeshift bed consisting entirely of Fern's cloak and his shed feathers.

Stretching—and wincing—Fern balanced the brush on the pot of wood stain and joined him. She regarded the rest of the shop's interior, now crowded with shelves just like the ones she'd been finishing. "Hmm. A few feet this way, I think. It'll have to be if we're going to line up the bookshelves in three rows." She closed an eye and framed the space with both paws.

Cal squatted to scratch Potroast behind one triangular ear. The gryphet snorted through his beak, rocking to the side to make his belly available. The hob obliged him, squinting up at Fern as he did. At least she was pretty sure he squinted. His eyes were mostly hidden by his bushy brows and the shadow of his cap. "So. You feelin' more plumb these days?" He angled his other hand so it ran straight up and down.

Fern's tail quirked in exasperation. "Honestly, everyone seems worried I might collapse in a heap at any moment." She hiked a thumb in the direction Viv had gone. "The building isn't going to fall down, and neither am I. We're both just a little crooked."

"Don't doubt you'll be fine a little crooked. But we're already in here straightenin' things out." He stood and slapped the wall. "Just figured you deserved at least as much attention as this old wreck."

She sighed. "Thanks. And I do mean that. But. *This* old wreck is just fine."

"Hm."

They contemplated one another for a long moment. Fern thought it was strange that she could in any way feel *related* to someone she'd barely said two words to, but the hob might as well have been an uncle, as far as that went. The kind you liked having by to visit, because they fixed all the squeaky doors, and they didn't embarrass everybody at the dinner table.

"Fair enough," Cal allowed. Then he pointed a gnarled finger at the shelf Fern had been laboring over. "S'pose since you're just fine and all, it'd be worth pointin' out that you've been fillin' that brush so heavy, you've got a little lake formin' on the bottom plank. Want me to show you how to do it proper?"

He had the good grace to cough to cover his chuckle when Fern turned the air blue.

As, of course, the best kind of uncle would.

Fern decided that the unending work of the following weeks had a therapeutic quality. She was too exhausted to fret about anything—funds, future, *or* friendship. Her new bookshop slowly took shape as the shelves found their places, fresh boards replaced rotted ones, wax gleamed on floorboards, paint refreshed the walls, and ancient stains vanished under lye and water.

Viv pitched in throughout any given day in dribs and drabs, especially when heavy objects needed shifting or someone more than four feet tall was required, but the balance of Fern's hours was spent mostly in the company of Cal.

She discovered she didn't mind that in the slightest.

The hob carpenter was soothing to be around, imperturbable and taciturn in ways that communicated more than they had any right to. More than once, one of them would appear unbidden next to the other to brace a piece of timber, offer a handful of nails, or top up a paint pot.

It wasn't that they *never* spoke. They simply didn't bother if they didn't have to.

As someone whose life had mostly been spent in the service of sharing words, Fern was enjoying keeping them to herself for a while.

It meant that when they did speak, it actually mattered.

Mostly, that happened during their lunch break.

"Thanks, Thimble," she said, as the little baker offered a platterful of sandwiches wrapped in brown paper, wedged next to two sugar-dusted scones.

He blushed to the ends of his whiskers, and then rummaged in a shoulder bag for a pair of flasks.

"*Coffee*," he whispered, offering one to Cal.

The hob took it with a nod and a tug of his cap.

"*Tea.*" Thimble didn't meet Fern's eyes as she accepted it from his outstretched paw.

An awkward silence swelled as he fidgeted as though he wanted to say something, and Fern waited patiently.

And waited.

"Um. It looks delicious," she tried, hefting the plate.

"*Thanks*," he squeaked and fled out the open door.

Fern watched him go, then shifted her gaze to Cal, who was already inspecting the sandwiches with great interest. "I think there's a conversation going on around here that involves me, but that I'm not part of. You wouldn't know anything about that, would you?"

"Hm?" replied Cal.

"Oh, come on. Every time that kid is in the room, I can feel the . . . the *matchmaking eyes*." She studied the hob's bushy brows. "All right, fine, I can't really tell with *you*, but Viv? Tandri?"

Cal took a bite of sourdough and cheese and ruminated as he chewed. At last, he replied, "I figure folk who lucked into findin' each other maybe hope it happens to somebody else, too. 'Specially somebody they're fond of."

"Oh, hells." Fern dropped onto an upturned bucket with a sigh. "Those two aren't talking me up to him, are they? Nudging him my way? Please, tell me they aren't."

He shrugged. "Doubt they're that ham-fisted. Prob'ly just watchin' you both like old ladies watchin' young folk at a summer picnic."

"He's practically a baby! I'm forty-seven years old!"

"Never could tell the age of a rattkin, m'self."

"My muzzle is *silver*."

"Hm. Distinguished. 'Sides, he's *all* gray."

"I can't tell if you're fucking with me."

Cal cocked half a smile and took another bite.

Fern laughed helplessly. "I hated the coffee, and now I'm going to disappoint them in a whole *new* way." She selected a scone and took a morose bite. "Fuck, he is a good baker, though. Maybe I'm being too hasty."

She felt the weight of the hob's regard and met his gaze. Or where it would have been if his eyebrows didn't obscure it.

"Hm. Yeah, the coffee thing *was* a real disaster."

It turned out she *did* know when he was fucking with her.

―――

"This is profoundly weird," said Viv, hefting a volume in one hand and flipping it open with the other. She brought it halfway to her nose for a sniff. "Gods, I got a little shiver up my back. I expect to look outside and see a boardwalk and dunes."

Fern looked up from the open crate before her, paws trailing over the cloth covers of the books stacked precisely inside. The ranks of shelves and freshly polished floors glowed mellowly under lantern light. The windowpanes fogged against an evening chill.

"My vision was a little sharper back then, but I can still picture you prying those crates open with your bare hands."

Viv snorted. She'd wisely used a pry bar for the task this time around. "And I can still see Pitts towing them up on that cart of his. Whatever happened to him?"

"Still trooping around Murk, hauling and fixing what needs hauling and fixing." Fern lifted three books from the crate, passing them over for Viv to shelve. A small smile. "And ambushing folks with a line or two of poetry when they least expect it."

They stocked shelves in companionable silence while the little woodstove in the corner pushed the temperature toward the sleepy side of cozy.

Once they reached the bottom of the first crate, Viv snugged the pry bar under the lid of the next. "I remember Gallina making some sort of terrible excuse to get out of helping with this."

"Said she was too short, as if *that* was a convincing argument." Fern swept a paw to indicate her own height. "Whatever happened with you two?"

"We ran together for years, off and on. Then back in a group for a good stretch until . . . well, until I was done."

Fern eyed her. "I'm sure she took it well," she said, in a deliberately neutral way.

"Better than you'd think. She evened out in her old age, just like the rest of us."

"Speak for yourself. I'm still salty as hells," said Fern tartly. She blinked, and a slow smile crept across her lips. "And on the subject of relics, that reminds me . . ."

She scurried to her room and returned carrying a misshapen bundle wrapped in brown paper. Hoisting it triumphantly, she said, "Open it."

Nonplussed, Viv took it and peeled back several layers of paper. "Are these what I think they are?"

She withdrew a wooden bookend, much battered.

"They are."

"The seagull bookends," murmured Viv.

"Or maybe rabbits." They shared a glance and chuckled.

There was a pause during which Viv handed over the bookends, and Fern wedged a few novels between them on the countertop.

"I'll be damned," Viv breathed behind her.

"What?" Fern looked back sharply.

The orc reached into the freshly opened crate and withdrew a red volume. *"Ten Links in the Chain,"* she said, flashing a big, tusky grin. "This is the same book you tricked me into reading."

"Tricked? That was honest saleswomanship, I'll have you know."

"I'm pretty sure you *guilted* me into it."

"You *did* break my boardwalk," Fern pointed out. "And then I gave it to you on credit, so I'm not sure what you're complaining about."

"And now here you are," said Viv.

The stove ticked and the shadows of moths flittered their way across the walls. "And now here I am," she whispered. A surge of some desperate emotion halfway between despair and hope squeezed the breath out of her.

"You got *me* here," said Viv solemnly.

That crushing sensation receded, mostly.

"It was you, more than anybody. You saved my life in a way I can't properly put into words. I found . . ." Viv stared away and through the walls. Fern knew that if all the stones were peeled away, she'd find Tandri at the end of that gaze. "I found things I didn't think were even possible."

They looked at each other with the red book held like a remembrance between them.

"Well," said Fern, with a comic shrug, "now I guess you have a chance to return the favor."

"If you need saving, then that's what we're going to do," said Viv. She shelved *Ten Links in the Chain* decisively.

She hadn't meant to, but after discovering Viv's change of fate, Fern had buried a call for help in that first letter she'd sent, and not particularly deep.

The lines still burned in her memory.

> I'd love to say that my life has been perfect, that I've seized every moment, that after you left there were no struggles or doubts, but that wouldn't be true. It has been satisfactory, though. There have been many good days.

Doing her best to chase any bitterness out of her laughter, Fern said, "You already did that once. Twice in a lifetime is asking too much."

"I don't see any reason to keep a tally if you don't." Viv regarded

Fern with a gaze much more perceptive than it had been a few decades prior. Then she sniffed and scrubbed a forearm across her eyes. "Hells. Lot of dust in these crates. Let's shelve some fucking *books*."

"Let's shelve some fucking books," replied Fern, relieved.

Hours later, with the shelves stocked, and the crates hauled to the alley, they leaned side by side against the gleaming counter that Cal had built.

Fern felt . . . fine. Maybe even good.

Viv looked down at her from a familiar great height. "So, whatever happened to Satchel?"

Fern smiled wistfully at the thought of the surpassingly polite homunculus made of bone and blue fire.

"Gods, I wish I knew. But I like to think he saw all the things he wanted to."

―⁕―

In the end, Fern named the shop Thistleburr Booksellers in honor of the place her father had built and raised her in, what seemed a thousand leagues to the west and as many years ago. Besides, she couldn't think of a better name that fit, and it was . . . comfortable.

As Viv pointed out, there wasn't likely to be any confusion.

Cal had chiseled the letters deep in a broad oak plank and carved the edges into fancy scallops. Fern had painted the name white with a small brush and a careful hand. Viv had barely stretched to peg it above the freshly scrubbed entryway.

It was the last thing slotted into place before opening day arrived.

Fern stood just inside the door with a single paw resting on the handle. She closed her eyes, drew a deep breath, and held it.

The shelves were stocked. The appointments sparkled. The spice of ink and paper enticed.

A veritable tower of Thimble's baked treats steamed and gleamed atop a round table in the center of the shop, beside carafes of coffee and tea and clusters of mugs.

Tandri's chalk artwork proclaimed OPENING DAY SALE, 5 BITS OFF! from a sandwich board. Fern was reminded of a similar effort by Satchel many years past, rendered in his precise, mathematical hand.

The echoes of that event swelled inside her, painting the inside of her lids until she half believed she'd open them to find herself twenty summers younger and staring into the homunculus's blazing blue eyes.

Then a warm hand fell on Fern's shoulder, heavy and strong, to deliver a gentle squeeze. "It's going to be fine," said Viv. "Better than."

Breathing out, Fern glanced up with a smile. "I've owned a bookstore for twenty-five years. I should be used to a feeling of impending disaster by now, right?"

"Twenty-five years, and no disaster yet. Doesn't seem like a real reliable feeling, does it?" Viv returned the smile.

Fern blinked. "That's an annoyingly logical observation."

They both started at a sudden rap on the door, and after an embarrassing series of fumbles with the latch, Fern pushed it open a few inches.

Tandri's face greeted them as she waited in the dawn light, wearing a soft sweater and stamping her booted feet against the early morning chill. "All set?" Then she glanced to her left.

Fern swung the door wider, revealing four townsfolk waiting on the step beside Viv's wife.

A coil of tension released inside the rattkin.

"Gods, get in here out of the cold! I'm *so* sorry I kept you waiting."

And from then on, scarcely a pause could be found.

~

Fern remembered the day as a series of little landmarks, like treetops rising from a misty valley.

Viv, waving *Ten Links in the Chain* at a bewildered dwarf, covering one eye with a hand and loudly describing a dismemberment.

The dwarf bought the book, but he had a hunted look in his eyes when he did. Viv winked at Fern over the top of his head.

Thimble, squeaking in dismay at platters empty of all but crumbs and rushing to refresh them with steaming cinnamon rolls, the scent of which caused an audible ripple amongst shoppers.

The startling appearance of a shaggy gray cat the size of a timber wolf that *nobody remarked upon*. Its tail crested the tops of the shelves like the fin of a shark roving shallow waters as it prowled the shop with an air of menacing indifference.

The arrival of a venerable woman in a red cloak, accompanied by a stone-fey in a very impressive hat, whose combined presence had an effect that Fern honestly thought the cat *should* have produced. The lady bought a stack of books two feet high, but not before sharply inspecting Fern with a flinty eye. Her escort carried her purchases for her when she left.

Tandri nudging Fern aside to take over the counter so she could eat a hasty sandwich, which Potroast ogled mercilessly until he received his half.

Cal ambling in the door and stepping to the side to lean against the wall, hands in his pockets. He nodded when he caught her eye, smiling his stubbled smile.

The steady accumulation of copper bits and silvers in the cashbox, and the impression of some great, impending wave curling back into the tide before ever breaking on the shore.

And with the closing of the door, the weary, bewildered, dazed, exhausted, triumphant, satisfied silence that followed, as Viv, Tandri, Cal, and Thimble clustered around the countertop, noting the many fresh gaps amongst the bookshelves.

The opening of Thistleburr Booksellers in Thune was an unmitigated success. A new chapter freshly opened in Fern's life—the page turned, the title printed, and ready to be filled with words of renewal, purpose, and peace.

3

"I fucking hate it!" sobbed Fern, her face in her hands.

Potroast glanced up with a hoot and a slow, concerned blink of his owlish grapefruit eyes. One of Thimble's hard cookies lay half masticated between his forepaws.

She let out a watery breath and scratched him behind the ruff of his feathers. "What am I going to do now, little man?" she whispered.

Fern gazed around the alley behind the shop, where she sat on the back step with her red cape rumpled around her. Evening painted the tumble of boxes, barrels, and bales there in shades of deepest blue. A scatter of puddles reflected the pale rind of the moon, and the nighttime murmur of Thune echoed from streets that felt very far away. The frosty air bit her toes.

A week had passed since the grand opening of Thistleburr Booksellers, and things had gone better than they had any right to. Viv's intuition had proven correct, and some kind of synergistic energy had built between the coffee shop next door and her own. A cozy magnetism. It was obvious to all and sundry that the bookshop *belonged* there.

And that was wonderful, Fern supposed.

Except that it didn't matter.

The hollowed-out feeling of dissatisfaction that had steadily eroded her center for the past few years was still there. In fact, it seemed to have *grown*.

Oh, she'd been distracted from it for a day or so, in the same way that sprinting until you're breathless makes it hard to focus on the growling of an empty belly. But now that things had settled into an easy—and profitable—rhythm, it yawned within her, sucking up all the light in reach.

"There you are," came a voice from the mouth of the alley, rousing Fern from her morose reflections.

As the shadow approached, it resolved into the craggy features and flat cap of Cal.

"Shit. Don't look at me. I'm a mess," protested Fern. She gestured at the detritus around her. "I came here to be with my people. This is a garbage-only meeting."

He ambled over and dropped to the step on the side opposite Potroast, who tucked both paws tighter over his cookie and gnawed it with wary determination.

Cal folded his hands between his knees and didn't say a thing. The smell of fresh sawdust tickled Fern's nose.

She mopped her cheeks with the hem of her cloak. "This is the part where you wait in silence until I unload all my feelings, isn't it? I've read a few books, you know."

"Hm."

"I wasn't *supposed* to feel this way."

"That so? Who says?"

"I thought for *sure* you'd do the silence thing."

Cal shrugged. "Can if you like. Just greasin' the wheels. Speakin' of." He rummaged in his overall pocket and withdrew a flask. He spun the cap off, sniffed it, and took a slug of whatever was inside. He passed it to Fern.

She took it, and without pausing at all, put it to her lips and tipped it back. The liquor hit her throat with a quick burn and her belly with a slow warmth that made her eyes water.

Fern coughed and returned the flask. Wiping her eyes with her cloak again, she said, "Okay. Consider me greased. I just . . . I feel . . . *empty*. And it seems like that's my fault. But I don't know what to do about it. I don't even know what I did wrong? If there was a choice that I made somewhere along the road that led me to this, I sure as shit don't know what in the hells it was."

"Seems your shop is turnin' out fine," observed Cal, tilting his head back toward it.

Fern snorted. "Better than fine. And that makes it *worse*. I figured a change of scene, an old friend, new acquaintances, it'd be something like a fresh breeze in a stale room . . . I leaned on the kindness of others to get here, it didn't fix what I wanted fixed, and now I'm *ungrateful* to boot."

She took the proffered flask again.

It traveled back and forth between them while Cal ruminated on that. Eventually, he pursed his lips and ventured, "Didn't get the impression Viv thought she was doin' anythin' more than helpin' a friend open a business. Maybe allow that she wasn't thinkin' of . . . fresh breezes, or what have you."

"Does it matter? I don't know if I can keep doing this. But I don't know if I can *admit* that to her, either. 'Oh, hey, Viv, thanks for all the help, sorry it didn't work out, but I'm questioning my very existence, and I can't keep on this way. So sorry!'"

"Any reason you can't say 'xactly that?"

"I . . . well, *obviously* I can't say . . . what?" Fern spluttered through a mouthful of whiskey.

Cal shrugged again. "What's the worst that can happen?"

"She hates me and never wants to see me again?"

"Remind me how long it was the two of you didn't trade a word?"

Fern gaped at him, her belly afire and head woolly with liquor.

"Awful quiet stretch for a friendship," Cal continued. "Longer'n most could stand. Seemed to survive okay though. Sturdy, I expect."

"All right, setting that aside, even though I am *not* saying I agree with you, what the hells do I do if I'm not doing . . . *this*? Who would I even be?" She stabbed both paws toward the shop.

"Seems to me Viv used to hack things up, and now she makes coffee. She's still Viv though, I guess. You'd know better'n me though, considerin'."

"I need some more of that. Seems to be working," said Fern,

extending a paw for the flask as a welcome cocoon of drunkenness enfolded her. "And it sure as hells beats figuring out a new career in an alley in the middle of the night."

Cal considered her before reluctantly handing the whiskey over once more. But not before taking another swig himself. "Never really was one for givin' advice. I'm more the askin' questions type." He leveled a finger at her. Fern had trouble focusing on it. "But I'm gonna break that rule and say you should talk to Viv. Tomorrow. Tell her what you told me. Don't figure you're gonna find anybody with a better idea of how you're feelin' right now."

Fern considered the mouth of the flask, which seemed very black and big all of a sudden. She sighed, and the alcohol on her breath curled her whiskers. "I guess maybe you're right."

"Hm."

"How do you turn a *hm* into whatever you want it to mean? How does that work?"

"Hob secret. Now, pass that back while there's still somethin' in it."

She did.

"Promise you'll tell her," Cal said with an uncharacteristic earnestness.

Fern slumped against his shoulder.

"I will, uncle," she mumbled.

She couldn't see his face, but even drunk and morose and suddenly half asleep, she thought she could feel him smile.

⁓

After Cal made his way home—tottering only a *little* unsteadily—and Fern made her way back inside—tottering a *lot*—she tossed and turned in her bed for a solid hour. Potroast sawed logs for the duration, and Fern was too cold, and then too hot, and then too queasy, and the room was spinning anyway, so she fiercely whispered *"Fuck it!"* and hurled her blanket back.

She seized her cloak from the peg to shrug into it, then took a moment to acknowledge exactly how drunk she was from a peculiar, muzzy distance. Mostly on account of the fact that she missed the peg three times with her paw.

"Ooh, too old to be this soused," she mumbled. And with the unjustified optimism of the middle-aged, declared, "S'not *too* bad, though. I'm not even slurring. Just . . . a li'l softened. Thass all."

She gazed around the darkened shop, the shelves and books bordered in wavering canary light from the streetlamps outside. On impulse, she snagged her battered leather satchel from the chairback behind the counter. A satchel once inhabited by an old friend, now home to parchment and quills and knickknacks and whatever book she was currently nibbling her way through.

Questing between the shelves, she slid out a few volumes until she found the one she was looking for. A red cover. *Ten Links in the Chain*.

"Sure, Fern," she murmured. "Some kind of peace offering. Appeal to rosy memories. That'll *definitely* help."

She hiccupped.

"Balls."

But she stuffed it into the satchel anyway, and then, before any more whiskeyed resolve could drain out of her, she unlatched the front door and went out into the night.

⁓

Fern didn't think to lock up after herself as she nearly stumbled off the step, only counterbalancing herself at the last moment with a reflexive whip of the tail and a small cloud of profanity. Clutching the satchel to her chest against the cold and blinking in the sudden blare of light from the nearest streetlamp, she peered next door at Legends & Lattes.

Candlelight still glowed through the mullioned glass of the front windows. Which meant she had no ready excuse to scuttle back inside and hide her head under the blanket she'd so recently cast off.

"You promised," she murmured to herself. And then, "Fuck."

The handful of yards between her and the coffee shop seemed very long.

"Just . . . a li'l walk to clear my head first," she mumbled, heading in the opposite direction. "Cool air. Sobrin' up."

She wandered, wobbling, to the next street corner, and then turned left. The cross street held mostly shadow, with lamps set much farther apart, but the chill was delicious on her overheated face as she walked.

Then another turn, and another, and by now, she should've been nearly back where she started.

She wasn't.

A rustle and creak to her right caught her notice.

Parked several doors down the unfamiliar lane, only just revealed by the borderlight of another streetlamp, waited a tiny, open-backed, two-wheeled horse cart. A canvas tarpaulin hid a lumpy assortment of something-or-other in the bed, and a shaggy draft horse in the traces nuzzled patiently at the cobblestones.

That wasn't what really drew her attention though.

A tall figure cinched ties at the edge of the tarpaulin, reaching easily over the boxboards.

A figure Fern *recognized*.

If the star-shaped pommel of the sword above one shoulder wasn't enough, the hacked-short silver hair and maimed ear would have settled it.

"Astryx?" mumbled Fern.

Well, it was definitely a coincidence to see her now, only weeks later. And after being the object of her rescue, no less.

"Coincidence . . . or maybe a sign," said Fern. "S'not every month you bump into a legend twice." She blinked, startled by the volume of her own voice.

If Astryx heard, she gave no indication. The elf scrubbed the horse's cheek affectionately before slipping into another alley, leaving beast and cart unattended.

Fern glanced around and at last spied a building she knew, a chandler's shop only a few doors east of Legends & Lattes. She wasn't lost. Hells, she could be back at Viv's place in no time at all, if she wanted.

Fern imagined the warmth within, a cozy fire, the lingering scent of coffee underpinned by cinnamon.

She imagined Viv's confounded expression when she opened the door to see Fern weaving on the step. Her easy smile when she ushered Fern inside.

The awkward silence, the halting, anxious beginning of the worst sort of conversation.

The way her smile would slip, and the light in her eyes would withdraw by degrees.

And suddenly Fern was moving, but not toward the shop.

In a trice, she lifted the tarpaulin on the cart and scrambled awkwardly inside before cursing herself—in a whisper, thank gods—for not removing the satchel first before she tangled in it on her way up.

Then she was on her back, hemmed in by crates and sacks, clutching the leather bag to her chest again. Her cloak was in rumpled disarray beneath her and wrapped around her tail. The canvas puffed up and down ever so slightly with every breath.

The horse stamped a hoof in surprise, but then fell silent.

She lay there for some minutes, holding every coherent thought at bay, focusing only on the rise and fall of the tarpaulin, the impossibly loud thudding of her heart.

No sounds came from without. Astryx did not return.

At last, the adrenaline leaked out of her, and the yammering in her head could not be staved off any longer.

"What in the hells, Fern! What in the fashionably fuckable *hells*! What is this? Really? Get your stupid ass out of this cart and march your paws down the gods-damned street like the grown rattkin you are and *keep your promise!*"

Fern paused and listened. She heard nothing but the occasional shuffle of the draft horse a few feet west of her head.

"What were you planning anyway? To stow away and flee the gods-damned city? Are you so drunk that that seems *reasonable?*"

She considered the idea. It seemed more reasonable than it ought to, actually, which was very distressing. *Definitely* drunk.

Fern surprised herself with an enormous yawn.

"All right, that's enough of that," she whispered, and gathered her resolve. She braced a paw against the bottom of the cart and began to sit up—

—and froze as footsteps approached.

She lay back down as quietly as she could manage.

Shit. At least this time, she had the presence of mind to say it only in her head.

It was getting warmer under the canvas. The minutes ticked by as Astryx fussed with this and that. She heard the creak of leather, and the jingle of harness, an oddly soothing chime. The cart rocked on its wheels gently as Astryx adjusted something on the buckboard.

Fern waited.

And waited.

And *waited.*

And then she was asleep.

4

Fern awoke to the sight of an alligator grin and eyes the red of a harvest sunset in a round, green face.

And daylight. Painful, *painful* daylight.

Supine as she was in the back of the wagon, and boxed in on all sides by, well, *boxes*, there was nowhere to escape to but up, directly toward that fierce and deadly smile. A direction no right-thinking rattkin would choose.

The hangover that battered Fern's skull confused the whole business to such a degree that *up* was exactly where she went, though, lurching to a sitting position, flailing with the satchel her arms were tangled in, and screaming her throat raw.

The sharp grin and red glare were suddenly three feet away, at the very back of the wagon. Through the sick thumping of blood behind her eyes, Fern saw that both belonged to a goblin with a mop of orange hair and bottlebrush pigtails, clad in some sort of enormous coat made entirely of pockets in a riot of mismatched colors.

Improbably, the goblin's hands were bound before her, and as if that weren't sufficient, several loops of cord were wrapped around her body, from her wrists all the way to her shoulders and secured to a ringbolt on the back of the buckboard.

"What . . . what in the faithless fuck?" wailed Fern. With an ungainly leap, she tumbled sideways over the boxboards of the cart and landed hard on a rutted track, with her cloak flipped over her head and her tail pinned underneath her.

She heard birdsong.

And smelled sweaty horse.

And heard a dimly familiar voice.

"How long have *you* been in there?"

Fern shoved her cloak out of her face and squinted upward, wishing not entirely hyperbolically that she were dead, for a variety of defensible reasons.

Astryx One-Ear stared down at her from a great height, one hand on her hip, the other combing through her silver hair.

Astryx narrowed her eyes in recognition. "Hang on, where do I know you from?"

With a mighty effort to keep the contents of her stomach inside her, Fern scrambled to her feet. She was aware that her fur was caked with the dust of the road and probably something horse-related.

She shot a glance at the goblin in the back of the wagon, who hadn't moved an inch and still grinned benignly at the both of them.

"I'm, uh . . . so, a few weeks ago I was in a carriage in some marshlands, and, er—"

"Oh. The pescadines. Mute couple in the wagon. That's it." She sniffed the air and caught a whiff of Fern's regret, judging by the face she made. "So is this on purpose, or did you just pass out in the wrong wagon?"

Still hung up on the idea of herself and the coachman as a couple and her head aching too much to formulate a lie, Fern replied, "Bit of both?" and winced.

Astryx nodded, thought about that for a moment, and then seemed to dismiss her entirely, shifting her attention to the goblin in the wagon. She pointed. "You. Back up front."

The goblin obliged, leaping nimbly across the cargo in the cartbed and up onto the buckboard, where she dropped onto her butt.

"Is she . . . some kind of prisoner?" Despite the sharpness of her smile, she didn't seem particularly threatening.

Fern crept gingerly off the road and found a grassy swell. She sank to the ground, hissing as every muscle along her spine shrieked in protest. She had no idea how she'd slept through the night, given that she felt like one enormous bruise.

"Bounty," replied Astryx as she tied the tarpaulin back down.

"Isn't that a lot of rope?"

"Trust me when I say it was not my first choice. You must've come aboard in Thune. Yes?"

Fern nodded mutely. Astryx couldn't see her, facing away as she was, but it didn't seem to matter.

"We're a day and a half out, and three days to the next town."

"A day and a *half?*" Fern exclaimed.

"By cart." Astryx was unperturbed. "There's a village back that way that we passed in the night. You should be all right. Safe country. Warm spots to sleep." Astryx finished what she was doing and turned to look Fern over. "Any food?"

It dawned on Fern what was happening. "No," she replied in a very small voice.

Not that food sounded like something she wanted again anytime soon. Her eyes squeezed with every heartbeat, and her guts didn't like the rhythm.

The elf rummaged under the buckboard and withdrew a hunk of thick-rinded cheese and a piece of bread that looked like it would clunk if dropped. Astryx held them out toward Fern without another word.

She didn't seem annoyed or angry. But she didn't seem interested, either.

She might as well have been waiting for her horse to finish relieving itself.

Which, yes, it was currently in the process of doing.

Fern performed some mental arithmetic. A day and a half by horse cart. On foot, that was . . .

With her head in her hands, she whispered, "Questioning my existence from the comfort of a warm bed sounds pretty godsdamned wonderful right about now. Fern, you *ninny.*"

"Hm?"

The elf's *hm* was as precisely calibrated as Cal's.

She hefted the food meaningfully.

Fern tried for an endearing but slightly pitiable smile. "Is there any chance I can convince you to take me to the next town or crossroads or someplace I could book passage back . . ." Fern trailed off, and her eyes widened. She patted at her waist with the sudden realization that she was wearing neither her belt, nor her purse. In a wild burst of optimism, she flipped open the satchel and rifled through it, hoping against hope that—

Nope. Not so much as a lonely copper bit gathering dust at the bottom. Only parchment, pencils, and a book she'd already read that was intended for somebody else.

Astryx had no trouble guessing her thoughts. "Seems like the walk might be the best bet."

It was very clear that the legendary Astryx One-Ear had no intention of retracing her steps to return a hungover rattkin to her shambles of a life. In a *story*, the heroine would have gallantly changed her plans to usher a naive villager back to the safety of their own home, no matter how inconvenient or obviously impractical that might be.

This clearly was not one of those stories.

"*Luffing shunks!*" chirped the goblin.

Both Astryx and Fern switched their attention to the girl on the buckboard.

"My thoughts exactly," muttered Fern, who knew a *lot* of goblin profanity.

"You know what she's saying?" Astryx cocked a brow at her.

Something canny in Fern that wasn't entirely debilitated by alcoholic low tide said, "Oh, sure. Why?"

"You speak goblin?"

"Does she not speak Territories?" Fern neatly avoided the question.

Astryx frowned. "Not so far as I can tell. What'd she say?"

"Well," Fern hedged. "Nothing polite." Not that politeness had ever governed *Fern's* speech before.

"Never really got on with the goblin tongue myself. They didn't even have one five hundred years ago. I understand it's mostly curses, so, that sounds about right."

Fern thought that if *she* had lived for a thousand years, *she* might have picked up a few more languages that were relevant to her line of business, but was wise enough not to say so.

Instead, she said, "Look, I've got a proposal. For the sake of argument, let's assume you take me with you to the next real stop. I can listen to what she's got to say? That's bound to make things easier for *you,* and as a bonus, I don't expire by the side of the road on my way home."

The elf pursed her lips in speculation. "You still don't have any money. How are you planning to hire your way back?"

Fern spread her paws. "You don't have to worry about that, right? I'll just have to find a way to scrape together the silver when I get there."

"Mmm. What's your name?"

"Fern."

"And what is it that you do?"

"I'm a bookseller," replied Fern, which didn't seem very useful at the moment.

Astryx appeared skeptical. "That doesn't bode well for your prospects."

Fern privately agreed, but said, "I'm a very *resourceful* bookseller . . . ?"

There was a long silence, during which the draft horse cropped several mouthfuls of grass from the verge and flicked away a few bothersome flies.

"*Ta shunka,*" declared the goblin.

Astryx glanced between the two of them and then raised both brows at Fern expectantly.

Fern sighed. "It means, 'you're fucked.'"

5

Dear Viv,
 I have no idea how to write this letter to you. This is the fourth attempt, in fact. All the others have started the same way, though.
 I'm sorry.
 And every time I write that, I immediately want to cross it out because it looks so small and stupid and useless on the page.
 I <u>feel</u> small and stupid. And I guess also useless.
 But I can't get around writing those words. This letter has to start that way.
 In the previous three versions, it got really pitiful after that point, and there was a lot of blubbering and wailing and abasement, but that feels self-indulgent, so I'm skipping it this time. Maybe that means I'll get further.

Fern looked up and made a sour face. "Gods, this is terrible." She took a moment to survey the green swells of countryside through which they passed. After several skins of water, half of the bread-slash-rock Astryx had offered—the pungent cheese was a no-go—and a solid afternoon of travel, Fern's hangover had fled at last.

Lupine bloomed along the side of the road, and hayricks studded distant fields. A windmill twirled lazily in the distance. The wind played through her fur, and the cart creaked gently beneath her, the motion of which was either very soothing, or like a hammer blow to the spine, depending on the condition of the road beneath. They were currently enjoying the nicer of the two options. It was a great relief.

She returned her attention to the parchment, and her charcoal pencil.

> *Cal may have already told you that I had a bit of a breakdown.*

Fern rolled her eyes and scratched that out.

> *I am planning to return as soon as possible, and I am probably standing in front of you watching as you read this.*

She put the pencil to her lips.

> *Or maybe I'm lying dead by the side of the road, and this letter found itself to you via some other mysterious means.*

"For fuck's sake," she muttered, and furiously scratched that out, too. The likelihood of scrapping this entire attempt was growing by the word.

> *The upshot is that a terrible feeling has been growing in me for years. The new shop was supposed to fix that, but the feeling didn't disappear, even with everything working out perfectly, and I guess I got scared. And then I got drunk. And on my way to explain all this to you, I crawled into the back of a cart and passed out, and now I'm far from home.*

Well, that was essentially true, anyway. Even if it did sound preposterous.

I hope Potroast is all right. I can't even write my apology to him. I don't know if he'll ever forgive me for disappearing. There might not be enough baked goods in the world.

Fern had to pause to arm away a tear. Bad as she felt about leaving Viv in the lurch after all her investment into Thistleburr, all the energy she'd poured into it . . . the realization that she'd left Potroast behind kept her stomach knotted long after the hangover had faded. She knew he'd be cared for, but . . .

I will find my way back.

Even though I'm riding in the wrong direction, Fern thought, but did not write.

You're never going to believe whose cart it was.

Astryx jogged easily beside the draft horse, the pommel of her blade tracing a silvery figure eight behind her in the afternoon sun. The legendary adventurer didn't seem to tire and never rode on the cart with the rest of them. Possibly it was a fitness thing. There didn't look to be an ounce of fat on her body. She also did not appear to sweat.

Or my other traveling companion.

The goblin, whose name was apparently Zyll, slept upright on the buckboard beside her. Her sharp-toothed mouth was open, and a pointed pink tongue lolled halfway to her chin. Occasional snores whistled from her nose, like the peeping of a new-hatched chick.

She's . . . unique.

When she looked up again, she startled. Zyll stared back with clear interest. Her mouth remained open, tongue still out, but she was very, very awake.

Another of those peeping snores escaped her nose, though.

The goblin did not seem at all uncomfortable, even swaddled as she was in hemp.

"What did you *do* to end up here?" Fern hadn't intended to say it aloud, but she didn't suppose it mattered.

"Maybe you should ask in goblin?" called Astryx, not even a bit winded.

Fern couldn't tell if the question was pointed or not.

"Would she tell me?"

Astryx's shoulders rose and fell. "Why don't we find out?"

Well, *that* definitely felt like a test.

The rattkin's mind raced, given that her goblin vocabulary was uniformly inappropriate for polite conversation.

"*Spenka tu drott?*" she managed, hoping Astryx didn't know that one.

Zyll's brows rose in surprise.

Which was only natural, Fern supposed, since she'd just been asked if she liked to drink her own pee.

An answer was not forthcoming.

―∽

"Tales vary. They usually do," said Astryx later that evening in response to Fern's now long-unanswered question about the goblin's misdeeds. The elf unbuckled her baldric and slipped the sword from her back, still in its sheath. She propped it carefully on the fallen log she was using for a bench, and then squatted before their small campfire.

On the hill behind them, an ancient, craggy dolmen framed a black window into starlight. The mournful, far-off *chuk-whooo* of a nightbird made their campsite feel unfathomably remote.

"One of the more recent ones involves the Seventy Saint army, up in North Territory." Astryx nodded toward the goblin.

"Allegedly, she disrupted their whole supply chain, and they ended up stranded for an entire winter in the mountains, eating their boots for breakfast."

Fern wrinkled her brow, gingerly extending a hunk of the detestable cheese toward Zyll's deadly-looking mouth. "That's enough to warrant a bounty on your head?"

The goblin's jaws creaked wide, her tongue lolling. Still bound and tethered on the ground next to the wagon, she waited, unblinking, until Fern tossed the rind of cheese, as though flinging meat to a starving dog. Zyll snapped her smile closed over it and swallowed without chewing once.

Astryx shrugged and prodded the fire. "The Seventy Saints seemed to think so. Probably objected strongly to the taste of boots."

"It's not . . . *evil*, though . . . ?" tried Fern, making a game attempt to tear a heel off the loaf of bread Astryx had provided for the evening meal. Boots were probably more appetizing.

"A bounty isn't a moral judgment," replied Astryx patiently. "Usually it's someone offering money for a person to be delivered someplace, usually a person who doesn't *want* to be delivered to that place."

Fern prepared to respond, but Astryx continued.

"Trust me, good and evil become a lot less easy to spot after a few hundred years of doing this."

Fern observed Zyll for a moment, wondering seriously whether she'd asphyxiate on the bread if she gulped it down like she had the cheese.

The goblin had developed a keen interest in Astryx's sheathed blade and appeared to be studying it. She caught Fern's gaze, winked at her, and said, *"Alstroon."*

Fern had no idea what that meant, so apparently it wasn't profane. "So I could just pay to have *anybody* hauled to my doorstep if I wanted? Isn't that kidnapping?"

"Doesn't work that way. There's a system. Requirements." Astryx waved a hand dismissively. "It's not very interesting."

"I imagine it's pretty fucking—I mean, I imagine it's pretty interesting if you're the one with a bounty on your head." For some reason Fern felt weird swearing around Astryx. Like she was cursing in front of her grandmother.

"If there *is* one on your head, then there's likely a good reason," replied the elf, with a mildness that Fern found very confusing and not at all in keeping with the swashbuckling mental image of the legendary Blademistress the histories had conjured. In fact, she was having a hard time squaring the entire situation with her heart-pounding first impression of the elf in the swamplands, too.

Fern fidgeted with the calcified bread, and then blurted, "It's just . . . I've read *books* about you. *The Flight of the Silver Hawk?* You're a living legend! And this . . . kind of makes you sound like a postwoman? Is this really what you mostly do?"

Astryx sighed, and for the first time her placid expression became something Fern recognized. Something a little weary. A little hollow. "Everyone always wants it to be exciting. For it to be worthy of a song. To buy you a beer and hear about a thrilling escape or a fierce battle or a vanquished demon. To write a *book* about it."

"But those *are* all things that happened, right?" asked Fern, hopeful.

"After ten centuries of doing this, do you want to know what's *really* exciting?" asked Astryx, ignoring the question. Her gaze was direct, and almost hungry.

Fern nodded.

"Dry socks."

～

Fern dreamed of Viv.

A distressingly *realistic* dream.

"I guess it's the risk we ran," the orc said, sighing deeply. She curled an arm around Tandri's back as they surveyed the empty interior of the new bookshop. "I didn't figure Fern for the sort of person who'd sneak off in the night and leave her obligations behind, but maybe the years changed her in a way I didn't expect. Or maybe I expected more than I should've. I'm sorry."

"No apologies from you," replied Tandri, cupping Viv's chin with a slender hand. "I know this is a huge disappointment, but we'll make do. You did nothing but try to help an old friend, and there's never any shame in that."

With no body and no agency, Fern was reduced to a powerless, floating perspective. She tried to speak but had no mouth. She tried to shift her gaze but had no body to direct.

I know this is a dream, Fern thought. *Of course it is. Because I might as well be reading this in a story. If it were real, I could change it. If it were real, I'd be here, and none of this would be happening.*

"I can run the place until we find someone to sell it to," said Tandri.

"Sell? There's still the chance she might come back . . ." said Viv, trailing off hopefully.

Tandri shook her head. "I doubt that'll happen. Besides, this bookstore deserves real commitment. It's something special. It needs someone special to care for it."

Fern's dream self had no stomach, but it knotted anyway.

Potroast whined, and her point of view tilted so that she could see the gryphet curled at Tandri's feet, giant golden eyes beseechingly pitiful.

The succubus patted Viv's hand and dropped to her haunches to run her fingers through his feathers. "I can't believe she left Potroast behind." The gryphet hooted mournfully, butting his head against her hand.

Viv smiled down at them both, hands on her hips. "At least he's found the home he really needed."

Oh fuck you, you fucking dream, thought Fern.

"We all just have to come to terms with the fact that she's gone," her old friend continued.

Then her gaze shifted and caught Fern's.

"She's gone."

Fern's eyes snapped open.

6

"She's gone. Wake up."

"Whazzat?" Fern startled awake at a hand on her back and searched her surroundings wildly. The disorientation of finding herself sleeping on the ground in the middle of nowhere was profound. Specters of guilt and dismay still haunted her from the fading tatters of her dream.

The heavy scent of cold grass in the shadowed valley and the sooty funk of a recently expired campfire quivered her whiskers. When was the last time she'd slept out of doors? Had she *ever*?

Struggling to a sitting position, Fern drew her cloak—currently serving as a woefully thin blanket—tighter around her. In the sharp morning chill she was spectacularly glad to have fur.

Astryx straightened and loomed above her, edged in what little morning light had made an early advance over the eastern hills. It took a solid ten seconds before Fern's recent memory slotted into place and she realized who she was looking at, where she was, and that she would not be stumbling out of bed to feed a hungry gryphet anytime soon.

"The goblin? How? Wh-Where is she?" Fern's mouth was still asleep. She glanced in muzzy confusion toward the wagon and the ringbolt, sans rope.

Even in the dim light, she didn't have any trouble interpreting the flat expression Astryx returned. "If I knew that, I wouldn't have bothered to wake you. I need you to watch the camp while I hunt her down. I've seen signs of hazferou in the area. The bounty doesn't specify that Zyll should be uneaten, but it *is* implied."

Nothing in her tone hinted that a *joke* was implied, though.

"Hazferou?" Fern scrubbed sleep sand from both eyes with her paws.

"A bit like a giant chicken. But with teeth. And venom."

That banished any lingering drowsiness, as surely as plunging through the surface of a frozen pond. "I thought you said this was *safe country* when you were sending me off to *walk* home?"

"It was. Now, it isn't."

"And you want me to stay here? Alone?" She snatched the red book from her satchel and brandished it. "If a bunch of devil chickens attack, you want me to, what, *read* them to death?"

Astryx plucked the book from Fern's paws and tested its weight. "I think you could get some power behind this if you used both hands."

That was a joke. Fern was *pretty* sure. Nothing seemed very funny at the moment.

"Fuck me."

"What a foul mouth you have."

"Seems appropriate to the situation? I'm coming with you."

Astryx glanced at the draft horse and scratched her ruined ear in a gesture that Fern was beginning to understand meant she was debating something. "I suppose if there are any cries of distress, you can translate."

Fern winced inwardly at that.

The elf approached the stub of a branch where the horse's reins were tethered and untied them. She looped the leather in her fist and then tucked them into his halter, patting his shoulder with her other hand. With absolute seriousness, she said, "All right, Bucket. You see any hazferou, you kick them and run."

"Your horse's name is *Bucket*? Is that a play on words, or just a really boring name?"

Astryx frowned. "What do you mean, a play on words?"

"Um. Never mind."

The elf shrugged, swept up her sword in its sheath with the baldric still attached, and strode purposefully west of their campsite and into the undergrowth with nary a backward glance.

Fern squeaked and hurried to follow.

───✦───

While it was technically dawn, and allegedly, this involved the existence of sunlight, the forest beyond the road was positively stygian. Fern also knew about enough woodlore to fill a teaspoon.

As a result, while she did her best to follow Astryx into the gloom, her cloak snagged on brambles, leaf litter clung to her fur, and whippy young branches slapped her in the face.

She tried to be quiet about it, but in addition to the general trampling and bumbling, the occasional curse made it past her lips, too. Sotto voce, but still.

After a few aggrieved glances over her shoulder, Astryx stopped, waited for Fern to catch up—scratched and panting—and without a word, slung the rattkin onto her back.

Fern squawked and hugged the elf's neck tight as Astryx hooked her forearms under the smaller woman's legs and set off again at a silent trot.

"You can let up on my throat," Astryx rasped. "You won't fall."

"Oh." Fern tried her best not to throttle her mount. "Sorry."

"Mmm."

Astryx didn't appear to mind the *weight* at all though, gliding with incredible agility through the dark woods without disturbing so much as a leaf.

Light slowly filtered through the canopy as daylight took the sky. Despite that, Fern quickly became disoriented as they passed in and out of glens, leapt over streamlets, and wove between crowded bastion oak. She had the sense that there was a method to Astryx's navigation. Fern just didn't understand it in the slightest.

Jouncing against Astryx's back wasn't comfortable as conveyances went and called to mind the horse cart traveling over the wrong sort of road. The elf didn't come with any built-in cushions, either.

Still, it beat stinging thorns and flesh-eating chickens.

At last, at some signal Fern couldn't detect, Astryx abruptly stopped and crouched. Her unspoken request was obvious, so Fern unlatched her bloodless paws and slithered off the elf's back.

Straightening, the Oathmaiden leaned on her sheathed sword, point down in the earth. She scrabbled a hand through her short, silver hair in an annoyed way.

"This isn't working," she said, at a normal speaking volume.

Fern opened her mouth to say something, and realized she didn't have anything to offer that wouldn't probably diminish her even further in the eyes of a thousand-year-old legend. She closed her mouth again.

Astryx quirked an amused smile and nodded once. Approval?

Fern experienced a tiny bloom of pride at maybe having put a foot right. Even if it was for choosing to do nothing at all.

"I followed her trail until it vanished. I crisscrossed the area, picked it up once more, and again it disappeared right here." The elf gestured at the glade they stood in. "No blood. No sign of a struggle, but still, there's a chance something got her. Or she's an unparalleled master of forest lore. But since she doesn't have the use of her hands . . ." Astryx frowned. "The former seems more likely."

An image of the trussed little goblin halfway down the beak of some malicious poultry flashed through Fern's mind. The goblin girl had an air of innocence about her, no matter what tales she'd given rise to.

"And that would be . . . bad, right?"

"Yes. That would be bad."

"Because she'd be hurt, or because of the bounty?" asked Fern carefully. She winced after she said it, but at the same time, she didn't wish the words *unsaid*. It felt increasingly urgent to find out what sort of person Astryx was, and while alone in the middle of a dark wood a dozen leagues from civilization *might* not have been the wisest place to discover the answer, Fern didn't figure it would get any safer in the future.

Astryx's eyes narrowed in speculation. "Neither would be ideal."

That was sort of an answer.

The elf continued, "If she's in dire enough circumstances to *want* my help, we'll try something else. It's convenient that you speak her language. That makes this a lot more straightforward."

"Oh. Um. Really?" asked Fern in a strangled voice.

"We'll spiral out from here, and you can call out to her, asking her to shout for help if she needs it. That shouldn't be a problem, should it?"

"Er."

An uncomfortable silence stretched.

Astryx sighed. "You don't speak goblin at all, do you?"

"Just the swears?" replied Fern in a tiny voice. "But to be fair, I never *actually* said I spoke the language."

The elf looked up and to the right as she appeared to review their previous conversation. "Hm. That's vexing. I can't believe I didn't notice at the time."

"Although," said Fern quickly, "I don't imagine she cares what language we're speaking if she hears us calling and needs help. Right?"

Oh gods, please don't leave me stranded in bloodthirsty chicken territory because I implied I knew more than a few dirty goblin words, thought Fern, with great fervency.

"Let's hope so," replied Astryx. "Still. You're walking from now on."

On balance, Fern decided she was getting off easy.

They tramped through the woods, hollering until they were hoarse. Well, Astryx's holler was more of a commanding shout, but it all amounted to the same thing. Sore throats for the both of them, and no Zyll.

"That's that then," said Astryx suddenly, dropping her hands from where they'd cupped her mouth. "She's gone."

She didn't seem particularly upset. Mildly annoyed, if anything. Like she'd forgotten where she'd left her toothbrush.

Fern found this challenging to wrap her head around.

It was solidly midday, and the bookseller's stomach continually registered displeasure at its total emptiness. Her feet hurt, her head felt swimmy, her cloak was a ragged mess, and she could barely remember why she was there in the first place. That mental thread led to a hopeless tangle she didn't dare tease out.

"Come on, the camp is this way," said the elf. She'd long since buckled on her baldric, freeing both hands, and she strode away without bothering to see if Fern would follow.

An ember of anger sparked in Fern's chest and wanted to flicker into something much hotter. "We're just giving up?"

Astryx didn't stop moving, but called, "Nothing else for it, really."

"But . . . she could be dead!"

The elf was getting farther and farther away. "It's likely. And if so, there's not a thing that can be done."

"But . . . *hey!*" Fern scrambled into a trot before she lost track of Astryx in between the tree trunks.

Panting, she mostly caught up to the Oathmaiden, who didn't so much as pause. "How can you be so . . . so . . . *indifferent?*" she sputtered angrily, if breathlessly. It was challenging to confront somebody who kept walking away, and whose stride length was easily double your own.

Astryx spared her a look at least, brows raised. "Do you imagine things always go perfectly in my line of work?"

"Well . . . *no*, but—"

"And when they don't, what do you imagine I should be doing differently?"

There was no heat in Astryx's voice. Just a sort of distant politeness. Possibly even a mild curiosity.

"It's just . . . *stop*, will you?"

To Fern's astonishment, Astryx did.

The rattkin clenched her paws by her hips and caught her breath. "Look. You said that these bounties, they're about delivering someone someplace. For money."

The elf didn't reply, only waited patiently, with that infuriatingly mild look on her face.

"So . . . if that person *dies* on the way, doesn't that mean you *fucked up?*" demanded Fern, with real heat.

"I'd like to point out that the goblin is the one who fled."

"In her position, that seems like a pretty reasonable thing to do!" hissed Fern.

"She was safe in my care," insisted Astryx.

"You *tied her up. All the time.*"

"Because of the fleeing," replied the elf, reasonably.

"Well . . . *shitkindling!*" cried Fern.

Astryx crouched so they were face-to-face, a distant candle-flame of empathy in her icy blue eyes.

"I understand what's happening here," she said. "It's easy for me to forget, but I think I know what you're feeling. Seven or eight hundred years ago, I might have felt the same. A sense of responsibility for events you can't control. A conviction that things could have been different, *if only.*"

"Why don't you feel that now?" demanded Fern, but quieter with the elf's face so close.

"In all the years I've been doing this, can you imagine how many jobs have turned sour? It's more than you'd believe. And after a while, it becomes clear that those feelings you're having aren't practical. Sometimes, the ill turn is your own mistake; sometimes, it's not. But that depth of feeling? It can't survive the *numbers.*"

"I think that's supposed to sound reasonable, but it only sounds awful," said Fern.

Astryx stood again. "I don't wish her ill, and I've done what I can to protect her. It's possible she escaped. Unlikely, but you never know."

"So . . . what now?"

"We go back to camp. We journey to the next village. We go our separate ways. And onward and again."

～

An hour later they trudged out of the woods and into view of the campsite—only one of them lacerated and aching. The first thing Fern noticed was Bucket calmly cropping grass by the roadside. Apparently the threat of hazferou had never materialized. Or he'd kicked them to death, she supposed.

The second thing she noticed was Zyll, just as calmly sitting beside the expired campfire. She perched atop a neat coil of the rope that had once bound her, her coat of many pockets puddling on the hemp. The goblin's sharp-toothed grin was barely visible over the creature clutched in her lap—a black-and-white hen the size of a turkey, with long feathered frills capping its feet.

"*Chuptik*," declared Zyll, lifting the bird and gesturing with it, much to the chicken's consternation.

No, *not* a chicken, Fern realized.

Chickens did not have cruelly hooked beaks and fangs and poisonous green eyes, nor did they hiss like a kettle on the boil.

The goblin hugged the indignant hazferou to her chest and snuggled her face into the spines and extravagant feathers of its back.

"Is she *really* a prisoner?" asked Fern.

Astryx scratched her ear. "Hm."

"Honestly, she's not very good at it."

7

Astryx made a game attempt to separate Zyll from the hazferou. This would have been easier had either of them cooperated, but the creature nipped at any approaching fingers that were not green, and Zyll's lips writhed closed over her teeth as she growled deep in her throat and clutched the hen closer to her coat.

Fern discovered that the goblin only seemed *truly* menacing when her incredibly sharp teeth were hidden.

The elf regarded the demon bird and the goblin with a frown and fists on hips, then squatted before them both, a choice that put her face far closer to that fanged beak than Fern would ever have dared.

Snagging the loose end of the coil of rope, Astryx held it up in front of Zyll's eyes. "I have a feeling you understand me perfectly. So, I'm going to offer you a bargain."

Zyll's eyes narrowed to calculating slits, but the growling ceased.

"I won't pretend to understand what *this* is," she said, gesturing between bird and goblin. "And I have no idea how you slipped your bonds, but I can assure you that I know *much* more complicated knot-work, and have dispatched plenty of hazferou in my time. It wouldn't even be an inconvenience to do it again. *However.* If you'll let me rebind you without a fuss—just the wrists this time—then I'll let this creature live." She tilted her head toward the hazferou, which clucked aggressively.

Zyll blinked very slowly, and with equal slowness her pointed pink tongue emerged from between her lips in an inscrutable expression. Lazy. Somehow catlike.

Then she stood, placed the hazferou carefully on the ground, and thrust both wrists in Astryx's direction.

"Holy shit!" cried Fern, shrinking away from the hazferou as it hopped onto the buckboard between her and Zyll.

This despite Astryx depositing the creature in the underbrush at least two leagues back.

Its evil green eyes regarded her with a species of malicious disdain before it shuffled closer to the goblin, who burbled happily and buried her face in its side.

The furry hind limb of some unfortunate woodland creature dangled from its beak for an unsettling moment until, with a gulping cluck, the leg vanished down its gullet.

Bucket whinnied as Astryx seized his bridle and brought him to an abrupt halt.

It was the first time Fern had seen surprise register on the elf's face.

"How—?" Astryx stood with mouth agape, one hand still wrapped around bridle leather.

"—did it get here?" Fern finished for her, gingerly sliding several inches to the right and as far away from the bird as possible. "Yeah, I'd like to know that, too."

Astryx's expression hardened, and she reached for the haft over her shoulder, striding purposefully back toward the cart.

Zyll's attention snapped to her approach, and she thrust her bound hands into the air and waved them significantly.

"The deal was that I'd let it live," said the elf. "Not that I'd take it on as a traveling companion. Hazferou fancy the eyes of their prey, and I don't like the idea of it fancying mine while I sleep."

The goblin hissed something under her breath at the hazferou. It clucked throatily, and at a single insistent nudge from the goblin, hopped back over the seat and onto the tarpaulin in the cart, where it waddled in a circle and then settled down to roost in the valley where the canvas spanned two crates.

Astryx stopped and regarded both of them narrowly, hand still gripping the haft above the starburst pommel.

After a long moment, she dropped her hand from the sword.

"So . . . it's staying?" asked Fern, hunched over and regarding the beast with distrust.

The elf stared at her levelly. "What's a second stowaway, I suppose?"

"What was that you said about them fancying the eyes, though?"

"Perhaps you should have a conversation with Zyll about that," replied Astryx with suspect cheer. She clucked to Bucket, and the cart got moving again.

To its credit, the hazferou made no menacing moves toward anybody's eyes.

Their little caravan continued along the road as it curved northeast, up a series of switchbacks and out of the wooded valley, into an increasingly craggy series of bluffs. Stronger, colder winds tugged at Fern's ragged red cloak, and low-lying mist poured slowly down the cliffsides until it tore away to form ribbons of cloud that glided above the valley below.

Fern stared back the way they had come, and for the first time could see the spare gleam of Thune's fortress walls in the far distance, and the glittering path of the River Briar as it cut through the heart of the city and disappeared into the western haze. She'd hardly spent enough weeks in Thune for it to feel like a home, but after only four days away, her heart still ached for what she knew she had left there. For *who* she had left there.

"For the fucking mess I left behind," she muttered to herself and dug her latest letter to Viv out of her satchel. Fern stared at it bleakly. "And now, I'm on a cart with a murder bird and a goblin with a mouth like a shark. A real improvement, Fern."

It also wasn't lost on her that every hour, every league they traveled, was one she'd have to painfully retrace at some point. There might as well have been a field of brambles behind them.

Her stomach growled loudly. Astryx had been free enough with the simple rations she had on hand, but the stone-hard bread and terrible cheese were a chore to eat, and none of it was a patch on Thimble's cooking. Or, indeed, *anyone's* cooking. The elf didn't seem to believe in the heating of foods. Fern was no chef, but she was increasingly appreciative of how many excellent ones she'd lived near.

The rattkin's fur was grimy, and a network of scrapes and scratches stung beneath matted silver tufts. She prodded some of the longer wounds with a claw, hissing as she did so. "What I'd give for a gods-damned bath."

She suddenly sensed Zyll's gaze upon her and met crimson eyes with her own.

"Um," she said.

The goblin cocked her head to the side, then shoved her bound hands into one of the many pockets that made up her coat. She fished around for a moment, tongue protruding, then, apparently dissatisfied, tried another. And another. And *another,* upon which she brightened and withdrew a fistful of what looked like aggressively moldy weeds.

Zyll extended them. *"Gul tatuk."*

Fern glanced at Astryx's back where she strode beside Bucket, and then at the tragic plants. "Um. What's this?" She wondered whether Astryx had searched those pockets. She must have.

The goblin's grin widened, and she waggled the handful significantly at Fern's legs.

Tucking the letter back into her satchel, Fern tentatively reached a paw out to take the offered weeds, or herbs, or whatever they were. She sniffed. "Whoof. Smells like . . ." Actually, it smelled astringent. The scent tickled some memory in the back of her mind.

While the plants were truly dire in appearance, squeezing them between her fingers pressed some sort of sap or oil from the leaves.

She eyed Zyll one last time, and then muttered, "Oh, what

the hells, it's been nothing but bad decisions for days. The odds are in my favor for a turnaround." With two fingers she rubbed some of the substance experimentally on one of her longest scratches. The smell intensified, heady and medicinal.

Immediately, a numbing coolness spread outward. The stinging fell away.

"Huh. Thank you," she said with honest gratitude.

Zyll did not reply, only settled back against the slatted bench back with a satisfied grin from which only two or three teeth escaped, and promptly fell asleep.

⁓

"So, bad debts?"

Fern shook herself out of a somnolent daze brought on by the rocking of the cart and stared in confusion down at Astryx.

The elf had dropped back to keep pace beside the buckboard, still loping along with her endless, effortless stride. Her voice was unaffected by the effort, as per usual. Bucket clopped stolidly onward, sure of his own business.

The stony ruptures of the uplands had dwindled to the occasional low upthrust of rock, peppered with scrubby trees Fern didn't recognize. Zyll's squeaking snores issued from beside her, although her eyes were closed this time. She sagged back and forth in dramatic, metronomic arcs that seemed implausible to sleep through. Broody grumbles issued from the hazferou in the cart.

"I'm sorry, what?"

"In my business, odds tend to favor owing silver, and not being able to pay it. I was just wondering what sort of trouble you were in."

"What makes you think I was in *trouble?*" Fern asked sharply.

Astryx shot her a look.

"I was just . . . drunk. And upset."

"Yes, I smelled the whiskey. And I might not be a terribly good judge of age as far as that goes, but aren't you a bit old to be passing out in random wagons? I thought that was reserved for the young and foolish."

Fern sighed and rubbed her face with both paws. "No age restriction for fools."

"So. *Not* fleeing." A pregnant pause. "You said you were a bookseller?"

"Hm." Fern figured that if everyone else could reply monosyllabically, then so could she.

"And you're anxious to get back to it, are you?"

It was Fern's turn for a long pause. "Why are you so anxious to know? You'll forgive me, but you don't seem like one for idle conversation."

Astryx shrugged. "I can be curious. Call it an essential job skill."

Two days ago, Fern's stomach might have fluttered at the thought of Astryx One-Ear's interest in *her*. Here and now, though—scratched and abraded, ass-aching, groggy, and existentially fucked-up—she was simply annoyed.

The elf continued, her tone offhanded. "It seems like relaxing work. Easy. Calming. Not the sort of thing to drive anyone to drink."

"*Relaxing?*" Fern sputtered. Her face burned hot with disbelief that wanted to swell into indignation if not anger. "I . . . you . . ." She was uncharacteristically lost for words.

"Sure." Astryx ticked items off on her fingers. "Nothing wants to stab you. Indoors all year long. Easy on the back. No risk of dismemberment, and, most importantly," she gave Fern a significant look, "the dry socks."

"Listen," said Fern, jabbing a finger at Astryx. Something far at the back of her skull shrieked, *Why are you wagging a claw at a thousand-year-old monster hunter, you numbwit!*

Something much older and more righteous ignored the warning.

"I have spent my *life* convincing people to buy blocks of paper with marks on them for more money than they want to part with.

I fill a room with them and pray to the Eight that I filled it with the right ones, and that I can get them into the right hands, and I *never get enough of that right*. It's like tossing fistfuls of fucking silver up a hill and hoping enough of it rolls back down that I have more silver to throw. I bet on odds that any self-respecting dice player would run screaming from, and half the time, I lie awake wondering whether I'll be able to keep at it for another week, or a month, or a year."

She was panting, and her eyes were probably a little wild.

"I only do it," she continued, "because I'm stupid enough to think it's *important*."

Astryx returned a considering look. "So, it's important. Then why did you run from it?"

Fern blinked. "I . . . no, I mean I . . . loved . . . it."

"I can tell from the impassioned defense." There wasn't a hint of mockery in the elf's reply, though it was clear she hadn't missed Fern's use of past tense.

The rattkin sighed and stared bleakly ahead at Bucket's patient progress. In the wake of her outburst, the emptiness that had gotten her into this fix returned, like cold, black water refilling a pool from an underground stream. "You know, I already bared my soul a few days ago, and that's how I ended up in this mess. You've been doing the same job for nearly a thousand years. Did *you* always feel good about it?"

"Nothing feels good all the time," replied Astryx.

Which wasn't exactly an answer.

"Only a day stands between us and Bycross, and then you can head back to where you belong," continued the elf. "To what's important."

And that was definitely the end of the conversation.

8

With Bycross less than a day away, Fern abandoned revising her letters to Viv in favor of working them out aloud. She was nearly out of parchment anyway. Zyll was a willing—or at least captive—audience. Whether she was fascinated or confused by the whole affair was beyond Fern's ability to determine.

The hazferou sat between them, clucking and cocking its head in every direction. It had reclaimed its space on the buckboard, but no blood had as yet been shed, and she decided not to tempt fate by trying to alter this state of affairs.

Astryx didn't comment on the one-sided conversation between goblin and rattkin, no matter how much the bookseller swore during the recitation. Still, Fern got the impression she was listening with half an ear.

Ha, she thought, with grim amusement.

"Maybe I should spend more time thinking about how to make it up to her?" said Fern, chin in paw. She arched a brow at Zyll. "Who wants to listen to somebody flog themselves, right? I'm here because I made a mistake. *Everybody* makes mistakes. So, focusing on minimizing the damage is what a responsible adult would do, yeah?"

Zyll stared back, neither nodding nor shaking her head. Or blinking.

The goblin slid her bound hands into a maroon pocket, withdrawing a spoon. It didn't look particularly clean. She slowly licked it, and then inserted the end into her mouth and closed her lips over it, sucking deliberately and never breaking eye contact.

"Um. Anyway." Fern cleared her throat, looking upward and appealing to an invisible Viv. "Look, I panicked. Everything was just too much, and I got maudlin and tipsy, then fell asleep in a wagon and woke up a day outside of town. Pretty fucking—I mean, pretty ridiculous, right? I'm sorry it took me so long to make my way back, but you wouldn't *believe* who I . . . okay, no, that's too much to start with."

Zyll hiked both brows up, still sucking on the spoon.

The cart jostled its way through an arcing turn, and Fern grabbed the edge of the buckboard with both paws while the hazferou fluffed and squawked in annoyance. They'd begun a slow descent toward Bycross, and the cart track noodled its way between humps of green hillside. Somewhere a brook gurgled, and three or four tendrils of smoke spiraled skyward in the distance.

Fern tried again, gesturing beseechingly. "I just want to fix this. So. How *are* things? Er. Whatever happened, whatever fell apart or cost you or made your life hells, I want to do something about it. I know I probably don't feel trustworthy to you right now, but I swear, it'll *never* happen again."

She stared down from Viv's lofty perspective at the humble rattkin before her. Coincidentally, this view coincided with one of Bucket's hindquarters. Deepening her voice, and already shaking her head, she replied, "'Fern, do you think I'm an idiot? You knew whose wagon that was. You knew what you were doing. You left everyone here to clean up your mess, and take care of your pet, and you know what? We *did* all that, and it turns out we don't need you for this, and apparently, you didn't need us, either, so—' Oh, gods, this is fucking ridiculous." She sagged and put her face in her paws.

Astryx's voice distracted her from her pity soliloquy. "If you want my advice, you're making this very complicated," she called, turning around to jog backward, which was honestly pretty impressive. "Simple is better. The guilty dog barks loudest."

"The what?"

"The quick cut is best. In and out before anyone can feel it."

"I want to apologize, not stab her. Have you spent a thousand years collecting these weird sayings?"

Astryx shrugged. "It seems a waste to agonize over something you've already run away from."

"I'm not *agonizing*, I'm *planning*. Those are two different things, I . . . Hang on a minute."

The elf must have seen something in Fern's expression that troubled her. "What?"

Fern raised a claw and pointed down the road. "I think somebody is waiting for us."

"Why would you think that?" Astryx replied suspiciously, already turning to face forward again.

Then her hand was at the pommel of her sword before Fern could even blink.

~

He stood before a wooden footbridge that crossed the slow-moving stream Fern had heard in the distance. The hills heaped up sharply on either side, casting shadows nearly to the bridge. The cool breath of the brook carried the smell of grass and dew to Fern's nose.

The waiting tapenti's coppery scales gleamed in the sun. The hood at his neck flared wide, the delicate pink of a conch's heart. His snakelike eyes glittered, half hidden in the shadow of a black, flat-brimmed hat. A red leather vest snugged tight over an otherwise bare chest, and red pantaloons were tucked into knee-high black boots, their tops folded down. A pair of magestones dangled from his leather belt like enormous silver teardrops, and he held a long, slim dagger out and to the side in his left hand, the right open and ready by his waist.

He used his free hand to adjust the brim of his hat and smiled, his tongue flickering out to taste the air. "Hail, wanderer." His accented voice caressed the vowels in the manner of his kind.

Astryx's stance managed to seem relaxed, despite the fingertips touching the hilt at her shoulder. "Hail," she replied patiently. "It appears you think you have some business with me."

"Oh, *shit*," breathed Fern, leaning forward despite herself.

"I do." The tapenti gestured at Zyll with his dagger, which looked somewhat anemic when compared to the impressive length of Astryx's blade. "A simple exchange. Her, for safe passage onward."

Fern blinked at Zyll, who was *also* leaning forward with great interest, her bound hands clasped between her knees in the folds of her ridiculous coat. "How high *is* the bounty on you, anyway?"

The highwayman's smile slipped for a moment into a confused frown. The point of his dagger dropped a handspan. "Is . . . is that a *hazferou?*"

Beside Fern, the devil bird made a very un-chicken-like hacking sound deep in its throat and ejected a handful of bones from its beak.

Astryx ignored them both. "I decline." In a sure, swift motion, she drew her blade and held it ready and slightly across her body. Her arms bunched and corded with lean strength.

"Ah, at last," sighed a voice that Fern thought she recognized. "Thank you, my lady."

A very *fussy* voice.

She realized with a start that it was coming from the *sword*.

The sword in question continued, "I'd be remiss if I didn't point out this one's, er, *magely* inclinations. Silver stones such as his are common as clay, of course. A favorite of hedge wizards, I believe." She could almost picture the blade fidgeting with long, silver mustaches. "Which reminds me of an amusing anecdote involving—"

"I'm aware, Nigel," replied the elf, in the resignedly affectionate tones of the long-married.

"Ah, an Elder Blade," murmured the tapenti, his reptilian eyes going wide. "Astonishing."

Fern was certainly astonished. She'd read any number of stories featuring the fabled talking swords forged of mooncraft and the souls of fallen warriors. She hadn't been aware that Astryx wielded one—much less one that sounded like the Territory's least interesting professor—which seemed like a huge oversight as far as the history books went.

And speaking of histories and legends, she couldn't hold her peace any longer about this one. She cupped her paws to her mouth and hollered, "Excuse me, do you have any idea who this *is*? I think you're out of your depth here."

"But of course," the tapenti called back politely, without pause. "She is Astryx One-Ear, Blademistress, Oathmaiden, the Silver Hawk, the Endless Blade. I am not so foolish as all of *that*. Still," he gestured in a general way at the cart, horse, and the passengers therein, "she has clearly fallen on lean times."

"I personally saw her dismember two dozen fish monsters, so I don't know, maybe you're a *little* foolish?" replied Fern.

Astryx looked over her shoulder at the rattkin and squinted.

The tapenti chuckled good-naturedly. "I warrant I am a greater student of her legends than any other you might chance to meet. I do not spring from ambush, nor do I come unprepared."

The Elder Blade in Astryx's hands pompously cleared its nonexistent throat. "We'll have to agree to disagree on that point."

"Astryx, Warden of the West, since there can be no accord without action, I, Chak the Pathless, challenge you for custody of the criminal, Zyll."

A thrill shivered up Fern's spine, and the daring tales recounted in *Scarred by Purpose* crowded to the front of her mind.

They seemed a lot less far-fetched all of a sudden.

"To death or disarm?" replied Astryx. She might have been asking how he liked his eggs.

Chak doffed his black hat and held it before him. "I would never knowingly deprive the Territory of your greatness."

"That's nice. You're very polite," replied the Oathmaiden. "It would've been a shame to have to kill you."

9

At some signal invisible to Fern, the elf and the tapenti broke into action at once.

Astryx loped forward, dust spitting from her bootheels as she closed the distance, the Elder Blade hardly swaying in her grip as she moved.

Chak tossed his hat away. His eyes narrowed to slits as he brought his slim dagger up into a middle guard, and he flung his right hand out to the side again. His fingers writhed, and blue sigils burned on his palm as he snatched arcane fire from the air. The magestones on his belt pulsed with a sympathetic glow.

And then there was no more space between them. Astryx's blade described luminous arcs as she wielded it with a graceful inevitability, every movement executed with such brutal economy that even Fern recognized that she was witnessing something otherworldly.

Fern discovered that she'd climbed down from the cart, one paw tightly gripping the clasp at the throat of her cloak.

Astryx hammered relentlessly at Chak's dagger with precise strikes, any one of which should have spun it from his grasp. Instead, blue fire splashed like phantasmal water with every impact, repelling the Elder Blade with explosive cracks of sound. Still, Chak retreated step-by-step under her assault, his right fingers busily plucking the air with the dexterity of a bard, each digit wreathed in rings of spectral flame.

With a snap of the wrist, he thrust his palm against the broad side of his dagger and barked something indecipherable. A ring of golden light burst forth from the impact, blowing the surrounding grass flat and tossing his black hat into the brook.

"My lady!" cried the sword.

Astryx slid back four strides, her shirt flapping so sharply that it cracked against her. She leaned forward, digging her heels in and grabbing the other end of the Elder Blade to hold it crosswise before her like she was barring a door. The elf kept her feet, and when the shock wave passed, she was immediately on Chak again.

He fell back, grimacing, his motions becoming more frantic as he sketched a new pattern with his magic-wielding hand. The magestones at his belt glowed even hotter, sizzling like fat on a hot skillet.

"Your legends are well deserved," panted Chak. "But all legends must eventually pass into memory."

With a harsh cry, he sketched a triangle in the air with the tip of his dagger, and the afterimage seared Fern's eyes.

When she blinked away the light, she gasped as Astryx's ankles clapped together as though lashed with cord. The elf teetered for a moment, overbalanced by the blade in her hands. A triumphant smile bloomed on Chak's face.

"Oh, fuck," whispered Fern.

Then Astryx reversed the blade in her grip and whipped it downward so that it passed between her booted legs, sending shreds of leather spraying out behind her and severing the invisible bindings in a burst of skittering sparks.

She snapped her left foot forward with a dry slap of leather, resumed her stance, twirled the blade in a precise half circle to level it at Chak's throat.

For the past several days, Fern's estimation of Astryx had drifted downward with every dogged step, bland reply, or fervent word of admiration for dry footwear.

It ascended again rather sharply.

Now the tapenti stumbled backward as Astryx pressed her advance. The splashes of blue flame that marked his frantic defense grew weaker, and the reports of the impacts less resounding.

His genteel demeanor crumbled into something desperate and savage, and he swore in ragged surprise.

"Mages often struggle to disarm their opponent," observed Astryx. "I find their options limited."

Did she *ever* sound out of breath, Fern wondered?

Chak grunted, his handful of magic stuttering as though unsure of itself.

"I release you from your word," the elf continued. "Strike a fatal blow without fear for your honor."

The tapenti blinked, flicking his gaze to Fern and Zyll as though they might object, and then with an unnatural twist of his knuckles, his fist boiled black, and the air went harsh with the smell of ozone.

A chill crawled up Fern's whiskers, and sudden pressure built against her eardrums. All sound went distant—the stream's chuckle impossible to hear, the clash of blades becoming a faint ringing of dinnerware.

She dimly heard Astryx's sword shout something. A warning?

Then, with a motion so casual it wasn't clear what she'd done until after it was over, Astryx flicked her longsword out and to the right and severed the belt at Chak's waist.

The magestones thudded to the ground as though each weighed ten stone—

—the black knot of deadly energy in Chak's fist ruptured into a tangle of silver light—

—and the tapenti was blown off his feet, back into the railing of the bridge.

His hips slammed against the wood, and he flipped up and over the side to sprawl in the shallow water below.

Fern's ears unplugged immediately.

She was so overawed, she almost forgot to feel miserable and small.

Sensing a presence to her left, she stared dazedly at the goblin standing beside her with hands unbound, the hazferou on her head, and a razor-sharp smile on her face.

"Zhu-chuk tah wrashoh," declared Zyll, and burst into applause. The hazferou was most displeased.

"Arcanists always forget about their vulnerability in the heat of battle," said Astryx. She leaned down to extend a hand to Chak, who crouched, dripping, on hands and knees in the brook.

He stared at her doubtfully for a moment before closing his eyes, drawing in a deep breath, and accepting her assistance to clamber out of the water.

"My thanks, Oathmaiden," he replied, with as much dignity as he could muster.

He did his best to regain some more of it once on dry land, despite his soaked pantaloons and the audible squish his boots made when he moved.

However, he lost it all again with a startled oath when Zyll popped up beside him to offer his bedraggled hat. Smiling, of course.

Still, he took the hat.

"Hm," said Astryx, frowning at Zyll's freshly unfettered hands.

"*Suvak*," said Zyll, apologetically. She plunged them into a pocket and immediately withdrew them again, freshly rebound.

The elf's eyes narrowed, but she said nothing.

Chak strode stiffly to where his belt and magestones lay in the dust, trailing a pitter-patter of brook water. He scooped them up, fussed over the severed belt for a moment, and then tied a knot in it and slung it over his shoulder.

He turned and bowed formally to Astryx, who watched, bemused.

"It is my honor to have been defeated by you, Lady Astryx," he said.

"It certainly is," declared Nigel the Elder Blade, in an aloof tone.

"Manners," said Astryx.

"Yes, well," muttered the sword. "It's only that—"

Astryx sheathed him, and his voice cut off abruptly.

She nodded at Chak. "I'm pleased you didn't die. Perhaps rethink the belt. Leather isn't the wisest choice."

"Ah. Yes."

Fern and Chak endured an uncomfortable pause while they all stood in front of the bridge. Astryx, for her part, appeared unperturbed and simply waited patiently, while Zyll rocked back and forth on her heels with a wide grin.

Fern wondered if *all* dramatic showdowns had such an awkward aftermath. It was more painful than a book group pretending they'd read the story. At last, she couldn't stand it anymore. "So. Um. Which way are you headed?"

Chak looked embarrassed. "My things are up the road." He pointed toward the chimney smoke of Bycross. "We are traveling in the same direction, are we not?"

Another pause.

The tapenti's embarrassment deepened. "I do not suppose you would like to join me for dinner?"

Astryx began to reply, but Fern was faster, thinking of loaves of bread you could load a catapult with and cheese that smelled of unwashed laundry.

"That sounds perfect."

10

Sparks corkscrewed skyward from their small cookfire, nestled back from the road in a green notch between the hills. Stunted trees with knotty, brambly trunks clung at improbable angles to the hillsides above, creating a wild sort of bower as evening shadows descended.

Chak retrieved his pack from where he'd stowed it amidst overgrown wildflowers. A sturdy gray pony was staked nearby.

After the tapenti kindled a fire, Astryx hauled three camp chairs from the back of her wagon and she, Fern, and Zyll now occupied them. The goblin's hands remained bound before her.

For the moment.

The hazferou clucked from atop Bucket's back, where he grazed next to the pony. The horse, surprisingly, did not object to his passenger.

Sitting cross-legged, the tapenti tended an iron pot that he rotated at the edge of the coals, prodding the contents with a long, two-pronged fork. Small, quartered red potatoes spat and sizzled inside, along with leeks, onions, a few eggs, and a handful of rosemary.

Fern's stomach rumbled loudly, and her whiskers quivered. She almost wept at the savory fragrance. She tucked away her latest attempt at a letter to Viv, which spent most of its words recounting the day's events. She might've gotten a little carried away describing the duel. The apology was getting a trifle muddled.

Chak smiled at her awkwardly. "Astryx, of course, I know. And the infamous Zyll, certainly. But you? I apologize that I have not asked your name."

"It's Fern." She buckled her satchel. "I'm, uh. I'm not anyone in particular."

The tapenti snorted. "In such famous company? I highly doubt it."

"She's a bookseller," said Astryx mildly. She glanced to the side, as though hearing a far-off voice, then unsheathed Nigel's white steel a few inches where he sat tipped against her thigh.

The tapenti cocked back his now-battered hat. "Ah, I see, I see. Mystic tomes? Legendary codexes?"

Fern coughed. "Uh. No. Just the, um, normal sort of tomes and codexes."

He frowned.

"I'm not supposed to be here." Fern spread her hands. "I, er, accidentally stowed away, and then it was too far to walk back to Thune, so I'm just along for the ride until Bycross, when I guess . . . I'll . . . go back . . . ?" She hadn't thought her last sentence would become a question.

"An *accidental* stowaway?" Chak's consternation deepened.

"She was *grossly inebriated*," declared Nigel. "And suffered a crisis of purpose, which led her to climb into the wrong wagon, and my lady has graciously allowed her to travel with us. For now."

Fern glared at the sword. It was hard to tell where to direct her annoyed gaze, though. "I wouldn't say *grossly* inebriated. Anyway, I don't know why we're talking about me. That was a *very* exciting duel, and she's clearly . . . whatever she is." She waved at Zyll. "I'm the least interesting thing next to this fire."

"Hm," said Chak.

Oh, for fuck's sake, not you, too, thought Fern.

The tapenti withdrew two battered tin bowls and forks from his pack and gestured with them apologetically. "Alas, I have only the pair. We will have to take turns."

Astryx waved dismissively. "I'll wait," she said, taciturn as ever.

He laid the bowls on the ground and grabbed the pot with a

bundled handkerchief, then tipped the pot and scraped a portion of the vegetables and eggs into both bowls. He offered them to Fern and Zyll.

The goblin accepted one with bound hands, opened her serrated mouth, poured the entire contents inside, chewed twice, swallowed, and handed the bowl back.

She smiled, and her teeth shone in the firelight.

Fern made an involuntary gagging sound and clutched at her throat with one paw. She could already feel the scalding heat of the food through the tin.

Chak opened his mouth, couldn't find any appropriate words, then closed it again before dishing another bowlful for Astryx.

As the elf methodically stabbed and consumed her meal in silence, Fern blew on her own, and couldn't contain her curiosity.

"You called her the *infamous* Zyll. How infamous, exactly?" She popped a chunk of potato crusted in herbs into her mouth. Her eyes fluttered closed with pleasure, and she moaned in a way she instantly regretted.

The tapenti arcanist didn't appear to notice the suggestive noise. He sat cross-legged again, patiently awaiting the use of a bowl. "Thievery? Skulduggery? Arson? Espionage? The tales are many. You have heard none of them?"

"Skulduggery?" Fern glanced skeptically at Zyll, who was now crouched very close to the Elder Blade, her pointed tongue out and a finger inching closer to his sheath.

"She appears in a place, and chaos follows. Magistrates deposed. Riots fomented. Treasures absconded with. Why, only two months gone, she made off with some kind of experimental relic from the college in Thune. You did not hear of this?"

"Before my time, maybe?" hazarded Fern. "I'm a recent transplant to the city. So, you're after the same bounty as Astryx? It has to be a lot of sovereigns to go to all the trouble, right? Like, a hundred?"

The tapenti and the elf exchanged a meaningful glance.

"*More?*" Fern almost choked on a second piece of potato.

"It is not only the money," Chak hastily amended. "There is the good of the Territory to think of."

"The Territory," scoffed Nigel. "You're like all the rest, only out to gild your own name."

"Nigel," warned Astryx.

"But it's true, my lady!" cried the sword. "Er, why is she touching me?" he asked in a worried tone as Zyll prodded the exposed steel of his blade.

"You're hardly bothered by the gilding of mine," replied Astryx, and with a sharp look at the goblin, she snapped Nigel's blade all the way back into the sheath. He protested with an affronted—but muffled—grunt.

Fern returned her attention to Chak. "I guess I'm just surprised you won't try this again. Never mind the fact that you invited us to dinner. For that much money, why wouldn't you wait until dark and . . . you know?" She made a stabbing motion with her fork.

"Well. It would not be honorable," he said, adjusting his vest. "I was bested fairly. Of course, there are many who would not see it that way, but I am not one of them. I will seek other adventures."

Astryx nodded as though that was only obvious. She handed back her empty bowl. "And on that note, we should be going."

"It is getting quite dark though, yes?" asked Chak, with a look of confusion. "Surely you will not set out until morning?"

Standing, and wearing a crooked smile, the elf replied, "Your honor is doubtless unimpeachable, but I still don't plan to sleep within a league of you. Too many elves abandon common sense after the first few centuries."

And with that, she folded up her camp chair and waved for Fern to do the same.

The bookseller stared forlornly into her own now-empty bowl, mourning in advance the loss of the warm glow of the cookfire and something that approached actual conversation.

Astryx didn't appear to notice and made short work of hustling Zyll into the wagon and stowing her things.

Fern folded her chair and made to bid Chak farewell, when she found Zyll once again by the fire.

The elf turned from un-staking Bucket and started in surprise.

Her surprise, however, was nothing in comparison to Chak's. He stared, bewildered, into the snaggle-toothed beak of the hazferou, which Zyll thrust toward him in a baleful bundle of feathers and fangs.

When he didn't immediately move to receive it, the goblin waved it at him insistently.

The hazferou was not amused.

"I am sorry, I . . . do not want it," Chak said.

If Zyll comprehended, she gave no indication.

Later, as the elf, the rattkin, and the goblin departed in the wagon—lit only by blue moonlight and the receding glow of Chak's cookfire—Fern could just make out the tapenti staring after them with a hazferou held awkwardly in both hands.

11

When Astryx first mentioned Bycross, Fern assumed it would be some sort of crossroads of a village with an inn, a tavern—possibly one and the same—a Territorial Post–slash–carriage stop, and a handful of shabby buildings.

She was spectacularly mistaken.

The brambled folds of hillside through which they traveled by starlight had wholly concealed whatever might have been visible of the distant horizon. Fern dozed off and on as the cart rocked and swayed, rousing occasionally to the same monotonous view of Bucket's moonlit behind. She woke again with the breaking of dawn as the earth sloped up to a small rise above a river valley, and Bycross came into resplendent view.

The valley itself seemed to have been dug from chalky stone by some titanic force, gouging deep while traveling roughly north to south. A narrow river squiggled along its basin, the waters an arresting blue-green. Directly ahead, a broad stone bridge crossed to the other side. Far to the south, the land receded toward a marshy plain crowded with towering, ivy-choked trees.

Fern had spent almost her entire life in Murk, and the carriage ride to Thune hadn't included much in the way of sightseeing, so the cliffs on the opposite side of the valley stirred a wonder she'd only experienced between the covers of a book. They towered high above, tall enough that scraps of cloud striped them here and there. Zigzagging up from bottom to top, a wide, white road was carved deeply into the sheer face.

At various points along the way, porticoes and spur roads had been chiseled out, symmetrically arranged like chunks of honeycomb. Complex sets of pulleys and cables studded the adjoining stone, with platforms depending from them. Fern thought some of these were moving.

Colorful banners fluttered from posts and pillars, and what could only be people and animals bustled and shuffled and shifted and strutted every which way. The cliff was positively alive with them.

"Assbiscuits," said Fern, with feeling.

"*Luffing shunks,*" agreed Zyll cheerfully.

"You certainly both have a way with words," replied Astryx. She had taken to striding along beside the cart, just ahead of the buckboard. Fern wondered why.

"You're driving the cart up *that*?" asked Fern, pointing in frank disbelief at the cliffside.

"Bucket will have no trouble. You're welcome to stay at the bottom, but if you want to book passage back to Thune, and you're short of coin, I'd suggest you come along."

Fern's stomach twisted nervously, and she wasn't sure if it was at the thought of the journey home and the mess awaiting her there, the precipitous climb ahead, or the looming unknown.

⁓

After gathering together with a few other tributary paths, their road ended at the bottom of the cliff, at a tall palisade constructed of quarried white stone. Pennants hung from evenly spaced iron spears atop the walls, each swath of red stitched with the symbol of a black crossroads inside a yellow circle.

Their cart joined a line of other travelers awaiting entry, many of them stone-fey, their gray skin and pale hair a fitting match for the cliffsides above. Fern also saw a few dwarves, a scattering of humans, a pair of tapenti tinkers with a carriage festooned with braces, buckles, and hinges, and a group of six rattkin penitents in gray habits belted around their waists with lengths of rope.

Beside Fern on the buckboard, Zyll drew more than a few

interested glances, and Astryx provoked several muttered conversations as she led Bucket with a hand on his halter. Nobody approached them though.

Even so, Astryx produced a stained old cloak from the back of the wagon and fastened it around Zyll's neck. The goblin made no complaint, only grinned and snuggled into it as it fell across her shoulders. When Astryx flipped up the hood, it obscured most of the prisoner's features, as well as her bound hands.

Fern climbed down to stretch her legs, wincing at the prickle in her thighs and the creak in her back. "Is it always this long of a wait?" She squinted up at the Blademistress.

Astryx frowned, idly scratching Bucket's ribs. "No. I don't recognize the men at the gate, either. You see the symbol on their jerkins?"

Fern leaned to peer around the folk in front of them. A blackclad man and orc flanked the passage through the palisade. They wore kettle helms, were armed with long oxtongue spears, and had sabers at their hips. On the breast of each, four white streaks radiated from a central point like rays of morning sun rising over a horizon.

"Guards?" asked Fern.

"Bycross never had them before. The walls, cliffs, and Gatewardens on hand have been defense enough against fools causing trouble. Strange not to see a Warden at all."

When they reached the front of the line, the orc stepped in front of Bucket and planted the butt of his spear in the road. Astryx stepped forward to meet him, and Fern hopped back into the wagon beside Zyll, who examined the guards with narrowed eyes.

"Morning," the orc said, his gaze drifting over Astryx's shoulder to linger on the now-cloaked Zyll. "Business in Bycross?"

This close, Fern could see that his black clothing was travel-worn. Dried red earth caked the boots of both men.

"It's afternoon, I think," replied Astryx. "After the long wait. And my business is my own."

"Do I recognize you?" He gripped his spear tighter.

"I wouldn't know. Is there trouble here these days? I don't remember things being so complicated." Astryx shaded her eyes to look up the cliffside, Nigel's hilt winking in the sun.

"Trouble? Definitely. Ever hear of Taltus the Venger?" The orc smiled at her in a knowing way.

"Can't say that I have."

He seemed taken aback. "Taltus? The bandit warlord?" When Astryx offered no further hint of recognition, he continued, sounding a little wounded. "Anyhow, he's moved into these parts, and the roads aren't as safe as they used to be. After it got a bit bloody a month back, Bycross hired the Four Fingers to set things to rights." He proudly tapped the four lines on his tunic.

"Well, that's fine," said Astryx, with profound disinterest. "At any rate, we'll be heading inside now."

"Afraid you'll have to pay the toll first. It ain't cheap to field an ongoing defense, and the Four Fingers have to make ends meet, too. Entry's thirty bits a head. That's . . ." He looked them over again in a performative way. "Ninety. And no questions about the hooded one in the wagon puts it at an even silver," he added with a magnanimous smile.

There was a long, quiet moment during which Fern could almost *feel* Nigel protesting from within his sheath. She held her breath, clutching the buckboard, and waiting for steel to be skinned and for the two guards to be decisively outmatched.

But Astryx slipped a hand into the wallet at her belt and withdrew a silver piece. She bounced it on her palm once, and then flipped it at the orc's face. He only narrowly caught it before it struck him in the nose.

Without another word she began moving forward. The orc fell back and gestured for the other guard to let them pass.

They rumbled through the gate and up the white road hacked into the cliffside. Fern watched over her shoulder as the two guards exchanged a glance behind them.

Fern slid the copy of *Ten Links in the Chain* across the countertop with both paws. Her fingers lingered on the cover before they withdrew, thinking of Viv and the hands she *should* have been placing this in.

She swallowed against a lump in her throat.

"I'm hoping to get at least sixty bits for it. It's an original printing, the spine is in perfect condition, and with the gilt edging and foiled embossing, you'd have a hard time finding a more pristine copy anywhere."

The bookshop in which she bargained was dimly lit by a variety of glass-hooded lanterns. Fern had been surprised to discover that much of Bycross was invisible from outside. Long hallways tunneled deep into the stone of the cliff, layers sandwiched one atop the other, accessible from the exterior road.

Tareben Booksellers was situated far from sunlight, where no errant breezes or blowing rain might spoil its stock.

When she crossed the threshold, Fern experienced a surge of nostalgia at the familiar weight of the books surrounding her, and the spice of ancient paper. That sensation was joined by a suffocating panic that she tried to wrestle down.

Bookshelves chiseled into white stone were stuffed with volumes and scroll-cases. Well-trod carpets in ornate designs covered the cold floor at odd angles, mirrored above by more carpets affixed to the ceiling. It conjured images of some exotic desert tent on a dune-scalloped island, the air rich with incense.

However, the only thing this air was rich with was the smell of cats. Of which there were at least five. A tortoiseshell tabby purred on the countertop, eyes half lidded.

The stone-fey proprietor—Tareben, presumably—gently opened the red cover and perused the interior, his other hand stroking the cat. He couldn't stop darting glances over Fern's shoulder at the imposing elf with her arms crossed, or at the *very* short becloaked figure by her side.

The hem did drag on the ground rather a lot.

"Yes?" prompted Fern, recalling his attention.

The stone-fey stopped stroking the cat to attend to his beard instead. "It's certainly a nice copy. But, sixty bits? There's hardly much demand for the works of Geneviss these days. I don't think I could go higher than forty." He smiled apologetically and pushed it back toward her.

Fern hadn't missed the man's obvious interest in the Blademistress, though. Honestly, how many one-eared elven warriors could there be? And with a bookseller's keen ability to seize any advantage in the face of insolvency, she looked back and said, "That seems a bit low, doesn't it, Astryx?"

The elf shrugged. "Could be."

The man paled. "Ah. The, er, Oathmaiden, is it? It's an honor, madam."

When they departed the shop five minutes later, Fern slipped sixty bits into her satchel with great satisfaction.

She did her best to ignore the pure relief she felt at putting this bookstore behind her, too.

⁓

"That won't be enough to get you back to Thune," advised Astryx, as they stepped back into the light and wind of the cliffside road. Red banners snapped in a fresh breeze, and a river of traffic swept by them on both sides. The sounds of footfalls and voices echoed off the weight of white stone above their heads.

Fern noted that the Oathmaiden reserved extra attention for anyone armed and kept Zyll close. Various ragged-looking individuals with the Four Fingers symbol on their tunics received even narrower glances.

The mercenaries didn't seem to be causing any trouble, though.

They were only three turns up from the base of the cliff when they paused by the rough-hewn railings, but still, looking directly downward brought on a wave of vertigo in Fern.

Paired with that dizziness was the queasy realization that reaching civilization made her feel even farther from home. And that she wasn't even sure what home meant anymore.

She stared out over the valley back the way they'd come, to the brambly hills and the lands lost in the haze beyond. "I'm sure I'll think of something," she replied, although she felt as far from sure as it was possible to be. "But, thanks for staying with me long enough to wring a few extra bits out of a haggle." Frankly, she was amazed that Astryx hadn't already cut her loose.

"You might make up the difference by selling the satchel," suggested the elf, as she moved to untether Bucket from one of the hitching posts along the broad avenue. They'd parked the wagon in a guarded enclosure farther down the way, apparently designed for the purpose.

Fern clutched the strap of the bag on her shoulder. "Fuck no!" she cried. ". . . I mean, no, I couldn't do that. It's . . . it belonged to someone I used to know."

Astryx paused in the act of untying the horse. "Someone who'd want you stranded far from home?"

"Ever heard of Varine the Pale?" Fern enjoyed a rush of satisfaction when she saw the elf's face pass through surprise to arrive at honest curiosity. It was nice to feel a little smug. "Ha! I guess so. Well, you might be interested to know that this bag was the home of her homunculus. Have you heard of osseoscription?"

Astryx considered her for a moment, rubbing at her ruined ear. "Just a bookseller, hm?"

"*Some* interesting things have happened to me," replied Fern as casually as she could manage. "I was there for the necromancer's last moments."

The Oathmaiden scratched her ear a little more aggressively.

"It's been a long journey," said the elf. "There's a place I always stop for a meal when I pass through. Why don't you come along and tell me about it before I go? I'm buying."

"No bread and cheese?"

"No bread and cheese."

"Deal," agreed Fern.

Although, given the warm glow that Astryx's invitation had sparked, bread and cheese wouldn't have been a dealbreaker.

12

Two more corners up Bycross's road—and a dizzying series of turns back into the cliff's interior—brought Fern, Astryx, and Zyll to the Oathmaiden's preferred restaurant.

When they arrived, Fern drew up short. She'd expected something more . . . plain. Honestly, she wouldn't have been surprised to discover that Astryx's favorite haunt was a wagon that sold dried jerky out the back.

Nothing could have been further from the truth.

The restaurant was a stone-fey establishment with its own private balcony, featuring a narrow wedge of the unobstructed sky outside. Inside, a sharp contrast of intricate shadow and firelight. Long, tasseled cushions served as seats, and tiny candles twinkled everywhere in tin cups perforated with delicate patterns. The carpeting of Tareben's bookshop was decisively outdone here by extravagant floor coverings and soft ceiling draperies that hid the bare stone Bycross was hewn from.

The cuisine was one Fern had never had occasion to try in the sleepy coastal town of Murk. Vast, shallow pans heaped with fragrantly spiced rice, peppers, cured meats, and mushrooms passed steaming before them to low tables of diners scattered around the place. Charred flatbreads arrived alongside them folded into padded mitts.

To their right, in the open kitchen, a cookfire blazed within a huge, white brick stove capped with iron cooking grates sizzling with kebabs and roasting capsicum.

The whole place had the feel of a desert prince's opulent pavilion in an ancient tale of the Westlands across the sea.

Fern's face flushed with the delicious sense of slipping into a story that you know welcomes you.

The staff recognized Astryx at once and ushered them to a table set back from the window and in heavy shadow stippled with candleglow.

With surprisingly gentle attention, the elf flipped Zyll's hood back and made sure she was seated comfortably. For her part, the goblin bounced on the cushion and grinned. After a thoughtful moment and a significant look, Astryx slipped her hands inside the cloak and unbound the goblin's wrists.

Fern barely marked Astryx ordering for them all, instead gazing around at the murmuring figures, listening to the frizzle of platters, the clink of dishware, the rustle of silk. She felt dreamily, profoundly outside of herself.

"So, Varine the Pale's sad end." The Oathmaiden recaptured Fern's attention, gesturing toward the satchel in the bookseller's lap. The elf didn't smile much, but one definitely threatened now.

"Oh!" The rattkin blinked. "Well, this was twenty years ago now, in Murk. You know it?"

"Few places in the Territory I don't these days," replied Astryx genially.

"Yeah . . . I guess that *would* make sense," said Fern. "Anyway, it all started when my friend Viv stepped into my shop for the first time. *Stumbled* is more like it, really."

"The same Viv you've been writing apologies to?"

"That's the one. You'd like her. Big girl, fond of swords. She saved my life in more ways than one."

Their food arrived, hissing in the pan and interrupting the telling.

Between hot mouthfuls of delicious food wrapped in flatbread and swallows of dry white wine, Fern warmed to her story.

She felt present. Clearheaded. Sharp-witted.

She felt like herself.

"And then Satchel lunges up out of the page"—Fern demonstrated with both paws, clutching at an imaginary necromancer's throat—"grabs Varine by the arm, and starts dragging her down, *into* the book, hand over hand."

Caught up in her narration, she spared a glance for Astryx, startled to find the elf hunched forward, elbows on her knees, expression rapt.

She looked so much *younger*. So *present*.

But after a life immersed in stories, Fern knew what a mistimed pause could do to the best of them, so she plunged onward.

"Viv seizes the opportunity and draws her sword, hauling back—"

"Blackblood," Astryx corrected softly.

"Blackblood, yes, but even as she's about to put an end to Varine while she's still struggling, the White Lady is already casting something nasty with her free hand."

"*Luffing shunks,*" whispered Zyll through a mouthful of flatbread, spewing crumbs all over the table.

"Then Potroast comes sailing in"—Fern arced a hand through the air—"and digs his beak into her other arm, and Varine *screams*. While she's off-balance, Satchel keeps pulling her in, down, down into the book, up to the shoulder, and then her head vanishes into the black . . . and the scream goes *silent*."

Fern thrummed with the retelling to the tips of her tail and whiskers. She felt the silence of the room as a physical thing, a weird impression of power in abeyance.

"It doesn't make any sense to look at as Satchel drags her inside. Even now, I can't picture it properly because the dimensions don't match, though she's still disappearing inch by inch into the book. But Potroast won't let *go* and then he's dragged in, too."

Tears quivered at the corners of Fern's eyes as she relived that agonizing moment when she thought she'd lost her little man forever—magnified now by the distance between them.

She planted both paws on the table and stood, leaning forward, glancing between the faces of her spellbound audience, dimly aware that neighboring tables were listening in as well.

Into the hush, she resumed. "Viv doesn't hesitate. She tosses Blackblood aside and lunges for the book, and she jams her arm in up to the shoulder. And the longest ten seconds of my life begin."

She released a shuddering breath.

"But after what seems like forever, when Viv's arm emerges, she's got Potroast by the scruff of the neck, hooting and gasping, and they tumble back to the floor together. She wastes *no* time, though, scrambling to her feet, grabbing the book, and slamming it shut, putting all her weight on it. The book *bangs*, almost knocking her off. Varine is not going to go quietly. She's doing her absolute best to smash her way out, *desperate* to live, or whatever it is she calls her existence."

She surprised herself with the savageness of her own voice, hammering a paw onto the table to punctuate every escape attempt.

Even Astryx jumped a little at the first impact.

"Again. And again. And *again*. But weaker each time, until finally . . . finally there's nothing. And still, Viv waits."

"But what about—" began Astryx, but Fern talked over her interruption, heedless and consumed with the power of the recollection.

"And suddenly, all the bones in the room—the lectern, the ones caging Gallina and me—drop at once in a cloud of bone dust. Viv yells, '*I have to get him out!*' and tears through the pages of the book until she finds the one Varine vanished into and sits there on her knees staring into the black of it. Will the necromancer emerge? Will Satchel? Will *anything*?"

Zyll's mouth hung open, full of teeth and half-chewed food.

Astryx's hands were clutched into bloodless fists.

"Then bony fingers crawl up from the page, and Satchel drags himself into the world again. Viv grabs the book, slams it onto a table, seizes Blackblood, and *rams* it through the cover and the table both until the steel hits the floor." Fern gathered her hands together and plunged them downward in a final, decisive thrust.

"A terrible wail pours out of the dying book. I can feel it in my tail to this *day*. And that," she finished, "was the end of Varine."

She stood there in the ensuing silence, candlelight feathering her fur, hands clasped on the hilt of an imaginary blade.

Then the energy rushed out of her all at once, and she slumped back onto her cushion.

"Fuck me. I don't think I've ever told the story that way before."

It was as though the telling had knocked all the rust off her memories, and she'd lived them again. She leaned back on her paws, panting, eyes locked on Astryx, who stared back just as intensely.

There was a glimmer in the elf's face. Of recognition? Or longing? Maybe both?

Then the Oathmaiden's eyes shifted, the lines of her body came alive, and the spell was broken.

"Zyll."

Fern followed her gaze to the cushion upon which the cloaked goblin had sat slack-jawed only moments before.

Empty of all but crumbs.

Also, all the silverware on the table appeared to be missing.

13

In the bewildering maze of Bycross, Fern had no idea how Astryx could possibly locate a goblin in a cloak who didn't want to be located, but the Oathmaiden moved without hesitation. She surged to her feet, snatching up Nigel and hurling a fistful of coins onto the tabletop, and then she was across the restaurant and through the heavy curtain shrouding the doorway.

"I, um . . . S-Sorry?" stammered Fern, shrugging an apology at the bewildered patrons gawping at them. She scrambled off her cushion and darted after the elf.

Fern was already puffing by the time she'd ducked out of the curtain and into the lantern-lit hallway lined with brightly painted arches, handcarts, and bins of exotic vegetables.

Astryx's shadow stuttered in the brighter light reflecting around a far corner, and Fern hurried to follow. "Why the fuck am I doing this?" she panted, hitching up her hem with one paw. A crazed giggle wanted to climb up her throat.

She'd managed to close some of the distance when Astryx paused to scoop something up from the stone floor.

The oilskin cloak.

Tossing it over her shoulder and without a backward glance, the elf was off around another corner.

"Wait!" cried Fern, but Astryx didn't bother to reply, or didn't hear her. "Hells. I'm too old for this!"

Which was depressing, given that the elf was over twenty times her age.

After several wrong turns and hallways much longer than she remembered on the way in, Fern arrived at the exterior road and stumbled to a stop in the thicker traffic there. Her lungs seemed packed with ice, and her vision had gone all swimmy.

Astryx was nowhere to be seen.

"Godsdammit."

A jostle from behind nearly sent her sprawling, and she spun to stare at the back of a long-haired orc warrior whose broad shoulders seemed familiar.

"Viv?" murmured Fern.

But of course it wasn't. As the orc turned, it was clear that she was younger, with a score of black braids and a frosty gaze.

"Watch your tail." The warrior gave her a dismissive once-over, before striding off into the crowd.

Fern stared after the departing orc momentarily, before a rising commotion from up the cliff face met her ears. She spied a group of black-clad Four Fingers mercenaries hustling toward it, and it became obvious which direction she needed to go.

"Chaos follows," she muttered, and with a groan, began the weary jog upward, satchel banging at her hip.

⁓

Fern's jog had devolved into an urgent stagger by the time she reached the source of the fuss, about three quarters up the ascent to Bycross's peak.

A massive concavity in the otherwise sheer cliff face created something akin to an open town square, if that town square happened to feature a deadly drop on one side. At least thirty strides above, enormous red banners bearing the Bycross symbol snapped and crawled across the vertical stone.

A statue of some important, famous—or very wealthy—stonefey dominated the square, one hand upraised in supplication, the other clasping the shoulder of a slumped figure at her side.

A mass of people blocked Fern's eye-level view, so she wormed her way forward until she emerged with a gasp into sudden open space.

Behind her and ringing the statue, folk of every race made up the crowd she'd just forged through.

But *within* that ring, another had formed of black-clad figures with the symbol of the Four Fingers on their breasts, oxtongue spears facing inward, kettle helms gleaming in the sun.

And at *their* center, at the foot of the statue, waited Astryx One-Ear, brandishing Nigel in guard position before her.

In the shadow of the elf—orange-haired, red-eyed, and grinning for all she was worth—Zyll the goblin held aloft two fistfuls of leather bags.

Fern looked closer.

No. Leather *coinpurses*.

"I'll thank the lot of you to pack away those *sad* excuses for weaponry," declared Astryx's sword, in the tones of a schoolmaster trying to be heard over a rowdy classroom. "You face the Oathmaiden! And in her hands, *Nigellus Primus*. No steel here can stand against her! Or *me*, for that matter, although I daresay that should be implicit in—"

"Thank you, Nigel," said Astryx dryly.

"Wouldn't give a tin shit if you were one of the Eight. Give her over!" hollered a thickly muscled mercenary, her black hair clubbed back, teeth white in an angry snarl. "Nobody steals from the Four Fingers. *Nobody*. Does the Oathmaiden protect *thieves* now?"

Fern blinked, then tried to count the number of bags in Zyll's hands. There were a *lot* of them.

The goblin jingled the purses gleefully.

"What the hells is she *doing?*" murmured Fern.

Astryx widened her stance and coolly evaluated the mercenaries, keeping the statue at her back. The prospect of fighting her way through a dozen Four Fingers goons didn't seem to upset her in the least.

Her gaze snagged on Fern for just a moment. A single brow rose ever so slightly.

"This one is mine," the Blademistress said, shifting her attention back to the warriors encircling her. "And I don't plan to relinquish her. If *these* are *yours* however"—she gestured with an elbow at the purses—"I'm sure that's something that can be sorted out. If not between us, then I warrant there are still Gatewardens in Bycross."

"Screw the Wardens," barked the black-haired mercenary, taking a decisive step forward. "We don't—"

"Screw the Wardens, eh?" came another woman's voice. A rising murmur in the crowd preceded its parting, revealing a stone-fey in a blue tunic with a silver lantern badge pinned above her heart, and an actual lantern on her belt.

The Gatewarden strode forth, flanked by two other Wardens with their hands on the hilts of their sheathed blades. Her flinty gaze passed over the mercenaries before finding Astryx. She hooked her thumbs in her belt. "Would anyone like to fill me in on what's going on here? I thought we were paying the Four Fingers to keep trouble *outside* of Bycross, not to start more in the heart of it."

The black-haired merc ground her teeth, and if her spear had been able to breathe, it would have already been throttled unconscious. "This . . . *thief*"—she jabbed her weapon toward Zyll—"is the only one starting trouble. Nicked the purses of a bunch of the Fingers. But, by the Eight, it's trouble we can damned well finish."

The Gatewarden studied the extravagantly pocketed Zyll. "You're saying that an unarmed goblin with a hideous coat you can spot a league away managed to steal from the lot of you, repeatedly, in broad daylight?"

"Well—"

"And we're paying *you* for protection?"

"I mean—"

The Warden held up a hand, forestalling any further explanation.

She spoke instead to Zyll. "Anything to say in your defense?"

The goblin closed her lips over her alligator smile and jingled the purses again thoughtfully.

Astryx opened her mouth to explain—

—but Zyll beat her to it.

"The Finger Folk, they are not *friendlings*." She waved one handful of purses dismissively, and her smile reappeared. "You are, ehh, how do you say . . . having the foxies in the chicken house?"

A long moment of silence reigned, during which Astryx let Nigel sag in her grip and stared, flabbergasted, at the goblin.

It was shattered when Fern cried, "You speak fucking *Territories?*"

─⁓─

Fern wasn't sure what possessed her, but before she knew it, she'd darted between black-clad figures to join Astryx and Zyll at the spot in Bycross with the most sharp things pointed at it.

"I know you, Astryx One-Ear," called the Gatewarden. Gasps of delayed recognition issued from the crowd. "Your reputation is the only reason I'm asking questions *before* letting the both of you cool your heels in a cell." She shifted her attention to Fern and her satchel. "But who's this, now? Did you decide you needed a scribe?"

"I'm her, um, traveling companion," gasped Fern, still winded.

Nigel snorted—impressive for a sword—and Fern spared him a glare.

Astryx, for her part, was scratching her damaged ear with an assessing expression on her face.

Fern rounded on Zyll. "I can't *believe* you could've spoken up the entire time," she hissed.

The goblin shrugged. The purses had disappeared, gods knew where. "Nobodies was ever ask-ling."

"I think the ask was fucking *implied*," sputtered the rattkin.

Zyll blinked back at her, very slowly.

"Quibble later," snapped the Gatewarden. "Astryx, what is this goblin talking about?"

"She's talking shit!" bellowed the black-haired merc, who seemed to have become the Four Fingers' de facto spokeswoman. She was clearly having a hard time mastering her need to say more.

Astryx stared at Zyll, and then at Fern, with that same assessing look. Fern wasn't sure she liked it.

"I'll let my scribe answer that," said the elf.

Now Fern was breathless for a reason that had nothing to do with the climb. Astryx might as well have seized her in both hands and dangled her over the precipice to tread wind with her paws. But there wasn't any malice about the Blademistress that she could detect. Just that feeling of intense speculation. *Amused* speculation.

All eyes fixed on Fern.

"I, um, well . . ." Then to Zyll in an urgent whisper, *"What the hells did you* mean, *foxes in the henhouse?"*

Zyll pointed mutely at one of the Four Fingers mercenaries. Then at another. And another.

No, not at the mercenaries. At their *boots.*

"Red," the goblin whispered back with an extravagantly rolled R. "*South-ly.*"

"I'm pretty fucking sure *black* is the color you—" Fern broke off midsentence.

The red mud caked into the seams of their black boots.

South.

"There's no red soil here . . ." murmured Fern.

"Do you have something to say, or not?" demanded the Gatewarden. "My patience ebbs."

Everything snapped together in Fern's brain at once. "The, um, the warlord! Tetanus?"

"Taltus?" The Gatewarden frowned.

"Yes, that guy! Taltus! The one to the south? In the swamplands? The one you're paying *them* to keep away? I bet the earth down there is pretty red, isn't it? Not like around here."

"What in the name of the Eight are you talking about?"

A slow ripple passed through the Four Fingers, and Fern's conviction grew. "In fact, I haven't seen mud that color anywhere nearby. Not for *days*. And nobody else's boots in this square seem to have picked any up, either. Nobody but the Four Fingers."

Fern experienced a blue bolt of inspiration. "And I'll bet after the trouble started, some local nob mentioned a crew you'd never heard of, but they insisted could get the job done? An easy hire?"

The Warden's eyes widened—a *direct* hit.

"I think you might want to have a little talk with them, whoever they were," added Fern, shaking her head woefully and really getting into the spirit of the thing. "If they're still around."

Astryx sighed. "I should have noticed. It's such a *classic* con." She flicked Nigel in an arc at the ring of mercenaries, addressing the Gatewarden in a loud voice. "They're all his crew. Taltus is fleecing you. You're hiring his own soldiers to protect you from him. Gods, this is a hoary old chestnut." She shook her head. "The Four Fingers don't exist. Or if they do, they're certainly not from around here."

The Oathmaiden leveled Nigel at the mercenary leader and smiled humorlessly, her ragged silver hair riffling in the wind. "Which means I won't feel the slightest remorse about doing what needs to be done."

The Four Fingers didn't wait for another word.

They collapsed inward as one, spearheads leading the way.

The Gatewardens pursued at their heels, already drawing their blades.

Astryx took a single lunging step forward, bringing her elbow high and her swordpoint low—

—and with a graceful turn and a long, looping slash, she beheaded seven of the oncoming spears with Nigel, who laughed his plummy laugh the entire way.

Then she danced among black-clad figures, deadly and purposeful, while the Wardens smashed into the circle from without, spilling violence into the crowd.

Fern gasped as she felt Zyll's hand knot into the hood of her cloak.

Then the goblin dragged her, choking, up over the statue's plinth and into the shadow between its legs.

To safety.

14

"You can come out now," said Astryx.

Fern stared in astonishment from around the toes of a massive sandaled foot carved of stone. Behind the Oathmaiden, black-clad figures sprawled across the square amidst shattered spears and a scattering of helms. A few of them sagged between the shoulders of Gatewardens leading them away.

Although the skirmish had been far from bloodless, Fern thought every one of Taltus's crew would be crawling away with all their limbs and most of their fingers.

The Gatewardens had pitched in, she supposed, but Astryx?

There was a reason they called her the Blademistress.

"That was the most incredible thing I've ever seen," breathed Fern.

The elf scrubbed a hand through her hair in a shower of sweat. "But not worthy of any foul language, I noticed." The corner of her mouth curled in the specter of a smile.

"Only appropriate," declared Nigel. "I'm pleased to see the bookseller expressing some *proper* appreciation. Er, my lady, do you mind?"

Astryx glanced at the Elder Blade in her hand, and with a casual whip, flicked a ribbon of blood off his length and onto the white stone. The sword made a contented noise deep in his phantom throat.

Her gaze found Fern again, then skittered away to search beneath the statue. "Now where did she get off to . . ."

Fern spun. Zyll had been crouched by her side for the entire battle, she was sure of it, but now—

"Hat-ling is verrry fashion-y, yes?"

When she turned around again, the goblin stood beside Astryx with both hands clapped to a kettle helm swallowing the top half of her face. Her orange pigtails barely poked out the bottom.

The elf rubbed furiously at her shortened ear.

~

Why am I still here? Fern asked herself dazedly as she followed Astryx and Zyll out of the crowded square. A respectful citizenry granted them a wide berth, which no doubt pleased Nigel immensely.

Fern's mind had been too occupied with recollections of dancing steel and legends in motion to register the ten minutes of post-battle politicking. There had been a conference between Astryx and the Gatewarden captain, and a lot of gesturing, and some further hushed words and hooded glances toward Zyll—who was still wearing the helmet.

But of course, none of that really mattered to Fern, did it?

Because this was the end of the road. The parting of ways.

Astryx would journey onward with her bounty in tow, Fern would find a way to earn another silver or two, and then she'd book another ass-bruising passage back to Thune.

Won't I?

She felt a painful *tearing* in the very center of herself, like a sapling being slowly peeled apart down the middle. An aching, growing tension that would either snap back together and resolve itself, or split forever into something unrecognizable.

At any moment now, Astryx would turn and utter words both perfunctory and final, a casual dismissal, and be on her way.

It was inevitable. Wasn't it?

And Fern was ready for it. Wasn't she?

She realized that she *did not fucking know.*

So she kept pace with the Oathmaiden, hazily half present, hoping and dreading at the same time. Fern withdrew her latest long letter of apology to Viv and stared at it while she stumbled along, forcing herself to reread the first few lines over and over, each review a tiny knife to the heart.

Dear Viv,
  I have no idea how to write this letter to you.
  I'm so sorry.

Fern was only startled out of her self-flagellation when Astryx stopped and faced her.

Oh fuck. Not yet, she thought with surprising desperation. The parchment crinkled in her paws.

"I just need to step in here for a moment," said Astryx, gesturing at an awning with something stitched across it that Fern didn't bother to read. "I realize it seems pointless, but watch her while I do?" She indicated Zyll, who couldn't have seen a thing through the helmet she still insisted on wearing.

Why is she asking me to do this? Fern cried within her mind. *Why is she drawing it out? What the hells is happening? It's like I'm drunk in the back of the cart again.*

But she nodded and said, "Of course!" in a perfectly reasonable voice, as though she weren't melting from the inside out.

When Astryx left, she stared at the goblin, who inched the helmet up with a thumb until she could meet Fern's regard with her shrewd red eyes.

Zyll studied her for several seconds.

"No rocks-es at the bottom," she said. "Jump, or no jump."

"Wh-What?" stammered Fern.

The goblin shrugged. "Jump," repeated Zyll. "Or no jump. Puts away the parch-ment." She pinched the edge of Fern's half-crumpled letter.

Dreamily, Fern stuffed it back into her satchel.

And then Astryx returned and knelt beside the goblin, a pair of bracelets in one hand. They were crafted of tangled silver wire, with dull gray stones knotted in the webbing.

"We'll leave your hands free," she said severely. "All right? But this *very* expensive artifact"—she held up one of the bracelets—"is going to make sure that I always know how to find you. Is that going to be a problem?"

Zyll let the helm fall back over her eyes and extended one wrist.

Astryx snapped the bracelet around it, where it drew tight against green skin. Then the Oathmaiden put its twin on her own right wrist, where it similarly contracted.

"This only comes off if I release the enchantment, or one of us dies. Understand?"

Zyll blinked lazily, which seemed like all the Oathmaiden was going to get.

"Oh, and before I forget," continued Astryx, fishing in her wallet. She withdrew a few silvers and offered them open-palmed to Fern. "This should see you on your way. No sense washing dishes for the next few weeks, hm? Seems you earned your keep as a translator after all."

Fern stared at the silvers in her palm.

And stared.

And went right on staring.

Astryx arched a brow at her. "Is something wrong?"

"No rocks at the bottom," whispered Fern.

"What's that?" asked the elf with a confused frown.

Fern took a deep breath, and felt the sapling split.

Dear Viv,
 I'm alive. I'm sorry.

Fern

The letter was very short, scribbled on her last blank piece of parchment.

Every word stung to write, but she didn't give herself time to equivocate or revise.

The Territorial Post station was stacked with crates and chests and bales, rich with the scents of horses and leather and paper.

When Fern emerged, it was without the letter and with an armload of fresh parchment and a fistful of pencils. She didn't know if she was lighter or heavier or falling or flying, but by the fucking Eight she was in *motion*.

Astryx raised a hand from where she was hitching Bucket to the wagon.

Zyll was already on the buckboard, sans helmet.

"No rocks at the bottom," Fern repeated to herself.

And, stuffing the parchment into the satchel—the vacant home of a friend who'd found a new one for himself out in the world—she ran to join them, red cloak flying behind.

15

I can't believe I'm delighted to be camping, thought Fern, warming her paws before the tiny fire with her tail draped across her knees.

And she *was* delighted. Giddy almost. She barely mourned the soft, warm beds they might have slept in if they'd lingered in Bycross until tomorrow.

A persistent chill crawled up under the hem of her cloak and teased the fur of her back, which only made the fire cozier somehow.

Ice-chip stars gleamed sharp in the sky, the red line of sunset long since erased in the west, where Bycross lay behind them. To the northeast? The city of Amberlin, their final destination.

Astryx sat across the fire from her, watching a soot-blackened travel kettle as it boiled nettle tea. Bucket formed a solid slab of night behind her. Zyll snored nearer to the flames than seemed safe, tucked up inside of her coat so that no skin was exposed, and she looked like a shabby quilt with a bedraggled orange cat sleeping on it.

Fern recognized a *talk* looming in the air above the fire—a needful discussion that would gather on the horizon until it broke. The tea seemed proof of that. Astryx had—in Fern's opinion—a very unfair talent for rolling over and immediately falling asleep the moment the day's duties were done. Obviously, Fern's sample size of evenings was small, but the elf had never once bothered to sit up late and brew *tea*.

The Oathmaiden clearly had something to say. A question? A demand? Some set of conditions to lay before her?

Fern didn't know, and the possibilities prickled her ears uncomfortably.

The *talk* just kept growing until she could almost feel the weight of it on her fur.

So, she waited.

And waited.

The elf poured tea into two battered tin cups, offering one to Fern, who puffed on it as she cradled it in her paws.

And then she waited some more as they both slurped noisily, and the fire snapped and spat and burned lower betwixt them, and the impending talk threatened.

Oh my gods, thought Fern.

It was dawning on her that the Blademistress didn't have the slightest idea how to start the conversation.

Is she . . . out of practice?

Fern thought she just might be.

She caught Astryx's increasingly distressed gaze. They stared at each other for a long, awkward span of time.

Then Fern did the only thing she could think of, which was to talk about something else entirely.

"So. How did you and Nigel end up together?"

The elf blinked and glanced at the Elder Blade where he leaned, sheathed and in easy reach, against a nearby stone. The distress vanished from her eyes, replaced with relief.

"Oh. To be honest, it wasn't very interesting."

And then silence again.

Gods and hells, thought Fern. She gulped the last of her tea in exasperation. The bitter taste was growing on her. Definitely better than coffee.

Thus fortified, she refused to abandon the conversational gambit. "I find that *very* hard to believe. I'm pretty sure Nigel would disagree. What does he have to say about it?"

Astryx looked ready to deliver what Fern was positive would be a refutation, then glanced at the sword and reconsidered. With a quiet sigh, she reached over to bare an inch of his steel. Too late, Fern realized her mistake.

Nigel didn't bother to wait to be asked.

"Why, there's no tale more worthy of the telling!" he declared. "Indeed, I can recall it as though t'were only yesterday, though it's seven hundred years gone now. Seven hundred and twenty-*seven*, to be precise. Or perhaps eight? Bah, no matter!"

"*Whathaveldone*," whispered Fern, but the Elder Blade either didn't notice or willfully ignored her.

Astryx made a deep study of the bottom of her tin cup.

"It was the dark of winter in the Bradden Heath, as it was called in those days. Now, of course, it's known as the Midland Fields, but that wasn't the case until the fall of the Red Shepherd, as I'm sure we're all well aware." He chortled. "Ah, me, the Red Shepherd. How times have changed, eh? Why, the blacksmith that forged me, Sandrum Temple, had a terribly amusing story about the Red Shepherd. Sandrum was simply stuffed to *bursting* with hilarious anecdotes—that is, until he grew ill with the blood fever in his latter days. You remember Sandrum, of course, my lady?"

The Oathmaiden looked as though she were about to reply, but he didn't leave her a sliver of room to squeeze into.

"My, my, the conversations we used to have, Sandrum and I . . . At any rate, where were we? Ah, yes, the Midland Fields!"

"Sandrum!" bellowed Zyll.

Fern and Astryx stared in surprise at the goblin, who lurched upright by the fire and laced her fingers between her toes, grinning avidly at the sword.

Nigel, blessedly, had been shocked into silence as well. Momentarily, anyway.

". . . Yeeesss, as I was saying . . ."

Fern clearly recognized the affronted glare in the sword's every syllable as he tried to resume his narration.

Zyll ignored him and rummaged through the pockets of her

coat while the elf and rattkin watched, and Nigel fretted over his distracted audience.

"*Shankling!*" cried Zyll at last, and from a hideous green pocket, she withdrew a silver breadknife. Brandishing it in the firelight, her sharp grin stretched wider as crimson eyes reflected the rising sparks.

"Is Sandrum's blade-ling," she declared, waggling the cutlery.

"I beg your *pardon*," scoffed Nigel, "but Sandrum Temple forged only the *finest*—"

"Gods, am I *glad* to be out of that pocket," gasped a new voice, wheezing like it had only just escaped suffocation. Then, sharp and annoyed, "Hang on, are we talking about *Sandrum*? Because, you'll have to forgive me, that guy was a complete *asshole*."

Nigel gabbled, apoplectic, and Fern realized with astonishment that the voice was coming from the knife.

"Another Elder Blade?" Her mouth dropped open.

"Kid, you're my new favorite person. Rat-person. Whatever, you get it. You wouldn't *believe* how long it takes some folks to figure that out. Look at this white steel! Snowy as hells, right? I've got that, you know, *weight of significance*. Runes all over the place. Soul of an ancient hero and all that. Anybody with a pair of eyes should be able to see that right from the jump."

"*You* were forged by Sandrum Temple?" asked Astryx, whose skeptical gaze couldn't seem to settle between Zyll or the knife in her fist.

"Oh, yeah, I definitely . . . was . . . um . . . *waitaminute*. One . . . ear . . . Are you—? Is that—? Frigging hells, you *are* . . ." The knife's voice bottomed out to a worshipful hush. "The *Oathmaiden*. Uh, that bit about the furry one being my favorite person was just, like, hyperbole, okay? I was only keeping the spot warm for you."

"Wow," said Fern.

"Look, kid, you can't see it, but I'm shrugging helplessly over here. No hard feelings, but my destiny is sitting across the fire from me, and I can't ignore that, you understand? Do you have any idea how big of a deal it would be for me to be wielded by the Blademistress? Still a big fan of *you* though, okay?"

Nigel recovered his faculties enough to bellow, "I beg your pardon, my lady, but this . . . this stickpin is *not* an Elder Blade! The greatest blacksmith of the Latter Age never stooped to forging . . . *tableware*! Speak your name, impostor!"

"Well, if you want to get technical about it—" the knife began.

"*Breadlee!*" interrupted Zyll, waving him around a little more.

There was a sudden, terrible silence, which was spoiled when Fern snorted and clapped her paws over her mouth.

"I go by *Bradlee*, these days," said the knife, in icy tones. "But as I was *saying*, my forge-name is Bradelys Tertius."

"Impossible," scoffed Nigel. "Bradelys was lost. And he was a *greatsword*. He did not spread *jam* on *toast*."

"*Was* a greatsword," continued the tiny blade, mournfully. "Sandrum and me had a, um . . . falling out."

"He *reforged* you!" said Nigel, and then laughed, a booming sound that actually made his blade rock gently from side to side. Fern thought she could hear amused tears in his voice. "Into . . . into dinnerware! What on earth did you do to earn his ire?"

"Did I *mention* he was an asshole?"

"So, Breadlee—" began Fern.

"*Bradlee.*"

"Is there a reason you're hanging around in Zyll's pocket?"

"This I am also interested to know," added Astryx, folding her arms and studying Zyll narrowly. "Since I searched every fold of that coat."

"I, uh. Do you want to tell it?" The breadknife's attention shifted to the goblin, somehow.

Zyll lowered Breadlee until he was at eye level, studying the length of his blade.

She licked him.

"Hey!" cried the knife.

"I have, how do you say . . . conf-is-klated him. He is murrrder weapon." Zyll purred the *R* in *murder* like she was savoring the taste.

"That's not a good way to tell the story!" Breadlee protested. "Look, I didn't murder *anybody*. I was barely involved. Except for the stabbing part."

"I have so many questions now that my mind has gone absolutely blank," said Fern.

"Give him here," said Astryx, extending a hand. Her tone was even, but full of steel.

The goblin narrowed her eyes in return, delivered another long and deliberate lick to the knife—who made a strangled noise—and then flipped and extended him, haft first.

"Thank you," replied the Oathmaiden.

She brought Breadlee up to her face to examine more closely, studying his bolster and running a thumb gently along his spine.

"Oh my gods," he whispered, reverently. "It's *happening*. I can't believe it! Hold me forever."

"My *lady*," said Nigel, reproachfully.

"Bradelys, was it?" asked the elf.

"Blademistress, you can call me whatever you *want*."

"*Breadlee*," insisted Zyll.

"Except that."

Astryx tipped the knife in the direction of the goblin across the fire. "I imagine there are a lot of stories you could tell about our mutual friend with the pockets, aren't there? Stories that might make it worth keeping you around?"

Fern decided that she very much wanted to hear them, too.

"Um. I mean, maybe one or two, sure. And, you know, I may not be a greatsword these days but, like, I can absolutely punch through a breastbone. I'm still *very* Elder. Plus, you go wandering around with some *longblade* on your back and everybody knows what you're packing—but me? Very, *very* concealable."

"Mm. I'll bear that in mind."

"My *lady!*" cried Nigel again, with a note of desperation.

"But for now," continued Astryx, "I think we could all use some sleep. Some words are best spoken in daylight."

She twirled the Elder Blade between her fingers and returned him to Zyll, who snatched him back, her mouth for once flattened into a thoughtful line.

"Wait!" protested Breadlee. "Hang on, I—"

The goblin stuffed him back into the ugly green pocket, extinguishing his voice.

Nigel breathed an audible sigh of relief.

A sudden night breeze fluttered Fern's cloak and made the dwindling fire struggle. She shook out her whiskers and shivered all over, as though waking from a lucid dream.

Her gaze met Astryx's. The talk brewing between them only minutes before seemed to have receded, and from the look in the elf's eyes, they both knew it.

Fern thought the talk was just biding its time, though.

Maybe Astryx was right.

Some words *were* best spoken in daylight.

―⁓―

Curled on her side with her snout to the fire and her back to the night, sleep continued to elude Fern as Zyll's peeping snores issued from the pile of pockets to her right. She couldn't see Astryx's eyes, as the elf always lay facing away into the dark with one hand on Nigel's hilt, but the Oathmaiden's shoulders moved gently with the slow cadence of her sleeping breath.

Fern closed her eyes, but images of the day crowded behind her eyelids. Bycross climbing up white cliffs in the dawn light. Astryx whirling amidst a sea of warriors, effortless and graceful and brutal. A goblin with bottomless pockets and a fistful of stolen purses. The Territory's most ridiculous Elder Blade.

She sighed and whispered, "If I read this in a book, I'd never believe it. It's too amazing and stupid at the same time."

Opening her eyes and blinking in the firelight, she patted around with one paw until she found her satchel. Quietly unbuckling it, she slipped her fingers inside and pinched out a sheet of the fresh parchment she'd bought, then rummaged for a pencil.

Squinting in the dying firelight, she began to write, until everything *in* her was *out* of her.

She had to use five more pages to finish the job.

When she was done, she repacked the satchel, and slept. Soundly.

16

Astryx had taken on fresh supplies at Bycross, and Fern was glad of it. They breakfasted on flatbread toasted over the last, elderly coals of the fire, then folded over strips of salted ham and sharp cheese.

As they journeyed northeast, the terrain rose and fell sharply, where the earth had been scoured away to expose chalk cliffsides. The stony, derelict road continually narrowed and hugged a series of ragged, white bluffs above a river valley blanketed in mist.

"What are those?" called Fern, pointing from her seat on the cart at a tall, pale pillar beside the way. They'd passed three or four of them already. Hints of a carved figure capped the stone, with the suggestion of a head and outstretched arms, now softened with time. It looked like a half-melted candle nested in a cloud of thistle.

"I've no idea," replied Astryx. She walked several yards in front of Bucket, keeping an eye on the road ahead. "They've been here as long as I've traveled these roads, and they never looked much newer."

"*Murden-tal*," offered Zyll.

"Now that we know you speak Territories, that's just exasperating," said Fern.

The goblin made an expansive gesture with both hands at the river valley below. "Water-watchlings."

"And what are *those*?"

Zyll shrugged, and Astryx answered for her. "If she means water-watchers, they're stone-fey effigies that purify underground streams. She must be mistaken. They're likely just forgotten old statues on a forgotten old road."

Dubiously regarding the route ahead, Fern asked, "If it's so forgotten, then why are *we* taking it?"

"Because if Taltus decides to send anyone after us, they likely won't think to try it. And if they do, I'll know long before they catch up."

With one paw at the clasp of her cloak, Fern took an involuntary peek behind them, half expecting to see a black-clad form pursuing them in the hazy distance. "Um, do you think that'll happen?"

"That they'll catch up? No."

Fern found that answer deeply unsatisfying.

The road continued to narrow and become more treacherous, and while the sun sometimes winked at them from rips in the cloud cover, the light remained silvery and close. At times, the fog from the valley clawed up and over the cliffside to tangle its fingers in the long grass and caress the feet of the water-watchers.

Fern clutched the buckboard with both paws and tried to anticipate the dips and bumps. As the exposed white chalk to their right crowded closer to the cart, and the margin of earth between the road and the cliff's edge melted away, she found herself leaning hard to the right, even though Zyll was nearest the drop-off.

Astryx now guided Bucket by the bridle, pausing from time to time to assess the state of the road and muttering to herself.

Then, the elf brought them abruptly to a halt. A raven coughed in the mist, and a series of tumbling stones echoed their chattering descent through the valley below.

"What is it?" called Fern, craning to see. Zyll hopped to her feet on the buckboard beside her and jumped up and down to get a better view, rocking the cart in a way that made the bookseller's stomach knot.

"The road is out," replied the Oathmaiden. She sounded exasperated. "I suppose it has been a few decades since I passed this way."

Carefully, Fern clambered down into the narrow gap between the exposed chalk and the cart, and squeezed past the wheel to join Astryx beside the horse.

"Assbadgers," she said, with feeling.

The ledge widened out for about thirty strides before it sheared away almost completely. Only a scrim of ancient stone still fringed a stretch nearly ten paces long.

Astryx said something delicate and beautiful in an elven tongue, but from the look on her face, Fern was pretty sure it wasn't that far from "assbadgers."

"What now?" asked Fern.

"Now, we turn around."

"And travel the whole way back? But that's—" Fern broke off with a yelp as Astryx urged Bucket forward, *toward* the gap.

The elf cocked a thumb back the way they'd come. "You'd both better wait farther down the road."

Zyll gamely hopped from the cart and trotted along the path, and Fern sidled past the cart to join her.

Then she watched, huddling close to the chalk wall, while Zyll perched on the cliff's edge. Fern couldn't bear to look at the goblin dangling her feet over the drop. It made her head go all woozy.

Astryx unhitched Bucket and led him carefully back past the cart, rubble clacking and skipping down the cliff face with every hoofbeat.

Parking the horse near Fern and Zyll, the elf then returned to seize the traces of the cart in both hands.

What followed was a delicate series of maneuvers during which Fern's heart never left her throat. Astryx laboriously turned the wagon by first rolling forward a few feet, then back, then forward again in a dozen tiny arcs. For the first time, Fern saw her look out of breath. Her ragged silver hair glistened with sweat.

The moments when the cart faced outward toward the dropoff were the worst. Fern had to shut her eyes tight, but even then, she could vividly imagine Astryx suddenly dropping out of sight to plunge over the cliff's edge, with the cart not far behind.

At last, their cart was turned around. Astryx, still dripping, rehitched Bucket, and they began the depressing journey back the way they'd come, except that Fern was now on the side nearer to the drop.

Zyll patted the buckboard next to her. "Closey-close," she said, with a sympathetic, razor-sharp smile.

Fern obligingly scooted over.

It turned out they didn't have to journey *all* the way back. After half a league, the chalk walls that rose to their left sloped away into a gentle rise studded with a cluster of three water-watchers in various states of decay. A hawk perched atop one of them, cocking its head at the cart in annoyance while it waited for the voles they'd frightened off to chance the open ground again.

Zyll eyed the bird and licked her lips.

Astryx led Bucket off the road into the tall grass and then stared up the rise with her fists on her hips.

"Woof," breathed Fern, as the muscles of her shoulders and back unknotted in a tingling wave. "Now what?"

The elf glanced over her shoulder. "Now I find another way. If I remember, the cliff road opens up a league or two past where it was destroyed. I'm going to scout ahead to see if we can make our way around to rejoin it, up this rise and behind the bluffs."

"And we—?"

"You wait here."

Fern frowned. "Remember when you said you took this road because some of Taltus's goons might be following us?"

"Following *me*. You should be fine here alone for a few hours. They've got no quarrel with you. You can watch her until I get back." She pointed at the goblin.

"I just think that if one of them *were* to have mentioned you, they might *also* have mentioned a suspicious rattkin and the goblin that stole all of their money. Actually . . . where *is* that money?" She narrowed her eyes at Zyll.

The goblin patted her coat as though searching for the purses she'd purloined, and shrugged.

"Yes, very convincing," said Fern dryly. She returned her attention to Astryx. "I feel a little exposed here in the middle of nowhere with maybe a bunch of angry bandits on the way and no defense. I don't think we can ask Bucket to kick them for us this time."

Zyll jammed a hand into a pocket and withdrew it to brandish Breadlee with great fervor.

"What's happening now?" asked the knife, sleepily.

"No," said Fern.

"I feel hurt, but I'm not sure why," complained Breadlee.

"There'll be no need of that," said Astryx, with a weary species of patience. "If they were following us, we'd have seen them already, especially now that we've backtracked. You won't need a . . . weapon."

"Why'd you pause before you said 'weapon'?" asked the knife.

Fern had no idea how, but she knew he was squinting.

The elf ignored him, unhitching Bucket to stake him near one of the water-watchers, where he promptly began cropping the grass. "You know where the food is. I'll return soon. If it gets dark, you can start a small fire. A *small* one. The flint is in the cart."

There was a heavy silence during which Fern conspicuously said nothing.

"Unless you don't know how to do that," said Astryx, frowning.

"I . . . will figure it out . . . ?"

The Oathmaiden and the goblin shared a look, which Fern didn't think was very fair.

"The longer we talk about this, the more likely dark will fall before I return. I'm going now. You?" Astryx pointed at Zyll and tapped her bracelet. "Don't cause trouble."

Without another word, she turned and strode swiftly up the slope and out of sight over the rise.

Zyll patted Fern on the shoulder and solemnly offered her the knife.

She took it and stared at it. Breadlee was surprisingly heavy, his steel gleaming with a faint opalescence. Some sort of sigils or runes had been inscribed into his handle.

The goblin promptly hopped out of the cart and trotted over to one of the water-watchers. She crouched until her feet disappeared beneath her coat and pretended to examine the spire with great interest, while sneaking hungry glances at the hawk atop it. The bird, no fool, launched itself skyward in search of less fraught hunting grounds.

Fern sighed.

"Hey," said Breadlee. "Look, just so I can calibrate my expectations, about how many people have you stabbed, would you say? Feel free to round to the nearest dozen."

17

"So, you just absconded in the night, huh?"

"I was *drunk*. It was an *accident*, Breadlee." Fern's paw clenched tight around the knife's handle, which she supposed was sort of his neck. It was weird talking to sentient cutlery.

"Bradlee," he corrected absently. "Seems like this is a pretty long-running accident though, if you don't mind me saying."

After explaining that no, she'd never stabbed anyone—not even once—Fern had felt compelled to justify her existence with a brief recounting of her life thus far. In the retelling, somehow it seemed to peak early with Viv, Varine the Necromancer, and a townful of skeletons, and she'd been on a steady downward slope ever since.

"But you were 'accidentally' a *murder* weapon?" She held him up and stared at a point halfway up his blade, which Fern had decided was where his eyes ought to be. Then again, maybe she was staring him in the ass. "I think it's time for you to tell *your* fucking life story."

"You got a real tart mouth, huh? Might interest you to know that the murderess was a rattkin like you. Name of Azula. Good kid. Bad judgment. Oh hey, that sounds familiar!"

Fern regarded him shrewdly. "I guess it's just that I assumed you were too important to be sidelined from the action, being an Elder Blade and all. I would have figured you had to be instrumental."

A shocked silence followed, during which the knife apparently had to reorganize his thoughts.

"I mean . . . I suppose it's fair to say that I was very *key* in the . . . let's say, 'events' both prior and after. Which may or may not have had a bearing on the result. Obviously, because of the weight of my—"

"—significance, yes, I know," finished Fern. "Significance to the murdering."

Another silence.

"Let's talk about something else. Like the fact that the goblin kid is gone."

"What?" Fern almost dropped him as she scrambled to her feet from the grassy spot she'd been occupying in the shade of the cart.

There wasn't a lot to investigate—only the three waterwatchers, grass and stone in all directions, and Bucket staring over his shoulder at her in horsey reproach.

She even checked underneath the tarpaulin at the crowded wagon bed.

Breadlee was right. Zyll was nowhere to be seen.

"Fuck!"

"Wow, how do you lose somebody in a coat that ugly on a totally unobstructed clifftop?"

"I was distracted and talking to *you*."

"Oh, is *this* an accident, too?"

"I am going to accidentally throw you into the fucking canyon."

"See, now we're getting to the bottom of what you would consider an accident."

Fern ignored him.

"Think," she muttered to herself. "Where would she go? She can't be far. Besides, she knows Astryx has that bracelet thing. She's not stupid." She was sure of *that* anyway, although she wished that she were the one wearing the other bracelet.

She glanced at Bucket, who was still regarding her with what she was positive was severe disappointment.

"You know who else isn't stupid?" breathed Fern.

"Is this a rhetorical question, or are you actually asking me? The list is shockingly short," replied Breadlee.

"Shush."

The knife harrumphed as Fern approached Bucket, standing on tiptoe to scratch his cheek under the bridle.

"Hey," she murmured. "You saw where she went, didn't you?"

"You're asking the *horse?*"

Paying him no heed, Fern unstaked Bucket and stared as meaningfully into his eyes as she could manage. "You're a smart boy. I see how she trusts you. And I think you know exactly where our little friend went. Can you show me?"

Bucket regarded Fern for a long moment, during which she felt increasingly moronic.

Then he shook out his mane, snorted, and began slowly clopping his way through the grass, in exactly the direction Astryx had gone.

She hoped like hells Bucket wasn't just following his mistress.

Keeping a tight hold on both his lead and that hope fluttering in her chest, Fern trotted beside him, leaving the cart behind.

She glanced back once and, squinting over the distance, Fern thought she saw a tall figure rummaging through the back of the wagon. It was obviously the tarpaulin flapping free, though. She must not have tied it back down.

⁓

Bucket was a smart horse.

It took a remarkably short time to find Zyll. As Fern had suspected, the biggest obstacle to locating her was the direction, not the distance.

The goblin was sitting with her hands in her lap atop the biggest in a whole jumble of stones. They crowded into the clifftop's edge like bad teeth into a jawbone. She was staring out over the river valley, where the fog pinked with late afternoon sun. The cloud cover had mostly disintegrated.

"There you are!" shouted Fern, still keeping up with Bucket as he picked his way stolidly up the rise.

Zyll glanced back at them, and then returned her attention to the valley below.

"Godsdammit," muttered the rattkin to herself. Then, louder, "You can't just run off like that! I don't need any help from you convincing Astryx to think less of me."

"Is that a thing that's happening?" asked Breadlee, with concern. "That's not going to rub off on me, is it? I gotta say, it doesn't really align with my long-term goals to be associated with mediocrity."

Fern bit back a sharp retort and panted the last few steps to the base of the cluster of stones. She shaded her eyes with the paw holding Bucket's lead and glared up at the goblin. "What are you looking at, anyway?" she asked, exasperated. "It's the same valley we've been traveling beside all day."

The goblin didn't remove her hands from her lap, or turn around. Her shoulders rose and fell in a shrug, but she remained silent.

"Shitwhiskers." Fern dropped Bucket's lead. "Stay here, Bucket. Um, please." Then she did her best to scamper up the stones to join Zyll. It had been several years since she had scampered, though, and she didn't remember the last time being so challenging.

When at last she stood beside Zyll, she glowered at her, and tried to think of something to say that would get the goblin off her ass and moving back in the direction of the cart.

Then she followed Zyll's gaze out over the valley, and all the annoyance leaked right out of her.

The mist churned in slow motion on its way up the channel to the northeast, blushing with conch pinks and delicate oranges. Here and there it tore apart like dough stretched too far, and the river below glittered in sudden sunfire.

Nearer, she could see the road they'd attempted earlier in the day, and at this remove, the water-watchers startled her with their regularity, a seemingly endless line of sentinels guarding the waters beneath.

A flock of starlings looped and bloomed and contracted as it described graceful patterns above the mist, dipping down sometimes to disappear, before reemerging in a plume of vapor.

The rush of the long grass behind them seemed to swell and retreat in time with the movements of the birds.

"Oh," said Fern.

Then she fell silent.

There atop the bluff, surrounded on all sides by a beautiful distance, Fern was consumed by a sense of remoteness that was not at all lonely.

A *safe* smallness wherein the horizon was infinite, and as such, judgment, too, must be impossibly distant.

The bookshop had never felt farther away. Thune, Viv, Tandri . . . they might have all been lost in that soft mist.

Or not lost, perhaps, but *enfolded*. Safely tucked away.

It was . . . relief. Somehow in this place, in this moment, she didn't have to strain for it. Her mind was quiet. Uncrowded with apologies or anxieties or anticipation.

Gods, to just *stay* there for a while . . .

"Uh, we should probably get back, huh?" prompted Breadlee. "I wouldn't want to lose the Oathmaiden's trust—or, you know, *we* wouldn't."

"Yeah. Sure," murmured Fern. "In just a second."

Then she dreamily slipped the knife into a pocket within her cloak and slowly sat down next to Zyll.

And thought about absolutely nothing.

The light was nearly gone when Fern stirred from her reverie. The mist below had thinned to purple threads that continued to wisp away, and the breeze had cooled considerably. The starlings were long gone.

Zyll was no longer beside her.

She staggered to her feet on numb legs, her ass suddenly awake to the fact that it had been parked on a stone for gods knew how long. Whirling, she found no sign of Zyll—again—and more worryingly, no sign of Bucket, either.

But before she had time to conjure up a curse suited to the moment, she noticed a figure crouched in the tall grass with one arm resting on a thigh, watching her.

A one-eared elf with ragged silver hair.

Fern's stomach, which had been plummeting downward, now jagged sideways.

The Oathmaiden's expression was unreadable.

"Uh, where are—" Fern began, her voice rusty.

"Back at the cart."

"And . . . *how* long have you been there? Watching me?"

Astryx stood, unhurried. "Does it matter?"

Fern couldn't decide whether the elf was upset or not. Remembering the previous night, she couldn't stand the idea of another awkward stare-off over unspoken words, and she was unsettled at having been observed without noticing.

So. Fuck that.

"It does if you're angry with me. Are you?"

"I am not."

"Oh. Well . . . then everything is fine?"

"I found a route back to the road." Astryx remained facing her, and Fern felt the weight of that regard. Was it curiosity on her face? Contemplation?

"That's good then?" she tried.

"It is."

Fern slithered down from the rock she'd been sitting on and successfully navigated the tumble of stones without twisting an ankle. As she approached the elf, feeling very much like a child being called indoors, Astryx spoke up again, this time with unexpected hesitation in her voice.

"What kept your attention for so long?"

It took a moment for Fern to find the answer, but at last, she did.

"I think for the first time in a long time, I wasn't looking backward . . . or forward, either. So maybe I was looking at whatever is between those things."

Astryx thought about that, then nodded, although her face seemed faintly troubled.

And then they strode together through the shivering grass, back toward the wagon.

18

The backcountry route Astryx charted did indeed bring them back to rejoin the old road.

Eventually.

It certainly wasn't conducive to travel by wagon, though. Zyll and Fern trooped alongside the Oathmaiden on foot while Bucket drew the cart, rattling and crashing, over lumpy terrain and hillocks hidden under the long grass. The going was slow, and more than once Astryx had to lend Bucket her shoulder to force the wagon over a stubborn fold in the land.

When at last they returned to the nominally paved road, even Bucket whickered in relief.

Two days later, as they arrived in the shabby, tumbledown village of Turnbuckle, it was amidst a sheeting downpour. Fern reasoned that at least she could be grateful that the storm had held its peace until roofs were visible in the distance.

She shivered miserably on the buckboard with her hood up and water pattering on her nose and whiskers, with Astryx crowded between her and Zyll, wearing a belatedly donned oilskin cloak. The elf almost never rode in the cart, but was willing to make an exception to avoid the ankle-deep mess of the roadway. Watching Bucket slog ahead, chin tucked, his massive hooves hurling great gobs of mud in all directions, Fern didn't blame her.

It was tough to make out much of Turnbuckle through the heavy curtains of rain, but lantern-lit windows suggested a handful of buildings hugging the road. They materialized one by one with the cart's approach, looking as sad and wet and bedraggled as Fern felt.

"We're stopping here, right?" asked Fern, doing her level best not to sound desperate.

"Gods-blast-it *yes*," replied Astryx, combing water out of her hair and off her brow. Apparently, given enough precipitation, even her stoicism could be washed away.

"Oh, thank fuck," breathed Fern.

The elf grunted in agreement, which felt like some kind of miracle. Fern was perversely pleased.

Zyll had her head thrown back and her mouth open and was making gargling noises.

At last, they spied an inn, which spilled more light into the street than any of the other buildings and featured a battered wooden sign that read THE SLIPPERY TROUT. Fern reflected that the badly executed fish carved into it was at last underwater, where it belonged.

Astryx drew Bucket to a halt, then stood and picked Zyll up one-armed before leaping down into the muck. She grumbled something beautiful in elvish again, which Fern was now certain she reserved for anything impolite.

Planting the goblin under the awning, she turned and held her hands out to Fern. "Come on, then." She made a get-on-with-it gesture.

"I'm not a toddler," said Fern, peevishly, standing and flapping her cloak in a failed effort to shed some water. "I can get *down*."

"Do you want mud up to your armpits?" Astryx squinted at her, hair plastered to her forehead and shin-deep in muck. Behind her, Zyll shook herself so vigorously that her orange pigtails slapped against her cheeks.

Fern muttered something ungrateful under her breath, clutched her satchel to her chest, and managed a begrudging, "Fine."

Astryx caught her easily and set her down next to Zyll. "Besides," she continued, "as far as I'm concerned, you *are* a toddler. I've had boots that were older than you."

"That's very funny," replied Fern. Then she blinked. *Is she bantering with me?* But she was too wet to seriously consider the possibility.

"Get us a room," said Astryx. "I'll see to Bucket and the wagon." Without waiting for a reply, she slogged through the mud to investigate the smallish stable that adjoined the inn.

~~~

Fern flipped back her sodden hood and heaved an enormous sigh of relief as she led Zyll into the great room of the inn. The door thumped closed behind them, subduing the roar of the storm to a low mutter. A fire snapped merrily in an enormous, misshapen hearth. The taxidermied head of a massive prairie-ox regarded them with sleepy alarm from above it. A crooked stairway at the back led to a second story. Water leaking from the roof dribbled into a scattering of mismatched tin pots, which threatened to over-spill onto the flagstones.

There were no patrons amidst the sprawl of old tables and chairs. Along the wall to the right, a counter ran in front of a line of cubbies and stacks of plates and cutlery, with a burlap curtain obscuring a doorway to a kitchen or office in the rear.

"Hello?" called Fern.

"Just coming!" hollered a rough voice from beyond the curtain. After a series of clatters and thuds, the broad back of a man preceded the rest of him through the burlap.

When he turned to face them, bristle-bearded and expectant, his face experienced a tortured journey which began with confusion, took a sharp detour into shock, and eventually arrived at outright dismay.

He nearly dropped the tray of tankards he was carrying.

"You!" he cried.

It only took a second before Fern realized that he wasn't talking about her.

Zyll grinned at the man and then made a curious motion with

both hands, hooking her thumbs together and flapping them like a bird's wings. "Howdy howdy," she said.

"Do you *know* her?" asked Fern.

"Aye," he replied sourly. He slammed the tray down on the counter and pointed one thick finger accusingly at the goblin. "Ain't got no grackle pie *this* time, neither!"

Fern didn't know what to do with that, and she was too wet to want to sort it out. "We just need a room for the night. Three of us, actually. Our, uh, companion is out in the stable, so, a night for the horse, too? I don't know how that works."

"Can't help you," said the innkeeper, crossing his arms. "This'n's nothin' but trouble, and I'll be damned to all eight hells if I'll have her under my roof for one night more."

Staring back and forth between the two of them, Fern couldn't help but ask, "What sort of trouble?"

"Chairs shattered to flinders. Gouges in the wall. Cutlery *missin'*," the innkeeper railed, flinging his hands toward all corners of the room. "And I only just got the damned ox head clean enough to hang again!"

"She did all that?" Fern eyed Zyll with skepticism.

"Well . . ." The man looked uncomfortable. "Maybe not *personally*." But then his resolve firmed. "She's an *instigator*. And I won't have it."

The goblin chose this moment to withdraw a fistful of spoons from a pocket, which she used a wet pigtail to polish.

"My *spoons!*" bellowed the innkeeper, at which point he became incapable of further speech. His mouth flapped open and closed, and Fern thought he might actually be approaching detonation.

They were all saved from the explosion by the door behind her banging open, whereupon a very soggy, very muddy one-eared elf entered the room. Nigel's pommel gleamed menacingly over one shoulder, and she had a leather haversack slung over the other.

"Good evening," said Astryx, in a dangerous voice. "You know, I feel absolutely confident that we can come to an agreement."

The innkeeper's open mouth snapped shut, and he gulped.

───

The chilly room had two beds, a rag rug, a small fireplace, and a wardrobe, all dimly lit by lantern glow through the rain-battered window. Upon shutting the door behind all three of them, Astryx strode to the opposite wall, kicked off her boots, unbuckled her baldric, tossed Nigel onto a bed, yanked open the haversack, and grabbed a bundle of dry clothes. She then immediately began shucking the ones she was wearing in a series of short, sharp motions.

Fern glimpsed a pale, heavily muscled back latticed with old scars before whirling around to give her some privacy, although the Oathmaiden clearly couldn't have cared less.

The goblin began wriggling out of her own soggy coat, revealing a moth-eaten nightshirt underneath. Zyll calmly wrung out the coat onto the floor, enlarging the puddle already soaking into the wood at her feet.

Fern joined them in disrobing, hanging her cloak and satchel on pegs to dry. Then she remembered Breadlee, and retrieved him from the interior pocket.

"Gah, thank the Eight. That cloak's wet all the way through. Aww, am I getting tarnished? I am, aren't I? And on my good side, too! Could you just give me a little buff? But not the kind where you breathe on me, that's disgusting."

"You're drier than the rest of us. Besides, I don't think Nigel *ever* has to be polished," replied Fern. "But maybe he's just especially well-crafted."

"That's not how—did *he* tell you that?"

"Mm," said Fern, noncommittal. She cast around for something to do with him, then deposited him on the mantel above the fireplace.

There was already wood in the grate, and a clay jar of long matches beside the hearth.

"I can start *this* fire," she muttered to herself, crouching. She fiddled with the logs and stuffed some splinters of kindling beneath them, before rasping a match alight on a sandpaper-wrapped brick and touching it to the tinder.

As the first tongues of flame crawled to life, a long sigh made her turn around.

Astryx finished lacing up her shirt, then sat cross-legged on one of the beds with her eyes closed. She breathed in through her nostrils, then out her mouth in a slow, meditative rhythm.

"You okay?" ventured Fern. "You seemed a little . . . put out."

The Oathmaiden opened her eyes and stared at her very seriously. "There is one thing that I have never gotten used to in a thousand years, and that is being soaking wet. It never, ever gets any less objectionable. Ever."

Clad only in her dirty nightshirt, Zyll bounced on the other bed alongside Nigel. The Elder Blade jounced up and down with every enthusiastic jump, and Fern could only imagine what he would have to say about the matter if he were unsheathed.

Fern and Astryx both chose to ignore her.

"Thank you for starting the fire." The elf let her exhaustion show as if she'd shed a cloak obscuring it. "Now, I'm going to lie down and sleep until I can't sleep anymore."

Astryx dug around in her wet trousers where they were hung over the footboard and withdrew the small brass key to the room. She tossed it to Fern. "It's best if she doesn't leave this room. If you go out, lock her in."

Snagging the key out of the air, Fern replied, "Um. All right. You're not worried she'll . . ." but the Blademistress was already flat on her back, her hands folded over her belly.

Her breath deepened, evened, and she was asleep.

"How do you *do* that?" muttered Fern, who had never been as envious of another person as she was in that moment.

"Sleepy sleep!" cried Zyll, going limp mid-bounce and falling to the bed like a rock next to the longsword, whereupon she instantly began to snore.

"Godsdammit."

Fern rubbed her eyes, seized Breadlee from the mantel and her satchel from the peg, and made for the door and the great room downstairs.

19

"This is gods-damned embarrassing," moaned Breadlee as Fern used him to sharpen one of her pencils. The growl of the storm seemed distant amidst the plink of rainwater in the tin pots and the pop of the hearthfire.

"It's a perfectly ordinary use for a knife. Stop complaining."

"A *knife*? Kid, there's no call to be disrespectful."

"That's what you are," replied Fern, serene.

"I'm a *greatsword* that has experienced a *diminishment*."

She snorted, shaving away another curl of wood.

"I don't see you selling any books these days, but you still call yourself a bookseller. That's rank hypocrisy, is what that is. *Oh shit, here he comes—*" The knife broke off as the innkeeper ducked his head into the great room. Fern was the only occupant, her fur slowly steaming dry before the fire, pencils and parchment on the table before her.

"Thought I heard somebody else," the man muttered.

She shrugged.

"Huh." The innkeeper disappeared behind the curtain again.

"Why'd you shut up?" Fern kept her voice low. "I figured you'd want an audience."

"Not *that* one. Guy has a weird thing for silverware. I don't need that kind of interest."

"That shouldn't be a problem. After all, *you're* a greatsword that has experienced diminishment. Can't imagine he has a lot of use for one of *those*." She blew the shavings off the table.

"Hey, not everybody is as perceptive as they oughta be."

Fern ignored him and began to write, while he grumbled quietly on the table.

Dear Viv,

I'm soaking wet. I've just finished arguing with a knife. This will require some explanation, and I can already tell this is going to run long.

I realize that as I write and rewrite this letter, I can't help but consider all the ones that came before as part of the same long message. I think I've resolved to give them to you in a bundle when I get back, then close my eyes and hold my peace until you read them all. One endless string of apologies with memories sandwiched between them. And at the end, forgiveness?

Maybe that's asking a lot. Maybe you'll put them down in the middle of reading. Maybe you'll never get through the first page.

I imagine you receiving the only one I actually sent. Were you furious? Disappointed? Relieved? All three? Hells, it probably hasn't reached you yet even now.

I realize I keep imagining your response and trying to write with that in mind. That feels like cheating, somehow, but given the circumstances, that's a weird thing for me to be hung up on.

Which reminds me . . . I <u>am</u> sorry. Sorry for tearing my life apart when I gave you every reason to believe you could rely on it staying whole.

I've caught the tail of something. I don't know what animal is on the other end.

I will see you again though, I know that—if it doesn't swallow me whole—

"Mind if I have a seat?" said a voice, startling Fern so much that she scrawled the trailing *e* across the page.

She glanced up to find another rattkin standing across the table from her. His fur was sleek and smoky, ears slim and back-swept, eyes interested and inclined to amusement. He had a dagger belted at his waist and a tartan sash worn crosswise over one shoulder. His tail quirked a curious curve behind him.

"Um," said Fern, glancing around at the extremely empty great room and its abundance of open seating.

"It's Quillin, by the way," he continued, ducking his head in the ghost of a bow. "Sorry to intrude, but I rarely see any of our kind on the road but penitent monks, and *hells*, they're boring conversationalists. If I can risk being rude, you don't strike me as a religious pilgrim."

"A *Tarimite?*" A laugh escaped Fern, along with a surprised, "Oh, fuck, no!"

Quillin's brows shot up, and a smile bloomed. "*Very* nonreligious. Thank the Eight. I'm starved for some honest gods-damned profanity."

"I . . . sure, have a seat," stammered Fern, flustered. "I'm Fern. Pleased to meet you." She self-consciously flipped the letter over in front of her, covering Breadlee with it. She thought she heard an indignant mumble from him, but Quillin didn't seem to notice, although he *did* eye the parchment.

"Just a letter to an old friend," explained Fern, as he slid into the chair across from her.

He raised both paws. "None of my business. And this is none of my business, either, but I'll ask anyway—what brings you to this absolute pigs-wallow of a town in the ass-end of no-place?"

Fern prepared to explain that she was a bookseller from Thune, which would inevitably lead to an astonished exclamation, a "How in the Territories did you get *here?*" and then the admissions and the justifications and the embarrassments.

Instead, with a curious shiver of delight, she replied, "I'm traveling to Amberlin with Astryx One-Ear. A sort of assistant, I guess you'd say."

The look on his face was *very* satisfying.

He leaned over the table and laced his claws together. "Eight *damnations*. Squire to the Oathmaiden? Well now, you are a singular lady indeed. Can I buy you something to drink? I *insist* you regale me."

It had been so long since Fern had felt the flush and tingle his attention produced in her that she almost didn't recognize it.

He *was* handsome, even if he had to be ten years her junior.

"Brandy makes me a talker," she said, self-consciously smoothing out her whiskers. "So don't say I didn't warn you."

"Consider me warned." He grinned and rose to summon the innkeeper.

⁓

Brandy *did* make her a talker, but she retained enough presence of mind after their encounter with Chak not to mention Zyll or the bounty. The tale of Taltus and the Four Fingers in Bycross was more than enough to sustain a good story, anyway, although it took some delicate omissions to subtract the thieving goblin from it.

Quillin was an attentive listener and an engaging conversationalist. Still, over the course of the evening, she didn't discover a great deal about him other than allusions to the breadth of his travel and knowledge of the Territory.

That didn't seem to matter much, though.

When she parted from his company, it was with cheeks, whiskers, and tail buzzing pleasantly with brandy-glow, and an invitation to meet the next day that she'd dithered over.

She closed the door gently behind her and locked it, then turned to find Zyll sitting up on the bed with her head cocked and Nigel across her knees, staring curiously at her. Astryx lay unmoving in exactly the same position, her chest rising and falling with sleep. The fire had burned low, illuminating them both in a rusty, pulsing glow.

"What?" whispered Fern, unnerved by the keenness of the goblin's gaze.

"You are, mmm, how do you say, kindled in the cheeks?" Zyll didn't bother to whisper, but Astryx didn't stir.

Fern frowned. "You can't see my cheeks. I'm covered in fur." Her cheeks, of course, instantly flushed.

"She and her sweetheart were practically canoodling," piped a voice from her satchel.

"Oh, shut up," hissed Fern, fishing him out. "Tomorrow, I'm finding a sheath to muzzle you with." She approached Zyll and offered the knife. "Stick him in a pocket or something."

The goblin ignored Breadlee, patted Nigel, and said, "I am liking *this* shankling."

Fern sighed, stuffing Breadlee back into her bag with a protesting squawk from him. "Whatever. Put Nigel on the floor and budge over. There's no way I'm missing out on a soft bed, and there's not enough room for the two of us *and* an old man."

20

It was hardly the most comfortable bed she'd ever slept in and in addition to her baby-bird snores, Zyll was a bit of a kicker, with sharp little toenails. None of it mattered. Fern had the most restful sleep she'd achieved since leaving Murk for Thune all those weeks ago.

When she woke to thin silver light filtering through the curtains, Astryx was folding her damp clothes before shoving them back into her haversack. Zyll continued to snore, a warm bundle of pigtails and puzzles at Fern's back. Rain clattered on the roof, and the fire was all but deceased.

"Are we leaving?" mumbled Fern.

Astryx scooped Nigel off the floor and buckled him back over her shoulder. "It's still pouring, and I don't fancy wading our way across the countryside. I have a few errands to attend to, then I'll see what the locals have to say about the weather and when they predict it'll break."

Fern sat upright with the quilt across her legs and scrubbed the sleep from her eyes.

The Oathmaiden shot her a look. "Have a good night?"

Something in her tone made Fern's cheeks flush again. "Um. Sure. Yes."

"Careful you don't end up in any strange wagons." A hint of a smile from Astryx.

Fern breathed on a paw and sniffed it. She could detect perhaps the *faintest* hint of brandy. The flush grew hotter. "I had *one* glass."

"Mm. Alone?" The smile had not departed.

"I—" Fern suddenly remembered relating their recent adventures in Bycross to Quillin, and wondered what Astryx would think about that. "No. I had a nice conversation. It was very normal." Then, with a hint of defiance, "And if we're not leaving today, maybe I'll meet him and have another one."

She wasn't sure if she expected a protest or another sly verbal nudge, but Fern got neither. "Mm. Be careful. And, rain or no, we'll likely leave tomorrow. I think it's best *that* one stays in this room." Astryx pointed at the sleeping figure of Zyll. "Don't leave her alone for long, or the door unlocked."

She reached for the latch, then paused and bent to retrieve something—a folded piece of parchment. Her brows rose. "This is for you." She tossed it on the bed at Fern's feet. "It must have been a *very* nice conversation." Then she was gone, quietly shutting the door behind her and padding down the hall.

Heart thudding, Fern snatched the note from atop the quilt. FERN was inked on the front in an angular scrawl.

Perhaps you found an answer in dreams. I'll be
downstairs at eleven.

—Q

"Could've asked for better weather," Quillin called back to her, as he trotted before Fern across a series of planks running from one boardwalk to the next. At least the rain had slackened to a drizzle for the moment, and occasional pale scraps of sky showed here and there.

He scampered under the next awning and turned to offer her a paw as she leapt to join him, her cloak mottled with dampness. Fern took it as she landed. "On the other hand, if it was any better, we'd probably be on our way by now."

In the light of day, it was obvious that while Turnbuckle was little more than a village, it had enough two-story structures to entertain pretensions of ramshackle township. It smelled strongly of fresh-turned earth and wet sheep.

"Then the Eight have my thanks," replied Quillin with a grin. He didn't relinquish her paw, and she didn't mind. "I was planning a hike to a pretty little lake west of here through some birch woods that're nice enough, but the path'll be a bog. You learn to make the best of a life on the road, though. We'll tour the local sights instead."

He squeezed her fingers for her to follow, leading her to the opposite end of the boardwalk, then nodded at a miserable lake of muddy water that occupied the entire intersection. A beleaguered man in mud-spattered Warden's blues slogged through it on the diagonal. Nobody else was about.

Quillin gestured grandly. "This, dear Fern, is known by the locals as 'Fuckery Wallow.'"

Fern laughed. "It isn't!"

"You're right," he amended. "They couldn't be bothered to name the roads around here at all, but you have to admit, it's appropriate." Quillin held a paw to his mouth and continued in a stage whisper, "Did I mention that Turnbuckle is an absolute shithole?"

What followed was a tour of a sad alleyway, a scummy well, a half-burned shed, and a muddy paddock filled with irritable geese—The Lane of Small Dejections, Hell's Least Important Bumhole, Cinder Estates, and the Quadrangle of Spite, respectively.

Fern nodded and effused appreciatively at each stop, grinning like a loon.

Turnbuckle was, indeed, depressingly lousy. She was having a fabulous time.

"Tourism is the beating heart of the community, clearly," she observed with great sincerity.

"Ha!"

"It obviously brought *you* here," continued Fern. "Do you always travel to such storied places?" She wondered what it might be like to journey alongside someone talkative and interested and with whom a tour of mudholes transmuted into something deserving of memory.

"When the work takes me there," he replied. "Come on, let's get back out of the rain." He waved a paw away from the grumbling geese and in the direction of what looked like a general mercantile.

Fern hitched up her cloak so it wouldn't trail in the mud and stepped carefully alongside him. "Fine, I've left enough openings, and you've passed them all by. I'm getting impatient in my old age. What is it you do, exactly, that brings you to what you've described as, and I quote, 'an absolute shithole'?"

"I've tried to make a habit of never talking about what I *do* until I'm out of anything else to talk about. In my experience, it's a terrible way to get to know somebody—at least if you want to know anything worthwhile. I want to learn what you laugh at, what makes you roll your eyes, what gets you upset, or passionate, or puts you at ease. Work is just . . ." He flapped a paw as they ducked under the eaves in front of the mercantile. "The stuff that holds the rest of it together. It's like describing a house by talking about the nails."

He studied her as they stood together under shelter, brushing dry their fur. "But all right, I'm game. I'll talk about the nails in *my* house if you talk about yours. I won't lie, I have been a bit curious, wondering what you're up to, swanning around with the Oathmaiden."

"Prepare for disappointment. I sell books. Or if you want to dress it up a little, a friend of mine once wrote, 'She traded silver for dreams in ink.'" Fern dried her tail with the lining of her cloak.

Quillin's jaw sprang ajar. "That's from Greatstrider, isn't it? Let's see . . . *Lovelorn by Lamplight*?"

"You've read it?" Fern replied, pleasantly surprised.

He chuckled. "Got to stay warm *somehow* on cold nights by the roadside. And Greatstrider is a *friend* of yours? Are you collecting famous elves? Does Martus Derrion do your laundry? Damnations. I know I just said that work wasn't important, but I'm so gods-damned intrigued that I may have to revise my rule. How in all eight hells does a bookseller—and acquaintance of Zelia Greatstrider, no less—end up trooping across the Territory with Astryx One-Ear? Actually . . ." He waved both paws and shook his head. "Roll that back. I've got the wrong end of the questions. Do you *like* trading silver for dreams in ink?"

"Well," replied Fern. "That's a complicated answer."

"Ah. We'll need fortification then." He peeked in the window of the mercantile. "Say I gather supplies for the Territory's dampest picnic, and we untangle it together?"

Fern didn't answer, shading her eyes to peer across the street through the drizzle. An orc strode down the opposing boardwalk, cast mostly in shadow. Heavily muscled, with braided black hair. *Was that . . . ?*

"Something wrong?" asked Quillin.

"I could swear she bumped into me in Bycross," murmured Fern. The orc didn't turn or appear to notice them but continued onward and out of sight around a corner.

"Hmm. I'm skeptical of coincidences, but are you sure?"

"Not positive. But I just got a tiny shiver of recognition."

"We'll keep a weather eye out then." He patted the hilt of his dagger. "No sense spooking ourselves on an empty stomach, though."

Fern opened the door before he could reach for it. "I'm half starved, and two steps ahead of you."

～

"So, your fire's gone out, and the coals are cold," observed Quillin through a mouthful. They sat beside one another on a bench in the stable adjoining the Slippery Trout, snacking on smoked cheese, walnuts, oatcakes, and currant jam. An opened bottle of raspberry shrub sat between them. Bucket watched them over his stall door, nostrils flaring with interest.

It was warm and cozy within, the air thick with the scent of horseflesh and saddle soap and straw. The rain had picked up once more, drumming insistently on the slate above.

"I wish it was that easy," replied Fern. "It's like I can see what I loved—still love?—about it, but it's behind a thick windowpane. I can't feel it or smell it or taste it, and I don't know that I'll ever be on the other side of that glass again." She popped the last of an oatcake slathered with jam into her mouth and followed it with a hunk of cheese. Chasing it all with a glug of the sharply vinegary shrub, she winced and continued, "But what am I going to do? I've tried everything I can think of to break back through. Do I wait around forever for the window to shatter on its own? In the meantime, I just feel so . . . so fucking *useless*."

"Are you worried that now that you've left it, you can never go back? And even if you couldn't, would that be so terrible?" he asked, licking his claws and taking a swig of the shrub himself. "You're in the company of a living legend. That's got to count for something."

"But what am I *doing*? Who the hells am I? Not a bookseller, that's for fucking sure. Somebody who follows a famous person from place to place writing a bunch of letters I never send?"

"It's not everyone that's beheld Fuckery Wallow, I can tell you that much."

Fern snorted.

"A more important question. Do you think we're here talking because you used to sell books? Yes, that's the current topic of conversation, but do you figure that's why I intruded on you so rudely last night? Or invited you to an *enchanting* trudge through the mud with me today?" His gaze was serious. Lantern light glowed pink through his velvety ears, and she wondered briefly—guiltily—what they might feel like between her fingers.

"All right, you're making your point," allowed Fern.

"I'm not sure I am. Have you asked yourself why the Oathmaiden lets you tag along?"

She blinked at him. At the beginning, it had been on the

pretense of translating and minding Zyll, hadn't it? But, neither of those reasons held true anymore. Why *did* Astryx suffer her presence?

Fern had no idea.

"That one's knocked you back, hasn't it?" observed Quillin. "Maybe ask her sometime, because the answers won't have a gods-damned thing to do with how you earn your way through the world. *I* liked you without knowing."

She flushed and fiddled with the clasp of her cloak. "Okay, that's more than enough about me for now. I'll sit with it," she promised, "but now it's time for you to hold up your end."

Fern worried she'd made a mistake by sidestepping his last few words, but Quillin didn't seem to mind.

"I always hold up my end," he said, letting the seriousness lapse and leaning back against the wall with his paws behind his head. "Which turns out to be useful in my line of business. I suppose you could call me an adventurer. Much less successful than One-Ear, but"—he shrugged—"I acquit myself well, I think, even though nobody has bothered to add anything particularly fancy to my name yet. I'm stealthy, capable with a blade when I have to be, and principled enough to get hired twice. I can stitch a wound and set a bone, and I'm very, *very* good at finding people who don't want to be found."

A cold knot suddenly formed in Fern's belly. "Really?" she asked casually. "Is that what brought you to Turnbuckle, then?"

He rolled his head to smile at her. "Just passing through in pursuit of the biggest bounty I've ever seen, and all for an unarmed goblin in a patchwork coat."

⁓

Fern slammed the door open so hard it banged against the wall.

She didn't see Zyll anywhere in the room—only an unmade bed, and her satchel hanging from a footboard post.

"Fuck!" she cried.

An orange mop of hair popped from under one of the unmade

beds, followed by the goblin, who clutched something wriggling in one fist.

Before Fern could identify what it was, Zyll had crammed it into her mouth and started chewing.

She was positive she'd seen more than four legs.

Feeling simultaneously green about the gills and profoundly relieved, Fern closed the door behind her and slumped against it.

For the last twenty minutes with Quillin, she'd endured wild swings of mood as she had done her level best not to bolt from the stable to check their room, to provide no outward indication that she knew anything about the goblin, and to continue asking thoughtful questions, while simultaneously wishing she'd never asked him what he did in the first place. She also couldn't help imagining that it would be very nice to scoot closer to him and find out whether he smelled as nice as she imagined he did. This was followed by an agonizingly protracted parting of ways.

Put succinctly, it was all just so much fuel for a bonfire of emotional garbage.

The blaze only leapt higher when the door snapped open and Astryx's voice came from somewhere above Fern's right shoulder.

"What is she *eating*?"

When Fern spun to face her, Astryx's face rapidly shifted from confusion to narrow-eyed suspicion. "And what happened?"

Fern couldn't marshal an explanation, and only managed to blurt, "Close the door behind you!"

Astryx did, without question.

Two possible futures spun out before Fern in that moment, with crystal clarity.

In one, she warned Astryx that Quillin was literally yards away, hunting for Zyll. Also, there was a high likelihood they'd been followed by the orc with the braids from Bycross, and given the way things were going, she was probably after the same quarry. She made it clear that if they didn't leave, secretly, and soon, *something* would happen, and they were all likely to deeply regret it.

In the other, the warning was nearly the same . . . but Fern stayed behind, and found out exactly how nice Quillin smelled, and didn't she need to be working her way back to Thune to tender that apology at some point? What did Astryx need her for, anyway? She was . . . *extraneous* to the whole enterprise.

Wasn't she?

Astryx's look of concern deepened. She crouched to match their eyelines. "Tell me."

Fern swallowed hard and started talking. She hadn't the foggiest idea which road she was going to choose.

I'm sure I'll figure it out by the time I finish, she thought.

"There's someone here after Zyll's bounty. In this inn. *Right* now. Maybe more than one."

Nope, that was not enough time.

She breathed in.

Her heart seemed to be buckling under an intense pressure.

No rocks at the bottom.

She breathed out.

"We have to go."

21

They departed Turnbuckle nearly as they'd entered it—in the middle of the night, under a shedload of rain.

There were a few key differences, however.

This time, Fern was the one driving the cart, alone—after almost foundering in Fuckery Wallow—hunched in her cloak with the hood up, and wet to the whiskers. Every other instant, she anticipated Quillin's voice calling out and asking her where in all eight hells she was going in such a hurry.

Worryingly, she wasn't positive she wouldn't answer if he did.

"Beats shaving pencils," chirped Breadlee from her cloak pocket. "Back on the thrilling road to adventure, am I right? Cold, wet, thrilling adventure!"

Fern peered into the moonless darkness as they slogged out of the village and up a muddy rise into a birch grove. She'd never driven a cart in her life, but Bucket didn't seem to need a lot of leadership, thank gods. Checking over her shoulder to reassure herself that nobody was following, she unshrouded the lantern on the buckboard beside her and blinked in the sudden light.

When they'd passed over the peak of the hill and the glowing windows behind them were no longer visible, she pulled awkwardly on the reins, and Bucket dutifully came to a sloppy halt, the wheels of the cart slithering through the muck.

"Come on, come *on*," muttered Fern, seizing the lantern and holding it high. The birch trunks cast twitching bars of shadow into the night. The rain pattered on her hood and splashed on Bucket's flanks, the only sound she could hear.

She thought of the cozy room in the inn. Of sitting beside Quillin in the stable, of the warmth of his fingers on hers. Of running away from something safe and good and possible.

Then, from the emptiness beyond her lantern's reach, Astryx threaded her way through the birches, her oilskin cloak bulging awkwardly on one side. In her hand, Nigel's bare blade glimmered in the yellow glow.

She slipped and skidded down a slope, and then dashed up the near side of the gully through long grass slicked down by the rain. She produced Zyll from within the cloak. The goblin blinked in the sudden light.

"No followers?" asked Astryx.

"Not that I could tell, but—" Fern shrugged helplessly at the rain.

"I don't like it, my lady," groused Nigel. "Absconding in the night? You should be marching proudly in the day's light, and let the hells welcome any who dare to hinder you!"

Fern held the lantern higher. "Oh, that's a *fabulous* idea," she hissed. "Then she can either kill or injure anybody in the way, and every bounty hunter within a hundred leagues will know exactly where Zyll is, which direction she's heading, and who has her. It'll make it so much easier for them to *ambush* us."

"Hush," said Astryx, sheathing Nigel even as he squawked about how damp he was. She leapt easily up onto the buckboard next to Fern and deposited Zyll between them both.

Before the elf could reach for them, Zyll snatched up the reins, snapped the leather briskly, and hollered, "Hup hup, Buckley boy!"

Bucket got moving again, as bewildered as anybody.

Astryx and Fern shared a look over the top of Zyll's sodden mop of hair. The Oathmaiden nodded, a strange expression on her face.

Fern couldn't help but think that a lot of things were packed into that expression and that nod. Acknowledgment? Gratefulness, maybe.

Respect?

Soggy as hells, cold to the marrow, her tailbone aching, Fern felt something straighten inside her that had been more than a little bit bent.

They disappeared into the night, leaving Turnbuckle behind. And Quillin, too.

~~~

"Merciful Eight, what a relief. Profoundest thanks, my lady. What *miserable* weather." Nigel sighed with contentment as Astryx polished him dry with a wad of cotton rag.

They camped beneath an overhang of black basalt beside the road, outside of which the rain poured in a perfect silvery curtain. Smoke fled in tendrils from a small campfire, feeling its way across the rock above them until it escaped into the sodden darkness.

The way had steepened throughout their nighttime flight, the air growing colder until pebbles of sleet sometimes joined the rain.

Fern rubbed her paws together before the welcome light and heat, which reflected off the black stone at her back. The three of them sat in a half circle, dripping and steaming, while Bucket dozed on his feet under the overhang alongside them. The cart remained parked out in the downpour, rain sheeting off the waxed tarpaulin.

She couldn't stop thinking about Quillin. About whether at this very moment she should be traveling in the opposite direction.

About not feeling alone, notwithstanding the company she kept.

Because what did she really know about her companions? How had Quillin put it? Something about what people did being nothing but the nails that held the house together?

She glanced at Astryx, absorbed in oiling Nigel's gleaming length while Zyll wriggled her toes dangerously close to the flames.

After days on the road, they were still practically strangers. What *did* she know about them—either of them? Anything at all?

That might not have been fair, since she'd done her part to

avoid the looming *talk* after leaving Bycross. At this point, Fern could only sense a misty silhouette of the person that she thought Astryx was, obscured by her legend and her reticence. She knew a *few* details, but . . .

"Mostly nails," murmured Fern.

"What's that?" the Oathmaiden asked, idly.

Then Fern decided that if she was going to turn fleeing into something more productive, she was going to have to take some fucking action.

While she was fretting over what action *meant*, however, Astryx surprised her.

"That was well done, by the way."

"What?"

Astryx held Nigel's hilt to her eye and peered along his blade, scuffing at his edge. "It was quick thinking on your part. You didn't freeze up. You were careful. Observant. You guarded your tongue." She nodded at Fern. "And now we've skirted trouble best avoided. It was well done."

"Oh. Thanks?"

For a wild, ridiculous instant she considered asking Astryx if anything made her laugh or roll her eyes, then came to her senses.

Astryx had just thanked her. She had been *useful*. If there was a time to press her luck, it was now. *And to forget about running off in the rain with handsome strangers*, Fern promised herself.

"After Bycross, I was pretty sure you wanted to talk about something," she said, with elaborate casualness.

The elf stopped attending to Nigel and slowly laid him athwart her crossed legs. She looked about to say something and then didn't.

"You don't talk to people very much, do you?" ventured Fern.

A long pause.

"I don't. Not so much anymore," said Astryx at last. Then, almost defiantly, "After enough time, it feels like you've had all the conversations."

Fern forged onward. "That must make it more comfortable to avoid them. Have you had *this* one before?"

The elf blinked, taken aback. Then she surprised Fern again by answering, "Yes."

"How long ago was that?"

Astryx returned her attention to Nigel. "Before you were born, I'm sure," she answered, with a hint of something like bitterness. Or regret?

"Is that the last time you traveled with anybody else?"

The elf snorted. "Hardly." Then, quieter, "Possibly the last time it mattered, though."

"Ahem. She had *me* to accompany her, of course," declared Nigel. "Hardly lacking for fellowship, eh, my lady?"

"That sounds pretty lonely," said Fern. She ignored the shocked noises of indignation that followed.

Astryx's smile *was* bitter now. "That's the inevitability of a very long life. People come and go, and you remain."

"It seems a lot *more* inevitable when you're traveling alone in the wilderness most of the time," observed Fern. "And it's not like you're the only elf in the Territory. Why do you still do it, after all these years? It doesn't seem like it's for glory or songs. Why not do something else? You've got the time."

"You suddenly have a lot of questions," said Astryx, sharply.

Zyll glanced avidly between them.

Fern spread her hands. "I told you every embarrassing thing that's happened to me in the past few weeks as part of my very stupid crisis of middle age. Maybe it's fair I know one or two things about you, too, apart from the fact that you hate being *damp*? So, why do you still do it? I sure as hells can't tell if you *like* it. Who could blame you if you didn't? It's wet, and lonely, and cold, and the two swordfights I've seen you in so far didn't even seem to elevate your heart rate. So . . . why?"

Astryx's mouth thinned. "Here you are with me in the cold, wet, darkness. You could have gone home. Somebody's even interested enough in you to slip a note under your door. So why aren't you back there?"

Sudden ire prickled Fern. What had begun as an earnest effort to unearth some of Astryx's character had turned into a wrestling match with a trout. "Because I can't go back to the same old thing. I can hardly breathe thinking about it. That's what I want to understand. How can you *still* be doing it after all this time?"

Astryx looked equally annoyed, stabbing one knee with a finger. "This life is like a sword. It's the tool I know how to use. I have sharpened it to a keen edge, and it accomplishes the tasks I set it to. It may cut me from time to time, but I know its *value*. If I put it down, what other tool is there to hand?"

"Oh, hey, can I make a suggestion here?" cried Breadlee, his voice piping from Fern's cloak pocket. "It's just when you put it that way, I can't help but think this clearly rhetorical question has a *brilliant* answer that maybe you haven't fully considered yet—"

Fern yanked him from her pocket and hissed, "This is *not* the time!"

"Indeed! M'lady is right—she has selected *precisely* the instrument that best suits her life's work and calling!" Nigel's voice vibrated with indignation.

"Oh my gods. You don't know what rhetorical means, do you? Sad." Breadlee affected unconvincing woe. "Probably the effects of Elder-rust on the mind. I've seen it before. Absolutely tragic."

Zyll leapt to her feet and produced fistfuls of gleaming cutlery. "More shanklings!"

And then the conversation-turned-argument went careening off a bluff and shattered to matchwood on the metaphorical rocks below.

When the Elder Blades had at last been silenced—Nigel in his sheath and Breadlee at the bottom of Fern's satchel—Astryx glanced around their tiny camp with both hands on her hips, as though looking for something else to set right.

"I think that's enough conversation for one night," she said.

Fern sighed and prodded the coals, filled with a foggy regret she couldn't put a paw on. "I'm sorry."

Astryx surprised her a third time. "Don't be. It's . . . Perhaps we'll talk about it . . . another time."

Zyll's head rose sleepily from the patchwork nest of her coat. "Daylight words."

She commenced snoring immediately.

22

They didn't exchange many words in the next day's light, however.

It was just too damn cold.

When they awoke, it was to frost furring the grass and glazing the mud of the night before. The rain had stopped, only to be replaced with intermittent flakes of snow. Above them, the basalt overhang dripped steadily from the melt their combined body heat and the dregs of the fire produced.

Fern's brain itself had frozen over, unable to muster any thought not related to her next movement or staving off the chill that penetrated her fur. Her head was too muzzy and her paws too stiff to even properly bemoan the warm bed she'd left leagues behind.

There was little to pack. After hastily breaking their fast with cheese and water for them and a pail of oats for Bucket, Astryx rehitched him to the cart. All three of them bundled themselves onto the wagon, Fern wrapped in a patched blanket and Astryx in her oilskin cloak. The frosted tarpaulin creaked and popped as ice shattered. Bucket's hooves cracked through the scrim of ice on the muddy road as he plodded onward, chuffing and blowing in an aggrieved way.

The temperature steadily plummeted until the ice no longer broke so readily beneath every hoofbeat, and the sound changed to a dull clunking that echoed eerily between the snow-sugared birches and bastion oak. Gradually, the grade increased as the road rose in a sinuous curve up the skirts of a prodigious mountain range. The snow line drew closer, a pearlescent white sometimes invisibly blending with the overcast sky.

Last night's conversation resurfaced when Astryx glanced at Fern, her lips blue and her breath a frosty plume. "Are you sure?" she asked, tossing her head to indicate the frigid ascent before them. "I know why I'm here. You didn't like my answer, but I didn't get one from you at all. Is your reason good enough for this?"

Drawing the blanket tighter around her shoulders, Fern replied, "Maybe my reason is just that I'm stubborn. Besides, it's a little late for second thoughts now, isn't it? I'm not walking back through this mess unless you toss me off the back of the cart and roll me down the hill."

Astryx glanced back the way they had come, calculating.

With some astonishment, Fern realized that Astryx was considering backtracking. She hadn't entertained that for a second when she'd first discovered Fern in the back of her wagon.

"It's definitely stubbornness," said Fern, tingling with bashful gratification.

The elf faced forward again, and they both shut up for a while, consumed with the business of being cold on a wooden bench.

Even Zyll had withdrawn mostly into her coat, with only a wedge of forehead and her eyes peeking from above her pocket-lined collar. Fern decided there was something satisfying about the fact that the goblin wasn't immune to the cold.

The road wended ever onward, although now in many places it was blown over with powdery snow that Bucket trudged through in misty fountains of white. Thankfully, it wasn't actively snowing, although flurries were sometimes borne on the wind that sighed and whistled down upon them from the peaks. It also brought with it a peculiar and intermittent, keening chime that Fern only gradually became aware of.

"What is that?" she mumbled through painfully chapped lips.

Before Astryx could answer, one of Zyll's hands appeared from within a sleeve and pointed into the snow.

Fern wasn't sure what she was indicating at first, although she saw what looked like a pair of low, stony walls studded with short capstones lining the road ahead. As they drew closer, however, she saw that the capstones were actually something like tiny bell towers, each with a brass bell suspended within, gently blowing in the gusts. Occasionally, a clapper would graze its bell, or even strike it more directly, and the chimes and shivery whines were issuing from them.

"Monks," explained Astryx, pointing up the slope. "There's a Tarimite monastery on the other side of that peak. The membership is all rattkin, if I recall."

Nigel, bared an inch, cleared his throat and adopted a lecturing tone. "Indeed, a rather curious circumstance, all of them worshippers of Tarim, the Sixth God, he of the One and the Many, ineffable and insatiable. Mm, did you know, each of his limbs has a *name*, inscribed upon every one of the bells the Tarimites tend. The brass itself is very particularly cast, what with—"

"Please stop," begged Breadlee.

Fern made a face. "Penitents," she said, with distaste.

Astryx studied her with bemusement, but said nothing.

They passed between the murmuring bells and though their eerie song put Fern ill at ease, she was glad for their presence when the road disappeared entirely beneath drifts, with the low walls the only suggestion of their path forward.

As the road curved in a meandering arc around a white-crowned bluff of dark stone, an involuntary gasp escaped Fern.

Before them the icy slope fell away entirely into a vast chasm whose other side was just visible behind sheets of snowdust skirling from higher peaks.

Spanning this yawning emptiness, a great, stone bridge, onto which their path directly led.

It was clearly a Tarimite structure, although how old, gods knew. Twin pillars bracketed each end of the bridge, with a narrow span of stone between them, several stories up. With a start, Fern realized that these pillars were actually towers, and the slim notches that ringed the top were windows. The span between them was in fact an open-sided walkway, which gave her vertigo even to consider.

Carved into the caps of the towers were images of the Sixth God, hooded and cyclopean and overly tentacled, and below, ranks of Tarimite penitents marched across the stonework, their tails curved back above their heads with lanterns threaded on them.

She shivered, and not from the cold. Encrusted with ice, the tower windows vacant, wind tugging spills of snow from every edge, the bridge filled Fern with an unexpected sense of sadness, loss, and the frailty of legacy.

"Fuckbuttons," she murmured, quietly enough that she hoped Astryx wouldn't hear over the breath of the mountains. Then, louder, "Is it safe to cross?"

Astryx seemed distracted, a slight frown on her face as she flipped her hood back to scan the snowfields leading up to the bridge. "It's absolutely safer than finding another way around." Then, without waiting for comment, she flicked the reins, and they got moving.

As Bucket's hooves rang on the wind-scoured pavers of the bridge, Fern braced herself for the whole thing to shiver or sway or crumble out from under them with a crack of shearing stone.

Nothing of the sort happened. Not so much as a tremble.

She began to relax.

Halfway across the bridge, everything went wrong.

A figure emerged from the right-hand tower at the opposite end of the bridge and strode to the center of the path where they stopped, facing the cart, their hair tugged sidelong by snow-flecked gusts.

"Well," said Astryx grimly.

She didn't pull back on Bucket's reins, and he continued to advance.

Fern held up a paw to shade her eyes, as though that would help her to see any better.

Nearsighted or not, she still knew who it was.

The orc warrior with the many braids.

She was bundled in a quilted jacket and heavy pants, and she held a hooked axe down and away from her thigh.

"Oh shit," Fern said, beginning to turn and look back the way they'd come.

Astryx brought her up short with a hand on the shoulder. "Behind us, too. Three of them." She looked disgusted with herself. "I should have checked the towers before we rode out onto the bridge. Foolish."

Then she reached up to bare an inch of her blade. "Nigel. I'm going to ask for quiet. If there's speaking to be done, I'll do it."

Fern heard what sounded like a sharp intake of breath from him, then a miserable, "As you wish, my lady."

"Another bounty hunter?" murmured Fern, gripping the clasp of her cloak so fiercely that the cold metal bit into her paw.

"Seems likely," replied Astryx.

Fern had seen the Oathmaiden single-handedly defeat a small army of Four Fingers thugs, so she wasn't sure why she was nervous this time.

Maybe it was the implication of patience on the part of the orc before them. She'd clearly been following them, biding her time until they were at their most vulnerable atop this forsaken bridge.

Maybe it was the memory of the look on the woman's face when they'd bumped into one another back in Bycross.

Maybe it was the deadly seriousness in Astryx's tone.

Or maybe it was just the precipitous drop on either side of their cart.

"What are we going to do?" whispered Fern.

"When I say the word, you both get down from the wagon. Put it between yourself and whoever is closest. You need to be able to move. To run. This isn't going to be like it was with Chak." The elf's voice was pitched low and freighted with deadly certainty.

Zyll started digging in her pockets.

"No," said Astryx, and for a wonder, the goblin stopped. The elf glanced at Fern. "Remember the knife."

The prospect of using Breadlee for anything but sharpening pencils had never once occurred to Fern and seemed ridiculous even now, but nevertheless, she jammed her paw into the satchel and found him at the bottom. Her fingers closed over Elder steel, warm to the touch.

Then there was no more time for discussion.

"Stop the cart," called the orc, hefting her axe and grabbing the shaft near the head with her opposite hand.

Astryx complied, making a peculiar clicking sound with her tongue and gently tugging the reins. Bucket clopped immediately to a halt.

Fern wanted them to do anything *but* stop, but she supposed trying to run the orc down was a good way to end up with that axe embedded in Bucket's skull.

"Once I start talking, get down from the cart," hissed Astryx. "Remember what I said."

She rose and tugged the tie of her oilskin cloak so that it fell away, tumbling in a gust. It caught on the edge of the wagon. Then she leapt down, unsheathing Nigel before she touched stone. He stayed quiet, as he'd been bid.

"Didn't say anything about getting out of the cart," drawled the orc. "But I guess for the Oathmaiden, I can make an exception."

Now Fern did look behind and saw the orc's three companions advancing their way. A rangy, red-haired man with a shortblade and a face as sharp as one, a stone-fey woman in black carrying an undrawn bow, and another orc in a parka balancing a heavy maul on his shoulder.

Their pace was unhurried.

Fern supposed she should be thankful she wasn't already riddled with arrows.

She slid Breadlee from the satchel.

"Thank gods, I can hardly see a damn *thing* from in there," he said. Fern got the impression he took in the scene. "Oh, hey, this may be your chance to finally get some real stabbin' in!"

"Shhhh!" she whispered fiercely. "I'm not stabbing anybody!"

"Gods, not *everything* is about you! This is my shot to show Astryx that I'm the kinda sharp that *matters*!"

Astryx had moved to stand a few yards in front of Bucket, about twelve paces from the braided orc who sauntered toward her, carving away that distance. The wind blew harder, fresh flakes borne on every gust.

The Blademistress shouted, "You know who I am. I'm waiting for you to tell me who you are or what you want, but it's cold, and I'm not feeling as patient as usual, so I'd appreciate it if you'd get on with it."

That was their signal. Fern threw off the blanket and tugged Zyll's sleeve to get her moving. She began to clamber down from the cart with Breadlee held clumsily in her right paw.

Fern froze mid-motion when she registered the humorless smile on the orc's face.

"I wasn't planning on any of that," replied the woman, pitching her voice to carry over the wind. "Not much of a talker, really. But like I said, I'll make an exception for the Oathmaiden." She pointed the head of the axe at Zyll standing on the buckboard, then at Astryx. "I'm Tullah. You won't have heard of me. I'm going to kill *her*. But first I'm going to have to kill *you*, because you're the sort of person that makes that necessary. Hadn't decided about the other one."

Fern could hear the consternation in Astryx's voice, even though she couldn't see her face. "The bounty's no good if she's dead."

Tullah's harsh caw of laughter echoed amongst the crags.

"I couldn't give a frigid fuck about a bounty."

Then she was sprinting.

23

It took three seconds for Fern's brain to register that her understanding of an already bad situation had been woefully wrong, and that it was significantly worse in every respect.

"What're you waiting for?" cried Breadlee. "That lady with the bow back there is gonna needle you like a pincushion if you just hang around!"

A frantic glance confirmed that the stone-fey did have an arrow nocked, but she hadn't fully drawn her bow yet. She only watched as the other two advanced, Zyll and Fern their obvious quarry, which was plenty of encouragement for Fern to get a move on.

Bucket moved first, though, and instead, she had to scrabble for a better handhold to keep from tumbling off. He surged forward, curving wide and then drawing the cart perpendicular to the bridge, blocking most of it and leaving several feet of room on either side before a laughably shallow lip of stone prevented travelers from accidentally stumbling over the edge.

"Thank-ly, Buckley-boy!" cried Zyll, and it dawned on Fern what he'd done.

Bucket had separated the two groups, giving Fern and Zyll something to hide behind.

"Good horse!" she fervently agreed.

They both scrambled to the side of the cart facing Astryx and leapt down to huddle behind the wheel.

Fern heard a peculiar whistling, distinct from the wind, and then the cart rocked as something thumped into the tarpaulin.

An arrow.

Peering around the wheel, she saw the red-haired man and the orc drawing ever nearer, still without any apparent urgency, as the stone-fey fitted another arrow to her bow.

She wasn't trying to kill them, Fern realized.

She was just keeping them in one place until the others arrived, so that *they* could kill them.

Fern ducked back behind the wheel, her eyes locking with Zyll's.

The goblin's sharp grin was nowhere to be found, and there was something in her eyes that Fern had never seen there before. Shrewdness. *Seriousness.*

Fear?

Zyll reached out, grasped her paw, and squeezed it once. "Zu-kenda."

A buzzing in Fern's ears ascended into a high whine. She hadn't been this terrified since her encounter with Varine the Pale, when she'd been absolutely certain she was going to die.

Her blood thumping at her temples, Fern put her back to the wheel and stared ahead, her mind whiting out, dimly aware that Zyll was rummaging in her pockets again.

Which is when she saw Astryx and Tullah.

Fern realized that this battle was nothing at all like the ones she'd witnessed prior.

Because Tullah looked like she was *winning*.

Astryx moved with the same liquid speed and unerring precision, but where before Nigel had flashed in blinding arcs of white steel, slipping past defenses and shedding parries, now he was deployed to different effect.

Tullah pressed her with brutal strikes, hacking with her axe in fierce and unpredictable chops that rang on Elder steel and flung blue sparks to mix with the flakes of snow, her dozens of braids snapping behind her like coachwhips. Fern could almost feel the impacts in her own bones, her fingers shivering with sympathetic vibration. Even as she watched, the orc heaved her weapon around in a diagonal cut that raked down the longblade with a scream of metal, catching between the steel and crosspiece—and then Tullah pushed her right hand all the way up to the axe-head and continued driving through with the left, smashing the haft into Astryx's sternum with a dull crack.

The Oathmaiden staggered back with a deep grunt, but her blade stayed steady.

"My lady!" cried Nigel.

At his pained voice, Tullah grinned even wider, lips skinning back to bare her tusks entirely. "Always wondered what it'd be like to handle an Elder Blade. Guess I'll find out."

She didn't even look winded.

"This is *just* when a knife would help!" cried Breadlee from Fern's paw, sounding near tears.

Astryx reset her feet and lunged forward, Nigel slicing upward in a rising angle, on the offensive for the first time.

Tullah's grin shifted into something like delight as she hammered the Elder Blade to the side, then looped around it with the axe's hook to fling the end downward.

"Why does she want to kill you? What did you *do*?" cried Fern, grabbing Zyll's collar.

The goblin looked like she might reply, but Tullah beat her to it, every word punctuated by steel on steel as she battered at Astryx's defenses like the hells' own woodswoman.

"She. Fucked. My. *Life*."

But then Fern could pay no more attention to Tullah or Astryx, because Bucket reared, shifting the cart, just as the red-haired man rounded the end of it with his shortblade up. A peek around the wheel's rim saw the orc's boots heading the other way, presumably to the horse's bridle.

Bucket whinnied angrily and reared again, rocking the cart back. The man with the shortblade put his free hand on it as though to steady it.

Fern saw his eyes widen in disbelief at Zyll, coughing an involuntary laugh.

The goblin stepped away from the cart wheel, brandishing two fistfuls of assorted cutlery.

He took in Breadlee in Fern's paw. "How 'bout that, Kell? Looks like I'm fine dinin'!"

"Get on with it, Marv," called the orc, sounding annoyed. "I got the horse."

Then several things happened almost at once.

A sharp, pained cry from Astryx, although Fern did not see its cause.

Zyll hurled a half-dozen forks and knives at Marv with surprising speed and ferocity. One of the knife blades glanced off his temple, leaving a long gash, and a meat fork embedded itself in his left thigh. His pained oath joined Astryx's.

And it turned out that Kell the orc did not, in fact, "have the horse."

"Shit!" he cried, as Bucket swung his head hard to the side and cracked him in the skull with his cheek. Kell staggered away, dropping his maul and clapping both hands to his face.

The horse surged backward, and the cart began to jackknife, clipping Marv, who was just yanking the fork out of his thigh with a shout. He stumbled sideways and went down as the wagon rolled toward the lip of the bridge.

Zyll leapt on him like a rabid weasel tangled in a quilt.

Fern chanced a glance at Astryx and saw her down on one knee, fending off a series of heavy blows from Tullah.

The snow was feathered red around her.

And then the cart shuddered as the rear right wheel jumped the lip of the bridge and went over.

Bucket screamed as the end of the wagon sagged into space. The tarpaulin came untethered, and boxes and barrels and loose gear tumbled out of the rear. With the reduced weight, the horse almost brought the wheel up over the lip again with a surge of effort, but his hooves skidded backward on the icy bridge, and the second wheel began to ease out over the abyss.

"Oh, fuck," whispered Fern.

Marv howled as Zyll clawed at him.

Tullah roared in triumph.

The moment stretched as Fern stared at the wagon in open-mouthed shock. It teetered on the precipice. She whipped her head back toward Bucket struggling in his traces, foam flecking his cheeks and chest, straining mightily against the dead weight pulling him toward a terminal downward journey. On the other side of the cart, Kell stooped to retrieve his maul, and in the far distance, the woman with the bow was shouting something.

"Bucket!" Astryx's cry was anguished. Fern saw her lunge to her feet with her right hand clamped to her opposite side, the left barely deflecting another of Tullah's attacks with Nigel as she retreated toward the horse.

The buzzing whine in Fern's ears ceased.

The white receded.

She darted toward Bucket's head, seized one of the thick bands of leather hitching him to the wagon, and with a sure, swift stroke, slashed it with Breadlee's glimmering steel.

He parted the leather like shears through silk.

"This is undignified!" the knife protested.

The cart jerked and tipped and now both wheels were over the edge and the wagon slammed down upon its bed, canting perilously, dragging the horse back several more handspans. His hooves left fracturing trails in the ice.

Fern dashed between Bucket's legs, heedless of the heaving weight of him, and grabbed the strap on the opposite side, slicing it in two effortlessly.

Trace-buckles higher on his chest popped at the rivets with a metallic snap, and the horse staggered free, even as the cart rumbled over the edge and out of sight. Several soundless heartbeats later, a terrific crack resounded as it struck the rocks below.

Free of the weight at last, Bucket wheeled and reared again, his massive hooves lashing out at Kell the orc, who stumbled away with an arm upraised.

Fern backed up, then tripped over Zyll, who still wrestled with

Marv amongst twisting serpents of windblown snow. As Fern rolled onto her knees, red cloak whipping up her back and around her face, she caught a glimpse of Astryx again. The Oathmaiden parried another strike and howled at Tullah, her voice raw with anguish and rage. With a mighty stroke, she caught the haft of Tullah's axe halfway between the orc's two fists and sheared it in two.

The lower length of her axe handle went spinning off the edge of the bridge, and the orc was left staring with nearly comical surprise at the much-shortened weapon in her right hand.

"Hells yeah!" hollered Breadlee.

Fern heard a feral hiss from Zyll, then a kick from one of Marv's boots caught Fern in the shoulder and knocked her sidelong, where she almost lost her grip on the knife. When she recovered, Astryx was sprinting toward them both while trying unsuccessfully to resheathe Nigel and free her hand. She snarled in frustration and pain and gave up, reversing her grip and tucking him under her arm where blood from her wound immediately spilled over his blade and poured down the fuller.

An arrow clattered off the stone between them but whickered away harmlessly.

The Oathmaiden did not pause, reaching down to scoop Fern up with one hand. In another two strides, she reached Bucket, tossed the rattkin over his back sideways, and seized his bridle with her newly freed hand to wheel him around.

Fern scrabbled frantically for the loose straps of leather still buckled to the horse and found herself staring into Kell's shocked gaze for a surreal split second, his maul forgotten in both hands.

Zyll landed on Bucket's back beside her with a puff of breath and an angry, *"Luffing shunks!"*

Then they were moving, plunging through the thickening snow. Astryx tangled her hands in Bucket's mane and wound her boot into the remains of his cart harness, dragging herself up so that she clung alongside the barrel of his chest.

Fern looked past Bucket's head and the fog of his heavy breath.

Tullah waited on the bridge before them, the top of her ruined axe still in hand, her face set in a snarl.

The horse shifted to pass the orc on her left, and as he did, Astryx pressed herself away from his side with a knee, slipping the blood-slick Elder Blade from under her arm. With no time to turn him blade-first, she drove the starburst pommel left-handed, directly at Tullah's shoulder.

The combined force of Bucket's gallop and the Oathmaiden's strike spun the orc off her feet and face-first onto the snowy stone. The elf grunted and almost lost her grip on her horse's mane, but held on.

And they were past, speeding over the last strides of the bridge and into the heavier snow beyond.

Fern felt Zyll drop away, snatching Breadlee from the bookseller's nerveless fingers as she did.

"What are you doing?" she cried, struggling to look back the way they'd come.

"By the fucking Eight," snarled Astryx.

It was the first and only time Fern ever heard the elf swear in Territories.

With a cluck of the tongue, the Oathmaiden brought Bucket to a skidding halt and struggled to untangle her boot from the wreckage of his tack.

Fern worked herself up to a sitting position, using her tail for balance as she watched the goblin dash back through the snow directly toward Tullah, her pocketed coat flapping behind her like the Territory's ugliest flag, Breadlee clutched in one hand.

"Hey, hey, you're going the wrong *way*!" wailed the knife.

The orc had found her knees and was staggering upright just as Zyll dropped to hers on the stone of the bridge. Breadlee flashed as she held him high, blade pointed down, then she drove him with all her might into the crevice between two massive blocks of stone.

He plunged in up to the hilt.

The goblin dug into a blue pocket with one hand—improbably to the elbow—then withdrew a long-handled metal soup ladle.

Tullah paused in absolute confusion as Zyll cocked the ladle back, then hammered the knife's hilt with it, producing a resounding, ear-bruising SPANG.

The sound that followed was loud, out of all proportion to what should have been possible, with a harmonic resonance buried inside it that seemed to build and build and *build*, reverberating between the peaks.

Tullah found her scowl again and began to advance.

Another arrow whistled through the air, blown off course and missing Zyll by only inches.

Kell and Marv both tried to catch up to Tullah, sprinting and stumbling respectively.

Then a terrible crack thundered through the canyon, and everyone stopped moving at once.

Snow sifted down in ragged curtains from the two towers at the end of the bridge. White powder suddenly seethed along the blocks of stone nearest the knife.

Zyll yanked Breadlee free and backed away, just as a long, dark line appeared horizontally in front of her feet.

From edge to edge, a section of the bridge three strides long dropped several inches as though it had been hammered from above by an invisible sledge.

Tullah began backpedaling, then turned and sprinted flat out.

The stone fell away all at once with a sound like an avalanche. Blocks the size of lockboxes tumbled into the chasm amidst snow and crumbled granite as their end of the bridge collapsed.

The far side, which Tullah and her crew still occupied, groaned as grit dribbled and blew away from its underbelly, held aloft only by one pillar still supporting the midpoint.

Fern watched in amazement as Zyll hurried back toward the horse with Breadlee in one hand and her mouth set in a line of grim satisfaction, red eyes blazing.

Another arrow buried itself in the snow just short of them.

Along the ragged gap in the bridge, Tullah paced back and

forth like a thwarted cat, fury in every line of her body, while her crew gathered at a safer distance from the edge.

As Zyll arrived, wading through snow up to her knees, Astryx stared down at her. The elf's right hand was wrapped around her belly to hold her bloody side, and her left used Nigel's crimson-streaked length as a crutch.

They regarded each other for a long moment marked only by the wind in the mountains and the ghost of a metallic whine.

Astryx opened her mouth to speak—

—and then her fingers slipped slowly off the Elder Blade's hilt, and she collapsed in the snow.

24

Fern stared at the elf's prone form in dull shock as snow skirled around her knees and Tullah shouted something across the gap.

Astryx lay half obscured and unmoving in a drift that slowly pinked at her side, her hair riffling in the wind.

Fern was dimly aware of Nigel's frantic cries from beneath the snow, and panicked noises coming from Breadlee. Zyll waded to Astryx and began tugging at one of her arms, to little effect.

These were things Fern registered as a distant observer, floating back and away and up into the silver sky.

A puff of vapor from Astryx's lips broke the spell.

The Oathmaiden was alive, but the weather would surely kill them all if their enemies didn't find a way to do it first.

"We have to get her out of here," mumbled Fern, dropping her satchel and struggling forward to join Zyll, seizing the other arm.

"Must be turn-ling over," said Zyll, her grin nowhere to be found.

Fern nodded and looped both forearms under Astryx's left shoulder, groaning as she heaved. The elf was hardly bulky, but she was twice Fern's weight, at least, and the sheath on her back fought them the whole way. Zyll dragged Astryx's other arm across her body, and with much puffing and struggling, they managed to roll her faceup.

"Be gentle! Oh, my lady, would that I had hands!" cried Nigel, his voice muffled by the snow that hid him.

The elf's chest rose and fell erratically, her closed eyes like bruises in the bloodless flesh of her face.

Sparing a look across the bridge, Fern saw Tullah watching, fists on hips, braided hair whipping in the wind.

"Like a fucking vulture," she muttered.

Gingerly inspecting Astryx's side, she peeled away the cloth of her tunic to reveal a long, clean gash that immediately overspilled with blood. Fern's knees went wobbly. "Godsdammit." She spun to face Zyll. "You have something in that coat of yours for this, don't you? In one of those pockets? You have to."

The goblin was already rummaging through them, pointed tongue out in concentration. Her hands emerged with a bundle of linen in one fist and Breadlee in the other. With a quick slice she hacked off a wad of the fabric and tossed it to Fern, who, amazingly, managed to catch it.

"Ugh, I'm still vibrating," said the knife. "Stop waving me around!"

"Holding *here*," said Zyll, indicating Astryx's wound with Breadlee.

With a nod, Fern first unbuckled Astryx's baldric and, with great effort, slid the sheath out from under her back. Then she pressed the wad of linen against the wound, where it immediately blossomed red. The goblin straddled the elf's chest, passing one end of the remaining strip of cloth to Fern. With one paw occupied stanching the wound, she used the other to assist Zyll in another awkward maneuver to lift and pass the wrapping under Astryx's back.

The elf moaned and muttered something unintelligible as they cinched the bandage tight across her chest and tied an ugly knot to keep it in place.

"Be *careful!*" pleaded Nigel.

Fur clumped with sweat, Fern panted and took a step back, overheated despite the frigid snow burying her paws.

She stared from the fallen warrior to Bucket, who stamped nervously nearby, ducking his head toward the elf in clear anxiety. Any satisfaction at sort-of dressing Astryx's wound vanished immediately at the impossibility of getting her up onto the horse's back.

"There's no way in all eight hells," she whispered, despair threatening to choke her.

"Help me . . . up," came a weak voice.

Fern turned to find Astryx's ghostlight eyes burning into her own. The elf had struggled to one elbow, trembling with cold or effort or shock. Her wound had already leaked through the dressing and was dribbling into the snow again. Zyll crouched at her other shoulder, providing grim support to keep her upright.

Fern's impulse was to protest, to insist that there was no way the Oathmaiden should in any way move, much less scramble atop a horse.

But that was stupid, because if she didn't, they were absolutely all going to die.

"Here, you can help," she said to Nigel as she slogged over to drag him from his snowbank.

She'd expected him to be heavy, but her estimate was woefully short of the truth.

His point trailed through the snow in a wavering line as she lugged him the short distance to Astryx, who wavered almost as much. Fern wasn't tall enough to stand him vertically with her paws on his hilt, so she gingerly grasped his blade and managed to arrange him pommel-up.

With a sharp intake of breath, Astryx wrapped one hand around his crosspiece, gathering her strength before hiking a knee and getting a foot underneath herself.

Supported by the goblin and rattkin, and using a blubbering Nigel as a walking stick, the elf squared herself with Bucket's side.

Afterward, Fern would have had a hard time articulating how the three of them managed to get the Oathmaiden astride her horse. The blood that painted his side was evidence enough of the battle.

With increasingly numb fingers, Fern and Zyll got Nigel into his sheath, then slid it through one of Bucket's girth straps. When Fern looked up from securing him with one of the dangling bits of leather, Astryx was unconscious and sprawled across the horse's neck.

"We have to get the hells out of this snow," she muttered, casting about for any sign of the road that had been buried in drifting white. She blinked. "The bells—where are the bells?"

Zyll seized a fistful of Fern's cloak. She cocked one of her enormous ears into the wind, then pointed upslope. "To be following. Bring Buckley-boy."

Fern couldn't hear anything but wind moaning through the crags.

Then the goblin began to forge her way in the direction she'd indicated. Fern retrieved her satchel and slung it over a shoulder, then stood on tiptoe to grab the side of Bucket's bridle. He obligingly dipped his head lower so she could reach it, and she led him after Zyll.

But not before turning back to holler at Tullah—

"I hope you fucking freeze!"

The orc probably couldn't hear her, but Fern didn't give a shit.

Fern had never trudged so thoroughly in her life.

The keenness of Zyll's hearing was confirmed as they came upon another low wall of bells. Even in high wind, the weight of metal and the windbreak of their stone housings meant they only occasionally rang, their silvery voices easily lost amongst the mountains.

They stumbled along seemingly forever. There was little room for thought, only relentless forward motion. Their passage reminded Fern dimly of a rolling theater she'd once seen in a shop in Murk's fortress town, cleverly painted on the outside of a cylinder of thick paper. The illustrated landscape unspooled in ceaseless repetition, lit by an interior lantern.

This was altogether less interesting, though. The terrain never changed, a world in black and white that drifted unendingly, marked only by the rise and fall of the shivering chime of bells.

Zyll's patchwork coat seemed the only scrap of color for a thousand leagues.

Occasionally, Fern would remember to look back at Bucket's passenger to make sure that she hadn't slid off his side and been lost to a bank of snow, but it was an increasingly dull and distracted observation. She couldn't hold on to dread or fear or any other sharp emotion for long.

As the light dwindled, the density and size of the flakes increased, and the temperature dropped further.

"Where the hells is this monastery?" mumbled Fern through frozen lips. Her whiskers drooped with ice. The satchel thumped against her hip, which ached at every impact.

Then, resolving from the ghostly gray, a dark, regular shape.

Her hope rose, then just as suddenly subsided as the relatively small size of the thing became apparent.

"What is it?" she shouted to Zyll.

The goblin looked back. "Camp-ling!" she cried, and made directly for it.

The structure was some sort of Tarimite way station for penitents, constructed of the same stone from which the ill-fated bridge had been quarried. Its walls curved inward halfway up, tapering to a blunted point at its apex. An arched portal flanked by a pair of bells led to a dark and icy interior.

Fern dropped Bucket's halter and hustled inside after Zyll. A precisely shaped stone brazier marked the center of the building, scooped out into a charred bowl that the goblin was already inspecting. Flakes drifted down from an oculus in the curved ceiling, ringed with carvings of tentacles. Four severe and unwelcoming benches circled the firepit, and alcoves in the wall looked as though they had once housed statues or offerings.

"Oh, thank hells," breathed Fern as she spied a neatly stacked pile of wood and kindling in one corner, dusted with snow.

A snort and the sharp ring of a hoof on stone drew her attention to Bucket's head peering in the doorway.

Like a specter swimming out of twilight, Astryx appeared beside him, one forearm against his neck for support.

A wan smile.

"I guess you can finally figure out how to start that fire now," she mumbled, before tottering to one of the benches, slowly easing herself down onto it and carefully lying back. Her eyes drifted closed. The Oathmaiden's breath came in shallow, whistling gasps that Fern didn't like at all.

Bucket snorted again, squeezing through the arch, then with much stamping, arranged himself alongside Astryx's bench. Nigel sagged in his scabbard amidst the tangle of leather on the horse's side.

"Fire," murmured Fern, moving to step outside and search the wagon for flint and steel, before remembering that there wasn't a wagon anymore.

No supplies.

No flint.

No *food*.

Her stomach hollowed out for more than one reason.

At a dull clatter behind her, she turned to find Zyll dropping an armload of wood into the stone brazier. The goblin stared at Fern expectantly.

The bookseller's mind whirled as Astryx's wheezing breaths acquired a troubling catch in them.

She dug a blank sheet of paper from her satchel and then shrugged it to the stone floor. Fern thrust out a paw. "Hand me the knife."

Wordlessly, Zyll drew him from a red pocket and offered him haft first.

"Hey, I don't trust that look," said Breadlee as Fern snatched him and inspected his length with a critical eye. "You're not thinking what I think you're thinking, are you?"

She crumpled the paper and stuffed it under the tumble of logs. Setting the flat of his blade against the lip of the brazier, she briskly drew him back with a terrible rasp of Elder steel on stone. Blue-white motes of flame sheeted into the bowl, snapping and bouncing with cold fire.

"Ow! You *were* thinking it! Stop that! This is . . . this is sacrilegious!" howled Breadlee.

Fern ignored him, dragging him mercilessly against the stone and shedding fountains of sparks onto the paper and cold wood.

"Come on," she hissed. "*Light,* you bastard."

As though her command had been heard by a forgotten god of campfires, a thread of smoke puffed into being amidst a sudden burst of light.

She slumped onto one of the cold benches and stared with blurred vision into the growing blaze as the first tentative fingers of heat reached out to embrace them all.

"*Sacrilege,*" sulked Breadlee where she held him loosely in one paw.

"Oh, hush," she mumbled and stuffed him into the pocket in her cloak.

The flames spread, crawling along the wood with increasing hunger as smoke twirled up and out the oculus to be torn apart by the wind.

"Good for you," whispered Astryx. "You managed after all."

The elf's eyes were closed, but that wan smile had returned. Fern might have imagined it, but she thought the rasp in the Oathmaiden's breath had eased a little. Her face seemed less bloodless, too, although perhaps that was only the effect of the growing glow of the flames.

Then Astryx's hand slipped from her chest and flopped to rest against the floor.

The bracelet of wire on her wrist loosened even as Fern watched, as though the meager heat were melting it. With a metallic *pop* it sprang open and clattered to the stone.

Fern gasped and struggled back to her feet to do . . . well, she wasn't sure what.

Zyll's voice stopped her, though. "Is still live-ly."

And Fern could see the feeble beat of blood in Astryx's throat.

"Is time for sleep-ling," said the goblin, who had crowded close to the fire. Her green nose was chapped and dripping, and she held her hands with fingers splayed toward the heat. Her own bracelet was still locked tight around her wrist.

Fern dimly wondered whether Zyll would disappear in the night. Then she decided that this was a concern for a Fern who was not stranded in a desolate mountain range with a half-dead elf and no reasonable idea of how any of them would survive the following day.

Gingerly taking her seat again, Fern tucked her cloak beneath her behind, for what little good that did. The heat slowly penetrated her fur, though, which began to steam. She wanted nothing more than to sleep as her eyes unfocused, lids fluttering against exhaustion.

"Fuck," she muttered. Fern glared at her satchel on the floor nearby.

With more grunting than was strictly necessary she climbed down from the bench, then hauled the bag back up beside her to withdraw a sheaf of paper and a pencil with fingers just beginning to prickle with returning life.

Dear Viv,
  I'm sorry.

—she wrote.

  And if you are reading this, there's this fucking orc I want you to kill.

Fern hadn't intended much more than that, but in very little time, she filled three entire sheets of paper with lines crabbed by the cold.

She jammed her letter back into the satchel, which promptly slumped over beside her as though it were just as exhausted as she. She couldn't be bothered to right it.

A huff of a laugh escaped Fern's lips as she glanced to her left at the pile of scrap cloth and orange hair crowded against her ribs, wheezing and whistling in its sleep.

She was dimly aware of a flitter of paper as the rising heat drew breaths of icy air through the entryway, but was already collapsing to the side as a tide of weariness rose to consume her.

Her cheek met a coat made of pockets and sank into it, and she was gone.

25

In her dream, she again fought through the snow, alone and pelted by stinging flakes, her fur crusted with ice. Fern chanced a look over her shoulder and glimpsed a tall figure following the trench she'd forged through the drifts.

She paused, shading her eyes against the white as the figure resolved.

For a moment, the person shifted like smoke, and then—

—Viv, arms bare, seemingly immune to the cold, moving with purpose.

Her curls writhed behind her in the wind. The pommel of her greatsword was visible above her shoulder, a simpler, more practical echo of Nigel's silver starburst.

Blackblood doesn't exist anymore. It melted in the fire, thought Fern, although this did not trouble her.

"Hey!" she cried, turning fully and waving with both paws above her head, overcome with relief. She grinned, suddenly giddy with joy.

Apologies seemed unimportant.

Then another smoky shift, and the orc shrank a handspan. Curls became braids, the greatsword's hilt vanished, and in her right hand, a hooked axe, whole once more.

Tullah, because of course it was—relentless, unforgiving.

The ice in Fern's fur doubled in weight as she turned and began to desperately surge through the snow again.

The white expanse before her rumpled like a sheet in a gale, fluttering, flapping, and a sudden cloud of ivory birds burst into flight. Their wings beat at her frozen face, and she was lost in the cacophony of their wings as they swirled around her in a whirlwind of feathers and sound.

Fern started awake to frantic wingbeats and bitter cold and immediately doubted whether she'd awakened at all.

Frigid gray light cast everything in pewter. One cheek was settled against something soft and warm, while something feathery tickled her whiskers. She squeaked and scrabbled at it with a paw only to discover a wrinkled piece of paper.

Dear Viv, it read.

Then she was fully alert, sitting bolt upright from where she'd been leaning against Zyll. The goblin blinked groggily at her from above the collar of her coat.

The fire had expired, and letters from Fern's satchel eddied around the room in fresh gusts of wind. Bucket snorted and shook his head to dislodge one that had plastered itself to his neck. Fern's satchel lay open beside her, two or three pages trying weakly to escape its mouth.

With a cry of dismay, Fern leapt from the bench to chase after the scattered letters, heedless of how they crumpled in her paws as she snatched them up.

When she'd caught the last one, she knelt, breathing hard, to stuff them back inside the satchel and buckle it tight.

Only then did she have the presence of mind to approach Astryx, where Bucket snuffled anxiously at her face.

The elf's chest still rose and fell in shallow, sipping breaths. Her hand still rested against the floor. Hectic spots of color in her cheeks hinted at fever.

Fern blinked at the Oathmaiden's wrist.

The bracelet that had fallen off the night before once more encircled it.

She glanced with perplexity at Zyll, but she'd withdrawn all exposed skin inside of her coat.

Fern approached, reaching out a tentative paw to gently wake the Blademistress, when someone else beat her to it.

"Tarim's patience!" cried a new voice, and the elf's eyes snapped open.

Three rattkin penitents crowded the entrance, all bundled in fur-lined habits, mouths agape. Shocked silence reigned.

Then the monk in front, a piebald fellow, broke it by casting aside his staff and hustling to Astryx's side. She struggled to rise, but he was already investigating the rusty red of her bandage with gentle fingers.

Fern's mind felt as though it were still battling through the snow of her dream. A profound relief wrestled with an old distrust, but she was far too tired to declare a victor.

The monk caught Fern's gaze from across the elf's prone body. "You look iced through to the whiskers. It's only luck we spied the smoke." Then, to Astryx, "Can you stand?"

"I can," croaked the elf. She levered herself up with a sharp intake of breath, then slid her legs off the bench in a series of deliberate motions. Ice crackled off her trousers.

"Hemlock!" snapped the piebald monk, and one of his black-furred companions hurried to stand on her opposite side as they both helped the elf rise. The other made soothing noises at Bucket and tried to get a paw into his halter. The monk's eyes widened at the sword slung through the mess of leather across the horse's ribs.

Zyll appeared beside Fern, nose and eyes just visible, but hands tucked up inside her sleeves. They shared a glance.

"Safe-ling," mumbled the goblin through her collar, then patted Fern reassuringly on the back.

"Safe," murmured Fern. Her eyes widened.

She spun, and, realizing she had no idea how to address him— Brother? *Sir?*—tugged at the piebald rattkin's habit. "Um?" she tried.

He looked back at her distractedly as he and his fellow did their best to support an elf twice their height as she tottered toward the exit.

"Rhubarb," he said.

"What?"

"My name. It's Brother Rhubarb. Be quick. We need to get her indoors." He grunted as Astryx leaned more of her weight on his shoulder.

"Right." Fern swallowed, throat dry and lips cracking. "It's just that the one that did this is still out there. And I don't think she's given up. I figured you should have fair warning."

"Tarim's patience," he muttered, with a grim shake of his head. "There's nothing to be done but move swiftly. There's a storm on the way. Look, there's a donkey outside. He won't bite if you act like you know what you're doing. The two of you should mount up while we figure out how to get your companion on her horse."

"Apologizing about the bridge-ly," mumbled Zyll, then scurried out into the snow.

"The what?" replied Rhubarb, brow furrowed.

Fern groaned. "I'll tell you on the way?"

~~~

She didn't, though. The journey wasn't conducive to conversation.

Zyll and Fern managed to climb onto the donkey that waited outside. It looked annoyed, and while it did bare yellow teeth at them, it did not bite.

With what little assistance the monks could provide, Astryx did succeed in muscling her way onto Bucket's back once more, but Fern's stomach went wobbly at the fresh streak of red she dragged up his side. The Oathmaiden slumped forward on his neck, and the way her arms trailed bonelessly over his shoulders was worse than the blood.

Then they were off through the snow. Hemlock led Bucket in the front, while Rhubarb trudged beside the donkey in the furrows of the larger horse's wake. The other monk walked between the animals.

The leaden sky became more troubled by the minute as darkening clouds lowered and snowfall became even thicker.

Despite all of that, Fern found herself drifting, readily abdicating all responsibility to the monks, the mountains, and Tarim himself.

Saved by a bunch of penitents, she thought. Then, *Too bad I'm out of the bookselling business. I bet they could really use some filthy romances.* The thunder of a distant avalanche swallowed up the sound of her delirious laughter.

She leaned forward into Zyll's coat and the heat that rose from the donkey's back, as time became elastic. A moment might be one second as easily as a year, and there was only the croon of wind, the flutter of snow, the creak of leather, the huff of donkey's breath, and the rustle of the goblin's orange hair.

They continued that way until a change in the rhythm of things tugged at Fern's consciousness.

"We arrive," called Brother Rhubarb.

Disoriented by the near darkness that had overtaken them, she gazed over Zyll's head and the donkey's bristly neck at slabs of black, outlined in white and marked by licks of flame. The shadows resolved by degrees into a series of stone buildings sprawled across the slope of the peak before them. Capped with heavily pitched but still ice-encrusted roofs, the structures were girdled with cloisters. A massive chapel dominated one side, a cluster of six spires lancing into the darkness. Two pillars flanked the road where it entered the abbey, crowned with the tentacles of Tarim as the god seemed in the process of swallowing each of them.

Fern's relief curdled somewhat at the sight.

Several monks looked up from the main path where they were shoveling snow aside in apparent anticipation of their arrival. In moments, Fern and her companions were surrounded by a lively sea of habits, fur, and tails as the denizens of the abbey ushered them through the pillars and past torch and lantern light, to the warmth of the church stables.

A pair of donkeys regarded their entrance with skepticism as the murmuring gaggle of monks led them indoors. A hiss escaped Fern as her frozen toes prickled in the sudden heat. Zyll immediately slipped off their animal's back and disappeared amidst the confusion of black and brown habits.

Then Rhubarb was helping Fern gingerly dismount. She became suddenly and painfully aware of the stiffness in her joints and the ache in her tail. Her knees nearly buckled under her own weight.

Using his arm to regain her balance, she watched anxiously over the monk's shoulder as they set up two stools and a stepladder next to Bucket. With a Tarimite tottering on each, they began delicately maneuvering Astryx off his back.

"We'll do our best for her," said Rhubarb, patting her paw with his own. "I'm no man of medicine, so I won't pretend to know her chances, but there's no better place to be spared Tarim's ill-regard. As for you, let's get something hot in both your bellies to warm you up before you meet the abbess. Your friend should—" His brow creased as he peered over the heads of his brethren. "Now where did she get off to?"

"She tends to turn up again," mumbled Fern, whiskers shivering.

"Mmm," he replied, frowning, then turning his attention back to her. "Now, what was that you were saying before about a bridge?"

26

Fern waited in the refectory, seated on a bench at one of three long dining tables, all rattkin-scale. The dark wood was much-scarred, but well-polished by the elbows of generations of Tarimites. Tall windows of cloudy glass allowed in reflected moonlight from the snow outside. Flakes pittered against the panes like anxious moths. Rafters ascended into shadowy peaks above, and the wind had withdrawn to whisper mournfully along the eaves. The whole place was surprisingly devoid of tentacular decoration.

She was belted into a loaner habit while her sodden cloak dried on a peg along the hearth's lintel, her satchel dangling beside it. At the last moment, Fern had remembered to transfer Breadlee to her new outerwear. The habit's fabric was heavy, softened from a thousand washings, and enfolded her in a soporific shadow that tugged her toward sleep.

Rhubarb had ensconced her blessedly close to the hearthfire before hustling out of the room to fetch her a meal. Of Zyll, there was no sign. Fern couldn't be bothered to worry about it. She sat alone in the cavernous space, although murmured prayers filtered in from the passageway at the opposite end. They did nothing to help keep her eyelids open, despite the yawning hole in her belly. She reminded herself that these were worshippers of a mad god of destruction and horror, but it was challenging to hold on to that fear at the moment.

Just as she was nodding off, a mumbling from the vicinity of her middle brought her back to wakefulness. She patted around the unfamiliar clothes until she withdrew the Elder Blade from a pocket and laid him on the table before her.

"Hey," said Breadlee. Fern had the sense that he was fidgeting. "So, is she gonna be okay?"

"I don't know," she replied. "But I'm too tired to consider that *I* might be the bad luck that ended her after a thousand years."

"Yeah," said the knife, with obvious relief. "You're right. You're not that important. But in, like, a good way."

"Obviously, it'd be the cursed magical object that's responsible."

"Wait, when did we get one of those? What did I miss?"

There was a long pause during which Fern was pretty sure Breadlee narrowed his nonexistent eyes at her.

"Um," he eventually continued. "Thanks for not mentioning my part in the whole bridge thing. Really great job making it sound like an accident we had nothing to do with."

Fern sighed. "You didn't see the look on that monk's face. We probably cut them off from all civilization for the next six months. If I told him everything, they'd be sacrificing us to Tarim come morning."

"Oh, is he one of those blood-and-fire gods? Gotta confess, I never paid much attention because of the whole immortality-of-the-blade thing. Didn't seem personally relevant."

"Just your garden variety cosmic being that might fucking swallow the world if he gets around to noticing it. Not sure the immortality of your blade would do a lot of good."

"And they *pray* to that?"

She laid her nose on her crossed forearms atop the table, burying it in the warm folds of the habit. "You've got a whole abbeyful of credulous idiots here that I'm sure would be happy to explain it to you. I don't know why you're asking me," she muttered crossly.

"Am I interrupting something?"

Fern jumped at an amused voice, slapping a hand over Breadlee and staring guiltily toward the small wooden door Rhubarb had disappeared through.

The piebald brother was nowhere to be found, though. Instead, an older rattkin stood in the open doorway with a tray in her paws and a curious tilt to her head. She was plump and silver and wore the same simple habit as the rest of the abbey's denizens.

"Um," said Fern.

The woman approached without waiting for an answer. She slid the tray onto the table and unloaded it in front of Fern with crisp movements—an enormous porcelain bowl of steaming stew, a round of sourdough sharing a chipped plate with a generous knob of yellow butter, and a mug of fragrant mulled wine.

The stew was crowded with parsnips and other root vegetables, rich with the savory scent of beef and pepper, and edged with a hint of thyme. A hungry moan escaped Fern's lips in chorus with her stomach.

The rattkin placed a spoon beside the bowl and cocked a brow at the knife under Fern's paw. "You travel with your own tableware?"

"Uh, no, this is a, um, letter opener," stammered Fern.

Breadlee vibrated with indignation under her fingers.

"Ah, yes. Obviously. For the letters," replied the woman, with no detectable sarcasm.

Then she settled on the bench opposite Fern and laced her fingers together in front of herself.

"Thank you," said Fern with real sincerity, while fervently hoping the rattkin across from her hadn't heard the bit about an abbeyful of credulous idiots. She wondered if the . . . sister? nun?—*Did you call a lady monk a nun?*—sitting across from her was going to watch her eat the whole meal. She didn't appear in a hurry to leave. "Er, Rhubarb mentioned the abbess would want to speak with me?"

She shoveled in a hot chunk of parsnip and then huffed around it as it scorched the roof of her mouth. Her eyes watered, but not so much she didn't notice the amusement of the other rattkin.

"She does," replied the monk-or-nun. "But I'm sure I can wait until you're done incinerating your tongue."

Chewing carefully with her mouth open, Fern gulped down the hot ingot of vegetable before actually registering what the woman had said.

"You're the abbess?" she wheezed.

"Abbess Bluebriar," replied the abbess. "But I don't stand on honorifics much. Or extra syllables. Blue is fine."

Fern didn't foresee ever calling her that.

"Fern. And again, I'm *very* grateful. *We're* very grateful."

A gracious nod. "You're most welcome. And for what it's worth, only Brother Trestle is particularly credulous, but he nearly drowned when he was eighteen and hasn't really been the same since, so we don't hold it against him."

Fern chased the burning in her cheeks and stomach with a solid glug of the mulled wine, which was *also* quite hot, and nearly blew it out her nose.

"There, there," soothed Abbess Bluebriar, who was somehow behind her and pounding on her back as she spluttered spiced wine all over the table and Breadlee both. His sounds of disgust were mostly lost amidst Fern's hacking coughs.

While Fern mopped her whiskers, able to breathe once more, Bluebriar resettled herself across the table again. She withdrew a pair of spectacles and a small book from her habit and commenced quietly reading.

Fern eyed the volume for a moment, but there was no title on the cover, and besides, it was probably just Tarimite nonsense. Although she felt a touch uncharitable at that thought, given said Tarimites *were* currently feeding her beside a roaring fire.

She returned to her meal—more carefully—and in hardly any time was scouring the gravy from the bowl with the last rind of sourdough. The wine had been the first to go.

The instant Fern slumped back, replete, the abbess tucked away her book, peering over the top of her spectacles at her guest. "Better? Excellent. Now, Brother Rhubarb relayed some very upsetting information about our bridge, as well as those responsible for your friend's bloody circumstances, but he was rather vague when it came to the particulars. I'm hoping you can shed a little more light on events, since your *other* companion is currently emptying the kitchen of tableware, and pretending she doesn't understand a word anybody says to her."

Fern began to speak, but Abbess Bluebriar extended one paw and rested it deliberately on Breadlee, who emitted a muffled chirp of startlement. She smiled. "There's no need to be concise. The nights are long and dull, and I so enjoy a good story."

Her smile appeared genuine enough, but there was something stern and unyielding beneath it. Something that might not hesitate to tie you down to a cold altar against your wishes.

Uncomfortably aware of exactly how hidden away the abbey was, and how *definitively* cut off from civilization or communication, Fern swallowed, organized her thoughts, and began.

⁓

". . . and then Rhubarb found us," finished Fern, gazing forlornly at her empty wine cup. She dearly wished she'd had the foresight to save some of it for the long retelling Bluebriar had demanded. She'd omitted a few details she thought she could get away with—no sense recounting her time with Quillin, or how velvety his ears looked—but the abbess had managed to extract the complete and embarrassing beginning of her adventure, brandy and all. Anytime the narrative got a bit thin, Bluebriar keenly prodded her to thicken it back up.

Now, the abbess regarded her in the waning light of the hearthfire, which was gnawing on a few blackened nubs. She reached over and plucked Breadlee up to examine him.

"Uh, hi," he said.

"And this wee fellow was enough to shatter our bridge?"

"Hey, it's not the sword, it's the wielder!" protested Breadlee. He seemed to consider for a moment. "Although that was pretty dramatic. Do you think Astryx was too wounded to notice? I am really conflicted about whether this is a credit or blame situation. I need to think about it some more."

"You might want to think about it quietly," observed Fern. Then, to the abbess, "How bad is this for you, exactly?"

The abbess sighed and placed the knife back on the table. "We're fortunate to have solid stores for the coming winter, since all our relationships of supply lie on the other side of that bridge. We've pilgrims who will certainly find their return difficult. We aren't trapped, thank the Eight, but we'll have to make do with harder roads. I'll send a few of our masons to investigate when the weather clears, although given it took a decade to build the thing, I hesitate to be optimistic."

Fern was about to offer another awkward apology when Rhubarb shuffled in and approached the table. After a pained smile at Fern, he whispered in the abbess's ear for several seconds.

She nodded as she listened, and when he'd finished, hoisted herself off the bench and addressed Fern. "It seems your friend the Oathmaiden will survive the night, and I've kept you from rest for long enough, I suppose. They've corralled the green one in the dormitory. I find her story vexing. A prisoner? It seems unlikely."

"It's very confusing," Fern agreed.

"Brother Rhubarb will escort you there, and you can sleep and recover."

"Can I see Astryx first?"

"Let's leave her to rest," replied Bluebriar. "Never fear, Brother Burdock is an artist with a needle and a poultice. We'll see what tomorrow brings, eh? These things always feel more hopeful in the light of day."

Removing her spectacles and tucking them back into her habit, she moved for the door. With one hand on the pull, she added, "I don't expect we'll suffer an assault from this Tullah person before dawn, unless she's sprouted wings. But let's not tempt fate and wander, shall we? Best not to get lost and fall asleep in any wagons."

"Asleep already," whispered Rhubarb as he cracked the dormitory door and eased his candlestick into the windowless room, revealing orange pigtails and a riotous coat of pockets in a pile on a narrow cot, like a heap of shabby laundry. He gave Fern a significant look. "Brother Yarrow is still counting the spoons."

As he opened the door wider, she caught sight of another cot against the opposite wall, and at one end of it, a foot-stove freshly topped up with coals.

Rhubarb passed her the candle, bobbed a short bow, then scurried down the door-lined passage of old, dark stone, presumably to his own room for the night.

Fern hauled herself, her satchel, and cloak into the room and eased the door shut behind her. The goblin didn't so much as rustle.

Tiptoeing to the empty cot, Fern set the candlestick on a small writing table along the wall, hung her still-damp cloak on a hook, and tossed her satchel on the floor.

As she slithered under the wool blanket, she briefly considered the latch on the door and whether she should engage it, but the effort of thought and action was too much.

"No blood sacrifice to Tarim tonight," she mumbled into the darkness.

27

"Oh, fuck," said Fern.

Astryx lay with a crisp, clean sheet covering her to the chest, bare arms pinning it to her sides. Her hair clung to her forehead in damp clumps like waterweed, and her shortened ear seemed somehow more cruel in the light of a wintry morning. The elf's skin looked bloodless but for a feverish blush in her cheeks, although her breathing had lost the terrifying whistle Fern had fretted over in the Tarimite shelter. It was even, if shallow.

They'd had to push together two rattkin-sized beds to accommodate her, which made her seem gigantic. Nigel stretched beside her on the sheet, her right hand protectively curled around his sheath, as though to keep someone from attempting to remove him while she slept. Fern reflected that they probably had.

Zyll had been predictably missing when Fern had risen to a chilly darkness, with little sense of time in the windowless room. The nature of Zyll's "captivity" seemed a peculiarity hardly worth dwelling on anymore. She'd opened the door to peer into the hallway and startled Brother Rhubarb, his paw raised to rap on the oak.

Now, he waited behind her with Brother Burdock, the physician, who was drying his paws on a cloth.

"She's remarkably sturdy," observed Burdock, with a surprisingly gruff voice for a rattkin. "Stitched her up last night and managed to get a bit of broth into her this morning. It's clear she's recovered from worse. Scars like she was rolled down a hill in a barrelful of knives," he added with a disapproving shake of his head.

"How—" Fern's throat clicked. "How long 'til she recovers?" She wondered, possibly uncharitably, if they'd collected any of Astryx's blood for some unsavory practices honoring Tarim while they were at it.

The black rattkin shrugged and tossed the rag on a table. "Never physicked an elf before. Your guess is as good as mine."

Fern glanced back at Astryx and found her ghostlight eyes slitted open and staring back.

"Little ... squire ..." she whispered, almost inaudible. Fern flushed with a sensation halfway between embarrassment and pleasure. Quillin had called her something similar, although of course Astryx couldn't know that.

One corner of the elf's lips twitched up just a hair, and she swallowed laboriously. "Looks like ... you can manage ... a fire ... after all."

Fern tentatively reached out a paw to lay it on Astryx's hand where it rested atop Nigel, the wire bracelet still tight around her wrist.

"You're going to be all right," said Fern, hoping she sounded like she believed it.

"Do something for me?" mumbled the Blademistress.

"Yes?" Fern leaned closer.

"He'll ... never let me hear the end of it, unless he can ... say his piece."

It took a moment for Fern to understand, but then she nodded, shifting to the head of the beds. It took both paws to drag Nigel's sheath down an inch, like a stubborn pair of wet trousers.

"Oh, m'lady, they've *butchered* you," he wailed immediately. Both of the monks squeaked in varying degrees of alarm.

Astryx's eyes drifted closed as the Elder Blade crooned his concern and demanded explanations from the monks in turn.

A creak made Fern turn to see Abbess Bluebriar peeking in the door. The silver rattkin gestured to her with one paw.

"I'll check in again later," said Fern to Astryx, although she didn't know if the elf heard a word of it. Her eyes remained closed as Nigel's babble washed over her.

Then Fern trailed the abbess into the hall and let the door shut behind her.

⁓

Fern followed Bluebriar through a heavy, iron-banded door and onto a covered, elevated walkway lined with thin pillars. Dry, biting cold and blinding brightness assailed her, and she stood blinking for a moment as snow skittered around her feet. Then she hurried to catch up as the elderly rattkin reached the door at the other end. Fern gazed out at the icy crags and snow-frosted buildings of the abbey as she went. Everything seemed curiously flat, with all subtleties of definition hammered out by the watery light of day.

Then they were indoors again, descending a cramped staircase, which opened onto yet another long hallway. A blue carpet writhing with embroidered golden tentacles stretched its length.

Wordlessly, the abbess passed through another door. When Fern entered the room beyond in her wake, she gasped and clutched at her cloak-pin in amazement.

It was a library, two stories tall, with narrow windows that traveled nearly from floor to ceiling. Balconies lined either side of the room, accessible by tight iron stairways. Rolling ladders clung to the shelves.

Two long, severe study tables ran down the center of the library, but more comfortable chairs and couches were scattered about the perimeter upon scuffed carpets.

"Whew," puffed Bluebriar, rustling the hem of her habit. "Frosty." The room was unoccupied and, indeed, bitterly cold, with no fire burning in the corner hearth. The abbess bustled over to it and began arranging stovewood on the andirons.

While she busied herself with kindling and striking steel, Fern drifted to the shelves and traced her fingers along the books there.

Expecting religious tomes or abbey records, her brow wrinkled as she read the embossing on the spines.

"What the fuck?" she muttered with honest surprise.

She turned at the pop of flame behind her to find the abbess rising laboriously from a crouch and regarding her with amusement.

"These are *real* books," said Fern, accusingly.

Dusting off her hands, Bluebriar approached and examined the volumes Fern had been inspecting. "If you mean books that have better things to do than enumerate the tentacles of Tarim, then, yes, they're real books. Although we have the other sort, too." She flapped a paw toward a far corner of the library.

At Fern's frankly confused expression, the abbess laughed. "As a bookseller—or ex-bookseller, I suppose?—I thought you'd be more at home here. We can't very well spend every moment in supplication. What do you imagine there is to do around this place in the dark of winter?"

"I . . . well . . ."

The abbess patted her shoulder genially. "We have a special wing for the sacrifices and torture."

Fern was fairly certain she was joking.

"Come and sit with me while the place warms. Over here, closer to the fire. I have a pinch of time before anyone notices I've been misplaced."

The abbess indicated a pair of wooden chairs with lumpy blue cushions. The wood was ornately carved with Tarim's tentacles. Presumably, woodworking was the wintertime hobby of at least one entertainment-starved worshipper.

When they were both settled, the abbess arranged her habit around her tail and surprised Fern again. "You know, the Tarimites aren't widely recognized for their charitable works. Apart from the more cosmic one, that is. I doubt that's a great shock, but, still, you and your friends are part of a very select group."

"The *cosmic* one?"

Bluebriar continued as though Fern hadn't spoken. "Although

we don't have many opportunities for philanthropy here in the hinterlands. Hardly any exposure to the mundane ills of the world, really."

"I can't decide if that's a polite way to show unwelcome guests the door," said Fern.

The abbess chuckled. "We won't turn you out into the snow just yet. Unless that other one absconds with the rest of our cutlery, and then I think our cook, Brother Yarrow, may take things into his own paws."

She studied Fern keenly. "I suppose I am circling my point, though, which isn't really like me. Lance the wound and clean up after, I say. Saves so much time and agony. I'll speak plainly. I don't think you like us much, and you're not very subtle about it. I don't *need* you to like us, although others might observe that courtesy demands you keep it to yourself. But since you're under our roof and eating our food and occupying our physician, I rather think you owe me an explanation. So. Out with it. Let's hear your grievances."

Fern flushed hot from nose to tail-tip with a freshet of guilt and a gush of irritation at having her social missteps baldly pointed out.

Opening her mouth to protest, the words already halfway up her throat, she instead blurted, "You worship an evil god that wants to consume the world, and that's pretty hard for me to think kindly of."

Bluebriar's brows rose. "Succinct! Although that begs the question, why aren't you in *more* of a hurry to leave."

Fern raised her paws and then dropped them in her lap miserably. "I don't think Astryx would survive if we did. And . . . I'm thankful. You've been . . . kind. I don't know how to square that with what you are. What you do."

The abbess nodded and thought for a long moment before replying. "What *do* you think we do around here?"

Squirming uncomfortably, Fern finally said, "Um. Worship Tarim . . . ? I heard the chants. Awful lot of tentacles around the place."

"Nearly correct. But please continue, what do you expect we get out of that?"

Fern blinked. "Um. Horrible divine favor? I guess . . . his will done in the Territory, or something like that? Doom befalling your enemies? A little casual smiting?"

Smiling humorlessly, Bluebriar stared into the brilliant glow of one of the tall windows. "We don't spend much time educating anybody on the finer points of Tarim's will. We're not proselytizers, so you can be forgiven for being so terribly wrong." She returned her gaze to Fern's, unblinking. "It's more accurate to say we devote our time to *preventing* him from enacting his will. Why do you think we're called penitents?"

"I guess I'm not sure."

"Tarim is a god of endless hunger and consumption. His will to devour is never-ending. But he is vulnerable to appeasement—penance, for the temerity of existing."

"Penance?" Fern asked, with a suspicious frown.

"Oh, not offerings of souls or blood or anything overly messy. As beings of infinite cosmic power go, Tarim is remarkably insecure." She gestured heavenward. "Fervent, frequent, and *sincere* expressions of our unworthiness before his terrible majesty are enough to shift his regard elsewhere."

"Hang on, *insecure?*"

The abbess nodded. "As a teenager at a barn dance."

"I'm sorry, I want to make sure I have this right. Are you saying that you all spend your days apologizing for how insignificant we are to preserve Tarim's self-esteem, because otherwise he'll throw a tantrum and eat the whole world? And that you believe that actually helps?"

The abbess cocked her head and thought.

"Yes, that's pretty much it."

"How do you *know* it's working, though?"

"We could pause to test the theory, but if we're *right*, then I wouldn't be around to be smug about it, which would be disappointing. I think we'll carry on, just in case."

"But . . . you could be wasting your entire life for nothing?"

Bluebriar regarded Fern shrewdly. "*I'm* carrying on because I believe a mad god would devour all of existence if I stopped. From what you've said, you're still wringing your paws about leaving behind a life that no longer suits you. The Territory will carry on existing no matter what *you* do, so rather than worry about *me* staying the course, perhaps you should abandon your fretting, and thank the Eight that you don't have to."

Fern's mouth fell open.

"Just something to think about," said the abbess as she heaved herself out of her chair. "Now, do enjoy the library. I really must get back to my duties. The world won't rescue itself, after all, and I have a wobbly celestial ego to soothe."

28

For the first time in her life, surrounded on all sides by books unread, Fern hadn't the slightest inclination to pick one up. In the emptiness the abbess's departure left behind, she turned Bluebriar's parting words over in her mind like an unfamiliar stone.

"Boy, she sure put you in your place," piped up a voice from her cloak pocket. "You must feel really petty."

"I'd take you out of there so that you could see the expression I'm making, but you don't have eyes, so I'm not sure how that works," she replied crossly.

"Yeah, sure, don't bother until you've got some *letters* to open."

"Mm. I think I'd need something sharper."

"You take that *back*," cried Breadlee.

Fern didn't reply, instead crossing the room to stand on tiptoe at one of the tall windows. She erased a circle of fogged glass with one paw, peering out across a snowy inner courtyard where a crowd of penitents hustled for the shelter of the cloisters along the edges.

The knife surprised her by timidly mumbling, "So . . . do you think the Oathmaiden is gonna be, you know . . . fine?"

Then she did remove him from her pocket, holding him up to the light. "She actually wanted to listen to Nigel, so that suggests hidden reserves," she said with a wry grin.

"Bleah."

"Don't worry, there's hope for you yet," said Fern. "I'm sure somebody out there can't wait to wield Bridgewrecker."

She sensed him perk up—something about the glint of light along his edge.

"Bridgewrecker?" he asked with cautious interest.

"Why not? Sounds pretty Elder to me."

"I dunno. I mean, do you think of a *big* bridge when you hear that? An important bridge? Or just one of those little wooden ones? There's a lot of room for interpretation. You want these things to conjure, like, an indelible image."

Fern snorted, then turned with a decisive twirl of her cloak hem and started for the door the abbess had disappeared through. "Hells if I'm waiting around here all day. She didn't say anything about staying put. Let's figure out where Zyll disappeared to, shall we?"

But Breadlee didn't answer as she slipped him back into her pocket, instead muttering to himself.

Fern wasn't positive, but it sounded a lot like "Bridgewrecker."

The abbey was larger than Fern had imagined, a veritable warren of corridors, stairs, crooked passageways, vestibules, and cubbies. Some stonework writhed with a profusion of Tarim's many limbs in elaborate etchings or mosaics, while around the corner might be nothing but sturdy and featureless blocks of granite.

She passed clusters of Tarimites, and while she merited a few curious glances and the occasional flummoxed stare, nobody cut her explorations short.

At one point, she stumbled into the cathedral proper to find dozens of monks kneeling in a ranked half-moon, paws and foreheads touching the cold flagstones before a massive statue of Tarim. Nested amidst an explosion of intricately carved tentacles, an alcove filled with burning pitch represented his blazing single eye.

After her conversation with the abbess, the cosmic god's terrible majesty was dimmed somewhat. Fern had a fleeting vision of Tarim as a cranky toddler and had to stifle a laugh as she backed out of the room.

Eventually, it began to feel like an impossibility to locate the goblin. There were too many places to hide, too many dark recesses and half-hidden nooks. Instead, Fern went to find the one individual that she knew she would find exactly where she expected.

The stable lay on the opposite side of a cobbled square at the terminus of the road to the abbey. The only reason Fern could tell it was cobbled was because a pair of penitents were industriously sweeping a fresh dusting of snow into piles with straw-bristled brooms.

She gazed off between the two pillars that bracketed the roadway. A salmon blush rouged the harsh crags where snow striped the rock and curved down into a valley basin softened by drifts.

Fern wondered where Tullah was at that moment. Still seething on the other side of the bridge? Or forging another path to find them? She tried to imagine what Zyll could possibly have done to warrant that kind of enmity.

Shivering, she hurried to the stable and through a small access door beside the equine-sized pair that was closed and barred against the cold.

Her eyes slowly adjusted to the comparative gloom of the interior, thick with the scents of sweaty horse and straw. Donkeys lifted their noses curiously in her direction, but her gaze went immediately to the larger stall in the far corner.

Bucket and Zyll stared back at her. The goblin stood beside his stall door with a brilliantly pointy smile, both hands cupped full of oats beneath his muzzle. The horse snorted and tossed his mane in Fern's direction, then snuffled another mouthful from Zyll's palms.

Fern sighed. "Of course you're here, in the last place I'd look for you."

She approached and stood beside the goblin as Bucket's velvety lips excavated the last oat from between her fingers. "I think Astryx will live," she said, because she wasn't sure what else to say. Conversations with Zyll tended to be like bottling smoke.

You mostly weren't sure if you were going to end up with anything for the effort.

Zyll wiped off her hands and turned to regard her, the lines of her smile sobering a hair, but still gleaming in the half-light. "Monk-lings are, how do you say, hospi-tala-bly." She nodded decisively, then held out her hand. "Where is shankling?"

"Shank—? Oh!" Fern slowly drew Breadlee and handed him over, hilt first, with a reluctance that surprised her.

"Ah, nuts," said Breadlee. "Not back in the pockets!"

But Zyll held him aloft, the bracelet on her wrist flashing, and solemnly proclaimed, "Bridgemasher, flames-maker. Good job, shankling."

Then she handed him back.

There was a long pause.

"Oh," said Fern and Breadlee both.

"Yeah, I like Bridgewrecker better," murmured the knife out the side of his nonexistent mouth.

Fern pursed her lips, then blurted the question that had been plaguing her off and on, in moments when she wasn't so exhausted she couldn't entertain it.

"Why are you still here?"

Zyll tilted her head.

Fern sighed. "I mean, I know why *I* wouldn't flee alone into the snow, but I don't get the impression that would bother you very much. Frankly, I think you could have left at any time if you wanted."

Stretching out a paw, Fern tapped the wire bracelet. "Even if this really does work, you've got enough table-knives in that coat. You could have stabbed her when she was out cold. That aside, I'm pretty sure you could disappear, and she'd never catch up to you once she finally recovers. So. Why are you *here?*"

Not dropping her gaze, the goblin patted a few pockets, stuffed a hand into one, and withdrew a knife that was very much *not* tableware. It was slim and wicked and designed for killing, not cookery.

Fern jumped at the sight of it, and Breadlee made a pained noise where she held him loosely in one paw.

With remarkable dexterity, Zyll used the tip of the dirk to excavate something between her teeth, which looked a bit like a feather. She blew it off the end of the blade, then tucked the knife away again.

"We goes when is time to be somewhere else," said Zyll.

Like bottling smoke, Fern thought.

A rumble issued unexpectedly from her belly. She'd declined breakfast before visiting Astryx, and now Fern's guts had apparently mounted a protest.

The goblin's grin widened, and she seized Fern's paw in both hands. "Come. We knows *all* about the kitch-lings."

In the days that followed, Fern understood better why the Tarimites had such an extensive library. As Astryx slowly recovered, the erstwhile bookseller found there was little else to do for those who didn't need to spend a goodly portion of their day engaged in penitent acts to deflect Tarim's not-so-benevolent regard.

Zyll's appearances were erratic at best. Fern was mostly left to her own devices, and now that she'd borne the abbess's keen interrogation, Bluebriar didn't call on her again. She ate amongst the monks in the rectory at mealtimes—which were signaled with a bell—but any attempts at striking up a conversation were met with polite, but unsatisfyingly brief replies.

She kept expecting a pointed question about when they'd be leaving, or at the very least a judgmental gaze when she was handed her meal, but none of that happened.

For worshippers of an evil deity beyond mortal conception, they were very hospitable.

So, she wandered, perused the library, and made excursions to keep Bucket company and sneak him handfuls of oats.

And she visited Astryx daily, where she read to her.

Fern wasn't sure exactly what prompted the idea, but on the

third day, she remembered the fancy volume of *Ten Links in the Chain* she'd hauled around in her satchel until she'd sold it in Bycross. The monastery had their own copy, although it was a cheap printing, much-battered and well-read.

She didn't ask, but simply took it with her on her visit to Astryx in the infirmary. The elf was sleeping and, although Fern was hardly a physician, she thought her color was continuing to improve.

Burdock had finally succeeded in moving Nigel off the bed and had leaned him in a corner.

She drew up a stool, cracked the book to the first page, and nervously cleared her throat.

"I don't know if you can hear this, but it seems like exactly the sort of thing you'd dream about."

Flicking her gaze to the elf's face, she detected no motion.

Then she read aloud, "'Chapter One. In which I dismember a man.'"

Astryx's chest rose and fell evenly as Fern continued. "'When I first tell you that I was wrongfully imprisoned, you may have some sympathy. But when I also relay even a few of the dire things I've done, your sympathy will, perhaps, become strained beyond its limit. I can only ask that you hear me out, dear reader.'"

She chanced a cautious glance to make sure she wasn't disturbing the elf's rest. "'Indeed, because I cut the man's head off and then his legs and his arms and stuffed them into three barrels of brine to survive the voyage, I may *seem* a monster. But by the end of my tale, I think you may again consider me worthy of your regard. Besides. He was a bastard.'"

She almost dropped the book at a sudden cough from Astryx, leaping to her feet in concern.

The curve of the Oathmaiden's lip was unmistakable.

It hadn't been a cough. It sounded like pebbles in a clay pot, but Astryx One-Ear was *laughing*.

As Fern relaxed and moved to settle back onto her stool, the elf's hand reached out and squeezed her forearm, gently, just once.

"Good storyteller. Keep going. Please."

Fern made it through four chapters before Burdock shooed her away.

⁓

On the fifth day, as Fern slipped into the stable to visit Astryx's horse, she discovered a new resident. A sturdy dun pony nosed curiously over her stall at a skeptical Bucket.

Further investigation revealed a brightly colored wagon parked beside the stable. From the little round windows in the sides—with curtains—it looked like somebody lived in it, although a rap at the rear door received no response.

"Huh," mused Fern aloud.

The mystery didn't survive long.

By silent and mutual agreement, Fern and the monks had fallen into the habit of leaving space between each other at mealtimes so they didn't have to endure her conversational gambits, and she wasn't embarrassed when they failed.

So, it was a surprise when, just as she was about to dig into her meal, someone plunked their bowl and cup decisively beside her and dropped onto the bench.

"You don't look much like a monk," said the dwarf, with a brilliant smile and an extended hand. Her black hair was pinned back with a jeweled clip, she wore a burgundy doublet with intricate gold stitching, and she had an open, earnest face.

"Um. No," replied Fern, and couldn't help but smile back. She took the offered hand in her own paw and shook. It looked like her conversational horizons were about to widen. "Definitely not. Fern."

"Staysha. Actually, Silver Sparrow is my traveling name. Maybe you've heard of me?"

"Well . . ." Fern hedged.

"Ah, never mind." Staysha laughed. "It's usually best for my sort not to ask questions like that."

"Your sort?"

"Bards. Minstrels." The dwarf mimed strumming a lute, then bumped her shoulder against Fern's. "So, you ran afoul of the bridge, too, eh?"

Fern blinked. "You could definitely say that."

"Whew, that monster of a horse in there can't be *yours*, though. You didn't *walk* here, did you?"

Laughing, Fern replied, "No. Absolutely not, I—"

But Staysha didn't let her finish. "Gods, I'm glad you're here." She leaned in close and held a hand beside her mouth before whispering, "Now, there's somebody to notice if I go missing. More tentacles around here than expected."

Her grin didn't seem overly worried, despite her words.

They chatted animatedly over their meal, although the dwarf held up her end, and then some. It turned out she'd been traveling west toward Bycross for some sort of long-running gig at a tavern there before she'd stumbled upon a bunch of monks inspecting the ruins of the bridge. One of them had escorted her to the abbey to resupply and reconsider her route.

When Staysha excused herself to retrieve her instrument from her wagon—"The cold's a beast for it!"—Fern made sure to let her know where the library was so she could find her later.

It occurred to her as she left that she'd never once breathed a word about Astryx or Zyll.

Although Staysha struck her as eminently likable, Fern thought she'd keep it that way.

29

"Remarkable," whispered Burdock, delicately probing Astryx's ribs on either side of her wound, while the elf hiked her shirt up to give him access.

The flesh still looked fierce and red to Fern, the stitches ugly and stark against the elf's pale skin; however, she couldn't deny that the Oathmaiden seemed much more herself. Her eyes were clear and bright, and she'd declined the sleeping tincture the monk had urged upon her.

Now, she sat on the pushed-together beds while the black-furred physician examined her under the frosted morning light.

"I'd normally advocate rest for at least another few days, but I suppose a bit of walking about would be all right. As long as you're careful of the stitching. Not that I could make you stay put if I wanted to," he grumbled.

Fern, seated on the stool with *Ten Links* in her lap, didn't miss the amused quirk of Astryx's lips.

"My thanks, Burdock," she said, dropping her shirt back into place. "I promise to go easy."

The rattkin rolled his eyes. "Tarim's patience." Then he muttered his way out of the tiny infirmary, closing the door behind him.

"So," said Fern. "No reading today?"

Astryx glanced around the room with obvious distaste, then eased herself off the beds. She shrugged carefully, massaging the back of her neck. The motion pulled the skin along her ribs, and she hissed through bared teeth. Letting her hands fall back, she said, "Let's get out of this gods-damned room. How's Bucket?"

"Why don't I show you?" replied Fern, tucking the book back under one arm.

Astryx sketched a glance over Nigel, propped in the corner, but left him behind.

Out in the hallway, she ran a hand through her tangle of silver hair, now in need of a trim. The Tarimites had built at a generous scale for rattkin, but that still meant that her head nearly brushed the ceiling.

The monks they encountered stared in awe at the elf as they passed, but she didn't appear to care. She moved more slowly than normal, wincing each time she had to duck under any lintel too short for her height.

When they emerged into the cold outdoors, Astryx breathed a long sigh of relief, closing her eyes and turning her face up to the wan light that found its way through the cloud cover. Errant flakes melted on her cheeks.

As they approached the stable, the elf spotted Staysha's wagon off to the side. At her questioning glance, Fern gave her the rundown on the Silver Sparrow, who, unsurprisingly, Astryx had never heard of. Fern was glad that they hadn't run into the dwarf along the way. There was something satisfying about being the one showing Astryx around an unfamiliar place. It was nice to be the person who knew what she was doing for once.

Inside the stable, the Oathmaiden spent a long while reassuring Bucket as he whuffled at her hair and uttered distressed whinnies. She ran her hands slowly along his neck and let him lip her fingers, murmuring into his ears.

Fern felt a bit like a voyeur, so she found a seat at a bench beside the tack-mending table and flipped idly through the book while she waited.

She glanced up when Astryx cleared her throat.

The elf leaned against Bucket's stable door with her left arm curled up under his chin, scratching his cheek. In her other hand, she held a sheet of paper that appeared to have been folded and refolded. She looked . . . embarrassed. *Shy?* It was an unfamiliar expression on the Blademistress's face.

"I, um." Color rose in the elf's cheeks. "I didn't mean to take this."

It dawned on Fern why the page looked so familiar. That was *her* crabbed writing on it.

At the no-doubt horrified expression on Fern's face, Astryx hurried to explain, "It caught on my leg, back at the waystation. I guess I stuffed it into my pocket. I'm not sure what I was thinking."

"Oh, gods," muttered Fern. "You read it, then? How ashamed do I need to be?"

Astryx gave her a confused look, then turned her attention to the page. Swallowing, she read, "*I'd seen her fight before, and I don't know how else to put it—she'd always been flawless, like she'd experienced the battle already a thousand times before and knew every beat. But against Tullah? It felt like a first. Like the layers of a legend were peeled back, and I saw the person underneath, the instinct and impulses that make her who she is. The sound of her voice when she saw what was happening to Bucket? I felt it in my heart. At the edge of what she could handle, caught between two disasters, hurting inside and out, I think I finally understood why people still tell stories about her. She was beautiful.*"

It was very quiet in the stable, and Astryx kept her eyes on the page.

Finally the elf broke the silence, her voice wobbly. "Is this really what you see?"

"Yes. I mean. Sometimes. I don't know." Fern massaged her eyes with her paws. "I'm sure I'm not the only one," she said in a small voice.

She heard the elf approach, and the paper crackled as she laid the page down on the tack table. "I'm sorry I kept it."

Fern sighed. "In your defense, you've been asleep most of the time."

"Still."

Astryx carefully lowered herself to sit beside Fern on the rattkin-sized bench, her knees awkwardly high. She looked endearingly ridiculous.

A long pause ensued.

"Thank you," said the elf. "For saving Bucket." Her gaze remained carefully fixed on her horse, instead of Fern.

"Oh," mumbled Fern, bemused. "Um. Sure."

"Little squire," added Astryx, with a faint smile. "Maybe you missed your calling?"

"I'm not sure I like the 'little' part," said Fern. "Makes me sound cute."

"Mm."

"Tullah's not going to give up, is she?" asked Fern.

"No, I don't think so."

"I didn't get a chance to tell you, what with all the"—Fern gestured broadly—"*everything*. I've seen Tullah before, I'm sure of it. Hells, she nearly knocked me down in Bycross, and I swear I saw her in Turnbuckle. She's been following us for a long time now."

Astryx shifted, searching for comfort she wouldn't find. "Then I'm certain I'll see her again."

Fern glanced at the elf out of the corner of her eye. "How do you think that will go?" she asked, carefully.

"I didn't live this long on accident, you know."

Reaching out, Fern tapped the wire bracelet on Astryx's wrist. Even as she did it, she was mildly shocked at the familiarity of her own gesture. "So, you can feel that Zyll is close with this thing?"

Pointing in the direction of the abbey, the elf adjusted her aim while squinting as though sighting down a bow. "There. Like little tugs on a piece of thread tied between us. It gets tighter the farther away she gets, and past a certain point, there's a pain that keeps increasing."

"Are you surprised she's still here? I know I am."

Astryx thought about that. "I suppose I should be. But I think I've given up expecting anything rational from Zyll."

Fern worried at her lip. "What if you just let her go?"

The elf turned to look at her, brow creased. "I—"

But the bookseller hurriedly continued, "She saved all of us back at the bridge. We'd be dead now without her, right? Okay, none of this would have *happened* without her, either, but that's beside the point. Is it really worth it to keep on? If she goes her own way, Tullah has no reason to find you. *Us.*"

"Setting aside everything else," said Astryx, "you were worried Zyll would wander into a hazferou's belly on her own. Tullah's a *great* deal more dangerous. I think it's clear that orc means to end her."

Fern considered the bracelet falling from Astryx's wrist back at the waystation, its reappearance the following morning, and who exactly might have replaced it.

Ignoring that for the time being, she forged onward. "Maybe. But I'd bet anything she's a lot harder to find by herself. What's to say that whoever's paying to have you haul her in doesn't have the same fate in mind? What if they're no better than Tullah?"

Astryx chewed her lip, but then shook her head. "What happens after is always unknowable. Good or ill, you'll go mad trying to anticipate it. There was a time when I tried . . . But I learned to forego such things long ago. I can't turn away."

"Why not?" cried Fern. "What do you get out of it? You keep going on and on, but for what? For who? You saved me back in that swamp, and I was *very* grateful, but to you it was probably not even worth remembering. You didn't even stick around to be appreciated, already off to the next thing."

"Because that's part of it. Part of being who I am. I see things to their end. I keep my covenants. I do what must be done."

To Fern, those sounded like old words repeated so often they'd lost all meaning, and she felt her ire rise. But she remembered their argument outside Turnbuckle and was determined not to repeat it. The abbess's words from the library echoed back to her.

"Penance to your hungry god," she muttered to herself.

"What's that?"

"You're worried about what will fall apart if you don't keep doing what you're doing," said Fern.

Astryx tried to link thoughts to words she'd probably never articulated before, not in a thousand years. It took her several long moments. "I . . . It's like walking a straight road when night falls. You know it goes on and on, even though it's too dark to see. You don't stray in the night, you keep moving straight, so that when the sun rises, you'll still be on the path."

Her ghostlight gaze was fierce. "I still believe that when morning comes, the road will be under my feet. So, I keep walking straight."

Fern winced at a feeling of painful familiarity and refrained from saying things like, *Well, maybe you should just stop for the night*, or *I've never seen a road that straight in my life, what are you talking about?* Because it felt like bad form to abuse somebody else's metaphor.

Astryx continued. "But this is *my* road. It doesn't have to be yours. You said before that you couldn't go back—but back is only one direction. You can choose a path to anywhere in the Territory. Step off this one at any time." Then she asked the same question Fern had asked of Zyll just days ago. "Why are *you* still here?"

Her mind's first defensive response was to muster a tart reply, but Fern strangled that impulse. Instead, she took a slow breath. She watched the dust motes dance in the light slanting through the high window of the stable while she considered the question, determined to give an honest answer. "At the start, I think this was just something to cling to when I was drowning, and as we traveled, it was easy to convince myself that dry land was getting farther and farther away. Even when I could've paddled for shore, a convenient storm made it simple to justify hanging on longer. The Four Fingers. Turnbuckle. Good excuses to pretend I had no choice. But now . . . Honestly?" She laughed bitterly at a realization that felt like an echo resounding through her entire life. "I worry you'd think less of me if I left. I know what I'm going to see in Viv's face when I go back, and I couldn't stand to see it in yours, too. Not that you *need* me or anything."

Astryx's hand fell on her shoulder. "Have you already forgotten the worthy things you've done? Bucket won't forget, and neither will I. You belong if you want to. But, if your reason for being here is only because of what I might think?" She squeezed, gently. "You should find a better one."

"Oathmaiden?"

Staysha's breathless exclamation brought them both up short as they emerged from the stable. The dwarf had stopped mid-stride, clearly on her way to her wagon with a bundle under one arm and black hair riffling under cold licks of wind. She shot Fern an accusing glance. "And you didn't tell me?"

Astryx answered before Fern could marshal an awkward explanation, laying a hand on her shoulder and making a show of leaning on the rattkin for support. "I've been recovering from a battle. You'll have to forgive her—my squire is very protective of my rest. That must be your wagon? Which would make you the bard. The Silver Sparrow, if I remember right?"

The shadow immediately cleared from Staysha's face, replaced with a gratified smile. "Oh, you've heard of me? Er, I mean—gosh, you were wounded? You'd never know it to look at you!" Her eyes were keen. "Can I convince you to tell me all about it?"

Pulling her cloak tight around her shoulders, Fern tried to look apologetic. "I've really got to get her in from the cold. She's already overexerted herself today, and Burdock will have my head if I keep her away too long."

The dwarf fought to hide her disappointment. "Maybe later, though?"

"I'm sure that would be just fine," allowed Astryx, with subtle pressure on Fern's shoulder to get them both moving.

"An epic ballad about the Blademistress won't write itself!" the dwarf hollered after them.

As they made their way back into the heat and shadow of the abbey, leaving a disappointed Staysha behind, Fern asked in a loud whisper, "*Would* that be just fine?"

Astryx snorted. "Gods, no."

―――

Over the following days, Astryx recovered with increasing speed, moving out of the cramped infirmary to a guest room with larger furniture for taller visitors. She took meals in the refectory and walked with increasing frequency and duration in Fern's company, making a sort of game of surprising Zyll wherever she was wandering. The goblin did not appear off-put. If anything, she seemed to delight in finding more obscure places to be, from wine cellar to widow's walk. Very often, there was something unexpected and possibly recently alive in her mouth.

Staysha, on the other hand, made herself too easy to find, doing her damnedest to corner the elf and tease out tales of adventure and battle. Astryx seemed to experience bouts of crippling and unspecific weariness whenever this happened.

She endured Burdock's daily ministrations with patience, though, even after her stitching was snipped and removed. Fern entered the infirmary after one such session just as the black-furred physician was leaving, grumbling loudly about Callis oil.

The Oathmaiden's skin was flushed red, sweat slicking her face, but at Fern's concerned look, she gritted her teeth and hissed, "Fine. I'm fine."

"Overanxious to be on her way, apparently," observed Abbess Bluebriar, waiting nearby with arms crossed. The woman regarded Astryx shrewdly. "Although I'd just as soon you not expire anywhere nearby. We don't do much to polish our reputation, but I'd also rather we not be remembered as the last place you were seen alive."

"I'll do my best to stagger a little farther down the mountain before dying," gasped the elf, one hand clamped to her side.

"May Tarim spare all who deserve it," said the abbess, with a long-suffering sigh, "and you, too."

―⁓―

Dear Viv,

I'm sorry, but, of course, you are keenly aware of that already unless you have somehow missed all the other letters I've written.

I look at the piles of pages I've scribbled to you, stained or smeared or wrinkled, and they look like the ravings of a crazy person.

Which is accurate, I guess.

As I think I wrote once before, this has clearly ceased to be a bunch of failed attempts at writing a single letter to you and has become an unending monologue. After handing you this thick stack of messy pages, I think at this point I'll have to come back a week later to see if you've made it to the last one, and how the end of it all added up for you.

I don't even know the end. How strange. I can't picture one now, and don't know if that's a terror or a relief.

We've been at this Tarimite monastery for weeks, and writing to you has almost become an obsession. I can't bring myself to read anything from the library. Isn't that odd? Words can only go out of me. None can come in. They pass through my mind without a trace when I try to read a page. I don't think I've ever experienced that in my life, not once. Pretty terrible liability for a bookseller. Fortunately, they have plenty of paper and were willing to part with some while we continue to abuse the hospitality of this pack of cultists in the mountains. So, writing it is.

I told you about the abbess and the conversation I had with her. Of course, there's not a chance in all eight hells I'd ever consider becoming a penitent (ha!), but I figure I will be less obnoxious to Tarimites in the future. It's hard to maintain one's cold aloofness when someone keeps feeding you hot meals every day and tending your wounded friend.

Astryx One-Ear is my friend. I'm pretty sure of that now. What an insane thing to write.

It feels like an electric thrill of importance should have coursed through me when I realized it, but no. I just say more embarrassing things in her presence than before. That's really the proof. Same as with you.

I think you'd like her.

Speaking of embarrassing, I had a conversation with her a week ago that made me think of you. It made me think of my father, too, and I find myself wondering if, for every hard decision of my life, I've put a thumb on the scale in favor of what I imagine somebody else's opinion of me might be. Is that true, and I've just stacked other reasons on top to hide it from myself?

Fuck it. I don't feel up to answering that question today.

I should be more like Zyll. I can't think of anyone more themself, although I'll be gods-damned if I could tell you who that self is. Zyll is . . . incomprehensible. Is she even a prisoner? None of us treat her that way, and for her part, she seems not to be bothered. Those bracelets Astryx clapped on the both of them just feel like a way of pretending she has some control. Zyll exerts a kind of gravity—I can feel the pull of it. Is Astryx taking her somewhere, or is it the other way around? I'm never sure. Here in this hidden place, far from everything, it seems that any natural order of things was left behind below the snowline.

That bard I mentioned is still around, but her excuses for staying smell like old milk. There's been plenty of clear weather in stretches of days. She could've easily been on her way by now. She's just hoping to excavate a precious story from the Oathmaiden to polish into a song, and is perpetually—deliciously!—thwarted. I am secretly amused every time.

I think our days here are nearly at an end. Astryx has been

practicing forms out in the square, longer every afternoon. Nigel is overjoyed.

Breadlee? Annoyed. I think he was hoping she'd have to settle for a lighter blade. He's destined for disappointment.

He's still very good for sharpening pencils, though. And okay, he's a very available conversational partner.

I miss Potroast. I miss you.

I hope you're well.

Sometimes, I hope you've forgotten me altogether.

But I never manage to hope that for very long.

Fern

30

A turn in the weather signaled the day of their departure. The sky burned blue in all directions with a cold clarity, and it seemed to Fern that she could see for a hundred leagues. Ice and snow groaned from the pitched abbey roof, occasionally sloughing in tectonic slabs to thunder to the ground below. Fern kept a wary eye on the eaves as she passed under them with Zyll in tow.

With her satchel over one shoulder, she carried a haversack stuffed with dried goods over the other. Yet another gift from the Tarimites.

In the center of the cobbled square, which gleamed with melt, Astryx fussed with the saddle the stablemaster had refurbished for Bucket, checking and re-cinching the girth strap. With Nigel on her back again, she moved with purpose, and Fern could almost believe she was as hale as when they'd first met.

She saw the carefully hidden evidence of suffering, though. Moments of subtle reorientation as the elf adjusted the saddlebags.

"Apologies, old man," Astryx whispered, patting Bucket's cheek.

"I'm sorry we can't part with one of the donkeys," said Bluebriar. "Unfortunately, with the restoration work to be done, they can't be spared."

The abbess, Rhubarb, and Burdock had gathered to see them off, and a pack of monks huddled near the main doors, whispering and watching.

"We'll manage. You won't hear a word from me that's not grateful," replied Astryx. She turned and fixed the abbess with a solemn gaze and bowed her head formally. "Yours are kindnesses

I won't forget. If ever you have the need, I will come. Only call for me."

Fern passed up the haversack, which the elf received with only a slight wince before tying it beside one of the saddlebags. Approaching the abbess, the bookseller extended a paw. "Thank you. I could wish you hadn't seen the worst of me, but I'm glad you looked past it until you saw the back of me."

Bluebriar smiled, amused. "Perhaps you'll make it up to us someday. If not, we're accustomed to a rather one-sided relationship with the world."

Fern thanked Rhubarb and Burdock in turn, and then Zyll appeared beside her, rummaging in her pockets. One hand emerged clutching a fistful of clinking leather bags that Fern recognized. She'd altogether forgotten about the Four Fingers' coinpurses.

"Thank-lings," said Zyll, dropping them into the paws of the shocked abbess, although several spilled onto the ground with a chime of silver. "Sorry for bridge-ly."

Then she turned, scurried to the horse, and held out her arms to be hoisted aboard.

"Tarim's patience!" exclaimed the abbess, as she teased open the mouth of one of the bags and saw what was inside. It was the first time Fern had seen her off-balance.

Bluebriar didn't get the opportunity to protest the gift, however.

"Wait!" cried another voice, as Staysha the Silver Sparrow came stumbling out of the abbey doors toting a battered lute case, her black hair falling free from its jeweled clip. Everyone turned in surprise as the dwarf came huffing to a stop a few feet from Astryx. "I . . . whew . . . hey, so, I had no idea you were leaving today!"

Astryx, bemused, blinked at her.

Catching her breath, Staysha continued, "Is there any chance I can travel with you, just for a while? At least until you reach civilization?"

Fern frowned, gesturing southwest. "But Bycross is that way.

We're heading in the opposite direction. Don't you have some kind of engagement to get to?"

The dwarf waved a hand dismissively and laughed. "Hells, they've long since given up on me showing. Time to pick a new horizon and see what opportunities I can find." She refocused on Astryx. "I won't be any trouble! Hells, with no cart, one of you is bound to be walking most of the time. There's room on my wagon. You can make better time that way. We can make better time."

"Well . . ." Astryx's expression clouded.

Fern thought she could see her weighing the prospect of endless prodding for tales of derring-do against Staysha's offer of a spare seat. If the elf hadn't been wounded, Fern had no doubt she would've declined instantly. She'd traveled on foot before, but as things stood . . .

Fern was amazed at how vehemently she wanted the bard to stay behind. There wasn't anything wrong with the woman, really, apart from her overbearing interest in Astryx. She was friendly enough. Still, Fern caught the elf's gaze and tried to transmit her objection with her eyes alone.

Astryx chewed her lip and stared eastward like she was gauging the distance left to travel. Fern saw the precise moment of resignation before the elf turned back to Staysha.

"All right," she said, with a reluctant nod.

"I think Zyll would probably like to ride in the wagon. Wouldn't you, Zyll?" said Fern, brightly. No matter how mixed her feelings toward the bard, she didn't strike Fern as a bounty hunter in disguise.

Staysha seemed to notice the goblin standing in Astryx's shadow for the first time.

Zyll grinned at her with savage cheer.

"Wait, who the hells is that?" asked the perplexed dwarf.

Rhubarb mounted a donkey and accompanied them back out the tentacle-flanked entrance and along a narrow, less-traveled path that curved around the perimeter of the abbey and to the northeast. The snow was crusted over and wet beneath, breaking up like ocean ice before Bucket's progress. Fern rode in front of Astryx. Staysha brought up the rear with her dun pony gamely following the larger horse, Zyll on the buckboard beside her.

Fern glanced over her shoulder and around the elf, and thought the dwarf looked vexed by her travel partner.

"Something the matter?" asked the Oathmaiden as the leather creaked beneath them and Bucket's hooves cracked through the snowshell with squeals and snaps.

"Nothing at all," replied Fern, smiling to herself.

They passed alongside three more of the Tarimite bell-walls before reaching a promontory of stone and snow overlooking a deep valley. Far below, a long, still green lake filled the notch it made, painting near-perfect replicas of the clouds above.

"I'll leave you here," called Rhubarb from the back of his donkey. "Follow the switchbacks down, and the path continues along the south side of the lake. Go slowly and be careful." He laughed ruefully. "No bridges that way. Even so, don't try Tarim's patience any further, eh? Leave us at least one way out."

With parting words of thanks, they continued along the promontory until the way plunged downslope.

The sun seemed warm for the first time in weeks, despite the snow in every direction. Fern closed her eyes and luxuriated in the unexpected heat of it on her fur, leaning back against Astryx's belly as Bucket navigated the decline. The clatter and clank of Staysha's wagon behind them was a lulling counterpoint to the rhythm of their motion.

It took the better part of the morning to make their cautious way to the base of the valley and the westernmost point of the lake. There, dark, round stones emerged to stud a snowy beach that had been skimmed thin by winds which were now still. The lake's surface seemed a mystic window into a verdigris world that mirrored their own.

As the way became easier, Astryx spoke unexpectedly from above Fern's head. "You never finished the story."

"Hm? Oh. *Ten Links*? Well, after you got up and around, there didn't seem to be time, somehow."

Astryx made a *hm* sound that Fern could feel in her back where their bodies couldn't help but stay in contact. "Plenty of time now."

"Oh, shit. I think I stole their copy. It's still in my bag." Fern laughed guiltily. "I'm not sure I can read and ride, though. I think it'd make me horse-sick."

"Ah." She sounded disappointed.

"But," Fern amended, "I remember most of what happened. I guess it depends on whether you're fine with the Fern version."

"Does that have more swearing in it?"

"Fuck yes. Also, fewer descriptions of the furniture. And I don't think I can tell it in first-person, since I'll be sort of summing it up."

"That sounds just fine."

"Where were we, do you remember?"

"Madger was trapped in the bell tower, with nothing but a stolen coat and Warrick's magestone," said Astryx without hesitation.

Fern cocked her head to peer back up at the Oathmaiden, who stared serenely ahead. "Damn. All right then. Let's see if I remember how this goes . . . Ahem."

Prepared for an embarrassed moment of self-consciousness, Fern was surprised to discover it didn't arrive.

Her chin rose and her tone shifted. She wasn't properly aware it was even happening.

"Madger leaned out of the tower, hanging on to the bell rope with one hand, staring down at the square far below. She couldn't even see the cobblestones for all the soldiers packed into the space, some with torches, a few with bows. Suddenly, one of them shouted as they spotted her, pointing at the top of the bell tower. She could hear boots on the stairs. There was nowhere left to run. Then, while her heart hammered in her chest and she searched the top of the tower for an exit that wasn't there, she spied a coil of spare rope in the corner . . ."

31

Fern delivered her best approximation of R. Geneviss's timeless classic as they wended their way through the trough of the valley with the great green lake slipping noiselessly by. The reflected clouds drifted past like ghostly ships.

The world itself was preternaturally still, with only the occasional puff of snow from a peak, like frigid spring pollen, marking the passage of the winds high above. The cold scent of snow and the mineral sharpness of the lake were bright in Fern's nostrils.

Those round, black stones advanced in an irregular squiggle along the beachward side of the path, which would have been impossible to find otherwise.

When Fern's throat became parched from the telling and she paused to wet her lips, Astryx wordlessly passed a waterskin to her.

They continued that way for hours until they reached the eastern end of the lake, where the valley opened out into a broad, descending wedge of slope between serrated ranks of mountains that were sanded away into hills and plains below.

For the first time in weeks, they saw the snowline ahead of them like a tattered white skirt. Frosted evergreens stippled the land here and there until they swelled in number and crowded together into a mottled emerald quilt that bunched across the lowlands.

The sight was a deep relief, but it also bathed Fern in an unexpected surge of melancholy. Despite everything, she had the sense of leaving a place of reprieve, no longer held outside of time. Even as she smelled the first prickling hints of pine and the musk of cold, wet earth, she had an impulse to retreat back up the slopes. The lake valley they were departing had harbored a feeling of secret holiness that the abbey never approached.

Fern was startled when their progress stopped along with her narrative. A glance upward found the Oathmaiden surveying the lands below with an expression that seemed a perfect reflection of her own feelings.

"What gives?" piped up Breadlee. "We were just getting to a good part."

Staysha's pony pulled alongside Bucket, puffing foggy plumes. The dwarf narrowed her eyes suspiciously at Astryx and Fern over Zyll's orange mop of hair. "Who was *that*? Don't tell me you've got another goblin stashed in your saddlebags."

"It's too much to explain right now," said Fern.

"Is it?" asked Breadlee, his voice skeptical.

"It can wait until evening," declared Astryx. She pointed north to where a thin cataract of water skated down a black bluff and disappeared into the forest. "We'll find the stream that waterfall feeds and pitch camp early. We won't push hard the first day out."

Before Staysha could protest, the Oathmaiden gently nudged Bucket's flanks, and they got moving again.

⁓

The stream was easy enough to find, since the road passed right through it.

They wended between pines and barrow-fir that steadily increased in density, until they reached a stony shallow that they carefully picked their way across.

Fern caught fleeting glimpses of brook trout flashing above speckled stones.

Astryx led them north along the burbling water until she found a clearing within sight of the bank. The fir-tops whispered in a sinuous dance high above, and a carpet of old needles muffled the water's song to a throaty hush.

With little conversation, they made camp. Zyll busied herself shuttling river stones for a fire ring, and to her credit, Staysha produced a small hatchet and gathered wood from a nearby deadfall.

After stringing a highline and tending to Bucket and Staysha's pony—Persimmon, who seemed delighted to have equine company—Astryx turned to find Fern crouched by the assembled firewood.

"This remains humiliating," complained Breadlee as Fern rasped him briskly across a river stone, shaving blue sparks on a cone of dry needles. "You're going to dull my edge!"

"Oh, hush. You're not telling me Elder steel is *that* fragile?"

"An *Elder Blade?*" cried Staysha, nearly dropping her armload of branches.

"'Blade' might be spreading it on a little thick," observed Fern, drawing the knife across the stone again and making a satisfied noise when the tinder popped with sudden flame. She pretended to think about it. "Pocketknife?"

"Shankling!" shouted Zyll.

"Hells with all of you!" grumbled Breadlee.

"He's a greatsword that has experienced diminishment, I've been told," said Astryx with a wry smile, as she unbuckled the longer Elder Blade from her back. Fern saw the skin around her eyes tighten as she did it, but she made no noises of pain.

"*Thank* you," whispered Breadlee, his tone pathetically grateful.

Then Astryx spoiled it by skinning an inch of her longsword's steel.

"Ahem. I don't believe we've had the pleasure of meeting yet," declared Nigel. "I am called Nigellus Primus. *U*ndiminished, as you can plainly see."

"Eight hells," breathed Staysha, and this time she did drop her armful. "I need my lute."

⁓

Staysha forewent breaking into song. At least long enough to prepare a makeshift dinner in a stewpot she produced from her wagon. The Tarimites had provided beans and heavily salted bacon and beef, as well as a dozen hard, yeasty biscuits. The dwarf settled the pot at the fire's edge and built a stew of beans, hunks of meat carved off with her belt knife, and a few of the biscuits, which dissolved in the boil and thickened it. She tossed in a handful of herbs and peppercorns from a jar.

Zyll appeared beside her, rummaged around in a pocket, and then held both fists over the stewpot. Before the dwarf could open her mouth to protest, she'd dropped in handfuls of mystery mushroom.

Staysha gave Astryx a questioning glance. "Those aren't deadly, are they?"

The goblin fished one back out of the pot. She crammed it into her mouth, swallowed, and bared her teeth at the dwarf, who recoiled.

"Guess not," observed Fern.

Astryx looked up from oiling Nigel's length. She nodded at the pot. "I'm afraid we lost our bowls at the bridge."

"No fear," said Staysha brightly, and scurried to her wagon. They heard a series of clatters and bangs, then a long pause. "Where are my spoons?" she cried.

Astryx and Fern both looked at Zyll, who stared innocently back at them.

Grumbling, the dwarf returned with a stack of wooden bowls and a tin ladle.

The stew was tasty, even though the beans were still chewy, and they all had to slurp noisily from their bowls. Zyll's mushrooms turned out to be meaty and fragrant. Night fell fully as they ate, and the darkening blue above the firs became star-flecked by degrees. Crickets chirred in the deep woods, underscored by the snap and rustle of something ponderously bedding down in the underbrush.

When they'd finished their meal, Fern scoured the bowls in the river by the light of Staysha's lantern. She returned to find the bard tuning her lute while Astryx stripped off her sodden socks and laid them across a pair of stones close by the fire.

"Oooh, a little entertainment," said Breadlee.

The bard cleared her throat. The gold thread of her burgundy doublet gleamed in the firelight. "Look, it's not lost on me that you seem reluctant to share your stories."

Fern gave herself credit for managing not to snort a laugh.

"But maybe I haven't done enough to reassure you that they'd be in good hands," Staysha continued, expression earnest. Her dexterous fingers danced over the lute strings, tickling out a musical flourish. "You may have heard this one before." She grimaced. "Or maybe not, but it's *possible*, anyway. If this is the first time, though, perhaps it won't be the last. I'm proud of it. It's called 'Kingfisher's Blue Cloak.'"

She strummed, her opposite hand busy on the frets. Fern had to admit, she was a hells of a lute player. Then she opened her mouth and began. Her singing voice was lower than expected, like sweet pipe smoke.

Fern set the bowls aside, pleasantly surprised. She sat crosslegged between Astryx and Zyll, leaning back on her hands.

> *"In the end, she found the beginning,*
> *In the beginning, she saw the end,*
> *From the froth of the river*
> *Did smoke, a-spinning*
> *The stair to the sky ascend."*

Huh, thought Fern, and shared a look of comic startlement with Zyll, of all people. *She's actually pretty good.*

Fern dreamed of Viv, again.

Even in the dream, she had the presence of mind to think, *Oh. Another one of these, then?*

She stood on the doorstep of Legends & Lattes once more, candleglow visible through the leaded glass, and a shadow passing through the light.

Her mind wasn't swimming with brandy. Her heart beat slow and regular. Her paw didn't shake as she knocked.

"It's late," said Viv, surprised as she cracked the door, her hair rimmed with gold. "Everything okay?"

"It is, and it isn't," said Fern. Her voice didn't quaver even a little. "Can I come in?"

A blur of time then, a smearing of the mundanities into an impression of talk and motion and the spaces they occupied.

When it resolved, they sat at the long table, which seemed less imposingly large now. In the curious way of dreams, her toes touched the floor, even as Viv fit perfectly well opposite her.

Without apparent effort or regret, dream-Fern reached out a paw to touch Viv's hand on the table and said, "This isn't working. It isn't what I need."

And here, Fern twinned so she was standing beside dream-Fern and Viv at the table, watching incredulously as this other-her calmly withdrew a silver knife from her cloak and brandished it. Dream-Fern pointed toward the door with Breadlee, who seemed to grow huge in her hand. "I've got to go. But you'll be all right. I found a better reason."

Now, Viv was Astryx, staring across the table with those ghostlight eyes. "No rocks at the bottom," the elf whispered.

As Fern left the bench and turned to the door, she saw that it was half open already, and Quillin stood just outside, peeking into the shop. Then he was crowded aside by Zyll, grinning her shark-grin. The hazferou was atop her head again, snaggle-fanged and savage.

"We goes when is time to be somewhere else," said the goblin, and then everything swirled into dreamlessness.

32

They traveled for three days through the evergreen forest, the terrain more frequently erupting with massive slabs of granite, hoary with lichen. Deer were plentiful, and many times they saw a doe leading a pair or trio of fawns deeper into the woods, away from the road. Once a young buck stood transfixed on the path until they were within a few strides of him before he bolted.

Four times, an eerie call echoed mournfully between the tree trunks and Astryx stopped abruptly to listen, erect and alert. To Fern, it sounded like a loon, but it trailed off into a peculiar chuckling cough, like stones dropped into still water, one after another.

Each time, the call was followed by silence, and they continued onward. Fern noticed that Astryx tossed extra wood onto the fire at night, however, and sat up later than usual, although the elf did not make any comment.

The way appeared little-used, with tall grasses crowding old cart tracks. Branches grew low enough that Astryx had to push them away from their faces, and they scrabbled at the sides of Staysha's wagon. The dwarf groused loudly about the damage to the paint.

Staysha entertained them in the evenings. Her range was pretty good, from twisty short stories that Fern had never encountered before, to nostalgic ballads, or the occasional dirty joke, expertly delivered. Fern had to grudgingly admit to both the woman's talent, and the fact that she didn't mind having Staysha along all that much. The Silver Sparrow seemed less and less pushy from one day to the next, and they settled into a comfortable rhythm of travel.

They never explained Zyll's presence to the dwarf, despite several gently probing questions.

"We share a destination," was all Astryx offered.

Zyll, of course, did not elaborate.

The particulars of the goblin's supposed imprisonment were murky, anyway.

Fern marveled at the familiarity of returning to life on the road, as though she'd been journeying with Astryx for years, instead of weeks. The days before the monastery had blended into a "before" that occupied more space than it had any right to.

She continued her retelling of *Ten Links in the Chain* to Astryx in fits and starts, but the hush of the place demanded quiet for long stretches. Their passage was peaceful, shadowed by barrow-fir and surrounded by the secretive murmurings of the woods.

Until the fourth day.

The forest village showed itself unexpectedly, hidden on approach by the bulk of a long rib of granite. Ice had sheared the gargantuan stone apart centuries ago, and the road ran straight through the notch between the halves for thirty strides.

Their progress between the close granite cliffs was cacophonous as the echoes of hoofbeats and Staysha's rattling wagon rebounded in the narrow passage. Only when they emerged from the other side were the buildings revealed, and the sudden stillness was startling. Even the rustle of the wind in the treetops seemed to have ceased.

From the first second, a terrible sense of wrongness pervaded the place, and Fern didn't need to feel the tension in Astryx's body behind her to register it.

"Maybe we shouldn't stop here?" said Staysha, drawing up beside them and surveying the area skeptically.

Astryx held up a hand for silence. Beside her, Zyll's eyes narrowed in suspicion.

Six buildings, their pitched roofs furred with crowns of dried needles, made up something like a village center. Fern spotted a few other dwellings tucked back into the trees.

A little river ran through the center of the barely-a-town, straddled by a crude wooden bridge. Upstream, the paddle wheel of a decrepit mill groaned with every revolution.

There were no people visible. No audible voices. No smoke.

Fern noted fenced gardens in clearings, but their contents seemed trampled and disrupted.

"It's like it's hollowed out," whispered Fern, wincing at how loud her voice sounded in her own ears. She pointed at the largest of the buildings. "Why are the windows boarded up?"

That peculiar, mournful call echoed again, descending into that throaty, wet coughing sound, and gooseflesh rippled from Fern's tail to the tips of her ears.

Zyll *hissed*.

"Okay, but really, what *is* that?" asked Breadlee. "Puts the jimjams in my haft."

Astryx didn't answer, but instead dismounted from behind Fern. "Stay on Bucket, or in the wagon," she said. With a grace that didn't betray her recent wound, she drew Nigel—who had the presence of mind to remain silent—and approached the door of the boarded-over structure.

It might have been something that passed for a tavern in this tiny community, although there was no signboard or outward indication other than its second story and the size of its river-stone chimney.

The Oathmaiden paused and listened at the door, then reached out slowly to try the latch. When that didn't work, she put a shoulder to the banded planks and pushed, unsuccessfully.

With a glance back at Fern and Staysha, she rapped sharply on the door with her free hand, thrice.

A moment of hush, then a scuffle beyond the door that Fern heard even from her place astride Bucket.

"If y'aint Haber's Five, best you go, and soon!" came a rough voice from beyond the door.

Fern almost missed a stiffening in Staysha's posture. She studied the bard's face, but found nothing in the dwarf's expression to explain it.

"I don't know who that is," said Astryx. "Is this door boarded from the inside?"

Another pause.

"Aye," replied the voice suspiciously.

"Enough force will knock the nails right out. You'd be better off pushing something heavy against it. I'm called Astryx."

A murmured conversation ensued, and then a different voice, reedy and querulous, piped up, "Oathmaiden?"

Nigel couldn't help himself any longer. "Indeed," he declared. "None other!"

"Someone's coming to help you then?" asked Astryx. "Someone called Haber?"

"He's late!" cried the reedy voice, although the rough one tried to shush it.

Astryx stared down the road through the village, scrubbing absently at her ear. With a small sigh, she appeared to arrive at a decision, then called through the door, "I think you should probably let us inside. I don't know Haber, but I know what's in your woods."

If it *was* a tavern, it wasn't much of one, and there was no bar. There were a few tables, but they were crowded against one wall amidst a tumble of old chairs. The place was lit weakly by oil lanterns hanging from the rafters and thin fingers of light that stabbed through the boarded windows. The hearth squatted cold and dead. A pile of planks and pulled nails lay beside the door.

The room also smelled pungently of goats.

Which made sense, because four goats joined the village folk in their makeshift refuge. A brown-and-white-spotted nanny regarded them with disdain as she chewed her cud beside a set of stairs.

Eight individuals occupied the maybe-a-tavern. The rough voice belonged to a sturdy woodsman-looking fellow named Booth whose red mustache devoured his upper and lower lip, and who still held an iron pry bar forgotten in one fist. An underfed stone-fey couple had protective hands on the shoulders of their waifish daughter. The reedy voice was the property of a tiny, crooked, and surpassingly elderly woman whose eyes were squinted closed behind a pair of cracked spectacles. Her silver hair was gathered into a bun pierced with two knitting needles. Fern thought she might be dressed in a feed sack held in place with about twenty turns of twine. Three gnomish women in kerchiefs who were clearly sisters murmured to one another near the goats.

Fern, Staysha, and Zyll crowded together near the door, now closed at their back. The dwarf shifted uncomfortably.

Astryx towered over all of them, Nigel once more sheathed.

It was very tight indoors, and with the animal smell pervading the close air, quite claustrophobic. A gabble of conversation and argument had broken out immediately after they'd entered, but Astryx had silenced it with a few quiet words that nevertheless seemed to drown out everything else.

"It's a verdigaunt."

After a beat of silence, the old woman adjusted her spectacles and peered balefully up at the Oathmaiden. "Don't know about *that*."

Astryx frowned back. She didn't appear to know how to respond to skepticism. Were Nigel's blade bared, Fern had no doubt he'd already have risen to her defense.

"Finny means we ain't seen one of them before," offered Booth, apologetically.

"If you had, I don't believe we'd be talking," said Astryx. "You've just seen the greenlings, I'd warrant."

"Greenlings?" asked the stone-fey woman, doubtfully. "That sounds too nice for what's been coming 'round."

"Bones and roots. Corpses run through with ivy. They're not fast, and not smart, but hard to kill," said Astryx.

Booth and the gnomes, who'd finished their muttered conversation, were already nodding. The little stone-fey girl's eyes were huge with recognition.

"The verdigaunt is nothing like them, but they belong to it. That's the call you must have heard—in the deep woods, where its tree grows. And that's what must be dealt with."

"Eight preserve us," murmured Finny, clutching at the front of her hideous dress.

"We sent young Lem to Trestletown with all the coin we could muster." Booth seemed to be trying to figure out what to do with the pry bar, but resigned himself to continuing to awkwardly hold it. "Haber's Five can be got hold of there, and we all figured they could see us clear of the trouble. Lem said they were s'posed to arrive four days after he came home, but it's been two weeks now."

Astryx scanned the assembled folk, but Fern was the one to speak up. "Where is Lem? Is he upstairs?"

A shadow passed over their faces, and the answer became self-evident. Fern thought Staysha looked a little pale.

"I'm sorry about Lem. And if it's two weeks, then I think your money is well and truly lost," said Astryx. "But I can help you. I've been done a good turn where I didn't expect it, and it looks like you're due one as well. We'll have to wait until the greenlings return, though. Once they're dealt with, I'll follow their back trail to the tree where it sleeps."

The Oathmaiden stared speculatively around the room.

Fern tingled as she sensed her gathering up the reins of authority.

"Will any of your other buildings fit a pair of horses?" asked the elf. "And I'm going to need a volunteer."

Fern wasn't sure how her paw ended up in the air.

―――

As twilight unfurled, Bucket and Persimmon were shuttered uncomfortably into a shed attached to one of the dwellings. Bucket registered his opinion of their lodgings with a bitter whinny.

Staysha's wagon sat on the other side of the wooden bridge, tucked out of the way.

Astryx ordered Booth to remove all the boards from the windows of the building so that they could see out, then attempted to usher all of them upstairs. Staysha was only too happy to join them, but Finny and Booth declined. Booth because he offered to help keep an eye out through the exposed windows, a hatchet at the ready, and Finny because she was a contrary old lady.

Zyll had regarded the elf seriously, before declaring, "Shall be scout-ling," and then scrambling onto the roof where she perched like a very colorful gargoyle at its peak.

Astryx waited inside, leaning next to the window beside the door that gave the best view of the road out front.

The goats bleated piteously from behind her, except for the one that stood beside Fern in the road directly before the tavern. It was the brown-and-white-spotted nanny, who had the sad misfortune of being the most tractable.

Fern held the end of its lead in one paw and Breadlee at the ready in the other—as though she was capable of anything more useful with him than slicing bread.

"What the fuck am I doing?" she mumbled to herself, with an unhinged giggle.

"Yeah, I dunno why you signed up for this," observed Breadlee. "There's already a goat. Why did we need more bait?"

"So somebody can drag the goat indoors if they come?" said Fern. "I don't want her to get killed."

"It's just a goat. It's not like it's sapient."

The goat lifted its upper lip spitefully in the knife's direction.

"Astryx will make sure I'm safe," replied Fern, with what she pretended was firm resolve.

But resolve had nothing to do with it. Her reasons had more to do with something Astryx had said to her in the monastery stable.

You belong, if you want to.

And maybe she did want to.

Hardly a feeling she planned to share with sentient silverware, though.

So they waited.

And waited.

Eventually, as moonless dark descended, Astryx lit a series of torch poles in both directions along the road and brought out a stool for Fern to sit on. She also fetched a lit oil lantern and placed it on the road beside the rattkin and the goat. It cast a wobbly pool of faded light that threw their shadows outward in dark stripes.

"Are you sure about this?" asked the Oathmaiden.

Fern settled onto the stool with a sigh while the nanny nibbled at her cloak. "Seems like a squire's duty. What about you? Are you sure about this?" She gestured toward the elf's wounded side.

"I'm hale enough," Astryx replied, with a collegial squeeze on the shoulder that made Fern sit up a little straighter.

Breadlee sighed wistfully after the Blademistress as she retreated to the building with Nigel held at her side.

"Oh, get over it already," muttered Fern.

Then a piercing, ululating cry split the air. The torchglow picked out Zyll's red eyes in flecks of fire atop the roof as she pointed into the woods.

"Dead-lings!"

33

Fern couldn't see anything to begin with.

Then a bristle of shadow penetrated the margin of torchlight several yards down the road. At first, she thought it looked like nothing so much as an ambulatory shrub.

This impression crumbled in moments.

The dirty gleam of mud-smeared bone, the wink of teeth, the stringy remains of cadaverous flesh—all became clearer as it drew near. As though a riot of ivy had tunneled upward through a grave and brought along everything it found along the way, greenery choked its battered rib cage, swaying in mossy beards as the greenling staggered in her direction. Its skull was misshapen, blown out and crowned with a tangle of holly that snaked in and out of its orbits. The lower jaw bobbed, disconnected, in the ferns choking its collar.

Each footfall was a rustle and clatter as it advanced unerringly toward her.

Fern stared transfixed at this shambling nightmare of creeper and decay. It moved so slowly that her horror and fear hadn't yet muscled their way to the forefront of her mind. The goat beside her shifted anxiously from hoof to hoof, panting in quick, hard breaths.

A noise behind Fern made her turn to discover three more of the horrible things, and they were much, much closer. Then her fear *did* find purchase.

"Astryx!" she cried. She forgot all about getting the goat back into the tavern.

The nanny's thinning patience with her snapped, and it jerked the lead from Fern's paw, fleeing into the darkness with a bleat of dismay.

The greenlings did not turn to follow it.

"Um," said Breadlee. "I'm not sure which bit to stab."

Fern's temporary paralysis ended, and she began backing away from the lantern, toward the tavern. "Astryx!" she called again, a note of desperation entering her voice. "Where the hells are you?"

Her foot caught in her cloak, and she went down hard on her tail. The second greenling's right arm creaked in her direction, twined through with roots. A profusion of green shoots bristled from half a wolf's skull, sagging slowly down its humanoid chest. She squawked in horrified alarm, nearly dropping Breadlee as she scrambled to regain her feet to escape.

Even as she did, she heard the door behind her bang open. The shadow of Astryx passed on her left, Nigel's silver length burning gold in the firelight.

The Oathmaiden whipped him around in a flat arc, crashing into the rib cage of the thing and smashing it sidelong. A pained grunt of effort escaped the elf's lips as the greenling folded nearly in half and sank to the ground. Straight away it began to rise again in eerie defiance of a living beast's physiology, thrust upward by the greenery that animated it.

Astryx didn't wait for it to gain its feet, bringing the Elder Blade down in a vicious chop that cleaved it in two halves that at once fought to draw themselves back together. As she pulled her sword back from the mass of bone and ivy, questing tendrils of green tried to cling to the blade, but skittered quickly away as they touched the steel.

"Get inside!" commanded the elf. "Hurry!"

Fern stared at the door, still yawning open, where Finny stood, slack-jawed. Suddenly, Booth appeared from behind the old woman and yanked her out of view. His eyes met Fern's for a fleeting instant, a question in his gaze.

When she didn't move, he heaved the door closed with a rattling bang.

Glancing back at Astryx, Fern saw that the crumpled mess of the greenling was smoking as though Nigel were a hot brand held against it. It did not seem able to rise again as it seethed and bubbled around the Elder Blade.

Two more loomed from the shadows and the Blademistress took a solid step back. Their advance was slow, but relentless. With a flick, she severed a leg of the leftmost, hooking it away with a swipe so that the limb tumbled off into the darkness. A snarl of foliage immediately blossomed from its hip, trying to prevent its fall, but Astryx was already slipping her blade between the ribs of its fellow and ripping outward, hurling it away.

She cried out and clapped a hand to her side as Nigel's point dipped and wavered.

"Steady on, my lady!" Nigel's voice was thick with helpless distress.

The one-legged greenling lurched toward her again with ungainly, undulating steps, supported by ropes of vines that spidered along beneath it.

"Watch out!" hollered Breadlee. Three more of the creatures staggered around the side of the tavern and directly toward the elf.

Astryx threw a look behind her and put both hands on Nigel's hilt to steady him, her eyes narrowing with cold resolve.

There are too many, thought Fern, wildly. *She's still too hurt. It takes too long to kill them.*

"Shit," she cried, glancing at the knife in her hand, then at the lantern she'd left behind.

Before she realized what she was doing, she was dashing to scoop the oil lantern up in her empty paw. Without even pausing for a terrified breath, Fern ran toward the group of greenlings and hurled it directly at the one in the middle.

Lantern-glass smashed against its bones and oil sheeted up in a vivid plume of flame that made her flinch back from the heat and light.

The greenling didn't react in the slightest. They felt no pain, it was clear. But as the vines and plants animating it crisped and curled, it began to stutter, like a puppet whose master had forgotten to twitch the strings from one moment to the next.

Ignoring the burning greenling, Astryx hacked the newly regrown limb from the creature at her back, taking its other leg with it, then turned to engage the others.

"We need more lanterns!" yelled Breadlee.

"There aren't any," said Fern. Then she caught sight of one of the torch poles, half again her height and jammed into the earth along the road.

Dodging around Astryx and skirting the grasping arms of the legless horror nearby, she seized the closest torch pole low on the shaft and heaved upward with all her might.

It didn't budge an inch.

"Fuck!" Tears of frustration pricked her eyes.

"Ah, shit," swore Breadlee. Then, in a tone of resigned exasperation, "Use me."

"What?"

"Use me to cut it, all right?"

"It's thicker than my arm!"

"Just do it!"

She stared at the knife in her hand, then quashed her doubt and began sawing at the wood while holding the pole above the cut.

Unbelievably, Breadlee's keen edge slipped deeper into the wood with each stroke, until after only six, Fern used her weight to snap the top of the torch free in a shower of greasy sparks.

Turning back to the battle, she saw Astryx shoving one of the greenlings off Nigel's blade with a savage kick of her booted foot. Her longsword made an inarticulate sound of triumph.

With a yowl, something plummeted from the roof to crash into a greenling topped with ram's horns and burdock—

—Zyll, clawing furiously at the creature as she rode it to the ground, before springing away and disappearing into the shadows before it could retaliate.

"Lady!" cried Fern as she ran back with the shortened torch pole awkwardly pinned under one arm.

Astryx half turned, understanding already plain on her face as she stretched out her free hand.

"Sorry," gasped Fern. Breadlee swore as she flung him to the dirt and used both paws to heave the torch in Astryx's direction.

The elf snatched it from the air, spun, and planted its burning end into the chest of her nearest assailant.

Fern snatched Breadlee back up, but then could do little but watch in exhausted astonishment as the sweeping arcs of the torch sketched afterimages of fire into her vision. Astryx dismantled the remaining greenlings, laying waste with fire and Elder steel, until nothing remained but smoking wrecks of bone and stem.

In the stillness that followed, she stood heaving in long breaths, leaning on Nigel for support, bathed in sweat and soot in equal measure.

"Gods-damn," breathed Breadlee. "We did it!"

Fern was about to suggest that Astryx was too tired to track down some more terrible creature deep in the woods when a haunting loon-call pierced the night, twisted at the last into a rotten, wet, chuckle.

Then the verdigaunt arrived.

Fern shivered with dreadful awe. The thing seemed to grow in stature as it emerged from the darkness with a thundering stride, rising above the smoldering remains of the greenlings like a lord of the Third Hell. It walked on two legs, and from its split hooves to the tips of its massive rack of antlers, it must have been thirty hands tall. Swollen eyes the glossy black of tar considered Astryx from the bearded, misshapen face of an elk, teeth bared in broken slabs within a lipless mouth. Its heavy shoulders dripped dead moss like banners of spiderweb as it moved. Three keratinous digits the width of shovels curled and uncurled at the ends of powerful arms as it regarded the Oathmaiden with the disdain of a vengeful god.

"Oh no," breathed Fern, sagging.

"Guess she doesn't have to find its tree after all," added Breadlee, his voice grim.

There would be no reprieve, no moment to regroup.

The thing hunched to survey the wreckage of its minions in the road, then twisted its remarkably flexible neck to stare at Astryx.

Fern wondered in a distant way where Zyll was, and if the goblin had anything in her pockets they could use.

Through the glass of the upstairs windows, she could see the spectral impression of faces, watching with mouths agape.

Astryx caught Fern's eyes even as she brought Nigel up before her, straight and still. "You can't help here anymore, little squire. You have to run. Now."

Something lost and tired in her voice bent a piece of Fern entirely out of true.

But she didn't run. She couldn't bring herself to abandon her friend.

Astryx snapped into motion, discarding the mantle of her fatigue. Nigel's steel whipped in a flashing arc, and the verdigaunt howled as a line of black blood appeared along its thigh. The greenlings might not have been mortal, but this beast certainly was.

Mouth yawning and breath smoking, the antlered beast swiped at the elf with one arm, and she narrowly evaded by falling to a knee. Its bony fingertips dug a trench in the earth. The Oathmaiden caught the underside of its arm with a shallow slice as she rolled inside of its reach.

"What do we do?" said Fern, seized by a mad impulse to run toward the battle.

"I don't think a torch is gonna help this time," replied Breadlee.

The verdigaunt dropped its hands to the road and charged on all fours, the wicked tines of its antlers advancing like a phalanx of spear points. The bottommost points carved squiggling furrows in the road. Astryx lunged to the side, but not fast enough. One outer spike caught her in the right shoulder and spun her off-balance.

She did not cry out, but Fern thought she saw a fringe of blood cast into the night from the impact, and she clapped both paws to her mouth.

The creature sensed the strike and dug its digits and hooves into the earth, skidding to a stop and wrenching its head, still held low, in her direction.

Astryx tossed Nigel to her left hand and continued the motion into a vertical spin of the blade that lopped the ends off half the verdigaunt's antlers. The tines spun away into the darkness like severed fingers, trailing ribbons of dark fluid.

It bellowed, bunching its shoulders to lunge again, but the Blademistress dashed forward, sprinting *up* its lowered skull, between the tangled thorns that flanked it, and onto its back where she brought her blade up in both hands, point downward, and drove it between the verdigaunt's shoulder blades.

With a reverberant roar it threw itself upright. Astryx crouched to maintain her footing, both hands still on the blade, but her eyes flew wide as her fingers slipped from his hilt and she was hurled away.

As the Oathmaiden hit the dirt and rolled, Nigel remained buried in the verdigaunt's back. It bayed with pain, flailing its blunt-fingered hands at its shoulders, trying to reach the steel planted next to its spine, and shifting its prodigious weight from hoof to hoof.

Astryx moaned, pushing herself to her feet with her hand once more at her side.

Fern reached her in seconds. "Come on, come on, you've got to get back!" she cried, putting her shoulder under Astryx's unwounded one. Fern could see a dark stain leaching through her jerkin where the verdigaunt's antler had caught the elf.

"You shouldn't be here," grunted Astryx. Then she hauled herself the rest of the way to her feet, blowing out a pained breath at the end.

"Neither should you!" retorted Fern, glancing up at where Nigel still stood in the back of the flailing monster.

Then, a flash of patchwork color in the torchlight.

Zyll scurried out of the darkness, leapt, and caught her fists in the shaggy hair of the verdigaunt's back.

Astryx and Fern stared agog as the goblin scrambled up to the Elder Blade. The beast seemed not to perceive her.

At least, until Zyll flung herself into the air, snatching hold of Nigel's grip as she went. Her weight and momentum dragged him free with an awful tearing sound, and then the blade cartwheeled over her head as she released him at the forward point of his spin.

Nigel whickered through the air, shedding black blood, until he thudded, point-first, into the ground.

Zyll disappeared once again into the darkness.

The verdigaunt cast about, bewildered and huffing in pain.

Astryx pushed off of Fern's shoulders and ran, curving her path past Nigel's still wobbling length. Without stopping, she jerked him from the ground and veered toward the towering beast.

It noticed her at the last, snarling and lowering its head again.

The Oathmaiden screamed, raw and ragged, and drove Nigel like a spear directly into the center of its skull.

Her momentum carried through and she slammed into its head with one shoulder, bounced back, and tumbled to the roadway as, with an awful groan, the verdigaunt dropped like a wagonload of boulders.

"Take this, Oathmaiden," said Finny, pressing a cup of something hot and fragrantly nasty into Astryx's hands.

"Oh, leave off, woman. That mend-all of yours is like to kill her as soon as cure her," groused Booth.

Astryx accepted it anyway, bemused and ensconced in a wooden chair draped with what seemed like every blanket the villagers could find. Her shoulder had been thoroughly bandaged and Nigel leaned, unsheathed, against the arm of her chair. The old woman in the raggedy dress fretted over a pair of cushions which she kept trying to jam behind the elf's back. The Elder Blade tutted in annoyance every time she bumped into him.

They had parked the Oathmaiden before the hearth, now loaded with logs that burned cheerfully.

Fern thought that while the elf looked rightfully exhausted—her cheeks and neck still smudged with soot, hair a messy tangle—there was something in her expression she hadn't seen before.

Her quiet, steely reserve had been replaced by something simpler and more open.

The tired smile on her face was disarmingly genuine.

That is, until she took a sip of whatever it was that Finny had prepared, at which point her mouth twitched in disgusted surprise.

From her own, less-padded chair nearby, clutching a mug of hot, watery wine, Fern couldn't help but note how thoroughly the tavern had been transformed.

With the windows unboarded, the fire roaring, and lanterns and candles scattered throughout, it was downright cheerful when compared to the dour, hopeless ruin it had seemed earlier in the day.

The tables had been drawn back from the walls, and the chairs and stools replaced in a semblance of order. The goats were also now outside, and the floor had been swept, which improved the smell tremendously.

Staysha chattered animatedly with the three gnome sisters, while Booth fussed with a round of cheese, summer preserves, and cured meat that he'd retrieved from one of the other buildings. He was determined to assemble something resembling a feast, even if they didn't really have the stores to support it after the past weeks of privation.

The stone-fey couple sat quietly and watchfully with their daughter. The man and woman looked just as gaunt and underfed as before but, every once in a while, evinced the ghost of a smile. Their daughter stared with open wonder at Zyll, who was parked in a corner murmuring to a bunch of forks she had appropriated from somewhere. Nobody seemed inclined to ask for them to be returned.

The bustle and noise continued, and Fern sipped her wine dreamily. Every muscle in her body ached, and all she'd done was dash around and throw things. She couldn't imagine how Astryx must feel. Still, those aches were sublimating into something like peace.

Finny cleared her throat, raising her hands for silence. She stared around the room, or appeared to. Her eyes never really seemed to open behind her cracked spectacles. The silver knitting needles in her bun flashed in the firelight.

"Oathmaiden," she addressed Astryx, with great solemnity. "We owe ya a great debt. Can't pay it, leastwise because we sent all that silver with Lem, Eight rest him, but t'wouldn't be enough even if we had it."

Astryx listened, but didn't speak. Which was all right, because Finny wasn't done, anyway.

"Our lives are little things in the Territory," she continued in her reedy, wavering voice. "We know that. But you've made us feel a touch bigger. Didn't have to stop for us. Didn't have to *bleed* for us. We thank ya, and though these words feel as little as we are, we'll remember ya. And we hope that knowin' it makes ya feel a touch bigger, too."

Astryx went to drink from the cup again, to give herself time to marshal a response, but thought better of it at the last moment. Fern saw her struggling and realized that this was territory the elf was uncomfortable with.

She never sticks around for this part, it dawned on her.

"I . . . Thank you for the kind words, mother," said Astryx, despite the fact that she was the old woman's senior by centuries upon centuries. Then she looked from one face to the next, appearing to mark them in some way. Fern thought the elf's eyes were shining with something other than lamp-glow, but couldn't be positive.

Finny approached and patted Fern on the shoulder, whispering, "You picked a good'un to squire for."

Then Fern was lost for words, too.

Staysha wasn't, though. The dwarf stepped away from the gnome sisters, already slinging her lute over her shoulder as Booth laid out a meager spread on the table beside her.

"I knew I chose the right star to follow," said the Silver Sparrow. She grinned brightly at all of them. "What's a celebration without music, eh? Hearing about great deeds is all well and good, but seeing them? Well, the words have never come easier."

"Oh, geez," muttered Breadlee.

"Hear, hear!" cried Nigel.

Then Staysha burst into song, strumming up a storm, while Astryx did her best to disappear into all the blankets.

"Oathmaiden, Oathmaiden, silver and true,
Forged in the shadow and—"

The bard broke off with a discordant chord as the door banged open, and all eyes turned to the man framed within it.

He was strong-chinned and clean-shaven, hair cropped close. He wore stained quilted armor, with a shortsword belted at his waist and a white ferret curled around his neck. The creature regarded them all with beady eyes.

"That's a dead verdigaunt," said the man, eyes wide as he

cocked a thumb at the road behind him. "I'm Haber. Sorry we're late, but we—"

He started, and his mouth flattened into a suspicious line. "Staysha?"

Fern glanced back to the dwarf, who laughed nervously and seemed to want to hide behind her lute. "Oh. Um. Hi?"

34

What followed was something remarkably like a family dinner involving a lot of estranged relatives. Haber and his crew shuffled awkwardly indoors—a pair of narrow-faced sea-fey, the shortest orc Fern had ever seen in her life, and a gnome illusionist who couldn't seem to find a color besides black to clothe herself in.

With everyone squeezed inside, the tavern went from cozy and convivial to close and crowded in a matter of seconds.

"So, you know each other?" asked Booth, confusion plain on his face as he gestured from the bard to the newcomers.

Haber frowned and seemed to be debating the merits of politeness versus accuracy. "We, um. Traveled together," he hedged. "For a while."

"Just chronicling their adventures," said Staysha, brimming with enthusiasm Fern thought was false.

"That's one way of putting it," muttered the orc, who looked like he wanted to throttle her with the hands that he was keeping very carefully unclenched at his sides.

"You were s'posed to be here ages ago," cried Finny, who couldn't be bothered with all of the dithering politeness going on. She stumped over to Haber and glared up at him through her cracked spectacles. "The Oathmaiden's gone and done your work for you. So, where's our silver?"

The attention of everyone shifted to Astryx in her throne of blankets. She waved mildly in return.

BRIGANDS & BREADKNIVES

A hushed conference ensued amongst Haber's Five, with many glances thrown the elf's way.

Eventually, Haber emerged once more as their spokesman. He approached Astryx and bowed formally, which the white ferret around his neck was not amused by. "Our thanks, lady. It's to our shame that you had to face such a threat on your own. You are clearly the equal of the tales that go before you." He shuffled his feet. "And on a personal note, I've admired you since before I was old enough to dress myself."

Astryx, unlike the ferret, appeared *highly* amused.

Turning back to Finny, Haber continued. "As for your silver, I wish I had better news. It was . . . misplaced." Here he shot Staysha a dark look that she appeared to studiously ignore. "But we'll do what we must to see you repaid."

Then everyone stood around awkwardly and couldn't figure out what to do with their hands. The rest of Haber's group started to inch for the door with many nods of deference in Astryx's direction and daggers stared in Staysha's.

Zyll was suddenly at Fern's elbow. "Very inter-lesting," she mused aloud, with a remarkable amount of discretion. "The bard-a-larding is maybe, how do you say, little shit-faced."

"I don't think that's how we say it," replied Fern, out of the side of her mouth. "But I think I know what you mean. And I'm going to find out."

"Hey, hang on a minute."

Haber turned back to Fern with a quizzical expression. The rest of his crew were already halfway to their horses, which shied and stamped nervously at the smell of the slain verdigaunt sprawled half on the road at the verge of the lamplight.

Fern pulled the door closed firmly behind her and gestured for them both to move farther away. Inside, she could hear Finny stridently arguing with Booth.

When she was sure she was out of earshot, she kept her voice low and said, "I need to know about Staysha. You were too polite or unsure to say something in there, but the looks you gave her could have spoiled milk. My tail isn't going to untwist until I know why."

The man glanced back at the door, while his white ferret blinked at Fern. "You're with One-Ear? And the Sparrow is traveling with you?"

"I guess so. For a little longer anyway."

"Everything all right, Haber?" called the orc, who had stopped to peer at them through the gloom.

"Fine!" Then, to Fern, "You don't know me, but I'm not the sort to speak ill. Tends to kick back and catch you in the face. And we can't prove anything, but . . ."

"I'm not a Gatewarden," said Fern impatiently. "You don't have to hedge."

"We didn't 'misplace' the silver. It's gone, though." He sighed. "Here's the thing. Staysha rode along with us for a few weeks—gathering material, she said. It's not a bad idea for an outfit like ours to have a few tales told or songs sung about them, even if it can be a bit embarrassing. Well, *usually* not a bad idea.

"Seems the Silver Sparrow may have taken too much artistic license in our case and given folks the impression we did some things we definitely didn't. Jance Half-Hand wasn't too happy to discover she was giving *us* credit for *his* work. She vanished just as he came calling, and wouldn't you know it," he jerked a thumb back at the tavern, "the purse these folks sent as advance payment disappeared right about the same time. We've been struggling to navigate the whole mess, which cost us most of the silver we had left and a big slice of reputation."

"Shit-faced," muttered Fern.

"Huh?"

The ferret hissed from his shoulder.

"Nothing. Thanks for telling me."

"Even if it does mean we owe these folks, make sure the Oathmaiden knows we're grateful, and she has our respect." He nodded at the bulk of the verdigaunt. "Not many I know could tackle such a beast alone."

"Yeah," replied Fern. "She's pretty incredible."

"And, like I said. I can't prove anything, but think about finding yourselves another travel partner." He looked thoughtful and scratched the back of his head. "Speaking of—the greenskin in there. She with you, too? I seem to remember something about a goblin. Big bounty. Colorful coat, even, now that I think on it. Not sure whose stew they pissed in, but there were a lot of sovereigns put up to bring them in."

Fern regarded him evenly. "Yeah, she's traveling with us. I don't know about a bounty, but if there were, I imagine Astryx would already be aware of it."

He searched her face, then nodded. "Sure, sure. Anyway, travel safe. And maybe suggest to your friend that she wear a different coat for a while."

⁓

Fern didn't have an opportunity to talk to Astryx for hours. After the departure of Haber and once Finny had finished venting her spleen with repeated angry exclamations of "three hundred silver!" things settled back into as festive a mood as could be conjured. Staysha seemed unperturbed by the recent appearance and departure of her erstwhile traveling companions and played songs to match the tone of the gathering, from cheerfully festive to quietly languorous, as the night deepened.

The little stone-fey girl with the big eyes escaped the clutches of her parents to edge closer and closer to Astryx until she was on a stool beside the elf, awed worship obvious in every particle of her body. Fern saw the Oathmaiden pat Nigel's hilt affectionately, then murmur something to the child, whereupon she nearly vibrated apart.

Astryx laughed with less reservation than Fern could recall, and looked . . . comfortable, despite her wounds and abrasions. Not a storied legend, but the fascinating aunt who'd traveled from one end of the Territory to the other, and slyly implied that you might one day, too.

Fern herself was too nervy to appreciate the celebratory atmosphere, turning over the conversation with Haber in her mind.

When Staysha paused to wet her throat at one point, Fern sidled up to her. "So, you traveled with the ferret guy and his group for a while?" she said, without preamble.

"Hm?" Staysha looked at her over the top of her cup. "Oh, sure. Just for a few days. A fun bunch."

"Yeah? And it went well?"

"I thought so. A few songs hatched, and it never hurts a crew like that to have someone like me out there telling their tale. Why?"

The bard was doing an impressive job of affecting innocent curiosity.

Fern shrugged. "I talked to him a bit, and I got the impression they didn't come away from it with the same feelings, is all."

Staysha laughed. "Well, they've been riding for days only to find out they're too late, and that means they don't get paid. That's bound to salt their slugs. Some people are always looking for some other peg to hang their misfortune on."

"I guess so," replied Fern. She thought about bringing up Jance Half-Hand, and the missing silver, but Staysha's unblinking smile told her it wasn't likely to provoke a tearful admission. Instead, she nodded to the bard and found her way to a seat near Zyll, who was already dozing in a corner.

"That girl smiles way too much," murmured Breadlee from her cloak pocket.

"Yes, she does," replied Fern, sipping at her wine and staring darkly at the dwarf.

Eventually, the fire died down and the party did as well. Astryx's tiny admirer was shepherded away by her guardians, the three gnome sisters fell asleep in their cups at the table, and Booth escorted Finny to her cottage.

When he returned, he immediately offered his own bed upstairs for their use, but Astryx declined, whereupon he brought down every cloak he owned, a few more blankets, and what Fern was positive were the quilt and pillows from his own bed, to assemble makeshift sleeping arrangements. He gingerly dropped a quilt over the snoring Zyll, then woke the gnome sisters and sent them packing.

Staysha left to sleep in her wagon, much to Fern's relief.

When they were alone, and Astryx was giving Nigel a quick polish at the table before resheathing him, Fern pulled up a chair across from her.

She cursed the bard for putting her in this position.

The Oathmaiden looked up from her labor with a gentle smile. Despite a shoulder wound that would have had Fern writhing in pain, she looked relaxed.

"Look, I think we need to leave Staysha behind."

"Oh?" Astryx stopped polishing.

Fern relayed all that she had discovered from Haber, and her subsequent unsatisfying conversation with Staysha.

"It *does* sound like hearsay," observed Nigel.

"You're just happy someone is writing songs about her!" cried Fern.

"As well they should be!" he retorted.

Astryx laid a hand on his blade to forestall a further outburst. "Songs or no songs, she *does* make travel swifter. Do you think we're in much danger of being robbed by her?"

Fern realized the question wasn't rhetorical, and there was no sarcasm in her voice. Astryx was asking her honest opinion.

She squirmed. "Well . . . no. I guess I have a hard time imagining that."

"Are you worried she'll cause us some sort of *musical* trouble?"

Fern felt color rise under the fur of her cheeks. "I mean. Um."

"We should be able to part ways as soon as I can secure another wagon. There's little to be had here, and these poor people can't part with much of anything, anyway, even for silver. Do you think we can manage her company for a while longer?"

Again, Fern marveled that it was clear Astryx actually wanted to hear her answer.

Fern sighed. "I guess we can."

Still, she didn't like it.

35

They departed the nameless village with barely any fuss, although Finny did insist on gifting Astryx with packets of pungent herbs to recreate her vile "healing" concoction at their leisure. The elf was gracious and didn't immediately throw them away. For their part, the villagers were indulgent and didn't comment on their missing silverware.

Astryx's parting words to each villager in turn, and the way she knelt before the little stone-fey girl and lifted her chin with a gentle finger, were a far cry from Fern's experience being rescued in the bog all those weeks ago. That had only amounted to a fistful of reins and a swift exit.

Fern suffered a pang of ridiculous envy.

She quickly squashed it, and even held her peace about Staysha.

And they resumed their journey.

According to Astryx, Amberlin was less than a week of travel away—

—which meant it was the end of *Fern's* journey as well, but anytime her mind threatened to open a window on what came afterward, she ruthlessly shuttered it.

Instead, she lamented the fact that they'd likely be stuck with the bard for the rest of the trip.

To be fair, the Silver Sparrow was nothing but cheerful and made herself useful about camp without complaint. Fern found it difficult to maintain a heightened level of suspicion.

They shortly emerged from the evergreen forest into a gently rolling, grassy prairie, stitched through with fresh streams of snowmelt that branched and branched again in gleaming threads. Mountains rose blue and shadowed behind them and to the north.

More than once, small herds of prairie ox skirted them in the distance, their shaggy backs seeming to merge into one long, undulating beast, spined with massive horns.

The little seasonal rivers intersected the road in dozens of places, sometimes washing it out entirely. Bucket traversed these obstacles easily enough, but they had to be cautious with Staysha's wagon, as Persimmon struggled mightily where the streams became bogs. Several times, they hitched Bucket in her place to make the crossing.

After one such ordeal in the early afternoon of the second day, Astryx called a halt so the horses could rest. Studying the Oathmaiden keenly, Fern thought that she might need a breather herself. Although the elf moved with remarkable agility, she'd suffered too many wounds and too much punishment in too short a time. Little hesitations and pauses in her manner hinted that it was all adding up. She'd also taken to strapping Nigel's sheath across the back of the saddle, which Fern found concerning.

After refilling their waterskins from the stream they'd just forded, they sat in long grass in the shade of Staysha's wagon, nibbling at the dried rations from the Tarimites. Zyll darted around in the tallest weeds in search of small animals, whose fates nobody wanted to think about.

Staysha brushed crumbs from her doublet and cleared her throat. "So. I haven't had a chance to finish the song I've been tinkering with after seeing you in action."

"Hm," said Astryx.

"The tune is solid, but I think the lyrics still need some finessing. Maybe if I had a bit more insight into how it *felt* to be out there in the dark, fire in one hand and steel in the other . . ."

Astryx was silent for so long that Fern thought she was going to actively ignore the bard, but the elf surprised all of them by murmuring, "I suppose if you think it'll help." She very carefully did not look at anyone as she said it.

Nobody seemed more astounded than Staysha. "Oh! Well, fabulous. Let's see . . . Let me find my way back to the snarl first." She hummed a few bars and sang softly, *"Oathmaiden, Oathmaiden, silver and true . . ."*

"Okay," said Fern, rising abruptly to her feet and shaking grass seeds from her cloak. "I'm going to stretch my paws and relieve the ache in my ass. Back in a bit."

Astryx opened her mouth, but Fern didn't give her the opportunity to speak, briskly rounding the corner of the wagon and striding into the rustling meadow across the road. Persimmon and Bucket didn't look up from grazing contentedly.

"Oathmaiden, Oathmaiden, barf in my shoe," grumbled Breadlee. "What a hack."

"You don't wear shoes," observed Fern tartly.

"Not with barf in them."

She stomped through the grass for a minute or two.

"I don't like her," she said at last. "But I don't fucking know *why*. Do I really have a bad feeling about her? Am I not giving her the benefit of the doubt because of Haber's word? He was clear he couldn't prove she did anything wrong."

"I just don't like music. I thought we were on the same page?"

"You don't like—? Never mind. No, it's not that. Gods, am I *jealous*? Do I just want Astryx to myself, like some kind of child?"

"Oh, well, wanting her all to yourself is totally natural. At least it better be, because if not, I'd have to rethink every one of my goals for the future. And I absolutely do not want to do that," chirped Breadlee. "If Nigel just happened to slip off that horse's butt and disappear into the grass, or plunge to the bottom of a canyon, or, like, a deep river, maybe? I wouldn't make a peep. Familiar feeling?"

Fern ground her teeth and didn't reply, because she wasn't sure she wanted to face the answer.

"Or maybe it's just because the end of the road is coming," said Breadlee more soberly, "... and you're mad because you feel like you're running out of time to do whatever it is you're doing out here. To be clear, I have no idea what that is."

Fern didn't want to face the answer to that, either.

―⁂―

She walked a wide loop and returned to the animals, where she fussed over Bucket until Staysha's singing voice trailed off.

"Finally," Fern muttered to the horse, who lipped her paw sympathetically as she scratched his chin.

As she turned to head back to the wagon, she was startled to find Astryx almost beside her already. The Oathmaiden joined her at Bucket's head, patting his cheek and inspecting his mane as though there were, in fact, something to be done with it.

Now Fern felt awkward about leaving, so she continued to stroke the horse's chin.

Two people pretending to have important business with a horse, thought Fern, and nearly laughed aloud.

Astryx surprised her by speaking first. "Anything the matter?"

"Of course not," lied Fern.

"All right," replied Astryx. There was also apparently something critical to be adjusted on Bucket's halter.

"Actually, she's very annoyed," declared Breadlee.

Fern withdrew the knife from her cloak pocket and hurled him into the grass.

"Hey!" he cried.

She ignored him and addressed Astryx. "All right, fine. I can't stand it. Why are you ... *indulging* this?"

The Oathmaiden frowned. *"Indulging?"*

"Yes! The song! Giving her *'insight'*"—Fern made a face—"when all she wants is to ride your coattails to, I don't know, glory? Whatever it is bards want. It's ... it's *beneath* you."

"Only days ago, it was *you* who told me that I 'don't stick around to be appreciated,' and am always 'off to the next thing,'" replied Astryx, with unexpected heat. "Now I pause for a moment and pay attention, say a few words to the people we helped, and listen to what they have to say in turn. I make time for someone that wants it, and it's beneath me?"

"Well, not all of it, but *this* part at least," said Fern.

"Are you just chronically dissatisfied, or is that only when it comes to me?" demanded Astryx, ghostlight eyes blazing with a fierceness Fern had never felt directed toward her.

She nearly quailed beneath it, but the upset she was wrestling with couldn't be subdued.

"I don't fucking know!" she shouted.

"Then you should figure that out first. Even if you did know what would please you, I doubt I could bring you to it. If you saw it on the horizon, you'd probably run the other way. I don't care about a gods-blasted song! I'm not trying to build my *legend*," snapped Astryx.

"No, you're just walking straight in the dark until the sunrise—whatever the fuck that means—which is why we're hauling Zyll in for a bounty and to gods-know what fate, even though you *know* it's wrong!"

"*We* aren't hauling her anywhere," retorted Astryx, with ice in her voice.

Then she spun on her heel and strode away from the road. "I think I need a walk. Look at all the good it did you."

Fern watched her go, the anger slowly leaving her body as Astryx disappeared over a swell in the prairie.

"Fuck," she muttered to herself. "Great job, Fern."

Behind her, she heard a muffled thud and a squawk, and assumed Zyll had caught something.

At least somebody around here got what they wanted, she thought.

At the gritty noise of a footstep on the road, she turned to find Staysha in the middle of the path, her lute case under one arm, heading Fern's way.

The expression on the woman's face was unreadable, her mouth a thin line.

Fern reviewed their loud argument and the words she'd shouted, experiencing a second rush of guilt. "Hey, I'm sorry. I don't know what you overheard, but—"

Then the Silver Sparrow grabbed the neck of the case with both hands and brained Fern with it.

36

"Hey! Hey, you gotta get up!"

Fern's consciousness bobbed just above a dark waterline before it sank beneath once more.

A little eternity ensued down in the shadows.

"Kid!"

She unwillingly surfaced again, lost in a forest of whispering green that seemed to heave up and down like the swell of ocean waves.

Something warm and velvety was brushing against one ear and the fur on the back of Fern's skull, which drew attention to the *front* of it, where her face throbbed. Hot shock waves of pain pulsed from her snout back through her eyes, which felt squeezed by her cheeks.

"Come on, come on. Hey, hey you, with the tail! *Damn, that doesn't narrow it down.* Bucket! *Horse! Bite* her!"

"Muphet," mumbled Fern into the dirt, eyelids flickering. "Nuh."

Her stomach flipped, and she thought she was going to be sick.

Then something nipped her ear, and a bolt of galvanizing lightning pierced the nausea. She yelped, pushing herself up onto her paws.

"Fuckass, ow!"

She was sprawled in the long grass beside the road. Turning her head made the ache inside it spill to the right side of her face, as though her skull was a bottle half full of liquid pain.

Bucket snorted, inches from her snout.

"Wuh."

"Oh, thank the effing Eight," said Breadlee, with huge relief. "You gotta get up. She's gonna be out of sight soon!"

"Who? Wh—" Then Fern remembered Staysha striding toward her.

"Oh, you bitch," she snarled, staggering to her feet.

Fern was not a vengeful rattkin, but she had never felt more murderous in her life.

"She tried to shoo the horse off, but he came back. Good thing, too, because I don't think you're gonna catch her on foot."

"She hit me with her *lute*."

The sky was coming down twilight, and the purples and golds pulsed brighter in time with Fern's heartbeat. She wobbled, listing to the side and steadying herself against Bucket's shoulder.

"Yeah, you're not the only one. She got little Miss Pockets, too. Tied her up, tossed her in the wagon, and off she went."

Fern remembered the thump and squawk, and then searched back a little further and recalled her own words, shouted at Astryx in the heat of the moment—"*hauling Zyll in for a bounty.*"

"Oh, no."

She gingerly probed her face, hissing at the goose-egg rising on her forehead, then did her best to take stock of her surroundings.

Nothing but grass, road, and one anxious horse. If she squinted—which hurt especially fiercely—she thought she could just make out a dust cloud in the distance to the east.

"Where's Astryx?"

"Dunno. Hasn't been back since you ran her off."

"Help!" hollered Fern, loud enough it rasped her throat. "Astryx! Can you hear me?"

The effort made her woozier.

She paused, listening intently, but heard no response besides rustling grass and the distant caw of a raven.

"Breadlee. Say something so I can find you."

"Would it kill you to use my *real* name?"

"That'll do."

She oriented on his voice and pushed aside the grass until she uncovered him, stooping to pick him up. Another wave of nausea from the motion broke against the shore of her forehead.

"Well, what are we waiting for?" prompted the knife.

Fern studied Bucket, who regarded her expectantly. She was suddenly very glad that Astryx hadn't removed his saddle. Nigel's hilt still stuck out from where he was strapped behind it, beside her satchel.

"This is not a good idea," said Fern, even as she tottered toward the horse and put a hand on his stirrup. Bucket stared back at her, tossing his head as though to urge her up.

She'd never climbed onto him without Astryx's assistance before, because, well, he was *mountainous*, and she was a rattkin. Picking up his trailing reins, she tossed them up and over his neck, gratified that she managed on the first go. Then, grasping the stirrup again with one hand, she tiptoed and managed to grab the billet strap with the other. The horsey scent of him filled her nostrils as she stood pressed against his belly.

Taking a deep breath, she leapt upward, scrambling from one handhold to the next, until she was spread-eagled across his side, with one paw on the cantle and the other on Nigel's haft. Scrabbling desperately with her right foot, she managed to snag the stirrup with her toes and slide her foot into it, lunging upward until she threw her left leg over the seat.

Facing backward.

She sat there for a moment, swaying with every thump of her headache.

"Well, you're up," observed Breadlee.

She managed to wriggle around and face forward without falling off, using her tail for balance, and then stretched to fumble the reins into her paw.

"I've never ridden a horse before," she said.

"Uh, seems to me like you've been doing it for days."

"I mean when I had to get it to *do* anything. My feet don't reach the stirrups. Fuck, this was a stupid idea."

Bucket shook his head, snorted, and began to walk after the distant dust cloud.

"Oh," said Fern. "Maybe this *will* work."

Then he began to trot. Without Astryx's steadying weight behind her, Fern bobbled in the saddle and felt herself slipping sideways. "Shit!" She grabbed the saddle horn and tried to hook her tail around Nigel's sheath.

Bucket broke into a canter, and it was all Fern could do not to judder right off the side of him.

Then he was galloping, and she held on for dear life.

○○○

Fern had never moved so fast in her life. Not once during their journey had Astryx ever urged Bucket into a flat-out gallop, and the sheer speed of him took her breath away.

He was *significantly* faster than Persimmon drawing a wagon.

They barreled through one of the streamlets and sheets of snowmelt fountained up from every hoofbeat.

The dust cloud grew closer and closer. Fern's eyes teared up at the speed of their passage. After the first floundering moments, she bit the reins between her teeth and used both paws to clutch the leading edge of the saddle beside the horn, her belly thudding up and down, cloak snapping as Bucket thundered toward their quarry. Her head boomed with every impact.

As they neared the wagon, Fern could hear an angry caterwauling from inside it, like a badger in a barrel, and she realized it was Zyll.

Bucket slowed his pace and drew alongside the buckboard until Fern stared over at an open-mouthed Staysha, whose eyes were wide in astonishment. The lute case she'd clobbered Fern with sat beside her. Her face and hands looked lacerated, and one cheek was going purple.

Apparently, Zyll's dangerous smile wasn't just for show.

Fern spat the reins out of her mouth and hollered, "Stop your horse, shit-face!"

The Silver Sparrow's incredulity transmuted into fury. "You should have stayed put," she yelled. "You're going to break your damn neck. There's nothing you can do from the back of that horse!" She snapped Persimmon's reins for emphasis. The horse fought to move faster as the wagon jounced dangerously behind her.

Fern stretched forward and pressed her nose against Bucket's neck, delirious with pain and anger and something like madness. "Run her off the fucking road, Bucket!"

But Bucket was a smart horse.

Ahead of them another streamlet approached, wider than the one they'd just passed. Boggier.

Bucket increased his speed, then angled in front of Persimmon as the ribbon of water drew ever closer. Fern glanced back over her shoulder as Staysha tried to steer her wagon out from behind him, but Bucket matched her move, obscuring her view.

Then he slowed down, and Persimmon had no choice but to do the same.

The bigger horse trotted through the muddy stream in sloshes of earth and water and Persimmon followed, then foundered to a halt as the wagon's wheels sank into the silty stream bottom.

"Good horse!" cried Fern, as Bucket pranced in a wide curve and returned to stare balefully at Staysha, apoplectic on the buckboard of her wagon, angrily snapping the reins and urging Persimmon forward.

This time, there was nobody to help push.

Persimmon snorted and reared, then strained with all her might, dragging the wagon forward another few feet, until the front right wheel dipped into a hidden hole. The entire wagon canted sideways, and Fern heard a terrific crack as the front axle broke.

Staysha squawked and spilled overboard to splash into the water and mud of the stream. Her lute case tumbled end over end after her until it popped open in the mire with a muffled *BONG*. Water filled the case around the exposed lute, and it began to sink.

At Fern's urging, Bucket approached, standing shin deep in the current.

"You're not going anywhere, now," she said.

Staysha struggled to her feet, her burgundy doublet and trousers caked in mud, black hair escaping her jeweled clip in a wild tangle. Baring her teeth, she drew the belt knife at her waist.

"We can take her," whispered Breadlee.

"Um," said Fern, as her guts filled with ice. "I actually hadn't thought this far ahead."

The wagon rocked on its remaining wheels as Zyll battered against its walls like a caged tornado.

Staysha began to forge through the stream toward her and Fern squeaked and scrambled down Bucket's opposite side, dropping into the water and just managing to maintain her footing. She drew Breadlee and stared at him blankly, then glanced up at the dwarf from under Bucket's belly.

"Remember when you said you'd never stabbed anybody before? That's an oversight we can fix now," said Breadlee cheerfully.

"I don't want to fix that oversight!"

"Good," said Staysha, moving to circle the horse. "Because I don't mind making this *my* first time. What do you think you're going to do with a breadknife, anyway?"

"*Bread*knife?" cried the knife. Then to Fern in a low voice, "Remember the torch? You got this, I know it."

Fern blinked as the chill water dragged at her cloak and numbed her toes.

Then she dashed forward, underneath Bucket, directly toward the bard.

Staysha's mouth opened in an O of surprise as she raised her belt knife to defend herself. Fern gave an inarticulate cry and slashed with Breadlee, cleaving the blade of the dwarf's weapon off neatly above the hilt.

"That's *Bridgewrecker* to you!" bellowed Breadlee.

The shard of metal pinwheeled off into the shallows.

"*Now* you can stab her!" finished the Elder Blade.

But Fern didn't, staring in frank disbelief as the Silver Sparrow staggered backward, dropping the useless hilt of her knife and casting about for another weapon.

The dwarf moaned when she saw her waterlogged lute but seized it by the neck and came at Fern again, brandishing it dripping over her head like a misshapen axe.

"Now!" shouted Breadlee, and Fern slashed a second time. A sharp, discordant twang erupted from the neck of the lute as the Elder Blade sliced it, too, in twain, leaving Staysha holding half of a ruined instrument and wearing a look of befuddlement.

"You . . . you . . ." stammered the dwarf.

Fern tackled her, and they both went down in the stream.

Her red cloak tangled around them both, sopping and heavy. She lost her hold on Breadlee as Staysha battered at her side with a fist. Suddenly Fern had a mouthful of water and she was choking, then she was above Staysha, staring at the dwarf's face where it grimaced at her from beneath the surface.

The bard bashed her again in the ribs, and Fern fell to her side. Their positions reversed again in a smear of light and nausea. She held her breath and gazed up through silvery ripples at the Sparrow's distorted face as the woman scrabbled for the bookseller's neck. Staysha found purchase and squeezed, bearing down with all her might as Fern tried fruitlessly to pry the fingers away.

Oh fuck, this is where I drown, and Viv is never going to know what happened to me, and Potroast is going to think I forgot him. Neither of them will ever forgive me. And this bitch will probably write a fucking song about it.

Staysha's face suddenly disappeared, as did the hands around Fern's neck.

She gasped and inhaled a huge glug of snowmelt.

Then she was yanked from the stream and hauled into the grass, spitting water as somebody pounded her on the back.

She blinked away mud and silt and stared up into Astryx's face, which instantly broke into an expression of exhausted relief.

"There you are, little squire."

"Sounds . . . too . . . cute," mumbled Fern.

⁓

"You can't leave me here," said Staysha.

The Silver Sparrow sat on the shore with her forearms on her knees, soaked through and muddy, glaring at them all with burning green eyes. Her jeweled hair clip was lost in the stream, along with the remains of her lute.

"We could let Zyll have her way with you, instead," replied Fern, cleaning mud from Breadlee with a sodden corner of her cloak.

It had taken her several minutes of searching to locate him in the stream, but he'd gurgled helpfully to get her attention until she spied the cold flash of silver through the running water.

"*Zu luffa dra gashmo*," hissed Zyll, snapping her teeth. She crouched atop the wrecked wagon, studying Staysha like a raptor eyeing a rodent.

"That *would* make it hard to sit down," agreed Fern.

Staysha gave the goblin a sullen and wary frown.

Astryx finished unhitching a miserable Persimmon from her traces and led her carefully over to stake her beside Bucket.

"We'll take Persimmon," said Astryx, looming over the bard. "And leave you your things. I'm sure someone will be along. Otherwise, you might have a long walk ahead of you."

Sneering, the bard retorted, "Go on. But expect everyone to know that Astryx One-Ear stole a poor woman's horse and left her to die. How's that sound for an immortal legacy?"

"To be honest," said Astryx, already turning to leave, "I've never paid much attention to that sort of thing. The songs are never very accurate."

"Plus, you'd have to have a lute," observed Breadlee.

Fern approached Staysha, dripping and cold. She didn't so much as twitch the knife in her hand, but still, trepidation crept into the dwarf's expression at something in Fern's gaze.

"Hey," said Fern, "I couldn't help but overhear you working on your lyrics back before you clobbered me in the face, and I just thought you should know that 'avenge' and 'scavenge' don't rhyme, you feculent sack of shitweasels."

Somebody snorted laughter that was quickly stifled, and Fern saw Astryx's shoulders shaking slightly as she strode toward the horses.

"I'll accept that as a stabbing," said Breadlee. "That's one! Onward and upward!"

37

"I'm thinking *Bardsbane* might be a good name. It's maybe a little more subtle than Bridgewrecker, but . . . bane. *Bane*." Breadlee's voice was wistful. "Do you think I could have two titles?"

"I'll just point out that bards might not look kindly on it," said Fern. "I mean, if you want your legend to spread."

"You make a fair point, but also, I *do* hate music. I'm conflicted."

"It's not the role of the blade to be the *subject* of the tales— merely the instrument of their creation," declared Nigel. Astryx had given him a bare inch of steel so that he could say his piece about the Staysha affair, which had taken a solid half hour.

While he'd rambled, Fern had been thinking about the many pages it would take to cover the last few days. An idea was forming in the back of her mind.

She rode on Persimmon with Zyll napping against her back. Since the pony had no saddle, Astryx led her by halter and knotted lead from astride Bucket. Persimmon was a well-behaved mare and seemed relieved that nothing interesting was happening anymore, placidly clopping beside the larger horse.

Night had stolen across the prairie, but a waxing moon glowed high on the rumpled black velvet of the sky like a clipped silver coin. Grassy hillocks and streams gleamed beneath it, preternaturally bright. Fall crickets trilled endlessly in unearthly chorus.

Astryx had insisted they ride farther after nightfall so that there'd be no chance of an unexpected visit from Staysha on foot while they slept.

Neither of them had brought up the argument that sparked the day's events. In fact, both were at great pains to pretend nothing had happened. To Fern, it felt like they were balancing a rotten egg on a plate. Nobody wanted to be the one to let it roll off and break.

Instead, Fern completed her abridged narration of *Ten Links in the Chain*. There wasn't much left to tell.

"'. . . and with a last look at the port all in flames, Madger sailed mournfully into the west, less a sword hand and the finest partner she'd ever known.'"

Cricket-song joined the hoofbeats to fill the space left behind by her narration.

"It was a good story," said Astryx after several moments, with great solemnity. "Thank you."

Fern thought that would be it for the evening, then. She was certainly all talked out.

Astryx wasn't, though.

"Your old friend, Viv. When you told us the tale of meeting her in Murk, and everything that happened after, you said she saved you in more than one way. What was the other way?"

The question was so unexpected that Fern had no defense and could only answer immediately. "She made me see what it was that I cared about. The thing I forgot when I was only going through the motions."

"Viv sounds like a worthy friend." Astryx nodded, then asked with gentle interest, "What was the thing you forgot?"

In recent weeks, Fern had thought about this more than was healthy, so the answer was easy. "That books are a weapon against loneliness. Putting them in the right hands lets people see one another. It makes us . . . *better* to one another. I think that's a worthy thing to do."

"But." It wasn't a question.

"But. That's not enough for me anymore, and I don't know why. I still *believe* it. Still *know* it. But I'm not content with it.

Which is apparently why I'm in the middle of nowhere, atop a pony I can't ride, with a goblin on my back, explaining this to the most famous person I've ever met. Still . . ."

The Oathmaiden offered her a wordless glance that prompted for more.

"I wonder if I misjudged what was happening all those years ago," said Fern, sighing. "Maybe it wasn't a fix. Maybe it was just a small piece of something bigger, and I fooled myself into believing it was the whole thing. Or maybe that sort of realization is like food. It fills you for a while, but eventually, you have to eat again."

"Do you feel hungry now?" asked Astryx. She fingered her ruined ear again.

Fern reached for what would surely be an obvious answer, except she couldn't find it. "I . . . don't know."

Her stomach growled, loudly and inconveniently.

"Or I can't tell over the sound of myself."

―――

"Give me your socks," said Fern.

Astryx stared at her, arrested in the act of stripping the soggy woolen things from her pale and wrinkled toes. "There aren't any stones to dry them on," she said.

"Come on, toss them over."

They had finally stopped between the two largest swells of earth they'd come across on the prairie, which formed a shallow bowl. It wasn't much, but it kept the meager fire Fern had built of ox pats from whipping around too badly.

Astryx wadded the socks together and lobbed them, her expression bemused. Fern snagged them out of the air, unrolling them again. She'd cut a pair of sturdy bulrush stems at a marshy spot over the hill, and now she planted each at an angle in the soft earth near the fire. She topped them with socks and dug them deep to stabilize them.

The wet wool began to steam almost at once.

"Dry socks," declared Fern, with a small smile. "You said they were the only thing that stayed exciting after ten centuries."

"I may have exaggerated slightly," allowed Astryx, with an echo of Fern's amusement. "But not by much." A regal nod. "Thank you, Li— . . . Squire."

Fern could still sense the rotten egg on the plate, but they were both doing their best not to tip it off the edge.

Zyll made a sound of disgust and stuck out her pointed tongue. Seated with her coat rucked up to her knobby green knees, she wiggled her toes close to the heat of the flames. "Socks-es is like hat-lings on horseys." The bracelet on her wrist winked in the flickering light.

The Oathmaiden extended her own pruned toes toward the fire and flexed them. "We should be in Amberlin in another three days."

"That soon," said Fern. It wasn't really a question.

Astryx cleared her throat. "I wanted to say. You were very impressive, with Staysha and the wagon."

"Yeah, we really were, weren't we?" chirped Breadlee, extra loudly.

Everyone pretended he hadn't said anything.

"Oh," replied Fern. "Um. Thanks." She fidgeted with one of the stems holding the socks, for no reason whatsoever.

"I have . . . liked having you along. Surprisingly."

Fern gave her a look.

"I mean that *I'm* surprised. Not that it's surprising that someone would like to have your company."

"Okay," said Fern, carefully.

"Afterward," said Astryx, as though stepping delicately from stone to stone, "if you find you're still . . . hungry. Perhaps you'd like to continue onward. With me."

Fern was seized by several different emotions at once—gratification, relief, fear . . . Excitement and trepidation in equal measure. And all with the sour aftertaste of her anger from earlier in the day. In other words, a real fucking mess.

"Afterward?" she said, more archly than she'd intended.

Astryx glanced at Zyll, who stared back at her with that savage smile and what Fern had no doubt was absolute comprehension.

To her credit, the elf maintained eye contact as she said, "After the bounty is delivered."

And the rotten egg rolled off the plate.

"Why do we have to do this?" demanded Fern.

Astryx frowned. "I've already told you, I—"

"Yeah, yeah. You keep your covenants, you *do what must be done*," said Fern, unable to keep the exasperation from her voice. "That's shit. That's a *slogan*. What would it cost you to forget all that *just* this once? What changes?"

"*Everything* changes! My life is built on principle because it has to be. It's the only thing that keeps it stable after all these years. Every chip in that foundation leads to another, and another, and soon it's cracked in two, and everything falls down around you." The elf was trying hard to keep the heat from her voice and only just succeeding. "People come and go. Moments like *this* come and go. Live to five hundred, and then you'll understand."

Fern leaned forward over her crossed knees and planted her paws on the ground. "Bullshit. We're not Tarimites. There's no mad god that's going to descend and consume the world if your principles get a little bent for a good reason."

"And the alternative is what? Tossing everything aside because I don't feel perfectly fulfilled at every moment? How is that working for you?"

The fire suddenly seemed overwarm.

"I guess well enough that you want me to stick around," retorted Fern.

They gazed balefully at one another across the fire as the air between them distorted with the heat.

Zyll abruptly stood, letting her pocket-coat fall back to cover her shins and interrupting their staring match.

She glanced between them, mouth closed, annoyance glittering in her crimson eyes.

"*Tua shunkata*," she declared, then marched away from the fire.

Before Astryx could ask, Fern sighed and explained, "She said we're both fuckheads."

Later, as she lay with her back to the fire and her eyes open, bruised and aching from Staysha's battering, Fern realized she hadn't answered Astryx's question.

She wondered what the answer would have been.

38

The last leagues of the prairie were characterized by regretful quiet. Words were exchanged, but precious few, and those mostly practical.

As they drew closer to Amberlin, the gentle swells of the grasslands grew in amplitude, the mountains to the north melted away, and bastion oak began to appear, first in lonely ones and twos, then in copses, and finally conservative stretches of forest. Early autumn zealously burnished their leaves.

Other, larger roads materialized to join and widen their own, and they saw and passed their first fellow travelers since leaving the monastery. Most seemed to be farmers or merchants, but several fine coaches made an appearance as well. Astryx awkwardly asked Fern to loan her cloak to Zyll, which she did without complaint. The goblin didn't protest, either, and kept the red hood up to shade her face.

The terrain rose gently over several hours into the first blush of dusk, increasingly wooded, until the trees drew away from the now wider and more trafficked road. Stone markers began to crop up at regular intervals beside the way. Little cottages and farms dotted the distance when the view was unobstructed.

When the slope began to descend again, Amberlin itself became visible in the violet haze of the horizon, a vast sprawl of white stone, red slate, and glinting copper, sprinkled with sparks of torchlight, that sprouted a thousand twists of chimney smoke. Satellite villages ringed it at irregular distances, all webbed together with a network of roadways, framing a patchwork of green-and-gold vineyards between. A white road broader than all the rest ran north-south between Amberlin and their own vantage point, meeting a spur of the city that extended like a finger to touch it.

A gorgeous twilight vista, framed by delicate shreds of cloud.

Fern couldn't appreciate it in the slightest.

Now their imminent arrival was a painful inevitability, flanked by remorse on either side.

Why did I have to spoil it so close to the end? Fern thought, increasingly morose as she watched a haycart trundle past on their left.

I ruined everything in Thune when it was all going perfectly fine, and here I am, doing the same again, but in a whole new way. Viv and Astryx should get together and compare notes. "That Fern! *Such a genius for fucking up a perfectly good thing at the last minute!*" She rolled her eyes and stared grimly ahead. *If I'd kept my stupid mouth shut, then we'd be having a nice conversation right now. Gods, a legendary adventurer* wanted *me to stick around and keep her company. I've spent my whole life dreaming of being inside the stories I read, and now I actually* have *the opportunity, and I can't even be bothered to answer the question.*

Although Fern had to admit to herself that even if she hadn't run them off the road into the ditch of another argument, she still wasn't positive what her answer might have been, and now it was difficult to untangle from the brambles of everything else around it.

"Crap."

Astryx turned to look at her with a question on her face.

Fern realized she hadn't kept that to herself. "Oh. Nothing. Sorry. Just . . . thinking out loud, I guess."

She considered a real apology but couldn't seem to put her paws on the right words. She experienced a sudden, vivid recollection of standing drunk in the street, staring at the candlelit windows of Legends & Lattes, trying to muster up the courage to make good on her promise to Cal by confronting Viv . . . and then failing utterly.

Potential conversations played out in her mind, halting, awkward, and with Astryx falling back to an unassailable position of literal centuries of experience.

So, it was surprising when the elf was the one to speak.

"This isn't how I imagined the end of the journey," she said in a thin voice, gazing toward Amberlin and rocking gently from side to side with Bucket's endless rolling motion. She cleared her throat. "I'm sorry for the words I said last night. And . . . earlier. They were unkind."

Fern sighed. "Truthfully, you were pretty restrained. Mine's the tongue that got away."

"No. I'd like to finish, please. I . . . I *shamed* you. A thimbleful of disdain poisons the entire well. It must never find its way into a friendship. It's been a long time since I've had one, but I remember that much." She drew both horses to a halt and turned in her saddle to find Fern's eyes. "And I would like to keep this one, even if we go our separate ways."

The sincerity in her voice and the intensity of her gaze hooked something in Fern's chest and unexpected tears threatened.

They became all but inevitable when Astryx dismounted and approached Persimmon to extend both hands palm up in a distressingly formal way.

"Stop that," whispered Fern.

Astryx ignored her, ghostlight eyes arresting. "I beg your forgiveness for the words I said. I beg your patience for the ways I fail. I do not expect it, but crave and strive for your regard."

"Gods-dammit," replied Fern, her voice gummy with tears. "I don't know how this works. Do I put my paws in yours?" She didn't wait for an answer and did it anyway.

Astryx's fingers were dry and warm beneath her own.

"Okay," said Fern, sniffing.

"I have not forgotten anything you said," murmured the Oathmaiden. "I will give your words the consideration they are due."

Fern didn't know which words she meant, because she'd said

a lot of them, but she didn't trust her voice enough to ask the elf to clarify.

Instead, she nodded, intensely aware that this was the part where she should apologize in return.

But Astryx dropped her hands away. "Nothing else need be said for now." Which was both awful and a relief at the same time.

The elf remounted, and they continued down the hill.

Uncomfortably aware that Zyll had been observing all this from behind her, Fern twisted to look back as they got under way. She caught the gleam of the goblin's eyes in the shadows of the red hood.

Zyll offered no comment.

Dear Viv,

This journey is almost at an end. It feels like I'm approaching a test that I've already failed several times, and have probably already failed again without knowing it yet. I feel a dreadful anticipation, like unbelievable possibilities lie ahead, if only I say the precise magic word required—but I don't trust myself to recognize it.

On the brighter side, I got into the first brawl of my life. Hells, I even swung a blade, although it was a little one. I also might have actually won, sort of. Maybe technically? I survived, anyway. Ha! You took up reading, and I took up armed combat. How about that?

This is going to take some explaining, though, and also some awkward admissions and the recounting of some conversations that I'm not sure paint me in a very good light.

Anyway, you remember Staysha, that bard I wrote about? Well . . .

It was their last camp before they'd reach proper civilization.

Fern stared at the four freshly written pages in her paws, then at the sleeping forms of Astryx and Zyll. As she opened the satchel—now positively stuffed with paper—to add the latest to her chronicle, she realized that for the first time, she hadn't told Viv how sorry she was.

39

As they approached the first, rather large, outlying village on the road to Amberlin, the morning had a crisp autumnal bite to it, and a low-lying fog seemed to burn off in retreat from their arrival. Traffic on the road swelled and began to evince an unexpectedly festive atmosphere. Fern spied wagons of kegs, and farmers in feast-day finery. Eager children tugged at parents, their faces scrubbed clean.

She caught the sounds of a fiddle and drums on the air. Crimson banners and unlit lanterns alternated across lines strung between roof peaks.

"Looks like a party!" observed Breadlee. "Shame about the noise."

"The grape harvest is over," said Astryx. "We've arrived in the middle of the Summerdusk festival." She checked to make sure Zyll's hood was drawn low enough to obscure her.

Although, maybe Astryx should have been the one to wear a cloak, since she was easily the most recognizable person for leagues in any direction. She drew plenty of glances from passersby, more than a few of whom stopped dead to watch her with open mouths. The Oathmaiden appeared practiced at ignoring the murmurs of onlookers and carried on, carefully weaving Bucket and Persimmon through the foot traffic.

Booths lined the main thoroughfare, selling jarred honey, cured meats, handicrafts, small kegs of wine and spirits, breads, spices, confections, crates of vegetables, handmade toys, and gods knew what else. Bunting decorated exposed eaves, ribbons fluttered from booth-poles, minstrels played on a temporary stage, and excited chatter swelled to a low rumble.

"It's foolish for us to go through," said Astryx, scratching at her ear. "Too many people, too much attention so close to Amberlin when we've no need. We'll circle around to the other side. It won't cost us much time."

"Wait. Would you mind if I met you there? At the other end?" Fern eyed the crates packed with ranks of green wine bottles and the neighboring tables piled with wheels of aged cheese. Since Astryx's earnest apology, the idea of some sort of peace offering had been brewing. This was probably the last, best opportunity she'd have to find anything resembling a gift. "I've got an errand I want to take care of. I promise, I won't be long."

Astryx followed her gaze and raised a brow. She seemed about to protest, but nodded instead. "We'll find you there."

Fern slithered off Persimmon and kept her feet under her as she landed, glancing up at Zyll, who blinked back.

"*Zu-kenda*," said the goblin, solemnly.

Fern didn't know what that meant, so it wasn't profane, but she also thought Zyll had said it before. She couldn't remember when, though.

"Thanks!" she called to Astryx as the elf handed down her satchel. Then she trotted into the village toward the stalls. When she looked back, they and the horses were nearly out of sight, heading southeast.

She had a sudden, wild premonition of emerging on the other side to find herself alone on the road, Astryx and Zyll long gone. She banished the thought almost as soon as it arrived.

Mostly.

Forging through the throng, Fern rediscovered what it was like for your eyes to be at navel height in a crowd. It was easy to get disoriented without a clear view of your destination except what you could snatch around moving bodies.

Grumbling to herself, she wove between legs, trying to keep

her tail out from underfoot. At last, she arrived at the spirit-seller's stall, where a generously proportioned tapenti woman was dickering with a customer over a case of wax-sealed liquor in little blue bottles. Fern moved to get in line, but drew up short when something snagged her gaze in the crowd.

Tartan. There, and gone.

Furrowing her brow, she forgot all about the spirits and struggled in the direction of the flash of color.

"Watch it!" she yelped as a dwarf backed into her and nearly knocked her sprawling.

She didn't even hear his apology as her gaze fell on the slash of tartan fabric again, and she did her best to dash toward it.

Squeezing past a pair of hips, she came out gasping behind a smoke-furred rattkin in a sash that she'd recognize anywhere. He wasn't wearing his belt dagger. With his back to her, he was glancing around as though looking for someone.

"Quillin?" she said.

He whirled, eyes wide. *"Fern?"*

The look of shock and delight on his face melted into something else almost immediately. Fear? *Guilt?*

He seized her forearm, bringing his face close. "Where are the others? The goblin?" he hissed.

"What? She's—"

Fern had never mentioned Zyll to Quillin. Not once.

She tried to shrug off his grip, already backing away.

"Fern, you have to listen to me. Are they here? You have to—"

Her back struck something solid.

"Shit," breathed Quillin, his shoulders slumping.

The dread that had been steadily building over-spilled its dam as Fern half turned and looked up into Tullah's flinty gaze.

The orc's many braids framed her face in dark curtains as she stared at Fern with a half smile.

"Yeah," said Tullah. "This should work just fine."

Tullah marched Fern through the streets with a hand on the back of her neck. She didn't dare call out. She could feel the spine-snapping strength of those fingers as they rested in her fur. Marv stayed beside them, his narrow face alert for trouble.

Kell the orc joined them just as Fern was steered into an alley. She couldn't move her head to see, but she could hear the patter of Quillin's paws as he trotted in Tullah's wake.

At a turn in the alley, Kell peeled off to lean casually against a plastered wall and keep an eye on the busy street while the rest of them moved out of public view.

The other member of their party, the archer, was nowhere to be seen.

Tullah spun Fern and pressed her against stone. In one hand she loosely held a plain, but extremely sharp-looking knife. Quillin was indeed behind her, head down and fidgeting with his belt beside Marv.

"You fucker," said Fern, her face hot. The rattkin didn't meet her eyes.

Tullah dropped to her haunches and seemed surprised at where Fern's ire was directed. With a glance at Quillin, she chuckled. "Huh. Well, if this goes well, you two can work it out later. Here, check this over, Marv." She tugged the satchel from Fern's shoulder and tossed it to him.

After rifling through it, he shook his head. "Nothing but a bunch of paper and an old book. A few silvers."

"That's fine, then. Here."

Fern was shocked when Tullah handed the satchel back to her, and it must have shown on her face.

"I'm not here to rob you. Hells, I want your *help*." She tried for a smile, unsuccessfully.

"My help," Fern muttered. She slung the satchel over her shoulder again, glaring at Quillin. "You were with them the whole time? You . . . you . . ." Fern was so furious, she couldn't find a curse sufficient to the moment.

"I wasn't!" he cried, glancing at her, and then away, which didn't seem particularly forthright.

"Him? Of course not," scoffed Tullah. "I had a feeling hauling him along was the right move, and he sure squeaked when we pinched him in the right places. Hells, it was easy. You can give him trouble about it later, if you're both still breathing."

Fern remembered that while she hadn't mentioned Zyll, she *had* mentioned their destination. She also recalled seeing Tullah when they'd been out walking the muddy streets of Turnbuckle. The sequence of events after the wrecking of the bridge seemed suddenly obvious.

Tullah misjudged the expression on Fern's face. "Young love's a bastard, isn't it?"

"Fuck you," said Fern. "I'm older than you, anyway."

Tullah threw back her head and laughed. "I respect that. Good for you."

Then she sobered.

"Let's keep this simple." She gestured toward Fern's belly with her knife. "You're going to put that shit of a goblin into my hands. And then I'm going to let you go. They're both here, somewhere, yeah? The Oathmaiden, too? You're planning to meet them later?"

Fern said nothing. Her eyes burned, and her breakfast tried to find an expedient exit.

"Think this through. You're bringing her in for a bounty, right? Hells, you're about to be shut of her anyway. Worst case, you lose your share of the take, but under the circumstances, that sounds pretty damn cheap."

Fern's paws shook at her sides. She wished she had her cloak, and Breadlee's comforting weight in the pocket.

A pause as Tullah studied Fern's face. "You *are* getting a share, aren't you?"

Fern blinked. The thought of collecting any of the bounty had never once occurred to her, and didn't seem important now.

"Wow," said Tullah. "Not even a piece of the action? What the hells are you even doing here? That should make this even easier, though. And, let's be realistic. If *he* talked"—she flipped the tip of her knife toward Quillin—"there's no way *you* won't. It's just down to how many inches shorter you want that tail of yours to be. You've got nothing but that left to lose."

"But Zyll does," whispered Fern, voice quivering.

"Yes," said Tullah. "Yes, she does."

"What did she ever do to you?"

"Look, Fern—pardon me for using your name, but after hearing about you from Quillin here, it feels like we practically know each other. Have you ever built anything? Poured your years and your blood and your coin into it, *willed* it to grow?"

Fern stared Tullah square in the eye. "Yes."

"Mm. Yeah, I guess he told me about your little bookstore. I think he was doing his best to convince us you wouldn't be a threat. Nice of him, really.

"Well, I built something, too, Fern. An army, or damn near one. But more important than that, I built a *reputation*. That's what everything balanced on—a story that people believe. You, of all people, should be able to appreciate the power of a story. It was the foundation for *everything*."

Then she reached out with her free hand and seized Fern's tail.

"And Zyll fucking obliterated it."

In the end, sadly, Fern wasn't as brave as everyone imagines they can be, but privately knows they are not.

40

After muttering something in Kell's ear, whereupon the sturdy orc vanished into the crowd, Tullah got them moving again, with her knife held hidden from any idle glances. They skirted the throng, hugging the side of the main street and heading toward the eastern perimeter of the village.

Quillin walked beside Fern, looking almost as miserable as she felt. She was finding it hard to think ill of the rattkin when she herself had so readily blabbed under threat of pain. Did she expect something more from him?

Fern fervently prayed to all the Eight that Astryx had noticed she'd been gone too long and was alert for trouble.

"I'm so sorry," muttered Quillin. "I swear, even if I'd known about the goblin back in Turnbuckle, I never would've . . . Not that you'll ever believe me. I understand why you disappeared, though."

"It doesn't matter now," replied Fern in a near whisper. A glance at Tullah revealed that while she could certainly hear their conversation, she didn't appear to care. The orc strode casually, easily, and didn't bother to look down at them.

"It *does*," insisted Quillin, soft and fierce.

They both fell silent as Kell emerged at the mouth of another alley and motioned them in his direction.

Behind him waited the black-clad stone-fey archer, her bow nowhere in evidence. Kell nodded at Tullah, handing her an axe and Marv a shortblade. They slipped them into their belts to match the mace hanging at his.

After a hushed conference, the archer vanished again.

They attracted a few suspicious glances, but ignored them and moved with greater speed, turning down side streets and charting a circuitous route. Marv and Kell drifted away but stayed in sight, scanning every intersection and roofline.

Fern's feet were like lumps of lead on the ends of her legs, her breath hollow in her ears. She saw several Gatewardens idling in the crowd, but didn't dare signal to them.

Any moment now, she thought, *I should run. Any moment. Dash away, surprise her. Warn Astryx.*

But she never did. Terror, and the presence of the knife a few inches from her face kept her carrying meekly onward.

Then the buildings thinned, replaced with gardens and low stone fences as they passed out of the village, and an unmown field of autumn gold came into view. Vineyards filled the leagues beyond, between them and the sprawl of Amberlin.

Traffic was sparse, with only a few folk heading home from the festivities still in full swing behind them.

Just south of the path, a windmill rose over the dead grass, tattered canvas clinging to its blades.

In front of it, clearly visible from the road, Nigel's starburst hilt and about a foot of steel stood tall above the rustling seed-heads.

There was no sign of Astryx, Zyll, or the horses. Fern had no idea what was going on, but some intention was plain. She rejoiced inwardly.

"I should be disappointed," muttered Tullah. "But I'm not, really. I never liked doing things the easy way. Come on, you two."

She nudged Fern to get her and Quillin moving again, directly toward the longsword in the field. The blades of the windmill creaked mournfully, rocking slightly on their axle.

"My lady, I see them," bellowed Nigel, startling everyone. Fern felt Tullah twitch and savored a moment of grim satisfaction. In lower tones, but no less commanding, he called, "Approach no further. Set free our companion, and you may go on your way."

"I don't think so," hollered Tullah, not slowing. "Behind the windmill, eh, Oathmaiden? That's a clever way to set a lookout." She squinted over her shoulder toward the village. Fern turned to follow her gaze, and at first saw nothing . . . then a black shadow on a rooftop in the lee of a chimney.

The archer.

"Leaves you unarmed, though," continued Tullah. She quietly ordered Marv, "Go. Grab the sword."

The red-haired man nodded once and began to jog toward the upright Elder Blade, looking left and right for any sign of an ambush.

Fern held her breath as he closed in, expecting . . . she didn't know what.

When the moment arrived, she still gasped.

As Marv came within a few strides of Nigel, already stretching out his hand, the grass on the far side stirred. Silver hair and a single ear breached the golden surface as Astryx pushed herself up and tore into a dead sprint. She reached the starburst hilt an instant before Marv, grasping it with her left hand and ripping Nigel from the earth in a spray of grass and dirt.

Marv squawked, grabbing for the shortsword at his waist, but the Oathmaiden let her momentum flow into an upward sweep of Nigel's pommel, clubbing the man in the skull. Temple bloodied, he dropped bonelessly in a heap, disappearing into the grass.

Astryx stooped quickly and seized him by the collar, dragging his unconscious head up beside her hip and laying Nigel across his chest. "The archer. Call her down. If I see her again, Marv here will regret it."

Fern fully expected an arrow to sprout in Marv's chest, or for Tullah to laugh and tell her to go ahead. That's certainly what would have happened in any number of adventure stories she'd read. The henchmen were *always* expendable.

Instead, Tullah gestured at the archer with a move-it-back motion. The woman melted away from the rooftop.

"So, you've got one of mine, and I've got one of yours," said Tullah. "Where's Zyll?"

"She tends to disappear," replied Astryx coolly. "Hard to keep track of, to be honest."

Tullah started pushing them forward again, pulling her axe from her belt. "Now what? I've got plenty of patience, and I don't plan to leave without the little demon."

"That's close enough," said Astryx. "Now we don't have to shout. But I imagine if we wait much longer, we're going to draw a crowd."

The orc stopped and studied her. "I notice you're using your left hand now. Something wrong with the right?" She shrugged. "We both know who won the last time we met, and you look worse off than before. I like my odds. Still, I'll suggest a trade. Let Marv be, and hand over the goblin. These two go free. We head our separate ways. You're out a bounty, but I guarantee, my need's greater. What do you say?"

"I'll happily exchange this one for my friend," said Astryx. "But as you can see, I don't have a goblin to barter."

Astryx wasn't wrong about drawing a crowd. Already, Fern saw that a few villagers had stopped on the road and were pointing. This wasn't lost on Tullah, who squeezed the haft of her axe until it creaked.

"I hate a fucking impasse," she growled. "But they always break, in the end."

And as though her words were prophetic, at that instant, it did.

"Hey!" cried Kell, pointing with his mace at the stone wall running alongside the field.

Zyll was sprinting across the top with Fern's red cloak billowing out behind her. Even as Fern caught sight of her, Zyll leapt spread-eagled from the fence and plunged into the grass, which rippled like water with her passage as she made a beeline for Tullah, pigtails flying.

"Finally," breathed the orc, widening her stance.

Quillin seized Fern's arm and yanked. She stumbled as he

pulled her after him, darting behind Kell, who noticed and began to turn. Tullah registered none of it, focused fully on the approaching goblin, her teeth bared and her axe waiting.

Then everything happened very fast.

Zyll growled in her throat, still barreling toward Tullah.

Quillin drove his shoulder into Kell's left calf, then bit savagely into the back of his knee. Kell shouted, and Fern sprang aside before he could crush her with his fall. She tripped and landed on her ass, scrabbling through the grass as the man hit the ground, hard.

With a triumphant grin, Tullah sliced her axe down and across in a savage cut to meet the place where Zyll would be—

—and howled in fury as Nigel's steel met the axeblade and drove it sidelong. She found herself face-to-face with Astryx, whose ghostlight eyes blazed into her own.

Zyll made a sharp left and skittered away from Tullah's thwarted attack. As she did, the clasp of Fern's red cloak came undone, and the red fabric billowed up and away from her, snagging on Astryx's hip and threatening to foul her step.

"Eventually," growled Tullah, turning her attention fully to the Oathmaiden, ". . . *every* legend has to end."

Kell moaned in the grass, one hand clapped to his wounded knee as he tried to rise, flailing with his mace at Quillin, who kicked at his exposed face with every opportunity.

Tullah hacked at Astryx in a frenzied explosion of motion. The elf backed away, wielding Nigel left-handed and barely turning aside the hail of blows.

Then Tullah let her axehead drop and punched Astryx directly in her wounded shoulder with a lightning-fast left cross.

The elf screamed and fell back, staggering unsteadily, tangled in Fern's cloak.

"I thought so," muttered the orc.

Astryx grunted with pain as she yanked the cloak from around her leg. She twirled it over her right arm and fist, eyes watering.

"Not much of a shield," observed Tullah, advancing relentlessly. "Let's get this over with."

She raised her axe and brought it down hard, not bothering to look for an opening. Every bone-jarring chop hammered Nigel's steel lower. Astryx's left arm quivered. With so much damage accumulated from recent battles, she couldn't muster the strength or vigor for a counterattack.

The Oathmaiden's eyes glimmered with the possibility of her own death as her defense was whittled away with each merciless stroke.

Nigel moaned something inarticulate, crying out at every impact.

Then Fern stared at the cloak on Astryx's arm, and something slotted into place in her mind.

"Astryx!" she cried. "The pocket!"

The Oathmaiden's face clouded for a moment before her eyes widened in sudden understanding.

Tullah's next stroke knocked Nigel from the elf's grasp and skinned along the outside of her upper arm, spitting blood across the dead grass.

Astryx let the impact spin her, bringing her right arm around and driving her cloak-wrapped fist against Tullah's belly with a meaty slap.

The orc grunted, eyes flying wide.

"Whu—" she choked through a mouthful of blood that stippled Astryx's face. Her brow creased in slow confusion.

Astryx raised her other hand and placed it open-palmed against the orc's chest. She pressed gently.

Tullah lurched backward, revealing Breadlee's bloody Elder steel where it had punctured fabric, armor, and flesh, and driven deep into the orc's gut.

Sagging to her knees, Tullah let her axe tumble from a nerveless grip and brought the hand dreamily to her belly, then up in front of her face. She marveled at the sticky crimson on her fingers.

Her eyelids flickered as she gazed past her trembling hand and Astryx, who was down on her knees and barely supporting herself with one arm. Zyll stood in the grass beyond, staring back solemnly.

"F-Fucker," gasped Tullah, and collapsed.

41

"Are you okay?" asked Fern, crouched next to Astryx and wincing at the ragged scrape running down the outside of the elf's arm. A dark stain slowly spread on her shoulder where Tullah had punched her. "Fuck, you look awful."

The Oathmaiden eased into a seated position, groaning as she did. Her smile was wan. "I appreciate your gentle understatement. I have felt . . . better." Coming from Astryx, that sounded to Fern a lot like "I am experiencing unendurable agony."

"Wow," said a hushed voice. "I mean, I imagined it a thousand times. I *knew* it would be amazing, but . . ."

They both looked to Breadlee where he had torn his way blood-slick through Fern's cloak.

"None of this is amazing," said Fern, with a frown.

"Did you not see what just happened? Bridgewrecker is a thing of the past, *that's* for sure."

She glanced over her shoulder at Tullah, unmoving in the grass. Only seconds ago, she'd been alive, vital, *deadly*. And now . . .

Fern felt sick, and an unexpected and profound sadness.

Beyond Tullah, Kell sat with a hand on the back of his knee and a look of dazed disbelief on his face.

"Let's worry about your new title later, maybe," Fern murmured.

The knife sheepishly conceded, "Okay, you make a solid point about the timing."

"My lady," whispered Nigel, from where he'd landed in the grass. "I have *failed* you. Shame chokes me from point to pommel.

I beg your forgiveness." His voice became strangled. "Perhaps I *should* make way for another."

Astryx gingerly unwound the cloak from her arm, withdrawing Breadlee.

"Well, I wasn't going to suggest it so soon, but . . ." the knife trailed off.

The Oathmaiden wiped him carefully on a trouser leg and held him point up before her face.

"Bradelys Tertius," she said, with sober dignity. "Your steel is true. You have my regard, and my gratitude."

He made a noise like a strangled squeal. Nigel gave the impression of holding his breath in dismay.

"But I think a better wielder has already found you." She flipped him around and offered him to Fern with one hand, the ruined cloak with the other.

Fern received them both solemnly.

"Whoof. I'm feeling a lot of things right now," mumbled Breadlee.

"Hey, I don't want to rush anyone, but there are Gatewardens on the way," said Quillin, cocking a thumb at the road. "That is, if you wanted to disappear."

Astryx followed Quillin's gaze to where three women wearing blue tunics with lanterns at their waists were detaching from the swelling group of spectators on the road.

She shook her head. "I don't think I can move that fast right now."

The elf stared at Fern for a long while as she considered something. She seemed to come to a decision.

Turning painfully, she found Zyll and beckoned. "Quickly, come here."

The goblin tilted her head, but drew nearer, her orange hair barely topping the grass.

Astryx reached out and delicately took the goblin's forearm, the one with the bracelet.

With her other hand she touched three points on the lattice of wire where the metal swirled in curlicues, murmuring something intricate under her breath.

The bracelet popped open and fell away.

"Go," said Astryx. "Now, before they arrive, and things become complicated."

For a long, breathless moment, Fern thought Zyll was going to stay.

Then the goblin vanished into the grass without another word or a backward glance.

Fern felt something splinter inside her.

She'd gotten what she wanted, but maybe Astryx was right, after all.

Maybe she *was* chronically dissatisfied.

Breadlee captured the feeling more precisely.

"I'm trying very hard not to be confused about how this is all working out."

~~

Things *did* become very complicated.

More Gatewardens arrived to assist the first three.

Astryx commanded both respect and the benefit of the doubt, but Tullah was, by the elf's own admission, dead by her hand, and Kell and Marv did their best to obscure the truth to their own benefit. Of the archer, there was no sign.

Fern sat quietly beside Quillin in the grass, staring at the bloody hole in her cloak. The only coherent thoughts she allowed herself concerned whether she'd be able to mend it and get the stains out, or if she'd have to find a new one. Her entire body felt like it was vibrating at high frequency.

Any musings on Zyll, or what would happen next, she drew back from as though they were aflame.

Quillin did his part to lend weight to Astryx's words, but still, they were all escorted back into the village to the Warden's garrison. Fern dimly wondered where Bucket and Persimmon were.

A physician was summoned to attend to their various wounds,

and more questions followed, although few were directed Fern's way. She remained mistily detached, until a freckled woman with a Gatewarden's badge snapped fingers under her snout.

"Are you with us? You've been very quiet."

"Hm? Oh. Sure," mumbled Fern.

"This one says you're a bookseller." She gestured at Quillin, who sat beside her on the bench. "Is that your trade, then?"

"I have no idea," replied Fern, honestly.

A frown. "Are you sure you weren't struck in the head? Still thinking straight?"

"Yes. No. I don't know."

"Well, you're free to go. No place to keep you anyway." Unspoken, but obvious, was the Warden's desire to be done with the whole affair and go home herself.

And so they found themselves in the street with nothing but a pointed suggestion to move on as soon as possible. Kell and Marv had been further detained, possibly only to prevent immediate bloodshed outside the garrison.

Fern felt adrift. Destinationless, literally. Amberlin had been their lodestone, and now it didn't matter at all.

Astryx, too, seemed disoriented, glancing blankly into the gathering dusk, her arm sheathed in fresh linen. The lost look in her eyes bruised Fern's heart.

Quillin cleared his throat. He extended a paw as though to clasp Fern's, but then reconsidered. "Well. I've got a long journey ahead of me. I feel like there are things I want to say, but I can't seem to find them, standing here in the middle of the road. Guess I'm too ashamed."

"No need," said Fern. She caught the paw he'd dropped and gave it a brief squeeze before releasing it. The motion brought a whiff of his scent to her nose.

Encouraged, he ventured, "Going to find someplace to stay the night before I find passage back west. The long route, if I can. With winter coming on, I don't fancy the mountains again." He glanced back and forth between Astryx and Fern.

"You're welcome, of course." It was clear that last was meant for Fern alone, though.

Resting a paw on the Oathmaiden's leg, Fern asked, "What now?"

The elf blinked and seemed to come back to herself. It took her a moment to find words. "We should get the horses, before someone makes off with them."

Not "I," but "we." Fern clung to that like salvation, however temporary it might be.

She glanced at her satchelful of letters, then caught Quillin's earnest gaze. "I'm not ready yet."

He nodded. "Well, if that changes someday, I take my summers in Cardus. Ask for me at the Red Roost."

"I'll remember," she said.

They stood awkwardly for a while, before he bobbed his head and departed slowly down the street without a backward look.

"Are you sure?" asked Astryx, when he was beyond earshot.

"I'm sure."

A long pause.

"You let her go."

"I did."

When they emerged from the town again to the forlorn cries of night birds, Astryx led them through the field, still mangled by battle and blood. The windmill stood stark and shadowy and still in the failing light.

They both stopped dead, lost for words as someone emerged from behind it leading two horses.

Someone small, in a coat made of pockets, wearing a huge grin.

She approached without hurry, halting a few paces away and studying them with crimson eyes.

"We goes when is time to be somewhere else," said Zyll.

42

They briefly considered camping under the windmill, but by unspoken agreement, continued until they were out of sight of the place where Tullah had fallen.

Instead, they stopped a league or two onward in a copse of oak, and didn't bother lighting a fire. Fern lay back on a bed of leaves with her torn cloak for a blanket. She stared through the shadows of balding branches at a sky salted with cold stars and did not sleep for a long time.

Tullah would not leave her mind, and when she tried to think past her to tomorrow, she found only a void.

When they rose before dawn in chill blue light, sniffling with the cold, Fern briefly considered asking Zyll why she was still there.

She knew what sort of answer she'd get, though—cryptic and short and deeply unsatisfying.

The last, brief leg of their journey was uneventful as dawn claimed the sky and revealed their destination creeping ever closer. They stopped once at a stream so that Fern could wash the blood from her cloak.

Then, at last, Amberlin's gates ushered them inside.

Fern reckoned the city was at least thrice the size of Thune, all plaster and ruddy tiles, with not a thatched roof in sight. She'd never visited a place so huge, where nearly every structure had a second or third story. The Summerdusk festival was still in evidence, with bunting and ribbons and vendors aplenty, although the celebrations were winding down. Some stalls were shuttered or packing up, and there was a general air of the morning after a drunken carouse.

Astryx guided them through the streets in solemn procession. The roads were wide enough that they continued to ride side by side the entire way. The decorations, stages, and craft stands dwindled away as they passed into quieter districts.

When at last they arrived at the bounty office—Fern realized she had no idea what it was actually called—she studied the building. It looked like a small prison, with brutal, utilitarian construction and iron-barred windows. There wasn't even a sign.

"Are we really doing this?" she asked.

Astryx dismounted and hitched both horses to the post out front. "I'm going to walk in the door and complete the journey. Beyond that . . ." She shrugged and glanced at Zyll in helpless perplexity. "I'll do nothing at all."

Making good on her words, she passed through the doorway and into the shadows beyond.

Zyll immediately slipped down from Persimmon's back and trotted after her.

"Well, fuck, what am I going to do, stay here?" muttered Fern, and followed.

Inside, the impression of a prison was even stronger. A cramped front office contained a battered counter, a small woodstove, three massive filing cabinets, a wallboard pinned with dozens of papers, two benches, and some very unfortunate mounted taxidermy of a pair of spineback heads. Beyond the office, a hall lined with barred rooms extended three cells back on either side, with a tiny slitted window at the end. To Fern, the place smelled of sweat and metal and the ghost of yesterday's stew.

The woman behind the counter was as tall as Astryx, with the substance of someone who'd once carried a lot of muscle, but didn't much use it anymore. A younger fellow, his face still spotty, sat behind her, laboriously perusing a stack of printed sheets and sorting them into piles.

Looking up with astonished recognition, the woman exclaimed, "Gods, the Oathmaiden in the flesh! That's my good fortune used up for the year." She extended a hand. "Tabba, pleased to meet you."

Astryx shook it and nodded, but said nothing. Her fingers hesitated at her belt for a moment, then she unsnapped a pouch and withdrew a folded and stained piece of paper.

Before the Oathmaiden could present it, Zyll came to a stop beside her and stole Tabba's attention. "Hang on, now."

The goblin beamed back with her dangerous smile.

The woman's eyes widened. "Hells, it can't be. Hemp! Hemp, get the record!"

The kid turned in his chair. "The record? Which one?"

"The *one*, the crazy one!"

His mouth made an O of comprehension, and he sprang from his chair to fumble through the top drawer of one of the filing cabinets. It didn't take long for him to triumphantly produce a big sheet of press-printed paper.

"Here it is!" he cried breathlessly, slapping it on the counter.

Astryx finished unfolding her own piece of paper and slid it onto the counter beside the other, much cleaner sheet. It was obvious they were from the same printing.

Tabba ran a finger down hers, then glanced up at Zyll with confusion. "That's her, all right. Description checks out. Although she seems awful . . . unrestrained."

She looked to Astryx for an explanation, which was not forthcoming.

Fern couldn't help herself. "The crazy one?"

The woman seemed to see Fern for the first time. "The most ridiculous reward any of us has ever seen. *Beyond* ridiculous." She shook her head. "Seemed a joke, if it weren't for the filings. All done proper, county's approval, a well-known client, and a hefty deposit to boot."

Thus far, Astryx hadn't uttered a single word. She was staring at Zyll with a troubled expression on her face. The goblin appeared oblivious.

Hemp leaned toward Tabba and whispered, "This is very strange."

"Aye, that it is," she murmured. "Don't think I've ever seen the bounty stroll in and hang about."

Then, nothing happened.

Astryx seemed incapable or unwilling to advance the issue. Tabba and Hemp grew increasingly uncomfortable.

Eventually, Tabba cleared her throat. "The, er, client will be paying. We don't keep sums so large in the office, you understand. Mister Delvyn is a highly regarded local solicitor, though, so he'll like as not be available right quick." She nudged Hemp with an elbow. "Get on to his office and fetch him, fast as you can."

He scampered.

When again Astryx said nothing, Fern prompted, "So . . . we just wait?"

"Well," hedged Tabba, gesturing at Zyll. "Traditionally, the, er, *bounty* would be held in one of the cells. That's the normal way of things." She still appeared confounded by Zyll's casual presence. Looking to Astryx hopefully, she asked, "What do you think, Oathmaiden?"

Astryx sighed, sat on a bench, and put her head in her hands. "I have no idea."

"Right."

Zyll trotted past her, opened one of the unlocked cells, and stepped inside, closing the gate behind her. She gripped the bars and peered out, the point of her sharp pink tongue poking between her lips.

"What in the hells," breathed Tabba, drifting over to lock it.

~

It couldn't have been more than half an hour before Mister Delvyn arrived with Hemp at his heels, although to Fern the wait seemed interminable.

Delvyn was thin, sharply dressed in an expensive-looking slate tunic and black breeches, his graying hair carefully coiffed, mustache neat. He wore a gold necklace of office and had a fine leather folio tucked under one arm.

Hemp bobbed around behind his shoulder like a baby owl.

The solicitor surveyed the room briefly, taking in Astryx and Fern on the bench. His brows rose as he noted Zyll at the bars of her cell.

"Thanks for coming so swift, Mister Delvyn," said Tabba. "I have to say I didn't see this day coming."

"Mm," he said, cracking his folio and perusing its contents. "Well, let's get her out of that cell, shall we?"

"Yes, sir!" Tabba hustled down the hall and unlocked the gate she'd locked less than an hour ago. Zyll obligingly emerged and toddled over to stand before Mister Delvyn.

"And am I correct that you consider the terms executed?" he asked.

It took Fern a moment to comprehend that he was addressing the goblin.

"Yep yep," said Zyll, nodding affably. "We are, how do you say, stuck with the fork."

"Excellent," said Delvyn. "Then all that's left is to settle up."

"What," said Fern, flatly.

Tabba had a hand to her mouth and a look that said she'd be telling this story for the rest of her days.

Hemp mostly looked politely confused.

"You put a bounty on *yourself?*" Astryx's expression had beached itself halfway between anger and disbelief.

Zyll shrugged.

"But why would you *do* that?" cried Fern, rubbing her forehead. The ache from Staysha's clubbing days before had since subsided, but now returned with renewed purpose.

The goblin considered, then replied, "Tullah, she is wanting to *whsscht*." She drew a finger across her throat illustratively. "She was very anger-ly. So."

Astryx rose and pinched the bridge of her nose. "Why didn't you pay someone to *escort* you?"

Zyll blinked back at her. "Would the Oaths-maiden have been esk-e-lorting?"

At the elf's expression, it was clear she would not have been. Fern thought she might also be reviewing precisely how challenging it had been to apprehend the goblin in the first place.

Astryx pointed at Delvyn. "How did you let this happen?"

He seemed unperturbed. "There's nothing legally preventing it. I'm merely an instrument of the will of the client." He shrugged. "Now, as to the matter of payment—a sum this substantial is obviously not practical to carry in coin, so instead I have a stamped bank chit for the full amount."

He withdrew from the folio an expensive-looking slip of paper and snapped it crisply. "As a friendly piece of advice, were I you, I'd transfer it to an account of your own, rather than hauling it around in saddlebags or whatever it is you're accustomed to doing."

Fern had some questions about how the goblin had amassed these apparently staggering funds, but on reflection, she decided that was the least improbable thing that had happened so far.

Delvyn offered the slip to Astryx, glancing between her and Fern. "I assume you'll be able to attend to any divisions between the two of you?"

"Oh," said Fern. "No, that's not—"

"I'm sure we can," replied Astryx at the same time.

A clatter arose from outside.

"Ah," said Delvyn brightly. "That'll be the last part of your request, miss."

"Round Boy!" cried Zyll, clapping her hands with clear delight.

Round Boy was, indeed, *very* round. The tiny, shaggy, extremely portly pony was hitched to an equally tiny four-wheeled cart, eminently Zyll-sized.

Delvyn departed when he was certain he was no longer needed, leaving Astryx, Fern, and Zyll standing in the street alongside three horses and a wagon, while Tabba and Hemp goggled at them from the doorway of the bounty office.

Zyll dashed to greet her pony, scrubbing him vigorously under the chin and on the cheeks and jabbering what Fern assumed were goblin endearments. Round Boy, for his part, seemed equally pleased.

Astryx and Fern stood beside one another, watching with a shared sense of unreality. The Oathmaiden held the bank chit beside her leg in one hand, forgotten. She looked adrift.

Returning to them, Zyll hitched up her coat of pockets and made a little bow. "Okay. Off to be going, with many thank-lings."

She patted Fern gently on the shoulder. "Be good to shankling."

"Oh!" Fern had forgotten Breadlee. She drew him from the pocket of her tattered cloak. Astryx had made a show of bestowing him on her, but . . . "He's not really mine."

"Glad we're clear on that," grumbled the knife. "Wielding is a *privilege*, not a right."

Shaking her head, Zyll pressed him gently back toward Fern.

She moved on to Astryx and stared up at her for a long, inscrutable moment. Then, startling Fern and the Oathmaiden both, Zyll seized the elf's legs in a full-body hug.

Astryx's mouth worked as she stared, bewildered, at the goblin. Tentatively, she reached down and patted her orange hair.

Zyll detached herself and backed away, blinking at them.

"Okay okay. Bye."

She crawled up to the buckboard of her cart beside the unlit lantern that hung from its awning, and with a brisk wave, twitched the reins.

Round Boy clattered off down the street, and they both disappeared out of sight around the bend.

"I'm gonna miss that little weirdo, theoretically," mused Breadlee aloud.

The strength seemed to leave Astryx's legs all at once, and she sat down hard on the curb, staring at the bank chit in her hand. Nigel's sheath twisted awkwardly on her back.

"Are you okay?" asked Fern, putting a paw on her shoulder.

"I feel like the road took a turn in the dark," murmured the elf, still gazing at the slip of paper.

She looked at Fern, her eyes rimmed red. "Like time is slipping away, except I've always had so much of it until now. I feel . . . rushed. I asked you a question before, but didn't get an answer. And perhaps it's possible you think better of me now. So, I'm going to ask it again, before I can't."

Fern's heart seized as Astryx shifted onto one knee and withdrew Nigel from his scabbard. She planted him point down in the street and bowed her head as though in prayer.

"What are you doing?" whispered Fern.

"Fern," said Astryx, her voice quiet and firm. "I, Astryx Arboren, last of my line, beg of you your companionship, your courage, your community. In return you shall have mine, and between them may loyalty bind us." She swallowed. "Will you accompany me on the roads ahead, treacherous or fair, as my squire and friend, for as long as it please you?"

Dizziness swallowed Fern whole. Before her, another friend who needed her, *wanted* her, to fill a space—a space she uniquely fit into. A need she could meet. A *thing* that she could be, to bridge a gap in someone else's road. Worthy. Useful. *Valuable*.

She tore her eyes from Astryx, awaiting her answer, to stare at the overstuffed satchel at her side. So many letters, all starting the same. *Dear Viv.*

So many apologies, stretching back weeks.

And before that, years, to a father long dead, to the dream of his that she'd inherited and lived for him.

Fern took a deep breath as tears over-spilled, wetting the fur of her cheeks. In a small and quavering voice, she uttered the hardest word of her life.

"No."

At the parting of ways outside the gates of Amberlin, they stood together beside the horse and pony, Persimmon newly outfitted with a saddle suitable for a rattkin.

Astryx had insisted Fern take a share of the bounty. Fern had accepted it uncomfortably, and certainly hadn't counted whatever was in the purse the Oathmaiden had tucked into the pony's saddlebag.

Kneeling before her, Astryx withdrew the bracelet that had last girdled Zyll's wrist. Delicate wire glittered in the afternoon sun. She offered it to Fern in an open palm. "If ever you need me, or decide you'd like to walk the same road together for a while, place this on your wrist, and we will both know how to find one another."

Fern took it in one paw and studied it. "Didn't you say that at long distances, there's pain?"

Astryx tapped the bracelet still around her own wrist and smiled. "I find that some things are worth pain. You'll know if and when this is worth it to you."

Sniffling, Fern nodded and tucked it away in her cloak.

"Oh, there's someone else who likely wants a word." The elf reached over her shoulder and loosed Nigel in his scabbard.

There was the air of somebody straightening their tunic, followed by the sound of a clearing throat, and then Nigel's voice declared, "There are few I deem worthy of my lady's regard. In you, however, I can find little fault. Be well, and travel safe."

"Can't help but feel *somebody* has been left out," muttered Breadlee.

Nigel harrumphed.

"Take good care of her, Nigel," said Fern, thumping Breadlee with a finger to hush him.

Mustering up the last of her courage, she took Astryx's hand in both her paws, and said in a wobbly voice, "Thank you for harboring me when I stumbled out of my life. Thank you for protecting me. Thank you for enduring me. Thank you for wanting me to be something you needed. And thank you for understanding when I couldn't."

Halfway through, her vision was a blur.

"Fuck," she whispered.

Then Astryx hugged her, burying her face in the fur beneath Fern's ear. "Goodbye, my unexpected friend," she murmured. "You have made my road a stranger, but I am so grateful to find my way by starlight again. I'm very glad you fell asleep in the back of my wagon."

43

On a frigid afternoon in winter's deepest heart, Fern stood once more outside Legends & Lattes. Snow caked the roofs of Thune and mantled the street, and a cloudless sky let the sun burnish it all in glitter and gleam. Her breath steamed in the sharp air.

It had taken weeks to make the return trip. She'd struggled astride Persimmon for two days before deciding that she was no horsewoman and that the mare would be better cared for by someone who knew what they were doing. The two of them weren't fast friends anyway.

After trading the pony, she'd booked a carriage to Thune. Again.

No pescadines waylaid them, and no fabled adventurer came to their rescue.

On a brandy-soaked night many months gone, Cal had sent her to say the words that needed saying, but she'd instead traveled half the Territory to avoid it. Now, she was where she should have been at the beginning.

To her left, Thistleburr Booksellers was clearly open and doing business. The windows were fogged, but the shadows of customers moved indoors past the yellow glow of lantern light. She did her best not to think about any of that just yet.

Instead, she raised a paw, depressed the latch, and entered Viv's shop.

The heat and steam enveloped her and made Fern's fur frizz, the scent of cinnamon tickling her nose.

She saw Viv straight away behind the counter, the orc's broad back turned, scrubbing at a mug with a cloth. A heap of Thimble's baked goods glistened with sugar under a glass dome. A couple of folks waited in line, and beyond, the tables were lively with conversation. Tandri was nowhere to be seen.

Then Viv turned and saw Fern, and dropped the mug she'd been holding. It shattered on the floor with a sound like an explosion.

Fern's heart squeezed tighter with every emotion she registered on Viv's face—surprise, confusion, joy, hurt, anger. *Definitely* anger in there.

That wasn't where it settled, but it had certainly been a stop on the trip.

"Gods," breathed Viv.

She rushed to fiddle with the counter door, which stuck, so she gave up and vaulted it, reaching Fern in two strides.

The orc scooped her up and crushed her in a back-cracking hug that made Fern squeak.

"*Gods*, you're all right," Viv said.

Then she set her down and stared at her in consternation. She opened her mouth, but couldn't seem to decide which question to ask first.

Instead, she turned to the rest of the shop and called, "All right, we're closing early. Everybody out!"

There was a great deal of grumbling and a few hasty refunds, but in minutes, Legends & Lattes was empty but for the two of them.

Viv turned back to Fern and put her hands on her hips. Her cheeks were flushed, and she was breathing heavily, barely containing an inner turmoil. "*I'm alive? I'm sorry?* That's all you could write?" she demanded.

Fern slowly opened the satchel at her side and withdrew a huge bundle of papers.

"Well, not *all*."

Viv set aside another wrinkled page, glancing up at Fern where she waited across the table. A couple of Thimble's cinnamon rolls languished on a plate nearby, but the bookseller couldn't imagine taking a bite of one.

Fern hadn't been silent for the two hours it took Viv to work her way through the letters, which she'd arranged mostly chronologically. Viv had plenty of questions, and there had been a lot of the journey Fern had never written down that she filled in on the fly.

"You got a lot wordier over time," said Viv, with a quarter-smile.

Fern couldn't find even that much of one. She shrugged helplessly. Viv hadn't said a harsh word since taking a seat, but it still felt like a slow-motion flaying to watch her face as she absorbed every word Fern had poured onto paper.

Finally, Viv set the last page atop the pile and sighed.

They studied each other in silence, with the gnomish coffee machine hissing and ticking along in the kitchen as it cooled.

At last, Viv said, "You have no idea how pissed off I was. Just . . . leaving like that, without a word? I thought you were murdered in an alley. Drowned in the river. I pestered the Gatewardens for *weeks* until that first letter showed, and then, sure, I was relieved—but also a different sort of pissed off."

"Yeah," said Fern, miserably.

"It was a *spectacularly* bad four-word letter, as letters go," said Viv, leaning on one arm and lowering her brows.

"Yeah."

"But." She rubbed her eyes. "Now, I think I know how Gallina probably felt when I quit our crew without even a backward glance. So, I guess that makes me a hypocrite. And seeing you again—alive and fine? It pushes almost all of that to one side. What's left will die down. I know that. It'll just take a little bit of time."

Swallowing, Fern ventured, "Thank you," in a very small voice.

"You didn't write the end of it, though," continued Viv, tapping the pile. "What happened with Astryx?"

"She wanted me to be her squire. Got down on a knee and formally offered and everything."

Viv blinked at her. "Eight hells. And?"

"In . . . fewer words, I said that it wasn't what I needed or wanted right now. And it was okay. Hard, but okay.

"Which is what I should have said to you before I got drunk and wandered off the map." Fern gestured in the direction of Thistleburr. "I can't do *this*—the bookshop—anymore. I don't know if I'll ever be able to again. I tried, and it *should* work, anyone with eyes can see that, but I shrivel like a dead leaf inside to think that *that* is my life. Not because it's wrong, or bad, or that it's not worthy of me. That dream is just . . . not *mine* anymore, if it ever was, and I'm not even sure of that these days."

She swallowed. "None of that would be so bad if I hadn't *pretended* it was. If I hadn't led us all so far down that road. Let so many people I care about invest in it, until . . ."

"Hey, look—"

"No, I have to finish. Because that's the part I need to apologize for."

Then Fern rose and rounded the end of the table, standing beside Viv, still seated on the bench. The orc eyed her with confusion.

Fern raised both paws, palm up, in a gesture made to her only a month ago on an autumn road. She swallowed thickly. "Would you put your hands on mine, please?"

Viv didn't question her, but gently placed her vast palms face-down upon Fern's upturned ones, dwarfing them.

It took a moment to work the moisture back into her mouth. "I beg your forgiveness for the words I did not say," Fern began, trying to remember Astryx's phrasing exactly. "I beg your patience for the ways I failed you. I don't expect it, but crave and strive for your regard."

"Fern. It's okay. You have it," said Viv, thickly.

"I'm so fucking sorry I didn't trust you with the truth," sobbed Fern, and burst into messy tears.

Viv enfolded her in her massive arms, and they stayed that way for a long while.

"Potroast!" cried Fern.

She'd thought she'd done enough sobbing for one day, but it turned out that there was still room for more.

The gryphet barked and shimmied at the sight of her as she stood in the open entryway of Thistleburr with arms outstretched.

If anything, he was rounder than before, with a little more silver in his fur, but his great golden eyes were clear and joyful.

He barreled toward her and had his forepaws on her chest in moments, licking her snout frantically, whining and hooting his delight.

"I'm sorry to you, too, little man," she whispered in his ear, kissing his forehead feathers.

Tandri stood open-mouthed with shock at the counter, a book in hand. Viv ducked into the shop behind Fern, edging around their teary reunion on the doormat and easing the door closed against the hard cold.

Fern barely registered the murmured conversation the two women had while she soothed Potroast and, if she was honest, herself.

Cal, predictably, found her later in the evening, after all the fuss. At least this time, it was on the front step instead of in the alley.

Fern sat on a stool beside the front door of the closed shop, wearing a heavy blue winter cloak that she'd dug out of her old things, with her ears tucked into a crocheted hat that she knew made her look ridiculous.

The shop didn't feel like hers anymore, and though they'd left her room alone and urged her to reclaim it—at least for now—it seemed like trespassing to sleep there. She hadn't decided what to do about that yet.

Finding a nice suite at an inn would be easy enough. She'd eventually given in and checked the contents of the purse Astryx had given her. The amount still seemed incomprehensible, and not at all deserved.

She glanced at Legends & Lattes, its windows still aglow. Viv and Tandri awaited her inside with Potroast. There was plenty left to discuss, and a great many arrangements to be made.

"Well," said Cal. He was wrapped in a muffler and a heavy woolen peacoat, stamping in the cold as he sidled up to join her. "Heard you were back."

"I guess I am. It's really good to see you, Cal. I'm sorry about all the worry."

She *was*, but Fern also thought she was wrung out of sorrow for a while, like a rag twisted dry.

"Hm." This was one of his more aggrieved inflections.

Under the circumstances, it seemed warranted. "Worry" was a terrific understatement for what she'd made them endure.

Fern reached out a mittened paw. Cal took it in his own bare hand, and she squeezed.

"You gave me some very good advice," she said. "I'm sorry it took me a little longer than it should have to finally take it."

"Ah. Well, just so long's you got there in the end."

She nodded. "I'll be leaving again. Not just yet. I have some things to do first." She thought of the satchel full of pages and all the missing pieces yet to be added. "But at some point, I'm going to be going. I'm not sure for how long."

"Appreciate knowin' beforehand," he said, with quiet earnestness.

"You're a good friend, Cal. I hope to do a better job of holding up my end, even if I disappear for a while."

"Well," he observed. "I seem to recall that some friendships can stand a quiet stretch. Sturdy, I think we said."

A long silence as they held each other's hands in the cold, still, blue.

"Hm," said Fern.

"Hm," Cal replied.

Epilogue

Fern slid the blue, clothbound volume from the bookshelf with a little thrill and turned it over in her paws.

The cover, amidst a gilding of intertwined leaves, read—

The Straight Road in the Dark:
Travels with the Oathmaiden
by
Fern Teverlin

"You should sign it," murmured Quillin, cocking his head close to hers.

"What?"

"You've got a pencil in there, don't you?" He gestured at her satchel, which was, indeed, loaded with pencils and several bound notebooks.

"I can't do that! That's . . . *vandalism!*" she replied, horrified.

"Are you telling me that back when you had a bookshop, you would have been upset if the authors all signed their books?"

Fern blinked. "Well, *no,* but—"

"But, what? You're an author. Your name's already on the cover. Do you want me to go ask?"

"No!" she almost shouted. Then she continued in a near whisper, glancing furtively at the ancient gnome sorting things at the shop desk. "*No.* And my stomach just did a weird thing. Let's go."

Quillin shrugged, his eyes delighted. "I'll give you two options.

I'll go ask for permission, or you can just sign it on the sly. Which is it going to be?"

Fern narrowed her eyes at him. "I don't appreciate having to choose between mortification and crime."

"Setting aside your definition of a crime, it seems suspicious that you have trouble choosing. I wonder what that says about you?"

As they left the shop moments later, Quillin still chuckling, she muttered, "Any second he's going to come running out and call for a Warden."

He put his arm around her shoulders. "I think we'll escape the law *just* this once."

A sharp voice piped up from the pocket of Fern's cloak. "If they do show, Fern still only has one stabbing on her record, and that was a technicality. We've got a *long* way to go before we can call it a respectable number," said Breadlee.

"Tell me more about this 'technical' stabbing?" asked Quillin, looking amused.

"Well, it started with the word *feculent,* and I don't even know what that means," explained the knife. "So, I think it had more to do with the tone."

Fern let their conversation fade from her attention as she glanced around the street, which was quite busy even at this late hour. Tall flick-lanterns lit the avenue in a steady, golden glow. It was strange to be in a place where everyone was about the same height—it had been quite some time since the Tarimite monastery. This was Fern's first visit to the gnomish city of Azimuth, although she'd heard tales of it from Viv. She had difficulty imagining the orc tromping around the place like an apologetic giant.

Quillin had found a bit of what he liked to call "detective work" in Azimuth, untangling the subterfuges of multiple gnomish enterprises who were nose-deep spying on each other's businesses. Better yet, they had *all* hired him independently, unbeknownst to their competitors.

Fern had mostly toured around while he worked and, of course, spent time with her notebooks.

"So," he said, rousing her from her reverie. "How's the new one coming?" He bumped her satchel with his hip.

"The book?" she asked. "I don't know. I've been writing down the things that happened in Murk when I was young, but I'm not sure if there's enough there to warrant the effort."

"From what you've already told me, I don't doubt there is."

"Maybe I should write down *our* adventures instead."

He looked thoughtful, putting a finger to his chin. "Crimes of illicit autography *do* sound compelling."

"Hush." Fern gave him a peck on the cheek. She still loved the way he smelled.

"Of course, if you need some fresh material, there's always this . . ." Quillin gently tapped Astryx's bracelet where it hung against her chest. She'd had it strung onto a necklace.

As they strolled down the curving street in the warm summer night, Fern scooped the bracelet up so that it rested in one paw, gleaming and delicate. It had almost no weight at all.

"Maybe someday," she said. "I'm not tired of you just yet, though. Give me a week?"

They both laughed, but Fern didn't release the bracelet.

She wondered where the last wrist was that had worn it. Fern thought she sometimes caught hints of Zyll's passage through the Territory in news of unexpected mayhem or preposterous coincidence, but she could never be absolutely *sure*.

Of Astryx, there had been much more to hear. She wondered if it had been partly because of her book—although she didn't flatter herself that it was read so widely yet—but the Oathmaiden was the subject of more and more frequent news. Surprisingly, many of the adventures relayed were small. And the *tone* of these stories was transformed. People spoke of the woman they met after the deeds were done, rather than the deeds themselves. Of a reassuring touch, or a concerned question. Of grace, and little kindnesses. Of being *seen* by her.

Fern wondered if she'd had a hand in making Astryx One-Ear less of a legend, and more of herself.

What had the elf said, there at the end?

You have made my road a stranger, but I am so grateful to find my way by starlight again.

Fern reflected that after wandering in her own wilderness, she was grateful for a clear night sky, too.

Acknowledgments

I'm eagerly anticipating one day writing an acknowledgments section that doesn't begin by mentioning that "this book was harder to write than the last one," but apparently that time has not yet arrived.

2024 was very tumultuous, and this book took much longer to wring out of me than anticipated. I was continuously filled with doubt. Would anyone want to read a cozy fantasy novel that was less cozy in every way than the ones that preceded it? There are easily more scenes of conflict in *Brigands & Breadknives* than the two previous books combined. Would readers be okay with Viv taking a backseat to Fern for the story I wanted to tell? Does anyone want a "cozy" story about the grief of disappointing your friends, and the agony of saying "no"?

Sadly, I don't have the answers to any of those questions as I draft this, so I'm almost as anxious as I was when I started. The thing is, I don't want to write the same book over and over. I don't want to pretend that fantasy small-business ownership is the answer to all of life's woes. I don't want to imagine that the solutions for every challenge are the same for everyone, or that they are neatly resolved—or that they *stay* resolved.

At the same time, I do want these stories to be affirming. While there is obvious whimsy in a hangover-incited road trip with a swearing rat-person, the things Fern wrestles with feel very real and relevant to me, and while there are certainly villains in this story, and hard decisions, and grief and bittersweetness and pain, ultimately, I hope it communicates a belief in essential goodness that makes you feel better after you've read it. It's a strange line to walk, acknowledging what is hard and painful and messy in life, while at the same time advocating hope. Still, I think any honest approach has to do some of both.

Thanks to my family. I love you.

Yet again, Aven Shore-Kind is the tireless champion who made sure I crossed the finish line. Frankly, she might as well have her name next to mine on the books. There's no other way they'd get done.

Forthright once more provided a detailed editorial pass that makes me look much better than I have any right to.

To Stevie Finegan, my agent—I remain ever grateful.

I'd be remiss not to thank Seanan McGuire in every book I ever write for the big push that started this snowball rolling down the hill.

Carson Lowmiller once more painted beautiful US cover art with immaculate vibes. I am so thankful.

To everyone who has made or sent me fan art—know that I am humbled and grateful for every piece.

To the many influencers in social media communities who have been such great advocates for me, I am vastly appreciative.

To the translators who have taken such care in handling my words, I appreciate you endlessly.

At Tor US, my undying appreciation to Lindsey Hall, Rachel Taylor, Eileen Lawrence, Aislyn Fredsall, Hannah Smoot, Sarah Reidy, Angie Rao, Peter Lutjen, Jacqueline Huber-Rodriguez, Heather Saunders, Russell Trakhtenberg, Rafal Gibek, Lauren Hougen, Jeff LaSala, Khadija Lokhandwala, Emily Mlynek, Tiana Tolbert, Michelle Foytek, Erin Robinson, Alex Cameron, Lizzy Hosty, Alexa Best, Will Hinton, Claire Eddy, Lucille Rettino, NaNá Stoelzle, and Devi Pillai. I am grateful for all of you.

At Tor UK, my huge thanks to Sophie Robinson, Bella Pagan, Grace Barber, Meg Le Huqet, Kieryn Tyler, Lloyd Jones, Becky Lushey, Jamie Forrest, Ellie Bailey, Emma Oulton, Carol-Anne Royer, Elle Jones, Ellen Morgan, Alexandra Hamlet, Andy Joannou, Will Upcott, Holly Sheldrake, Bryony Croft, Nick Griffiths, Stuart Dwyer, Kadie McGinley, Richard Green, Rory O'Brien,

Becca Tye, Leanne Williams, Joanna Dawkins, Lucy Grainger, Jon Mitchell, Anna Shora, Mairead Loftus, Elena Battista, Toby Selwyn, and Hannah Geranio. Thank you so much.

Last, but not least, I want to thank Kel, Jory Phillips, Kalyani Poluri, Linnea Lindstrom, Mark Lindberg, and Bao Pham for all your help and care.

And to you, dear reader—be well, and be kind to yourself.

About the Author

TRAVIS BALDREE is a number one *New York Times* bestselling author, a Locus, Nebula and Hugo finalist and a full-time audiobook narrator who has lent his voice to hundreds of stories. Before that, he spent decades designing and building video games like *Torchlight*, *Rebel Galaxy* and *Fate*. He is the author of *Legends & Lattes*, *Bookshops & Bonedust* and *Brigands & Breadknives*, and he lives in the Pacific Northwest.

If you liked *Brigands & Breadknives*, please turn over
for an extract from

First loves. Second-hand books. Epic adventures.

Viv's career with the renowned mercenary company Rackam's Ravens isn't going as planned. Wounded during the hunt for a powerful necromancer, she's packed off against her will to recuperate in the sleepy beach town of Murk – so far from the action that she worries she'll never be able to return to it. What's a thwarted soldier of fortune to do?

Spending her hours at a struggling bookshop in the company of its foul-mouthed proprietor is the last thing Viv would have predicted – even though it may be exactly what she needs. Still, adventure isn't far away. A suspicious traveller in grey, a gnome with a chip on her shoulder, a summer fling and an improbable number of skeletons prove Murk to be more eventful than Viv could have ever expected.

Sometimes, right things happen at the wrong time. Sometimes, what we need isn't what we seek. And sometimes, we find ourselves in the stories we experience together . . .

Available now

PROLOGUE

"Eighteen!" bellowed Viv, bringing her saber around in a flat curve that battered the wight's skull off its spine. She laughed and rammed her shoulder through its body before it could begin to fall, shattering bones in all directions. In two more steps, she'd already brought the blade back in an upswing, catching another in the ribcage. Splinters sprayed like woodchips from a felling-axe.

"Nineteen!" She grinned savagely, baring her fangs and forging ahead with massive strides.

Every breath sang pure and clean in her lungs, her muscles bunched and released in perfect rhythm, her blood roared in her veins. She was youth and strength and power, and she meant to push all three as far as they would go.

Varine the Pale's army of gaunt, skeletal soldiers crowded amidst the bastion oaks, nimble despite their desiccation. They battled in deathless silence, short-swords and pikes snapping toward Viv, and she dodged or hacked them aside, relentless as the tide.

She was far ahead of the rest of Rackam's Ravens, leading the charge. Old warhorses, the lot of them. Old and *slow*.

They'd tried to keep the new blood in the back, but that wasn't what she was built for.

Somewhere ahead, the necromancer lay in wait, and Viv meant to reach her first. When the stragglers finally caught up, they'd find her with her blade at ease and their quarry in a heap at her feet.

Her count increased with every stroke as she laid about her with her saber. Still not fast enough. She yanked her maul from its loop and went to work with both hands, crushing and shearing through the skeletal ranks with hammer and sword. Their shields were bashed aside. Their ring mail tore like paper. Their skulls collapsed like winter melons.

Harsh cries echoed behind her as Rackam's crew dealt with the chaff she left in her wake or the wights that tried to flank them. Someone shouted for her to slow down. She huffed a scornful laugh.

And then her leg lit up with a cold fire that turned hot in half a second. She staggered and pivoted on the other foot just as a pike's rusty head withdrew from a long wound in her thigh. It darted forward again, and she stared disbelieving as it disappeared through her trousers and into the meat of her leg in a perfect parallel slice. Then the blood came. A lot of it.

She roared, knocking the pike aside with her maul and following with an upward slash of her saber that ripped the wight in half. Its horned helm spun skyward in an absurd twirl. Viv would have laughed if agony hadn't overtaken her when her weight shifted from the swing. Her wounded leg collapsed under her like a cornstalk.

Suddenly, she was on her side in the moss and muck, bleeding everywhere.

Another skeletal revenant loomed above her, curls of blue

light flickering in its empty sockets. On its forehead Varine's symbol burned bright—a diamond with branches like horns. It hauled a rusty tower shield into the air, preparing to bring the edge down in a crushing blow. The only sounds were the creaking of its sinew and Viv's own ragged breaths.

She just caught the edge of the shield with her maul, knocking it to the side, but she lost her grip on her weapon. Tears of pain blurred her vision. Viv hadn't managed to disarm the thing, though. Implacable, the revenant raised the slab of metal once more. This time, the angle was all wrong to shift the saber between her and the falling edge. In shocked disbelief, she could only watch as the steel dropped toward her neck.

A ragged cry, but not her own.

Rackam barreled into the creature with his shoulder. As the wight staggered back, the dwarf obliterated the thing with a single swing of his flanged mace.

He glanced down at her, and the disappointed grimace on his lips made her nausea double. "Hells-damned fool. Clap a hand to that. Stay put, and try not to die, if you can."

Then he was gone, and Viv was breathless with shock as Rackam's Ravens charged past in a line of blades and bows and arcane fire that leveled the foe before them.

They disappeared into the mist, and she was alone, staring in disbelief as her life pumped out of her leg.

―⁂―

"Still with us, hey?"

Viv groggily regained consciousness. She felt like she was going to be sick. Maybe she already had been.

The first things she saw were Rackam's flinty eyes, glittering above the braids of his muddy salt-and-pepper beard. Viv shook her head and looked around; the edges of her vision seemed smeared with grease. Somehow, she'd braced her back against one of the oaks. She'd apparently also had the presence of mind to tear off the bottom of her shirt and bind her wound around a handful of moss. The cloth was soaked through, and the earth underneath was a churn of mud and blood.

At the sight of it, she began to drift, and Rackam brought her back with a surprisingly gentle slap to the cheek.

He sighed and shook his head.

The battle was done. If his presence hadn't been enough to tell her, then the unhurried movement of the warriors behind him would have.

"I figured it when you signed on. Hoped I'd be wrong, but nah, I knew this was the way it would go. Younger is always dumber, and wising up takes blood and time." He looked away, as though into some other possible future, then back at her. "Every new prospect, I give them even odds. I look at the hands, the arms. No scars? Then it's even odds that the first one they get kills them."

With one gloved hand, he patted her massive forearm. Corded with muscle, but the skin unblemished. Viv stared past it to the wreck of her leg.

Rackam stood, and she still didn't have to look up far to meet his eyes. "Is this the one that kills you, then?"

Viv swallowed down her nausea and narrowed her eyes, feeling stupid. Feeling stupid made her feel resentful. And resentment was only a half step from angry. "No," she said through clenched teeth.

He chuckled. "Don't guess it will, at that. But you're done for now."

She blinked. "Did we get her?"

"We didn't. Wasn't even here, near as we can tell. Only a little trouble she stirred up just for us. We're heading north. We'll find her."

Viv struggled to push herself to standing against the trunk with her left leg. The other felt too big by half, and every pump of her heart was a dark drumbeat all through it. "When do we leave?"

"We? Like I said, you're done for now. They tell me it's only a few miles to some sea town. I'll send you that way. You'll heal up, and we'll pass through when we're done. If you're still around and able when we roll through, we'll take you back on. Probably a few weeks. If you're gone when we show . . . ?" He shrugged. "No shame in calling this the end of it."

"But—"

"It's done, kid. You survived a stupid mistake today. If you want to make another so soon after, well . . ." His gaze was hard. "Want me to tell you the odds I give on that?"

But Viv wasn't a stupid orc, so she shut the hells up.

1

Viv lay on the floor of the tiny room. Well, almost on the floor. The place hadn't been built with orcs in mind, and the bed was too short by at least two feet. Someone had wrestled the straw-tick mattress onto the floor, and though her legs still went off the end, they'd positioned her pack so her foot was propped, keeping the wounded leg elevated.

It hurt like all eight hells.

She'd caught a fever while bouncing along in the litter behind a pack mule, coughing through all the dust it could raise. Which was a *lot*.

Viv might've been bedbound for two days, in and out of consciousness, a muddle of circular dreams and throbbing agony. The surgeon had come and gone multiple times. Or maybe he hadn't, and she'd just been hallucinating it over and over. She half remembered the man's face, tangled up in a shame she couldn't identify.

Now, her head was clear. Which mostly meant she could also *feel* everything with complete clarity. It was a debatable improvement.

What's more, she was absolutely ravenous.

Staring around the room, the place was mostly barren. A crude bedframe and a tiny table with a lantern and a basin on it. Gray, raw wood for walls. A small, slatted window. She smelled the sea, and dry beach grass, and fish. An old sea chest sat opposite. Her saber leaned against it, alongside a crude wooden crutch. Her maul was missing. There wasn't much else worth considering.

The building was absolutely quiet. The only sounds came from outside—the hissing of grass, the remote grumble of waves, and the occasional call of a seabird.

Viv had been lucid for less than a single hour, and she thought the view might drive her insane if she had to endure another.

Her leg was cleanly wrapped at least, splinted so the knee wouldn't bend. Her trouser leg had been cut away. The bandages showed some discoloration where she'd oozed through, but it was a big step up from moss and a dirty wool shirt.

"Well," she said. "Shit."

She made it up by degrees, hauling her butt onto the bedframe and sucking air through her teeth as she swung her damaged leg around. Her left boot fit, but the right foot was so swollen, it would have to stay bare. Tottering to her feet, she made it to the basin of tepid water, where she scrubbed herself as best she could with the rag she found there. Feeling less foul, she limped toward the door, but each thud of her heel against the floor pulsed black at the edges of her vision. Gritting her teeth, she changed direction and grudgingly seized the crutch.

It galled her to admit how much better that was.

While she was there, she belted on her saber out of habit.

Unfortunately, she discovered that the room was at the top of a flight of narrow stairs. She fumbled down them, catching herself every other step with the crutch. The saber did nothing to make things easier. With every impact, she found a new, more colorful epithet for Rackam. Not that it was his fault, of course. Still, it was a lot more satisfying to curse someone by name, even if that name should've been her own.

She could smell the ghost of bacon as she descended, which was plenty of incentive to carry on.

The stairs opened into a long, rough-timbered dining area in an inn or tavern or whatever they called it around here. A big, stone hearth crouched cold along one wall, yawning like a disappointed mouth. An iron chandelier hung askew, entombed in candlewax. Glass floats and storm lanterns were strung or nailed up in the rafters, alongside netting and weathered oars with names carved into them. The handful of scarred tables were unoccupied.

A long bar ran along the back wall, and the tavernkeep leaned against it, idly cleaning a copper mug. He looked as bored as the place warranted. The tall sea-fey's chin was grizzled gray. His nose was a hatchet, his hair hung kelp-thick past sharp ears, and his forearms writhed with tattoos.

"Mornin', miss," he rumbled. "Breakfast?"

Viv couldn't remember anyone *ever* calling her *miss*. ·

His gaze sketched over her, brows rising as he spied the saber, then returned to the mug he was polishing.

"Bacon?" asked Viv.

He nodded. "Eggs, too? Potatoes?"

Her stomach grumbled aggressively. "Yeah."

"Five bits ought to do it."

She patted at her belt for her wallet, looked toward the stairs, and swore.

"I'll get it next time. Worst case I climb those stairs myself."

The man smiled wryly. "Don't think you could outrun me, could you? You'd better fall onto one of these stools while you still can."

Viv was so used to her very existence being an obvious threat that it was honestly startling to hear a casual joke at her expense, even such a mild one. She supposed clunking around on one leg tended to dull one's fearsomeness.

As she accomplished the suggested maneuver, he disappeared into the back. Viv dragged another stool close enough to prop her bare foot on one of its low supports.

Drumming her fingers on the counter, she tried to distract herself by studying the interior further, but there *really* wasn't much else worth marking. The sounds and smells from the back were all her mind could dwell on.

When the tavernkeep brought out a skillet and set it on the counter along with a fork and a napkin, she almost seized the hot handle with her bare hand in her hurry to drag it closer. The hash of potatoes, crispy, fatty pork, and two runny eggs was still sizzling and popping. She almost burst into joyful tears.

Viv caught him watching her devour the food from the other end of the bar and tried to slow down, but the potatoes were salty and rich with the egg, and it was hard not to shovel it in without pausing. The noises she made as she ate were not polite, but they were definitely sincere.

"Feel better?" the sea-fey asked as he slid the empty pan off the bar-top.

"Gods, yes. And thanks. Uh, I'm Viv."

That wry grin again. "Heard when you came in. We've met, actually, but I'm not surprised you don't remember. Not with all the commotion."

She didn't *remember* the commotion, but his amused tone made her wonder. "So, did the Ravens pay up my stay?"

"Hoped I'd see Rackam himself," said the barkeep. "Still, the fellow he sent to put you up was practically a gentleman. Paid four days. Said you'd be able to foot it past that. I'm Brand."

He held out a hand, and she shook it. They both had hard grips.

"Back to your ease then?" he asked.

"Hells, no. I'd go crazy. Um. Where exactly *am* I?"

His wry grin went all the way to amused. "Let me be the first to welcome you to Murk, jewel of the western coast! A very *small* part of the western coast. And this here is The Perch, my place."

"Seems awfully quiet around here." She'd almost said *depressingly* quiet.

"We have our loud moments when the boats are in. But if you're looking to rest and recover, most days you're not going to be bothered by the noise."

She nodded and hopped onto her good foot, easing the crutch back under her. "Well, thanks again. Guess I'll be seeing a lot of you."

With hot food in her belly, Viv felt more herself. The thought of hobbling her way around a little of the town was a lot more attractive than it had been a few minutes ago. She rapped a knuckle on the counter. "Think I'll take in the sights."

"See you in ten minutes then," said Brand.

Viv laughed, but she had to force it.